FIVE LORDS OF DUSK

DUSK LORDS
BOOK 1

F. MALBECK

Edited by Kat Betts of Element Editing Services

Book cover design by BRoseDesignz (www.brosedesignz-bookcovers.com)

Map design by T. Munro (www.feedthemultiverse.com)

 Formatted with Vellum

To the Suggan gals
(even if some us are no longer strictly gals)

I'm glad I found my people. Thank you for everything.

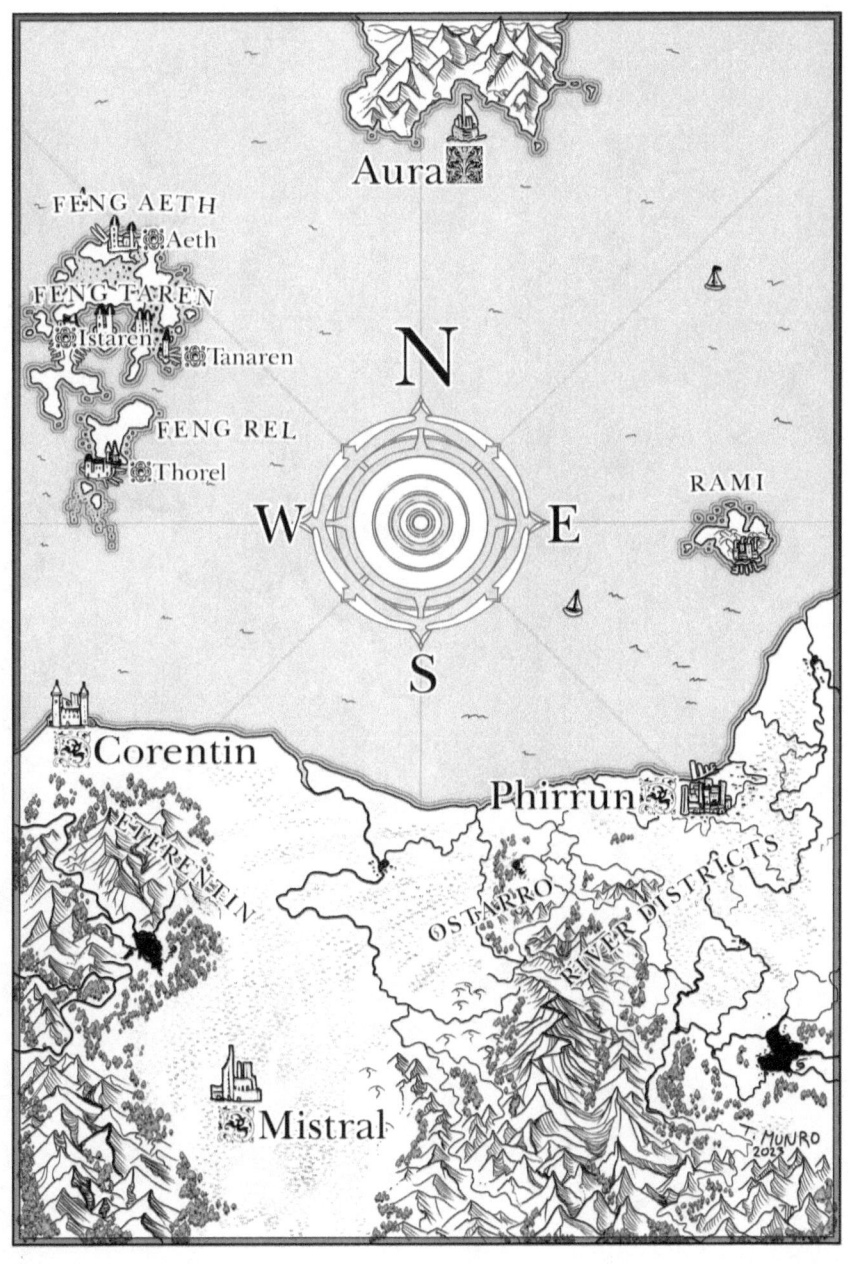

CHARACTERS

Prologue

Haith | Stormborn and Dusk Lord
Camillus | Dusk Lord
Prosper | Dusk Lord

The Royals

Cassius Sands | Crown Prince

The Hunters

Dorian Locke | Guild Hunter
Ever Locke | Huntsman, Dorian's Paternal Grandfather
Leon Payne | Guild Hunter, Dorian's Best Friend
James Locke | Guild Hunter, Dorian's Father

Lord James's Faction

Amabilis Bellhall | Guild Hunter
Lord Veredan | Guild Hunter
Lord Mysander | Guild Hunter
Lord Ashea | Guild Hunter
Lady Fenrent | Guild Hunter

Crew of the Oathbreaker

Ezra Creed | Captain of the Oathbreaker
Alice | Quartermaster
Muse | Bosun

Edge | First Mate
Butler | Surgeon
Mercy | Cook
Shye | Stormborn

Other Characters of Note

Master Fox | Merchant
Julius Bosworth | Harbour Master
Lady Tanith | Master of Accomplishment
Lorqin Mansel | Captain of the Border Guards
Jin Jensing | Lordling
Ayslin Jensing | Mother of Jin

PROLOGUE
PRIOR TO THE FIRST KING'S RISE

HAITH WAS FINALLY ALONE. THE LIGHTS OF THE CITY GLOWED BELOW the Brightspir palace and the wind on the quiet balcony they had retreated to welcomed them softly, the ruckus of their coronation celebrations left far behind. The new weight of the crown was heavy at their brow, the culmination of all they had worked for.

They were a Dusk Lord at last.

"It has always been the Stormborn's place to lead the seasons and our people. Though my Lord Haith is still young, none should be surprised by your capability."

The words rang out at Haith's back, cutting above the faint strains of music floating down from the spire of the palace, and Haith had not needed to turn to know who had broken into their quiet refuge. Leaning toward Haith, Camillus continued, "But leaving the party so soon on your coronation night, how will you survive a whole season of this gaiety?"

Haith wasn't so sure themself, but said, "Even if the season is not my choice, I still plan to make a worthy servant to the crown and my people."

Camillus's attentive gaze tracked the bright moon and violet night spread above, the light and sound cascading down from the spire. "Not your choice. Oh, it would be mine."

Haith felt a rare smile twitch their lips in response.

Camillus looked away from the echoes of gaiety, sighing wistfully. "I too hope to serve one day."

At that, Haith's smile froze.

"Camillus, you are—" Haith started and stopped, the flicker of the city below sliding away in favour of truly noticing the man across from them.

Human, was Haith's only thought. Too human.

They laughed.

Next to Camillus, Haith was shining evenspan and frostfall storms made flesh. They were golden like the stars that came out in that time before lightrise faded and nightrun fell and silver like a flash of lightning without thunder. The glow of Haith's eyes, paler and brighter than the moon, reflected in the deepness of Camillus's gaze, Haith's burning hair, the colour of lightning turned to pale liquid, sending his into deeper shadow. The power of their truth and the potency of their Dusk Blood granted them dominion over the storm and with it light and water and the wind. Amongst most of the Blooded, Camillus's half-blood could be hidden beneath his intelligence and the intensity of his attention, but next to Haith . . .

Haith remembered every truth they spoke, the words that had prefaced it, and who had asked it of them. Before this night, each truth of Haith's had been carefully given. Such a gift could easily turn against them, so they had grown practised at simply holding their tongue against the honesty that was one part of their power, one part the reason they had been chosen to lead. But this time, they found themselves giving Camillus what he had not asked for. A truth that Haith could not take back.

"If you were to try," Haith said, every word dripping with dangerous foresight, "your weak blood would not command this crown as I do. It would command you, send the world into disorder and disarray, and send *you* mad."

Camillus's long fingers had reached for them, snagged, and

caught around Haith's wrist as they turned away. The slight pain pinched on Haith's skin, and they turned back to loosen it, expression severe in the face of Camillus's unrestrained intensity.

"It is not traditional for the crowned to give gifts on this night of splendour. Especially as your gift of truth does me little credit, considering I did not ask for it. What ominous words you have given me without cause. But even the purity of your gift makes you no oracle. We cannot know its worth until it is tested."

Camillus's burning, pinpoint gaze on Haith flickered, and the intensity of his attention on them slipped into a courteous ease and a slow smile curved his lips, some dark humour lingering in its edge. His grip on Haith loosened with the lightness of his expression but did not entirely let its captive go. The pad of a finger pressed into Haith's pulse point, leaving a trail of gold in both their hands and up their wrists as the Dusk Blood in Haith's veins reacted to Camillus's own. Camillus admired the light that trailed beneath his skin as though its presence in both of them was enough to make them the same.

"I can do it, Haith. I want to be a Dusk Lord."

"Even so, we have no seasons to spare for you."

Haith slid free of Camillus's grip, the joy that suffused the nightrun suddenly bitter, the lights below suddenly dim.

"You may do what you will, Camillus, but do not wish for approval from me. You will not get it."

Camillus reached out and tugged at the chains which were belted at Haith's waist, a symbol of the Dusk Lords' commitment to service. His gesture made Haith freeze with how familiar it was, but Camillus's smile was guileless when he replied, "My only wish is to serve, my Lord Haith."

Do what you will. These had been dangerous words and Haith should have known better than to speak them to Camillus.

The clean snap of wrought glass echoed through the council room. For a Dusk Lord to break their chains of service was once a sign of irreparable difference. Camillus didn't even blink when Haith snapped theirs.

"Something wrong, my Lord Haith?"

"You invite your father's court to the end of our season," Haith bit out, surprised at the anger that was building in them, fuelling the spark of light in their blood. "Why? He is charged with conspiracy against the crown. He is not to return, and this is not a human-born land. The exiles"—Haith did not miss the way Camillus twitched at that—"the shipwrecked, we accept those, but the people from across the sea, their kings and courts, should stay there."

"One of these rises, Haith, it would be refreshing if you came before me with a little sweetness. I've seen you with Prosper's Raven, I know you can."

"You haven't earned my regard, let alone anything more," Haith countered. "You've claimed a crown that you cannot command, disbanded the court mid-season, sent guards to stand at my door and trail me about the palace, and don't think your 'terms' for Feng fool me. Feng is an independent Blooded territory. We are not an Empire."

"Not yet," Camillus responded lightly.

Haith fought the urge to yank Camillus off the throne and dash the damned crown that had started this into broken splinters. "You are not a king, Camillus! Dusk Lords do not rule alone or eternal—"

"My Lord Haith, you have never been careful with your advice and your lack of faith but let us not forget that it was you who said, 'Do what you will.' I heard you. If you had some other truth to share, you cannot blame me if I did not hear it because *you* did not share it!"

Camillus stepped away because Haith would not, turning away and then turning back again, before continuing. "Even you should know by now that my only wish is to serve. Isn't that what Dusk Lords do?"

Haith shook their head. "You make me wonder. You command the Lords as though you have no intention of releasing the crown to Prosper come next season. Is one not enough for you? Or must you have them all?"

Haith saw Camillus's eyes flash and squared their shoulders in response, tilting their chin in defiance.

"Don't you ever get tired of this, Haith?" Camillus opined suddenly. "Wouldn't it be easier for everyone if you could accept that I am exactly what I seem?"

Haith stoppered the insolent laugh that bubbled up in their chest. "I do accept that, Camillus. I'm the only one who does. The other Lords will ignore it for the sake of peace but to me, what you seem is exactly what you *are*."

"For one so famed for choosing their truths carefully, I must admit I cannot wait to hear what you think of me after all this time," Camillus answered darkly, returning to the dais and waving a condescending hand for Haith to continue. "Don't be shy, Haith. Tell me who I really am."

Haith bristled at the way Camillus's smirk lifted in false indulgence and stalked over to the dais. "You are the son of an exiled prince and a Dusk Lord, so you thought you were owed a crown, despite having nothing to recommend you. You want the truths I have not shared; I shall provide them."

Haith enjoyed the way Camillus's easy smirk quickly dropped away and made no move to hold their truth-laden tongue, as they had been doing all season. "You're not a real Dusk Lord, Camillus, you didn't do this to serve your people. You did it to serve yourself. If you wanted a crown, you should've followed your father across the sea. Ours isn't yours to take. We have no kings here."

They gave a short, insulting bow to finish and said, "Will my truth serve, my lord?"

Camillus sat frozen for a moment, still staring down at Haith, before slowly thawing, as though Haith's words had been cold enough to turn him to a frost-rimed statue. Eventually, he shook his head, a war for control raging across his face until he finally settled on a scornful smile.

"Your gift of truth does me little credit," he said, repeating the words he'd spoken that first time and Haith struggled to hide a flinch. "You judge me harshly, Lord Haith."

He slid purposefully off the throne, reaching out to snatch Haith's hand with the chains still clenched within. "But as I said all that time ago, we cannot know the true worth of your gift until it is tested. I don't think it will matter who is a real Dusk Lord for much longer. Because if Mistral has no kings, then I guess something, or someone, should stop me from becoming one come end of season. The first king."

He pulled the chains from between Haith's fingers and stalked out of the throne room. "Let's put your words to the test, honourable Haith, and see if you lie."

Haith followed and stopped just inside of the heavy doors flung wide open. Pulling on the threads of power within them, Haith summoned the wind to their side. The doors rocked in their sockets.

"Camillus, I remember every truth I speak, the words that preface it, and who has asked it of me. And I have just one more for you. Test it all you want. You will not be king forever . . . and no king of your line will ever sit on this throne."

Haith pushed on the doors and though Camillus rushed to try to stop them, the doors slammed shut with a booming gust of wind. Haith marked it with the blood that blossomed from the chain marks dug into their hand. Closing their eyes, Haith pulled on the well of power that infused their blood, the whispers of the wind still strong in their ears, and light shattered across the throne room. Haith disappeared.

A storm cracked across the skies, clouds rolling in dark across the warm evenspan and bringing with them the last frostfall of the season. But there was no one in the throne room to see it and the doors were sealed shut.

And they remained shut.

CHAPTER 1

THE *OATHBREAKER* WAS ROCKING ON SHALLOW WAVES, THE SOUND OF creaking wood a familiar lullaby to her inhabitants. The sky above the jutting topmast was dark, cut through with dull golden stars and a dying moon, closing its second run across the violet night. The light had been long during the previous rise, the evenspan that followed brief but welcome, but silence had taken an unusual hold over the port city of Phirrun and every ship in its docks with the coming of nightrun. Nothing issued forth from the *Oathbreaker*'s sleeping crew, and even the scratch of the captain's quill was missing where it should've been lost under the former's snores and shifting. The cook wasn't humming gently in the galley, and there wasn't the slightest trace of Edge's bare feet padding around on deck as he took his watch. An unexpected slumber had befallen the ship with the season's warm sunning wind and a calm sea.

Then, in the distance, a bell tolled.

The quiet was broken like a twig being snapped in two. Sound returned to the ship and the city beyond it with sudden ferocity, and movement immediately followed. Feet began tramping up and down the wood floors and voices rose from all points of the ship, without care for any still abed. The silence retreated from every crevice and dark corner, finding no place to rest on the now alive *Oathbreaker*, excepting one.

A heavy door remained unopened despite the din and calls to work. Behind it, all was still and quiet, punctuated by soft breathing only to remind the room that its occupant was still, in fact, alive. The bundle of bedclothes that formed a vaguely human shape could just as likely be mistaken for another heap of clothes, like those that littered the floor, the chair by the desk, and the chest by the bottom of the bed. Or perhaps a collection of trinkets like those that filled the shelves, drawers, and desktop alike . . . If not for the fact that the bundle was breathing.

Two sharp knocks on the door banished the only refuge for the all-encompassing silence, but the sound vanished without conclusion as the body under the covers answered the knocks with a resolved muteness and a practised stillness. The silence took hold again. One sharper and more impatient knock rapped out against the heavy wood of the door before it was thrown open with surprising ease. Lightrise poured in, along with the scent of hot food and salt-sprayed air.

The body rolled over with some difficulty and bright, unnatural eyes glared sleepily at the man standing with a wide grin in the doorway.

"Is the sun even up yet?" the Strange-eyed boy demanded, scrunching his eyes in distaste and shifting away from the lighted doorway and the captain of the *Oathbreaker*'s expectant expression which was boring into him.

"No, but work begins when I say it does, run or rise. Present company included," the captain answered, the lift at the corner of his mouth growing more amused at the theatric whine that issued forth from the covers, gracing his handsome face with good humour. His green eyes, capricious and twinkling, were now the colour of grass, next cooling jade.

He toed a pile of clothes by the foot of the doorway. "What a mess."

A questioning grunt surfaced from the direction of the bed.

The lift on the captain's face turned provocative. "Alice will be disappointed." He turned and stepped back through the door as the figure emerged from the bed in a flurry of tangled sheets and into the slanted light.

"Be on deck shortly. And clean this mess up at some point, won't you, Shye?"

The man stopped short in the small hall beyond the room and turned on his heel to face his charge once again.

Shye propped himself up against the bed, one hand buried in his hair, while the other fiddled with a broken hair tie. He swore quietly to the room as he tried to coordinate the two to work together.

"Don't go back to sleep," the captain commanded, as he wandered away again and up to the deck.

Shye struggled a few moments more with the tie before securing it around his tousled curls, and jammed on a pair of oilskin boots. He threw his worn green cloak over his shoulders and drew up the hood. The seams were lined with weights so that it hid most of his face from view and wouldn't fall prey to the billows of wind up top or any curious, catching fingers. Leaving the room behind, he followed after his master.

The ship beyond was a hive of activity as crewmembers darted up and down the gangplank, depositing crates of merchandise to be transported to both reputable and disreputable storehouses and buyers within the Empire, while the captain stood at the quarterdeck with Alice and Edge, and Butler hauled cargo up to the main deck for disembarkation. Shye looked around but couldn't spot Muse; probably vanished somewhere up the main mast checking the sails, before fixing the cargo net. *He'll have a hell of a time fixing that*, he thought, *and Edge won't make it easy*. There was no doubt that Edge had been enjoying watching Butler haul all the cargo off the boat by himself from his prime spot on the quarter deck. Even Shye had noticed how attentive Edge was to the big man's labour and the covetous look in his eyes.

Shye considered scrambling up after Muse to warn him not to fix it, if it meant ruining Edge's good mood.

He preferred Muse's easy, rough ways over the handling he got from some other members of the crew, but with the itch of the broken tie digging into his scalp, he stepped up to Butler instead. Intercepting the next create with some difficulty as the weight of it bore down on him, though Butler hauled them up from below with relative ease, Shye gave a quick nod to his guardian above on the quarterdeck and joined in on tramping down the gangway onto solid land for the first time since leaving Feng, a whole season ago.

The streets of Phirrun were sheeted with pale, grimed stone; the short-lived sun baths of the current season too quick-moving to give them a good washing like next season's frostfalls would. The moon would hold more sway then, the light shines would be short, and the falls would come for several rises and runs, and between there would be fires and foolishness in the evenspan as the big cities of Emin Rif closed their businesses against the dark and threw festivals. The spidered veins of mineral that ran through Phirrun's stones would glitter in the frosted nightrun.

Ammolite, gem silica, sunstone, moonstone, labradorite, and bone scarred the stone to show just how old the city was. Sealed stone could only be found in the original territories of the Dusk Blooded. The original people that had shaped these lands and cities had been conquered and cast aside by human inhabitants before the written histories of the Empire even began, but their ghosts could still be seen in places like Phirrun. In people like Shye.

The capital and seat of the crown, Mistral, was the only other one in the Mountain and River Lands that had the seals. Though, it was not the only other in the Empire – or at least in the lands they claimed. Whether those lands felt the same was another thing altogether.

Shye had not seen the streets of Thorel on the Islands of Feng, but he could dream they were deeper and cleaner than these, and the rivers that glittered in them would be brimming with something more than Shye's own Strangeness. Something of the Old World, something from the same place as him, that wasn't covered in the waste and ruin of more than a thousand years of neglect.

Shye dropped the crate among the others marked with the Feng-Tanaren clan insignia, careful not to mix it up with those from Feng-Rel. The symbol of a spiral with a trailing tail was used by every clan in Feng to represent the islands. Colour and the clan name attached were the only difference. Feng-Tanaren used painted garnet dust to mark out their merchandise. Shye double-checked the side of the crate and hissed out a breath of relief to see the crimson mark. He toed an errant patch of wet weeds with his boot, imagining the damp warmth of the stone beneath his bare feet. Would he hear it sing under him when his skin touched it? Would the seals of his folk, those veins of coloured glass, carved into ages-old stone, remember him? Like *Oathbreaker* remembered him, was almost a part of him, from her sails and the wind that moved them, to her wooden heart, and every heavy door. They were his, and if he called them, they would listen. Could a city be the same?

Shye.

Shye whirled around, his hair flinging out of its hasty tie and tumbling to hang about his face and neck. But for once it wasn't the wind through the *Oathbreaker* that whispered his name, it was old stones and old earth somewhere far from the docks. The feeling of storms breaking across dark waters, like the ones the *Oathbreaker* crossed at nightrun hit upon by a flash storm, suddenly rose up in his middle from somewhere deep inside. He blinked and the feeling subsided as he pulled his fingers away from the patch of moss and stone they'd reached out and brushed without permission. Through the heavy material of his boots, the stone was solid and dead, and his name wasn't coming from within the city anymore but from the deck with the rough husk of an irritated and impatient Edge. Shye turned towards the city and waited a moment, but whatever it was didn't call his name again, leaving only Edge and his growing agitation. Shye tapped the nearby load with fine, light fingers and sprinted back up the gangway to collect another, quickly forgetting the whisper he'd thought he'd heard before Edge had called out his name.

Every step away seemed to drag with an inexorable pull back into the city. The possibilities waiting there were only made more alluring by the scrape of loose hair against his neck and the promise of fixing that first. Setting down the crate on top of another cart sent by one of many secretive buyers the captain maintained dealings with, Shye glanced up at the ship. He trailed his eyes along her sleek lines and well-loved trimmings before he met the captain's gaze.

Shye started, flushing. Guilt began to drip into his stomach, not because he wanted to run off, abandon his duties, and explore a city he'd rarely been allowed to see, but because doing so was dangerous, and more dangerous was the temptation to seek that feeling of connection beyond the shelter of the *Oathbreaker*.

He busied himself with securing the load. When he peeked over the crates, the captain had moved onto more important things and was arguing with Alice, while he grasped a roster firmly in hand. Shye blew out his breath in a huff, in reproach of his restlessness. Scuffing the wet weeds free with the toe of his boot and glancing again at the busy ship, where few of the crew had care of him at the moment, Shye watched the captain move off from the quarterdeck and pass out of sight.

Shye.

He flinched. His mind twitched towards freedom, and he forced himself back to the ship. It took him more than half the lightrise and sixty crates of merchandise to give in to the whispered command and slip away, leaving the rest of the unloading to Butler and the sorry crew responsible for it. Part of him was sure the guilt would slip down inside him again, but to wander a city or even just its docks and bays without a crewmember present was a rare occurrence and this errand didn't need company.

His broken tie was a clumsy excuse, but then the captain didn't usually care for excuses, and Shye was sure he wasn't going to get away unnoticed for long. At least, if he was going to get caught, he'd have a new tie and no complaints about how he'd spent his time in the port city. After all, there were few better cities to play hooky in than Phirrun.

CHAPTER 2

ONCE PAST THE WIDE STRETCH OF THE DOCKS, PHIRRUN WAS A MESS OF alleys and streets, narrow and wide and curving often into dead ends. The buildings of the city collapsed in on each other but were so tightly packed that they stayed upright only by virtue of their co-dependency. The only people Shye passed on the streets whose guild he recognised were the sun-browned sailors, scarred from brawls, hard labour and, unlike many of his captain's operations, various services for the crown. The anchors inked into the back of their hands united them under the edicts of the Empire.

Shye's apprentice mark of faded camphire dye had washed almost out of sight and would need to be redone soon, along with the rest of the crew's black ink fakeries. The captain preferred that all legality required by the Empire be flexible on board the *Oathbreaker*, guild inkings included.

"We're not thieves, Shye," he remembered his captain saying once, "we're nautical tax dodgers helping other tax dodgers move their product. There isn't a high guild for it, but no one gets hanged for it either." But even Shye knew it wasn't that simple, even if he was not included, required, or wanted on the subject of how not simple the *Oathbreaker*'s work really was.

Among the crowd of the city, he could vaguely spot the minor noble, and knew a merchant from Feng by their braided hair, their skin smooth and dark, and flecked with gold, like Muse's. The insignia inked on their graceful necks were different from guild inkings by the clan colours they displayed and the defiant nature of the mark. Singularly Feng and only barely imperial, like the islands themselves which still vied for independence. He had little idea who the ladies with sapphires in their knuckles were, only that sapphires were not the only gems those sorts of ladies carried embedded in their skin, and that it meant something significant for a lady to flaunt a gem in all ten. Many only bore them in a single hand.

What Shye did know was that any one of them could be a Raven and he stopped himself from examining those around him too closely, just in case. What criteria the crown used to select their spies was unknown, but they were everywhere, their eyes watching in every city, their intelligence stretching from the throne room to the edge of the Empire. And should a Raven be looking to examine Shye, he kept his head down and his hood up, for each and every one of the crew's usual superstitions. Mostly for the rational ones, like Ravens and secret stealers, along with the irrational ones, like weather nymphs who giggle and whistle up the winds, and marsh witches who summon quickening fog, and to end his captain's jibes that only princes hold their heads that high – princes and swans.

Shye had not appreciated either attempt at a nickname.

He had been born with an experienced sailor's sunning-dark skin, which wasn't unusual on the islands that dotted the coast or around the ports on the mainland, especially among his own folk. No man nor Raven could find fault in that at least, though he couldn't claim ancestry from any clan in Feng, as many did. But if they looked closer, there had been some that picked Strangeness in the structure of his face, with its noble high cheekbones and a nose that had never been broken. A miraculous feat for almost any sailor except for Muse, the captain, and himself. If they looked closer than that, they'd see his eyes.

Little more than pure Strangeness existed within those.

With his hood up, Shye looked like every other one of those sailors, with only the lowest denominations of imperial glass to their name, a few jade fans and some night's eyes at most.

He weaved around a couple strolling through the dim street. His eyes caught on the gems lining the woman's knuckles, the long, needle-thin knife sheathed next to the bunch of blood lily and lemongrass tucked into her belt, and swerved to brush by a plum-spice drunk sailor staggering down towards the way Shye had come. Rubbing shoulders couldn't be avoided in such close quarters and the sailor didn't even notice the heavy impact as he careened into Shye's side and staggered onwards. But Shye didn't like the look of that lady. She might've felt the whisper of his cloak as he passed and perhaps, when she looked at him, she'd see through his hood and steal the secrets right from his eyes.

People let the couple pass into a lane that was wider, brighter, and cleaner than the rest of the city put together. Round candle-lamps bobbed on long poles overhead, even during the lightrise, and a million scents wafted from the lane into the rest of the city, all of them so rare to Shye that it wasn't only the spice that seemed intoxicating. Once the couple had disappeared into the crowd, Shye skipped over a fallen barrel spilling fish onto the grotty street and joined the heaving crowd at the top of the street, taking in the view.

Stalling Alley was the entire Phirrun market district stretched into one long, wide, snaking street. Stalls lined up along its length, from one end of the city to the other, each one selling as many different wares from as many different places as one could walk, ride, or sail to. The air was heavy with perfumes and soaps, food, liquored spice, oils, and powdered goods, and just when the crowd seemed like they were drowning in it, along would come the sweeping sea wind and blow it all away.

The street rang with voices, merchants – and the traders a rank below them – haggling and spruiking, while those ladies that could take leisure giggled behind gloved hands to hide their inkings and laced fans to hide their whispers, while others with less leisure hurried along at a business pace. Roughened sailors like Shye made beelines towards the stalls whose services they sought and were off again before too long. The clientele of Stalling Alley was many and varied, yet not even the lowest or the least imperial among them would test the punishment for petty crime.

Shye liked to believe it was the influence of the old stones that protected wares and marketgoers alike from light fingers, rather than the risk of losing them. Scouring each stall as he passed, he glanced up at the signs that decorated the tops and sides of each booth, searching for a familiar brand. Jewellers, smiths, medicinalists and medicas, haberdashers, milliners, so-called rarity sellers, and liba-tionists, all called out to him and the rest of the crowd to buy, look, touch, and taste their wares. None had what he was looking for.

Finally, he saw it. Burned into a wooden sign above a stall was a curling spiral with a trailing tail, this time in bright white for merchants from the city and clan of Feng-Aeth. The booth sat, colourfully arranged like the set of islands its wares came from, between a woodcarver and a lock maker, with clothes, cloths, threads, ribbons, and even beads hung over the windows, chairs, counters, and on the wall behind at the back of the shop. Every colour, shade, material, style, and texture had some presence on display.

Shye slipped through the crowd towards it.

The Feng trained the masters of weaving and dyeing, producing the softest fabrics and the longest-lasting cloths, though their record-keeping, spiced liquor, and governing council were also to be feared in their efficiency and quality of purpose. Their islands, which lay to the north-west of the Mountain and River Lands – what the imperials called Emin Rif – could more easily export their goods by legal trade to Corentin and sell their merchandise in the Empire's smaller port city in the west. Despite this, there would always be a Feng presence in Stalling Alley where the business was frequent, and the crown's fees for import could be recouped in trade or, for some, made avoid-able. Like the taxes on those crates Shye had been hauling for most of the lightrise.

The last tie Shye had bought had been from the market on a small island off Phirrun's coast and had lasted half as long as the one before that, picked up for him by the crew in the Islands of Feng, in their capital of Thorel. Quality paid for itself sometimes.

"Ah," the Feng merchant's voice rang out, clear and strong over the counter, despite the tiny, corded frame, and dark hair threaded with silver string. "A gentleman customer. How can I help you, friend?"

Looking over the Feng merchant's wares, Shye poked and prodded at the selection of ribbons. Too thick for his purpose, too nice for a sailor, too flimsy, too colourful; none of what he could see were fit for a little wear and tear. Shye leaned in closer to the small merchant, who had been eyeing his search with keenness and a small smile that said they were already well aware of what Shye was looking for. There was a certain something about the Feng, the imperials probably would've termed it Strangeness and tossed his captain and crew in with them, as if all Strange things came from his Dusk Blooded kind and were not simply just strange.

The imperials couldn't even use the title. They called them Strange or simply 'folk' out of remembrance, even fear, of what they had been. As if those two words were enough to wake them from the dead. The Dusk Blooded had been known to this world, like Shye was known to the *Oathbreaker*, like nightrun knows its stars and a bolt of lightning knows the storm it's born upon. There were things they'd been able to do, manifestations of will and wonder, things that died with the rise of the Empire. *And now, we are something less than we were*, Shye thought bitterly, *not wonderous, just different. Just Strange.*

The merchant coughed politely, and Shye was knocked from his contemplation, eyes darting across all the options of ribbon before him.

"I need a thin length of material ..." he began, heat flushing in his face, and was stopped by the small laugh that bubbled up from the merchant.

"No need to be shy," they said, voice neither high nor low but perfectly balanced, with a thread of enthusiasm running through it. "Is it for a friend of yours? No, I know. Airy always does."

They paused and then went on, puttering about the shop, only half addressing Shye, "No. What colour and material? Let me see."

Shye thought that was what it was about the Feng, not Strangeness but keenness; sharpness. A seized understanding. The merchant looked at him, seeing only the pull of his cowl and the skim of cheekbones, mouth and jaw, and ran their fingers over silks and ribbons of different shades of brown, black, grey and blue, sensing without input that they were not right.

"In all practicality," the merchant continued, "you want a strip of good-quality leather, preferably oil skin. It lasts for an extensive period of time, can handle various weather conditions, and draws no more attention than the rest of you."

The keen gaze travelled swiftly down and then back up. Their mouth quirked upwards.

"I have something better, I think. Not too thick, strong and durable. You would want it so long." The merchant made a gesture of measurement with their fingers, needing no more input from Shye than he had given in the first place. They turned away and opened a drawer draped in velvety fabrics beneath the benches, before retrieving a reel of material the like of which was unfamiliar to Shye. The merchant measured the length again, cutting the reel through and holding it up for Shye's inspection. It was ice-blue, with a dull shine like polished metal; tough, but yielding like leather.

"It's called winterhide, recently developed for the Imperial Navy. Admittedly, it has a brighter colouring than you would probably like, but something to brighten you up might not be a bad thing, and its advantages in durability make it worth the unusual dye. And the price."

Shye nodded. The merchant dropped the length into his palm where it coiled, glinting against his skin.

"Two suns."

Shye flinched a little. Good-quality leather was five eyes at most. Two suns was extortionate. The captain would not be happy he'd paid so much for a simple hair tie.

He handed over the required glass. The captain was already unhappy with him anyway.

The merchant waved him away from the stall with a gentle hand. "Thank you for your business, friend. And fair winds on your next journey, sailor."

"Thank you, Master."

Shye took the winterhide and melted back into the swelling crowd. On his way back to the *Oathbreaker*, he vaguely perused stalls. Stalling Alley may have been the most popular marketplace in Emin Rif, but that didn't make it honest. Most vendors offered illegal and sometimes impossible things after market hours and in tavern back rooms for the right price, or to the gullible-enough client; from mood and performance enhancers made of honey-like amber globules and folk-crafted storm-glass daggers, to blue smoke grenades and witching sticks. The stories had been surfacing again of the Imperial Navy policing the smaller islands of Feng and going missing in the lightrise fog. Witching sticks were in high demand again among the merchants, with rumours of marsh witches being responsible for the disappearances.

Yet if there was one thing Captain Creed vehemently protested – aside from shipping taxes, and all other taxes for that matter, plus the Imperial Navy, and the Empire as a whole – it was the Blood Manifest. His kind's ability to move this world and to make it something else, to bend jewels from stone, bloom seasons from hard ground, heal grievous wounds with only breath and silver string, and to split the sky with howling gales, their Dusk Blood and its connection to the world made manifest – all that was gone. The land that lived did so in silence without the Dusk Blooded to give it voice.

According to the captain, all that was left of the Old World was bad luck, thinning blood, recessive folklines, and Shye. All that was left of the Strange ones were the stones beneath Shye's boots.

But Shye felt there was something deeply wrong with that. Surely, he could not be the only one who had more Dusk in him than just a waning folkline in the entire Empire. The only one whose ancient blood was so evident he had to hide it away, the only one the Empire might think still had power.

The bell tolled down by the docks and Shye startled. He had run out of time to follow the snaking trail of Stalling Alley all the way around, and he had delayed the inevitable too long already. The captain was rarely impressed by anyone skimping on their duties, even less when it was his charge. Shye doubled back, twisting through the thick crowd and the maze of streets, till he arrived at the docks just as the last chimes echoed through the quay. He rolled up to the *Oathbreaker*, heels skidding on the wet patches of weed poking up through stone, and found he was awaited on deck.

The crew had dissipated to all but one.

Muse was sitting on the deck railing, pulling a jaunty tune from the strings of a violin.

Shye relaxed at the familiar sound of bells swinging in the wind, woven into the braided black lengths of the man's hair, and the counterpoint of well-tuned strings.

His mouth curled upwards at the familiar sight and his song, and as he dropped from the gangway onto the deck, Muse's melody turned ominous, before drifting away altogether. His hair jingled with the movement of his head as he turned from the instrument to Shye.

"All right there, Shye? Captain's in a pretty tizzy over your runnin' off this afternoon," the smiling man greeted, teeth flashing in contrast to his burnished complexion. His eyes were gold like bright sunstones and melted treasures – one of the many thinning folklines that had found their way onto the crew of the *Oathbreaker*.

Muse's folk blood had left him with his talent for unmatched persuasion and for drawing sweet music without a thought from any instrument he set his hands to, though he had always played his violin for so long as Shye had known him. Most of the crew had a touch or two of the Strange, even the captain, but none so much as Shye.

After the king's suppression in Mistral all those spans ago, it was no surprise that the captain took to the water and found himself some company. There weren't many refuges left in Emin Rif for their rebellious kind after that, and the crew weren't the type to settle quietly in Feng. Shye could count himself lucky to be from Aura, so far out as to rarely be of interest to the Empire that claimed to own it, though he was luckier still to be on this crew.

The light tinkling of Muse's bells came again as he twisted his body back over the railing and dropped down onto the deck.

"He said he'll be seein' you when you get back from your 'adventure in truancy'. He's in his cabin."

Muse turned back to the city, his smile sinking into a simple contentedness, and struck up his violin again. This time, he was ringing out a sea shanty that when sung told of a group of folk-born pirates who robbed a passing ship of all their hats, because they had robbed so long that no true treasure remained. It sounded like something this crew could have done, before the suppression, if they'd had the chance to meet before then. And before Shye had come along and made them complicit in his survival. Now, they took their jobs and pleasures under the cover of nightrun to keep him safe, when they could live rich and name their terms to the prince if they turned him in instead of keeping him.

He stayed until the song had finished, quietly singing the verses as the lights of the city flickered into the violet evenspan, before going below.

CHAPTER 3

SHYE STOOD BEFORE THE DOOR THAT WAS BETWEEN HIM AND A MAN HE was in no hurry to see. He raised his hand to push it slowly open before changing his mind; his fingers curling into a fist instead. He raised it to rap against the wood when a voice called to him from within.

"Don't dally at my door, Shye. Get in here."

The captain of the *Oathbreaker* stood within his spartan quarters, behind a desk that belied the simplicity of the rest of room, piled high as it was with paper, accounts and charts. The captain stood before a selection of books, lined up on one of many shelves, while his fingers danced across their spines.

His coat was clean and fine; a neat, deep grey with silver embroidery, the ends of the sleeves done up in double cuffs held by minor gems in sets of three. It was an unusual indulgence in finery that meant Shye's master had important business to attend to. Very important, if the neatly bound hair and clean shave were added to the tally.

Shye knew the captain had once belonged to an ancient house, but it was rare that crew ever got to see what that might have looked like.

Shit, Shye thought miserably, *I really am in trouble this time.*

At length, just enough time to start Shye shifting uncomfortably on his feet, the captain selected one book and turned to face his ward. His eyes faded from their grassy green to something deeper and quite unimpressed.

Among those books, Shye wondered if there was one on the possibility of Dusk Bloodedness being reflected in the eyes, or better yet how to control a disposition, as his had a tendency to get away from him and continued to be his greatest liability when it came to the captain's displeasure. Either way, at least Muse and the captain could get away with theirs. No one could say that persuasion and intuition weren't useful in their line of work. Truth was an inconvenience at best and potentially deadly at its worst.

How to will an element would also be helpful. If Shye ever wanted an opening for rediscovering the Blood Manifest, both disposition and element were crucial. But Shye had never heard the voice that was supposed to call to him, never noticed any raw component of the world bend towards his voice or show him any favour. Not even the *Oathbreaker* could really be said to speak to him, not the way Muse seemed to resonate with the wood of his violin when he played his music.

Undoubtedly, even if the captain had such a book, it would be the last thing he would ever hand over to his ward.

"We missed your presence at unloading this afternoon. Care to share what required such immediate attention?"

"I needed a tie."

Shye met his master's eyes with no regrets, but coloured a little in the silence that followed. The captain broke contact after a moment, releasing Shye from his commitment to not be the one to break first, and turned his attention to the book resting beneath his hand, deftly switching it out for another. There was a frown hiding at the edges of captain's mouth that made Shye wince. His attitude was only sometimes endearing to his crew and difficult to rein in regardless.

"You know how I feel about attending to your duties," came the stern rebuke. "When you came here there were a few things agreed upon by all. Namely, that you would do as you were told, go where you were you told, keep your head down and eyes out of sight."

The captain's green eyes shifted in what many assumed to a be a trick of the light, but Shye knew was not that at all. From clear emerald, they cooled further to something dark and vast enough as to almost be black.

Shye locked his muscles in place, ducked his head and fixed his gaze firmly on the straight, neat lines of the planked floor. Like many of the things he'd experienced out on the *Oathbreaker*, the only thing he could do when it came to the captain's disapproval was to weather it.

He flinched when a book slammed down on the desk, fingers twisting behind his back as the captain continued.

"This was the price you agreed to. A time will come when you do not have to hide what you are, but unfortunately it isn't this one. It comes when I say it does, when it will not cost me my crew or you your life. Do not doubt that if you break our deal, there will be consequences."

The captain paused, fingers tapping lightly on the cover of the book, the ornate ring that Shye had never seen him without winked back and forth, sending a play of light across the floor. His tone turned to a command that brooked no argument and Shye felt himself involuntarily pull up straight in response.

"Tonight, you'll be woken before the first bell, and you will come with us to meet Master Fox and attain some supplies."

He tossed the book to Shye.

"Read that too. It will afford you no enjoyment and waste your preciously ill-timed freedom. Unless, I suppose, you stumble upon a chance to philosophise with anyone on the subject of greater purpose. Trudging joylessly through it should be punishment enough to remind you not to shirk your duties every time we enter a city bigger than that floating Aurian dockside you were born on. Try to remember these rules protect more than just you."

The captain sat languidly down behind his desk and made a

shooing gesture in Shye's direction; his fingers coming up to twist the ring there three times around.

"Go play."

The captain's eyes were green as grass again when they bent down to his work. Not that that meant much at all. Anyone who thought those eyes made Captain Ezra Creed in any way honest, did not know him well.

Shye ducked out of the room and made his way back up to the deck.

Muse had put away his violin and was sitting at the railing by the time Shye crested the stairs, idly splicing rope with practised ease, while waiting for the rest of crew to reappear towards the close of evenspan. His eyes barely shifted from the lights of the city to check the movement of his fingers, relying on the feel of the coarse material to guide him, but he flicked his eyes away from the view to give Shye a curious side-eye as he clambered up to plop down next to him. Muse's mouth quirked in profile.

Shye pulled at his hood out of habit, not that he could hide from what would be said when Muse chose to say it.

"Where's Butler, Edge, and every other useless cretin on this boat? And Alice?" Shye asked, giving his hood another tug before letting his grip fall from its edge. Looking out over the docks, he tried to guess which lantern-lighted doorways his crew had wandered into in search of comforts they only had on land, whether that be drinks, fights, both, or otherwise. Alice had probably found a bathhouse with a spa.

Muse breathed a laugh as low and rich as the bells in his hair were light and chiming. "They'd be mighty sad to hear you callin' them that," he said, with the sliver of a grin. His fingers worked over the stiff rope without faltering.

"Sad? Doubtful," Shye answered, nose wrinkling. "Irritated, maybe. I'd prefer vaguely amused, but I'd settle for sufferance."

Muse's fingers paused in their work and his golden eyes shifted as though to see through the darkness cast by Shye's hood. "You've been spending too much time with the captain and his books."

His gaze moved back towards the city. "They're off enjoyin' themselves, but they'll be back before lightrise to make the run. They're
reliable like that."

Shye felt the small jab for what it was meant to be. His hand was
halfway to his hood already when he noticed and pulled it back
into his lap. Rampant pub melodies filtered out from the nearest
closed door beneath their dangling feet, and Shye wished Muse
would pick up his violin and drown it out with something better,
but instead he knotted the splice, put it aside and shifted to
face him.

"So, boyo of ours, what was so important it was worth gettin' woke
before bells tomorrow?"

Shye grimaced at the thought of so much sleep lost. He pulled the
strip of winterhide free from where he'd tied it around his wrist,
holding it out between them, where it glinted dully. Muse's eyes twinkled as he took hold of the fabric; icy blue and burning against his
dark, rough palm.

"Hood off," he commanded, with a brief spill of anticipation
seeping into his voice. Despite the dark emptiness of the *Oathbreaker*
and the street below, Shye still paused. His fingers were so used to
pulling his hood forward that he hesitated at pushing it back. The
captain's words rang out again in his head.

Muse snapped the fingers of his other hand impatiently.

"No one's here. Hood off."

Shye shuffled round to bare his shoulder and back to Muse, and
the cowl fell against them with the deliberate finality it always had
when it came to bearing his face and eyes to the world, even the one
that existed just inside his room or this one now, blanketed in darkness. His hair scratched his collar, the unbound curls tangled into
knots, sometimes brown, sometimes something else.

Muse cooed mockingly at the sight, producing what Shye knew
from experience was a comb and a box of matches from somewhere
on his person. He combed the tangles and snarls away with quick efficiency. His question floated into Shye's ear over the pull of the comb.

"May I?"

Shye took a breath and flicked his eyes over the dark street. He should be careful, but he nodded anyway. "Go ahead."

He heard the strike of the match, and in the corners of his eyes saw his hair turn in the pale-yellow light it threw. Strands turning violet-white, running with the pallid glow of lightning, consuming every curl of dusty brown. From his roots slipping down to his ends, it ran with the multitude of his old-world blood; one of many gifts from the folk. The Empire could hardly be called fond of Dusk and Strangeness. And those ran in Shye more than most.

When Muse touched it, combing out the twists and snarls, he felt the sputtering of embers and the veins in his hand flashed gold, and then he blew out the match and the light faded away.

Shye's hair crept back to unassuming brownness.

Muse gathered it, twisted, and bound it low on Shye's neck, tugging proudly at the bow when he was done.

"It almost matches your eyes."

Shye shuffled back around and faced Muse's slanting grin. Muse immediately recanted after a thought, "Well, it's hardly as bright or piercin' and it certainly is missin' that Stormborn spark, but there is a similar quality."

Muse's expression turned teasing, taking the rare chance to meet Shye's gaze without hindrance. "All worldly treasure pales in comparison."

He took the folds of Shye's hood in his hand and pulled it up again. Shye settled it back into place, his features sitting once again in shadow. Muse hummed and pressed his hand down onto Shye's head with an approving jostle, before picking up his violin. His eyes moved away to track the group of swaying figures making their way down the docks to their ship. As they got closer, he looked back at Shye, trying and failing this time to find his gaze beneath the cowl. He touched two fingers instead to the skim of light across his jaw.

"One rise, we might find a place where you won't have to hide them."

Taking his hand back, Muse struck up as the figures reached the bottom of the gangway and began to lurch upwards in their direction.

"Go on below," he continued. "Rest while you can."

"What about my second lecture?" Shye asked dryly, hopping down onto his feet and leaning against the rail, a little surprised Muse would let him get away without one.

Muse plucked at the strings of his violin and somebody below groaned. Edge's voice followed it, rising up over the side. "Unless yer've got a song which cures headaches and a broken finger, I suggest yer put that bloody thing away." This was only answered with a chuckle and what sounded like the beginnings of a lullaby.

More grumbling rose, getting louder. Complaints of headaches and bruises, the odd bitemark or clawed scratch, mixed with victories crowed from inebriated mouths about who won what or who took who and then immediately devolving into squabbling on the same subject. Muse kept playing, guiding them over the rail like a lure and fulfilling their ridiculous superstitions of sirens.

He flicked a glance towards Shye and said plainly, "Do you want to leave us, Shye?"

Shye was silent. He focused on the city spread out beyond them and then his attention caught on Butler; a hulking shape in the dark, his teeth flashing pearly at Edge's grievance with his impolite but efficient medical attention. Butler could mend blood and bone with more skill than any imperial surgeon and had, through talent and training, developed an expertise in refashioning the body to better match the spirit that even Shye – who had never doubted the architecture of his own form – could appreciate. Edge was so proud of Butler's work he bared his sculpted chest whenever possible. But no one could claim those hands were tender when Butler was mending the minor stuff.

Shye's mouth lifted at their exchange. Butler ever calm and cool where Edge was rough and unreasonable. For all Edge complained, there was no doubt he'd keep his finger splinted for as long as Butler instructed.

Muse's voice came to him again, breaking through the scene the crew were making around them. "Do you know what happens if you do?"

A breeze rustled through the *Oathbreaker*'s sails, her wood creaking underfoot. Shye did know. Or, at least, he had an idea. If he left, the world out there would change. It would change maybe even enough to halt the prince's upcoming, highly imperial coronation, and wouldn't that be something. But not something worth dying over or losing his freedom for, and not enough to stop the crown from caging him, maybe killing him. An old thing like him could not live free in the Empire. They'd have to make him theirs or destroy him completely.

The ship lurched unexpectedly in the harbour and sent the next crewmember, Senate, tripping over the railing, where he sprawled onto the open deck. Alice brought up the rear, stepping over Senate's cursing form, before reaching down to help him up. Her skin glowed in the weak light. Muse quirked a lip at Shye, who felt an echo of the voice he'd heard on the docks at lightrise slip away from the *Oathbreaker*'s stowed sails, an unconscious pull within him slithering back down to curl in his stomach, and he swallowed heavily. The *Oathbreaker* returned to a shallow rock.

Muse set his eyes back on Shye.

"Then, there's nothing I can tell you that you do not know. Whatever the captain has set will not teach you to obey the rules, but it will have to be enough. What more's to say, my dear? A disposition is one thing, an element another. Without both and Dusk strong enough to awaken it, the Blood Manifest remains a forgotten craft. Even with what power I have, I cannot will it. Without it, this ship is all we have. It is our protector and our home."

His focus flicked away, to the crew lingering around and to his soft music, and he jerked his head at the stairs. "Go on below."

Shye jostled his shoulder against Muse's in acquiescence and wandered back along the deck and then down into the heart of the ship.

CHAPTER 4

SHYE WAS DRIFTING OUT OF SLEEP. THE WARMTH OF A LANTERN WAS close, splashing red across his closed eyelids, and his bed seemed to be rocking in time to the folk shanty being crooned into his ear. His eyes cracked open just as the singer hit the chorus and he hissed from the bright glow of a lantern hanging over his face. Jerking away, he smashed his shoulder into the wall, the flickering light illuminating the dips and hollows of his captain's face as it leered at him, one booted foot propped firmly on the bed frame as the captain moved it in time to the song.

The captain's voice escalated from crooning to something rowdier, and it echoed pervasively throughout the ship by the voices joining in from above, with far too much cheer for a rise that was still on the edge of the nightrun before.

Depositing the lantern on the desk, the captain removed his foot from Shye's bed, threw Shye's cloak in the direction of his head, and sang loudly enough on his way out to make sure Shye understood the point, even in his barely cognizant state. He obediently tore himself free of the sheets and followed, joining in on the chorus as they trudged upwards from the bowels to the main deck, where the rest of the run crew was already waiting.

There were six of them, including the captain and Shye. Shye put the lantern down on the stairs to the quarterdeck, where the slight filtering of light revealed the four crew that had been just outlines in the dark before. Shye's mood soured.

His shoulders set with indignance, and he muttered to the night air, "You really don't trust me."

Muse's gaze inched away from the captain to send Shye an apologetic look, while Edge greeted their youngest crewmember with a grin that was dominated by slightly too-sharp teeth, turning his handsome face into something else entirely. Butler was silent and remained so. Standing back from the circle light, he was merely a hulking outline in the pale nightrun, leaving Alice awash with flame from the lantern from her rich hair and painted lips to her custom-dyed boots.

The captain didn't register his complaint with even a glance. He was still dressed so finely that it made Shye nervous. The circle of bodies awaiting instruction made up all of the captain's most trusted crew and his rebellious ward. Shye was suddenly quite sure he'd never heard of Master Fox – though that title was almost certainly a sort of face name, which meant the person they were meeting was serious business.

"Well, shit," Shye cursed to himself. Perhaps the babysitting was warranted, if still a little wounding.

The captain sent him a swift look of reprimand, with a contradictory hint of pride at how quickly he had deduced the situation, before grabbing the handle of the lantern and swinging it towards the docks with a wide gesture.

"Fox is waiting for us a little way down there. Let's make this quick and we can be on our way by lightrise."

He looked back to Shye and said, for his particular benefit, "Keep your mouths shut and load the goods," and then to all of them, "And I'll hear no complaining about babysitting, you're all well-fed, pampered, and knew what you were getting into."

He cast a special look at Muse and jerked the signal to get moving, handing off the lantern to Alice. Pushing Shye into place just behind the violinist's shoulder, so close he could see the gold sun-specks dotting his skin, the captain ordered, "Stay close to Muse," before loping off after Alice and the sway of light.

Butler stepped in, looming over him from behind, and the three of them tramped down the gangplank. Shye was neither tall nor wide enough to be seen between them, except for the odd impression that perhaps the two men had more legs and arms than was normally required for humans or folk.

A little way down the harbour, just as the captain had said, a figure was sitting delicately on a crate, peeling an apple with a mean-looking knife. The spiralling apple skin swung to a stop with the last pass of the knife, just clear of the dark silk pants, the stiff damask coat the figure wore tucked around her side and draping down to the ground. The knife winked silver with its final glide, meant for slicing other things, and hungry for it.

The captain sidled up to the lean figure. Fox, just as leisurely, wiped the knife on the hem of her pants and shucked it back into its sheath. She slipped the skin from the apple and threw it into the water; her sharp nails glinted with pale lacquer.

With talons like those, Shye thought she looked more crow-like than fox-like. He was familiar with the illustrations, but he'd have go deep into imperial territory to see either outside of a book.

The make of Fox's jacket and the silver pins lined along its cuffs denoted her as something above the lower denizens of the harbour city, and her thin face and dark eyes complimented Shye's personal imaginings of the Ravens – when he remembered they were people and not haunted shadows and spirits stalking the nightrun. Master Fox's chosen name seemed more and more an error the longer Shye stood near her, but perhaps even Fox balked at holding a face name that belonged to the siblings of the Ravens.

Thinking of Ravens so much had Shye fighting off a shudder. He felt Fox's eyes catch on him and then slowly drift on.

The captain drew up to the crate, his coat making a soft swish through the air, deliberate in its cultivated, curated finery. It looked imperial, even.

"Ezra Creed."

The captain's name was ground out like a particularly nasty curse, and the woman looked away from the shadowy crew to look the captain up and down, inclining her head slightly in greeting. Her grim face managed to pull a thin, crooked smile from the set of her mouth, though Shye thought it looked rather painful.

"Or perhaps, I should say, *Captain* Ezra Creed. Though, I'm certain you stole that title along with everything else, in replacement of your old one."

The captain traded a cursory smirk with the woman and clasped her forearm the way businessmen did, finishing the introduction of their polite exchange. Drawing away, he signalled the crew and they snapped into place, lining up at his back.

"You are looking fetching this run, Fox," the captain remarked, as one by one, Alice, Edge, Muse and Butler bounced their heads and repeated the greeting of "Master Fox". Shye clumsily followed suit between Muse and Butler, but Fox's sharp eyes were on him in an instant for it. She swivelled deliberately back to the start of the line.

"Alice ... Edge ... Muse ... Butler ..."

Fox's gaze skittered over each of them, passing over Muse but never making it to Butler. "Who are you?"

She turned to the captain.

"Who is he?"

Beside him, Butler moved off to collect some of the crates and started loading them onto the small cart they'd brought. Alice, Edge, and Muse moved after a moment to join him, leaving Shye quiet and still in the captain's shadow, until Muse returned and shoved a crate into his chest.

The captain moved towards Fox just as Fox took a curious step towards Shye, and the captain commandeered her shoulder. "Have no trouble, Fox," the captain said.

Muse suggested in Shye's ear, "Maybe you want to walk this one back to the ship?"

The captain leaned in close to the grim-faced woman and pointed at Muse and Shye with his free hand and continued, "The boy's

Strange is all. A bit folk-touched but still crew and, unlike Muse, he's sensitive to the eyes of others."

The captain shot a quick but significant look at them. "But he'll cause no trouble for you, he's just here to load the spice."

He let go of Fox's shoulder and shooed them off with a finger in the air. Muse grabbed a crate from the back of the cart and began marching Shye towards the ship, away from the two masters now discussing payment, though the fixed point of Fox's probing gaze remained on Shye's retreating form.

Ditching the load on the ship, Muse looked tempted to leave him behind, his gold eyes darkening in consideration. But with a sigh, he jerked Shye back down the gangplank and herded him towards the glow of the lantern. His voice whispered roughly through the dark, "Listen, that's a cold collector in a lady's dapper skin. The things she owns, now they are useful to us and they sell for good glass, so we keep good business, but we don't want her thinking it'd be interesting enough to collect you. You don't move from my side, and when someone hands you a crate, you walk."

Muse stepped deftly in front when they reached the cart and the rest of their run crew, while Shye trailed in his shadow until another crate was pressed into his hands. Fox's eyes no longer tracked the dark beneath his hood. Instead, they sized his feet and then his legs, lingering as he walked alone back to the ship, leaving a trail of phantom feeling, like spiders creeping down the backs of his shins.

Shye repeated the agonising process till the wind picked up and the sun began to warm the horizon. His eyes dipped low with want of sleep, his feet dragging slightly returning to the run and the wandering gaze of Master Fox. He heard Edge call, "Last one," as he came upon the cart and his limbs sagged in sweet relief.

Fox and the captain closed their business efficiently, shaking hands. The captain shifted back to the crew, who stood in a disciplined yet untidy line in front of the cart, while Fox's eyes skirted the group, winding their leisurely way to Shye.

Muse shifted uneasily at his shoulder.

Fox wandered till she stood in front of Shye. The line of the crew was between them with the captain at their head, but tension came in on the air like a sudden stiff wind. Swift bellows and blusters of this strength rarely rolled off sunbath storms without something Strange about, yet still Shye felt as though the air had sharpened suddenly.

The silvery pin Fox displayed glinted harshly at Shye; a circle of untarnished steel with a line spearing through it. If Fox was superstitious, such a symbol would grant her the luck from the lightrise sun if in gold, health from the nightrun moon if in silver, and protection from the folk if in black iron. Shye couldn't see the point of it being forged from steel.

He felt the catch of a hand at the edge of his hood, quickly followed by the *shick* of a cutlass being thumbed slightly out of its sheath. Fox and Shye drew away in the same breath, and the captain's hard eyes fell on Fox.

The woman shifted towards the captain, but her eyes continued to linger where Shye wished they wouldn't. He felt the phantom legs of silk spiders again, prickling at the tops of his ears and along his cheekbone.

Fox tittered a little to herself and said to the captain, "He's pretty. What I can see of him, anyhow."

"He's crew," the captain warned and let his cutlass sink back into its scabbard, judging that as all there was to say about it.

Master Fox folded her arms and slinked over to Shye once more.

"Is he expensive?" she asked, with the look of a surveyor in her eyes; interest and prospect colliding.

"He's not for sale."

The captain's gaze was cut like glass, but Fox's held greed. She removed them unhappily from Shye.

"It never hurts to ask."

Muse and Butler slid firmly into place, bracketing Shye on either side, their bodies angled to guard him, though by now it was far too late to divert Fox's attention. The captain took two deliberate steps towards them, but Fox stopped him in place with a question.

"I wonder what makes him so Dusk that you would make him hide such a fine face?"

She paused to deliver a cruel smirk at the captain. "Or is his face the reason you hide him? A coronation just around the corner and this little one with such a fine, lovely face all shadowed. Almost noble," she teased, and then paused as she peered closer. A slow incomprehension turned across her face like clouds crossing the moon.

"Almost . . . familiar," she drawled and then smiled wickedly again, her mood shifting as the clouds cleared. Fox lifted a hand, her fingers wiggling. "Shall we take a look?"

Five swords hissed free of their scabbards and Fox's face lit up; delight playing across her features with ravenous abandon.

"Did you steal a child of the Empire?" she pressed with glee, even as the swords took a pointed offence in her direction.

Muse's pistol cocked over Shye's shoulder. The sound snapped into Shye's ear, and his gaze darted up from the grimy streets to meet and catch on Fox's.

"Quite the opposite, really," Shye whispered, as Fox's face grew pale. In his bright eyes, she saw all the promise of the Blooded. The dark of her own eyes grew darker against the waning pallor of her skin, and her features twisted into something beyond horror. Fear and an unexpected sorrow twinkled like jewels in the darkness of her frozen gaze.

Shye quickly looked down again, grimacing at his mistake, his hood falling back into place, but Fox had already seen. Already realised from one look that some pure form of the Blooded remained and the cage that contained it bore Shye's face and a radiant, unforgettable gaze.

"It can't be," Fox breathed, just before Butler and Muse grabbed hold of Shye and whipped him behind them, their hands reaching out for the woman as Shye stumbled. Alice and Edge slid over, closing the gap and hiding him, and Fox, in turn, from view.

The captain broke through to shove Shye roughly against the cart. His slanted brows and twisted mouth spoke of cold fury, but there was something in his eyes, in his expression, that Shye could not decipher. Expectation, resignation, perhaps even understanding; Shye wasn't sure he'd ever be able to tell.

"That's twice this span you've disobeyed me. Believe me, you will answer for it."

He did not order Shye to go.

Stepping around the wall the crew had made between them, Shye heard the captain step up to Fox and crouch to the level that Muse and Butler had forced her to.

"That boy of yours is not good company, Ezra," Fox hissed. "He should not be crew. You shouldn't have brought him here! This is no place for one like him."

If Shye listened closely, he could hear the sound of skin and leather and cold metal. Together it was not a sound he could describe with words, but he knew what it meant. The captain was freeing his pistol from his belt.

Shye squeezed his eyes shut. This was not how he'd expected this run to go. Damn him for looking up.

"And I've heard quite enough from you in regard to the boy—"

"You should put him back where you found him. Before they come for him. Before *she* does."

Cold metal met the dank air between the captain and Fox.

The captain continued as if Fox had never interrupted. "Now, I trust you'll spread no rumours about me and mine after we've had such good business with you. I should kill you, but I think leaving you alive is a reasonable exchange for your silence. Agreed?"

The tang of metal and powder left the air. Shye's eyes popped open again and he sagged against the cart in relief.

Fox's voice whispered out in answer, bitter and condemning, "Oh, Ezra, silence won't save me, and you can't save him. He'll burn you worse than the king ever did."

Then, there was scrambling and the sound of boots escaping away down the pier. When the crew parted, Fox was gone, and Muse was adding her mean knife to the collection he kept on his person.

The captain strode forward, hauled Shye away from the cart and pinned him with his gaze.

"I'm not impressed, Shye."

His grip sealed itself on Shye's shoulder and forcibly turned him towards where the *Oathbreaker* was docked, serene against the violet night.

"Get back to the boat," he growled in Shye's ear, before pushing him forward and letting go. Shye stood there for a moment, dazed, the ghost of the captain's fingers still digging their way into his bones. He felt the tip of a cutlass at his back and, at last, he started walking.

CHAPTER 5

THE DECK WAS QUIET, THOUGH THE SUN WAS WAXING OVER THE SEA, and it wouldn't be too long till the whole crew was roused and ready for another lightrise. Slowly, figures appeared at the top of the gangway and dropped onto the ship. Alice, Edge, Butler, Muse and, lastly, the captain. Not one of them looked at Shye, not even Muse. The captain snapped into weary action, doling out orders in a low, strained voice.

He had given Shye many things over the years. His skills, his learning, his first cloak, his family; he'd also given him a set of rules to follow and impressed upon him the necessity of every single one. They'd never discussed exactly what would happen if one season Shye broke them. Perhaps, the captain had assumed it was implicit or had simply trusted the threat of consequences would be enough for Shye to obey. Shye had never questioned it either, never thought to ask, and now it was far too late to do so.

Breaking free from this unpleasant train of thought, Shye caught the end of the captain's decisive commands, his fingers brushing at the edge of his hood without permission.

"Consult the maps. I want us away by lightrise next, so do whatever you need to make that happen. We'll move this"—he gestured to the last of the spice that hadn't been secured—"and reassess."

He threw a dark glance towards the dock and then at Shye, who was trying to contain the captain's unease by loitering out of the way. Shye dropped his hand as a guilty surge washed through his gut.

"And somebody fix the damn cargo net between now and our inevitable ruin."

He turned away from them and his crew split off, going their separate ways to prepare for what would need to be done and passing on their orders to the rest of the crew.

Shye stepped cautiously in behind the captain, because that was how it had worked before, and until judgement had been passed, he could only act like nothing had changed down at the docks. The captain's shoulders stiffened as Shye trailed him down below. Then he stopped suddenly outside the galley, without continuing to his office. He still would not look at Shye.

"You're demoted. Mercy's waiting for you in the kitch."

Shye nodded at the back of his master's head and remained almost silent. Any other ship, any other captain, and he'd be tossed off the ship, whipped, or dead. Or, worse, given over to the crown.

Mercy, indeed, Shye thought contritely.

He moved off towards the galley and the captain pivoted on his heel, instead of walking on, his chin jutting with displeased intent at the wall, his eyes an unfamiliar jade slate. Shye stopped and waited to see if there would be more.

The captain threw him a bare glance, but it was something at least. Shye forced his eyes down, his mouth twisting with the sick feeling that was sitting heavy in his stomach.

"I didn't—" Shye started, uncertainly.

"No, you didn't," the captain interrupted. "And you're sorry."

Shye's fingers rose again to touch his hood, but he stopped himself, shifting guiltily on his feet. The captain stared at the wall, his expression clearing from cold fire into forced detachment. The sick queasiness swirling up Shye's throat was choking. The captain swivelled to look at Shye properly, though Shye couldn't return his gaze.

"Do you want to leave, Shye?"

The same question Muse had asked him earlier. He blew the stale air clogging his lungs out through his mouth, spilling over his teeth-marked lips, and the sick feeling went with it. Wind snapped and whipped in the sails, as salt air whispered past them into the dark. Shye felt the slide of air caress his skin, and he breathed in through his nose and felt the ship all around him in a deepness he didn't understand. His eyes started to water remorselessly, and he squeezed them shut to stop it. He sniffed quietly, embarrassed, and swallowed to keep his answer inside.

The captain's body shifted in time with the swell of the ship and his expression broke, his withdrawnness ceding to rigid disapproval and annoyance.

"Then your penitence would be better spent convincing me it's worth the trouble to keep you."

The captain turned away.

Shye slipped into the galley with relief and found Mercy boiling pork that had been picked up from the street vendors, and hastily chopping what vegetables they had, while they still had them, and throwing them into the pot as well. It seemed the crew could expect to ingest something lively and nutritious that wasn't sliced golden citrons and dried peaches. Cabbage was also popular with Mercy but could hardly be described as lively.

Mercy didn't pause her work when he walked in, though she did share with a compassionate lilt on her tongue, "Young'uns, so hard to raise."

Shye coloured, knowing she had heard them outside her door and would, before long, know all. Mercy usually did.

A knife slid through the air under his nose, flipped to the handle side, and Mercy flapped an efficient finger in the direction of a stack of onions resting on a bench, away from the hearth and its stoked fire. She hummed over her stew and then said, "Stormborns, so hard to contain."

Shye smiled at her under his hood and took the knife, resigning himself to his station of onions. He started to chop. The heat and the privacy of the room made the idea of taking off his cloak both tempting and sickening. His value to the crew was not in being a kitchen hand or even a working crewmember, but in what he was; the embodiment of their personal stance against a homeland that was barred to them and questioned what was left of their kind.

There was no point fighting for that home anymore, but they didn't have to bend to the crown on the open waters.

What he was also presented a certain potential for the ease of their trade, not that he'd manifested many tangible outcomes from it aside from Fox's reaction, and that certainly did not compound his worth to his captain or crew. If Fox told anyone what she'd seen, and if a Raven caught wind, Shye's value was imperial bounty. The Empire's spies were invisible, they had no guild, no public presence but their network of information had kept the crown in power since the downfall of the Blooded. The Ravens were silent in their work, resourceful and pervasive in their service to the crown. He didn't even want to consider what the captain would find more priceless; his kitchen boy or his livelihood, maybe his life, once they found out about Shye.

The captain saved him once, but Shye couldn't say with confidence that he'd do so again. Not after this.

He frowned at the sliced onion under his knife, before reaching up and swiping a fist over the wetness gathering on his lashes, this time a blessing from the pungent vegetable. Mercy blew past on the way to the stores and spice racks and tugged his hood down with a gentle pinch.

"Take it off. Ain't no one to tell on you in here."

Shye lay down the knife and shrugged out of his cloak, wiping his face on the back of it and tossing it over a sack-heaped chair. Mercy breezed past him again, humming along with the voices that rang from above. Shye picked up the knife again, rolled another onion over and went back to chopping, leaving the unhappy thoughts swirling around in the back of his mind.

CHAPTER 6

THE FULLNESS OF THE LIGHTRISE SUN BLAZED OVER THE OCEAN, BALMY and in its season. Gentle heat beat down on the road from the river districts near Ostarro, heading into Mistral, making the lone horse, its rider, as well as their limping cargo, grow sticky with sweat. The winds off the ocean brought blessed relief until the road turned away, past fields of pale-gold grass and rosy buds, and the wind couldn't find them anymore.

Dorian Locke pulled a soaked handkerchief out of a water canteen that swung from the side of the saddle and tossed it around their neck, the tails dripping down their collar and leaving damp patches on their streaked white shirt.

Passing between two black slabs of stone sticking up from the ground on either side of the road, the rider called back to the trailing cargo in a merry tone.

"Welcome back to the capital, Master Moon."

The man stumbled along behind the horse, where a rope attached him to his captor's saddle and chafed his wrists red and raw. The bounty that had been placed on him by the Empire had not specified that he be alive, so he could only assume it was the cruel justice of the guild and this rider that meant he was here, without rest or reprieve for spans, instead of blissfully dead. He swallowed, his tongue thick in his mouth, sticking to his teeth, as he tried to speak.

"My name is S-Swift, uh ..."

He broke out in a coughing fit. He knew well who this rider was, though he remembered only vaguely the council announcing that Lord James's lady had borne a . . . well, he wasn't about to make assumptions on the architecture of the hunter's person in any case lest he offend again against the Empire and bear a harsher punishment.

The rider interrupted his thoughts, taking advantage of his pause. The freckled face of the rider turned to smirk at him and watch him colour before turning to face the road ahead. "On account of the fact that you didn't have time to clothe yourself before we left, and since you are currently strapped to my horse with no chance of escape, not forgetting the fact you are a fugitive from the justice of the Empire, I rather think I get to call you whatever I like."

The rider leant over and fished a wide-brimmed, blue-and-silver atrocity of a hat from one of the saddlebags, before sending him a grin on the way back up and plopping the hat over their rampant mass of auburn hair, shielding from the sun. Two maroon plumes bobbed along behind their head, stuck haphazardly into the hatband.

"Ain't that right, *Master Moon*."

The man accepted the rider's word without further complaint; the same way he'd accepted his capture, this torturous journey and even that hat. Some things just weren't worth fighting for, and his miserable life was currently one of them. A spike of pain jabbed into the point of his foot as he stubbed his toe on a sharp rock. Cursing, he limped onwards, too tired to even really care about the pain.

The rider spoke again, unperturbed by his foul words.

"And evidently," Dorian started, turning back in the saddle once more to regard him, as the terrible jut of Mistral's border wall stretched ahead of them on the path, "you are not swift enough."

Swift watched the monstrous black wall ascend above them with dread in his stomach, while the guards of the border wall stopped their patrols as Dorian approached. The dry inland air and fragrant breezes off the south-west peaks made for easy work, even under the lightrise sun. There was an atmosphere of laziness and jovial chatter among the guards on duty, as they leant over the black obsidian lip or slouched against the North Gate and called out warm greetings. The old dogs hustled everyone back to work with well-meaning coarseness, though little haste was being made to do so. Their rough voices called out orders as they waved the stragglers onwards, though some paused to nod at the hunter as they passed.

"Welcome back, Locke," the gatekeeper hailed in a high, warm voice, as she waved them through. "Another 'rise, another hunt, ey?"

Out past the entryways of the border wall, nothing of the city could be seen except for the sharp rise of the Brightspir, the king's palace, in the centre of the city. The wall stretched the entire circumference of Mistral's sprawling, circular districts and warrens. Beyond it, the city crept to the edges of its protective circle; the circle for which the city's labyrinthine districts took after, leading in all directions to the guild houses and the palace ensconced by them.

A laugh sounded from above as Dorian came through the other side. A man with two crossed swords inked on the back of his hand, and a helmet mounted beside him where he rested on the edge of the wall, looked down at them.

"Justice comes to another runner, I see," he called down with a smile, casting an amused glance at the naked man Dorian was pulling along behind the horse.

"Justice didn't do any of the work. I'd hate to see her get all the credit," Dorian called back with a chuckle.

"Aye, that goes to the magnificent hunter. Give my regards to your grandfather, would ya, Locke?"

Dorian turned away, raising a hand in acknowledgement, and continued into the city, slowing the pace of the horse as Swift lumbered behind. People stopped and nodded, parting down the folk-stoned avenues to let them pass. The wide-brimmed hat shaded Dorian's face, but nothing covered the hourglass inking marking the back of their right hand or the glinting of their burnished hair as they rode through town. The people of Mistral were well acquainted with Dorian in some way; they would know Dorian's face, name, or family, and if by some small miracle they did not know those, all would know their trade.

Young voices cried out in ruckus from the length of an alley that opened onto the main way Dorian and their cargo were ambling down, and a group of youths burst from the skinny street and out into the road. One of them, the smallest among the lot, careened into Dorian's mare and grabbed a hold of the saddlebags to keep from rolling onto his backside; his dirty face beamed at the mounted hunter.

"Good rise, Locke," the youth piped, familiar and cheeky, his fingers and face smeared with dust and soot. The other youths scattered, their fun taking them elsewhere, away from the hunter. The boy dropped his smudgy fingers from the saddlebags and took up trotting alongside the horse. Despite his change of dress, Dorian knew to whom that dirtied face belonged.

"Good rise to you, young lord. Get lost on your way to the forge?"

The boy laughed and flicked his fringe out of his eyes, before lifting a finger in a hushing gesture and pointing to Swift, who lurched along behind.

"What about you? Get lost on your way to a bigger mark?"

Dorian gave a faux offended gasp and swatted the boy with a hand. "I go where the guild assigns me; you know that."

The youth dodged away, then danced back to the horse's side as quickly as he had skittered away, his smile growing wide. "There's been rumours about you on the streets, you know? After a meeting with the Head Huntsman. They were saying you were bringing in something"—the boy gave Swift a disappointed look—"else."

Dorian's mouth quirked at that. They kept one hand loose on the reins; the hunting horse was home now and would need little direction to guide them back to the guild halls.

"Well, look at you, young Spymaster Jin," Dorian teased. "Or are you a Raven now? Though I suppose if you were, you wouldn't tell me."

A stricken expression darted across the boy's face at such a casual mention of the word, and Dorian snorted, waving him away. "You should go. Before your father catches you dwindling sun shine with someone like me."

The tea houses were clearing now, and beyond them rose the Guild Circle. Dorian's hunting horse trod confidently towards the roads that divided the houses into bannered sentinels guarding the four entrances to the Brightspir. Flags were painted across the rooves and hung from the outside walls of their squat forms to mark each of the four main guilds as belonging to the crown's hunters, guards, scriveners, and gemwrits, the last also known as the Guild of Glass.

The high guilds and lower trades competed for the right to join the Guild Circle, but the four had too high esteem with the crown and held tightly to their place at its seat. None had yet to be dislodged from their place of power.

Dorian watched the boy run past Swift and back out into the city.

The naked man called out, "Who was that?"

Dorian threw him a smile and flagged down the guards stepping out of the central tea house, which hosted all guild members regardless of profession; the guild stables were hidden out back behind it, in a district all their own. The guards acknowledged Dorian's wave and stepped forwards.

"That was the son of the man you stole from, Lordling Jin Jensing, and if you aren't swift enough to escape, you're definitely not swift enough to steal from a Jensing."

The guards reached them and reached out for Swift, cutting him loose with practised efficiency and marching him away. Dorian turned in the saddle to watch them go.

"Best of luck, Master Moon," Dorian called out with a wave. "You'll need it!"

Swift looked back and nodded grimly, submitting to the guards' whims with an almost relieved obedience, but it didn't matter anyway. Swift wasn't Dorian's problem anymore. A man who couldn't steal, couldn't lie, and who was definitely hired by the Guild of Glass

just to piss Lord Jensing, and now Dorian, off, wasn't worth more of
the time and energy that he'd already taken up.

With a gentle kick, Dorian spurred the mare towards the
stables.

Dismounting, Dorian handed off the reins to a waiting groom and
pulled a small wooden chest free from the saddlebags, leaving the
rest to be handled by the attendants. A water serpent locked the chest
closed, carved from diamond, its tail and body curving to its head,
closing into a circle. Thin, filigree wings speared through its centre,
with no clear place for key.

Dorian hadn't asked but was pretty sure this box belonged to
Lady Jensing, and unfortunately for Swift, any secrets that were
locked within it ran stale with the knowledge that she had long
retired from court and all public life. A choice that, in some aspects,
Dorian could well respect. Besides, even she wasn't mad enough to
keep her husband's notes on his highly sought glass works in any old
box. Swift really hadn't stood a chance.

Dorian carried the box from the stables, following the paths
around the Guild Circle till they reached the door hung with the
banner of an hourglass. Slipping through the open doorway banded
by silk curtains into the antechamber, Dorian could hear a curious
uproar coming through the double doors at the back, accompanied
by shouts and general murmur.

The Head Huntsman must have called a meeting.

Handing off the box to one of the clerks in residence to be
accounted for, Dorian headed to the doors and slid them open.

The assembly room was alive and in uproar, despite the hour slipping from lightrise to evenspan, and it seemed that every single
hunter still present within the capital had put in an appearance. They
clustered around the room in a group, yelling at each other.

Dorian hesitated at the edges of the room until someone caught
their eye. The Head Huntsman stared down at Dorian from his
slightly raised bench across the hexagonal meeting space, while the
crowds of hunters stood or paced in the middle; their abandoned
benches closing them in.

The old man smiled at Dorian, his blue eyes pure where Dorian's were faded. He inclined his head to the empty space at his side.

Dorian skirted around the room, enough swagger in their gait to go unnoticed by the hunters, who would've smelled blood at anyone acting shy in their chambers, especially if it was Dorian. Edging onto the bench, Dorian sat down next to the Huntsman, pulling up their legs to rest their elbows on them. Dorian leant over and said, "Lorqin Mansel wishes you well."

The old man's eyes began to twinkle, and he responded, "The captain of the Border Guards? I had heard he was fishing for a promotion."

He paused with a familiar smirk – one that often found itself upon Dorian's own lips – and surveyed the room, saying with a provocative lilt to his voice, "Or he has somehow already heard the news that I have strived to keep within this room, which would be highly suspect."

Dorian sat up straighter, gaze flying to meet the old man's and then tracking across the groups on the floor; ears straining to hear the conversations all happening in unison. There were too many speaking at once to discern any useful information, but Dorian was well aware there hadn't been a meeting scheduled until three spans after they had been expected to return from hunting Swift.

"News that causes this ruckus and forces you to call an emergency assembly must be interesting news, indeed," Dorian remarked, the corner of one lip curling up, eyes slanting a look towards the old man.

The Huntsman looked back, his own mouth pulling to mirror Dorian's. "Oh, well, interesting enough to call an emergency meeting, yes. This, however"—he gestured to the throng of passionate voices rebounding around them—"is the result of telling them I was going to send our youngest and most *unconventional* hunter to deal with this news."

Dorian's eyes widened, and their hair swung to hit them across the neck and cheek as they whipped to face the Hunstman. Dorian's hands unconsciously curled into the fabric of their pants that were still dusty from the road. Their breath stalled as the Huntsman nodded and continued, "I've been waiting patiently since then for them to tire themselves out."

He clicked his tongue, turning back to look over the room at large. "I rather hoped they'd be done by the time you arrived."

Dorian's fingers unlatched and grabbed onto the edge of the bench, throwing their body forward, unable to wait longer. "What's the news!"

The Huntsman's eyes flitted back over, and his brows rose, amusement flickering across his face. Dorian leant back, colouring.

"I mean, the assignment. It is mine, right? That's what you meant."

The Huntsman held his gaze steady, brows high, till Dorian's colour faded and their expression threatened to split into a smile at him. When he kept his silence, Dorian's body swivelled on the bench, hands coming up to rest on their lips, together as in prayer.

"Grandfather?"

The Huntsman hummed and said, "Not yet."

He pointed a crooked finger at a group in the crowd.

Dorian immediately recognised the two men among them that the rest of the crowd seemed to gravitate around; the younger of them gesticulating and no doubt mouthing off at the elder, while Dorian's father, looked down his nose at Dorian's best friend, Leon, and met his rousing lip with glacial scorn.

In retribution for his own name, Ever Locke, Dorian's grandfather had chosen the subdued name of James for his son and the slightly more adventurous Dorian for his grandchild, in keeping with an imperial tradition that he surely did not believe in. Though it could be said that Dorian more than lived up to the adventurous name they had been gifted, there was, unfortunately, very little that was subdued about Lord James.

Dorian sighed.

The old man elbowed Dorian gently. "Now, now, I think before I give you your assignment, we should use this opportunity to revisit our lessons on relative worth."

Dorian rubbed their forehead, because of course James Locke

and Leon Payne were the two sides of a whole assembly debate over Dorian's personal and professional worth. Head nearly between their knees, Dorian said, "We discussed that when I was six."

"Yes, when you hocked the watch your father bought you for some impeccable tailoring. Any regrets on that decision?"

Dorian remembered shredding their clothes and marching into their grandfather's couturier in the business district, demanding he make them right this time. With what was left, there wasn't much he could do. So, before making them a whole new wardrobe, the tailor amended a hat he had in storage for another customer, who had never come back in to pick it up.

"Every rogue must have their signature," he had said, as he placed it on Dorian's head with a satisfied air.

Dorian remembered how excited they were and the slow slide of confusion on their father's face that devolved steadily into furious outrage as they grew and continued to refuse to conform to the life he had chosen for them, the ways he demanded they look and act. Every skirt, pant, long coat and shirt expertly tailored, each standing for the wildness and obstinance that Lord James could not accept in a perfect and only heir. Because while it was acceptable to amend an unjust body in Mistral, Dorian's body, or even really what they attired it in – varied though that was – had very little to do with Lord James's ire. It was that Dorian had used every choice along the way to build a reputation that ignored him, that deliberately sought to escape him, blatant and flaunting. A whole, perfectly customised scene. And Lord James detested any scene that he was not involved in, in which he held no power, and no say.

Dorian raised their head and answered, "Not particularly."

Ever's mouth twitched, and he began with enthusiasm, "Perhaps then, keeping that in mind, you might decide that there are other things worthier of your considerable talents than the small world between these walls and the attention of a father who no more understands you than he deserves you."

Ever fished a scroll out from the pockets of his vest and held it out for Dorian to take. "Your assignment. If you want it."

The old man's eyes were sharp and intelligent but not cold. Nothing about Dorian's grandfather had ever been that.

Dorian took the scroll carefully. Reverently.

As Dorian unrolled the paper, Ever remarked, "Some would kill for this, Dorian," and then fell silent while Dorian took in what was written within.

There was a short letter, addressed to the Huntsman – E for Ever, signed just as simply with a C. It looked personal, though its only message was a set of what looked like navel coordinates for the imperial port at Corentin. Dorian's brows drew together in confusion as they pulled out the larger sheet from underneath and found an incident report from the port city; a ship of smugglers carrying cargo precious to the crown. Dorian stalled.

In place of a signature was a smudged dark bird. A Raven.

A small steel ring with a line spearing through it, like the wings of the serpent on the box Dorian had retrieved earlier, slid out from between the two pages. It glinted, almost cruelly, over the inked black bird.

The Huntsman droned over the buzzing in Dorian's ears, as though he was far across the room instead of right next to them, "...And some still might."

One word kept jumping out from the page, throwing all other words into blurry slants of dark writing, standing out in stark relief, as though even its lettering carried power. A word that only a Raven could write and have it come before the Huntsman as truth, instead of legend. Like the stories Dorian's grandfather still told guild children and had told Dorian, in turn, many years ago.

Stories of mountains that moved to allow folk to walk through them, of earth that rent itself to carve the city in which Dorian now resided, of four high lords who shared a crown – chosen by their people and the lord of the wildlands as being worthy of the chance to serve their world – and four seasons for those lords to rule, two of sun and two of frost. Stories of other potent Blood, which served the earth and sky, pulling the stars into line and championing even the most forgotten of the folk, the Blooded rarities that carried lightning in their eyes.

The Stormborn.

Dorian's intake of breath was audible.

The Huntsman looked smug; his hands folded placidly in his lap, eyes twinkling still.

Dorian thumbed the circle of steel into their palm and held it under the Huntsman's nose. "What's this?"

The Huntsman pushed their hand back, closing their fingers over the pin. "You have your friends, Dorian, as I have mine, and none of them would think us to be fools, though perhaps to give credence to this is foolish, indeed."

He patted the hand he had closed over the pin gently. On his third finger rested their family ring. The sunstone sphere. Inside it, three stalks of wheat in black opal split the ring in half, and it was cold and yet warm somehow against Dorian's skin. Dorian could only consider the similarities to be coincidence.

"On the outside, this is a symbol for a world in balance, one that is popular among those that claim the Blood and those that see Strangeness in every shape, but it is also assurance for me that what is written in those papers is no lie."

Dorian looked across the room at their father, and was startled to find him looking back; mouth twisted in derision. James's eyes skirted the papers in Dorian's hands and his scowl deepened. He'd never forgive Dorian if they took this job, and Dorian would never shake him off if they didn't . . . and if it was true, James would never be able to rise above Dorian and take from Dorian what they'd worked so hard for.

James would lose.

Ever's eyes twinkled, three shades brighter than Dorian's.

"It's yours, if you want it."

CHAPTER 7

Stormborn.

DORIAN TOSSED THE REPORT AND THE LETTER INTO THE HEARTH, watched it blacken into ash and erase the word. Still, it was stuck firm in Dorian's mind, sitting there fat and heavy and full of doubt. The Blood was nearly gone and now a Stormborn had appeared. What sort of last stand was it attempting? The Empire's peace had stood for thousands of years. The forces of the Stormborn and all their Blood belonged to the Old World. Their folk moons and the whispering, wild winds had not been seen or heard since the Horned Crown had graced the head of Camillus, the first king. There were no Lords of Dusk anymore, no princes to rule the seasons, only those unfortunate enough to inherit the remnants of what they'd been.

The heat from the fire licked teasingly across Dorian's face from where they crouched in front of it, the private tearoom verging on too warm to bear. Dorian's coat, rumpled but of excellent quality and with none of the embellishments popular among the imperial elite, was slung across the back of the chair. A pot of cooling tea gave off dying wisps of steam across from it.

Still, Dorian thought, *the rumour of a Stormborn, a true remnant of Blooded power, now appears, and with the prince's coronation looming, a gift like this would not go unrewarded.* Though, this town hardly needed another noble house.

The wooden door a distance away from the abandoned chair and table slid open with a low trundling sound, and Dorian's father stood backlit in the threshold. Mistral's penchant for metal and gem works were splashed all over his layered coat, and the shoulders and back of it dripped in pinpricks of amethyst and swirling silver, while his dark hair was pushed off his face, leaving his cheekbones stark, with a sweep of amethyst powder at his temples.

Dorian picked up the fire poker and gave the coals a few pointed jabs, while their thoughts coalesced darkly into, *But I'd do it to get out of mine.*

"You are foolish," came the smooth, cultured tones of Lord James, all wrapped up in perennial disappointment, as though it would hide the small slip of resentment there as well.

Dorian stabbed the poker deep into the coals and left it there, sending a waft of smoke billowing up the chimney with a crackle of sparks. The reprimand was met with a slow shift in Dorian's body as they moved to look over their shoulder, brows raised, expression politely disinterested.

"You are welcome to think so, Father," Dorian replied, slinking up from the crouched stance.

James Locke's noble face clouded and, casting a derisive look behind him to the occupied communal tearoom, he slid the door shut with force, trapping the two of them in deceptively small quarters.

"You make mockery enough of our family as it is and yet, some-how, I still thought you'd be better than this." He waved a hand in Dorian's general direction, somehow also encompassing the rumpled coat into their detriments as well. Dorian preferred a simpler style to their father, if only so as to distinguish themself in contrast.

James glared at the firelight bounding across Dorian's matching flame-coloured hair. His mouth twisted sourly, no doubt at the reminder that Dorian took more after Ever in colouring than after him, more after their defiant mother in thought than of him, more after anyone else, even their princely cousin, Cassius, than after him. And Dorian, his personal disgrace, was to be his heir – his *only* heir, if Dorian did not outstrip him first.

The features they did share Dorian was quick to mask behind a wild grin and a wilder show for the masses, their talent for hunting and the tales of their varied and provocative attires and exploits at the last few festival seasons forever colouring Dorian's name with a sense of dangerous indifference to the expected comportment of a noble. The youngest hunter to ever be on guild registry after Lord James himself, Dorian's existence seemed a spectacle specifically designed to shame him.

A spectacle that reminded him of his wife, with all her wilfulness and none of her quiet precision. That lovely lady who could pickle vegetables with a single word, a single flash of her eyes, when faced with any form of idiocy or ineptitude. Her name a sardonic blessing in the highest orders of Mistral; a wish of long living, up to the neck and marinated in brine. "Lady Lis preserve you."

This her dishonourable child, who had never listened to better wisdom and never learnt how to muzzle their insolence and restrain their compulsions. This child who just wouldn't follow the grace of their family name.

Lord James glared at Dorian as if hearing the turn of their thoughts.

"This assignment is ridiculous," James accused, and he was not wrong, but only if the information proved false, and Ever did not seem to think it would.

Dorian crossed their arms over their chest and replied, "The Huntsman doesn't seem to think so."

"When *I* am Huntsman—"

When I am Huntsman, you will not be granted these freedoms. When I am Huntsman, you will not disgrace my name any longer. When I am

Huntsman, you will obey ME, Dorian. Dorian didn't need him to finish the sentence, their mind was already fast conjuring the ending.

His intonation went up on the "I" with the sort of self-righteous assurance that could make one forget that guild masters were not hereditary titles.

"You're not, though," Dorian interrupted.

James shot Dorian a poisonous look, his lips curling with such acute frustration that Dorian became wary of the fact they'd inherited their shape. Such decided expressions were well enough for James Locke, but Dorian preferred not to be known so well simply by the curve of one's mouth. Nor would James appreciate that particular inheritance.

James continued, with the most restrained of snarls, "Don't think you'll ever ascend to the title if you take this contract. Our name will blacken for it. Only the mad go chasing sea breezes hoping to find a Strangeness that doesn't exist, and no man can catch a storm."

Like an oracle who only knew what had been said before, James guessed at Dorian's dreams and fears as if they were echoes in every human who'd ever lived; an ambition that burned in fury, but it was only his own. His chase and his madness entwined within his own legacy; the title a means to control it. His need to hold Dorian in one place was stifling and offensive.

Dorian could never let him have it.

Dorian picked up their coat from the chair and shrugged it on. Gesturing to the tea in open invitation, they sidled towards the door and threw back, "Then either I'll be the first, or you have nothing to worry about."

Dorian was tempted to slam the door on the way out but years of training and lectures on everything from image and reputation to the weak points of certain architectures forbade it. Instead, the frigid temperature drop that always accompanied James Locke whenever he was displeased – and trying to be polite about it – made itself known to the other patrons of the tea house, emanating from the younger hunter. Prying eyes turned away and one patron even shivered, which pulled a pleased little smile from the corner of Dorian's mouth. Another inheritance from James, though none of them the ones he'd wanted.

There was always a part of Dorian that wanted to leave right away, itching for an assignment, for the chase, for the small freedoms that being away from the capital provided, but Dorian was well aware they'd have to beg forgiveness if they left without a word with Leon first. Dorian didn't go in much for begging, even with their oldest friend.

Glancing around the room, it became obvious to Dorian that Leon wasn't frequenting the tea house with a teapot and two round steaming cups, waiting for Dorian to emerge. Not much of a surprise, but just once it would've been nice.

Flicking up the collar of their coat, Dorian stepped out into the street and set their feet in the direction of the nearest wine garden.

Shye took a deep breath; his hips propped against the railing at the stern. The night air was crisp and a little biting for the sunning season, but intimately familiar all the same. Freedom from the galley was cautiously doled out, though there was little trouble for him to find – or to find him – now they were sailing again, for which Shye was thankful.

He was bearing his demotion with as much grace as he could muster, but the residual guilt that had kept him quiet and content at first was slowly being chipped and blasted away by the sound of knives hitting wood and the heat of the galley, like a well slowly drying up under the lightrise sun, at the same rate the crew began to thaw towards him. The fact that he now meant food had their disapproval cooling quickly, though the captain was not so easily swayed.

If the Empire heard news of Shye, they would send someone after the *Oathbreaker* and the crew would be forced into a fight. They wouldn't let Shye go without one, even if the captain ordered them to. The captain made his living operating independently of the Empire, which was already dangerous, but to actively fight against it would be tantamount to treason. The Empire had a history of devastation when it came to folk who didn't stay in line.

No, Shye wasn't getting out of this anytime soon, but at least Muse had passed by the galley and stopped to alleviate the monotony with a smile and a song after too much silence from all of them, their thoughtful faces trying to puzzle out where he'd landed them with this stunt. Edge had patted his head as Shye had handed over a bowl of Mercy's cabbage surprise, and Alice had stopped by to tell him to clean his room. He'd actually listened this time, but it hadn't stayed neat for long.

Mercy, herself, had taken to instructing him in her disposition of patience.

The combination of disposition and element were different for every Blooded, but these spans most only had a disposition. Though the family lines which carried folk blood still persisted, few retained the strength of it or had its gifts.

When Shye was younger, he had snuck many books from the captain's library about the Blooded, hoping to understand who his people had been. One was notable for a single sentence on the Blood Manifest, more than any other book had written on it. It had said: Disposition guides, Element speaks, Manifest makes.

It had taken a while of hanging around the crew before Shye understood the first two. Like an instinct you couldn't restrain, a disposition was an integral part of who a person is.

The element came from the outside, a phenomena of the world that a Blooded being connected to. What little Shye knew of the manifest was simply that it was the meeting of those two things. Blood and element. Somehow it made things. Real physical things and effects and things that were ephemeral, changes that were harder to see, like the early turn of seasons, or the fullness of the moon across the nightrun sky.

Shye thought it was amusing, considering Mercy's element was so clearly the fire she coaxed into being every day. A cook with no burn scars was unusual, one that literally teased the fire into doing her bidding could only be the thinnings of a folkline. The remainder of a manifest.

Through patience, she had been on the *Oathbreaker* longer than Muse. The first of the crew who had found their way to the *Oathbreaker* while it had docked in Phirrun for the first time. Like the legends of the whispering winds, Shye imagined Mercy could have heard the hiss of the lanterns that lit the dock. Whispers of the *Oathbreaker* and the man who'd bought her. A man of shadow and smoke, fleeing for the open waters from the king's suppression in the capital, the stench of embers still clinging to his spirit.

When he'd asked – still new to the *Oathbreaker* and relegated for the first time to kitchen duty – that was what Mercy had told him in her lilting tongue. Her fingers had pulled the crackle of fire upwards, illustrating her point by blowing a cluster of embers into his face. And she had said nothing more about the captain, but Shye had stayed. There hadn't been anywhere else for him to go.

And, as he reflected, there still wasn't.

Shye breathed out and tried to force his worries out with it, but the concern over the delay to make for remoter waters remained snake-like in his gut. The lights of Phirrun glittered a good distance away at the shoreline, rising and falling across the mass of nightrun like the ghost flares that trailed their ship when they were farther out.

They had gotten away by lightrise as the captain had ordered and anchored just beyond the reach of a spyglass, as the captain and the main crew decided what they would do.

This was the final reason the crew had forgiven his transgressions much too quickly. There wasn't much else to do when they weren't going anywhere other than to move on or let the bad feelings fester, and more trouble could only follow that. None of the crew wanted to linger over what had happened when they needed to focus on what lay ahead.

The spice was supposed to be bound for a warehouse in Corentin, but if it made the captain's brows furrow in concern enough to form a little V between them, surely, they could conceive to dump it elsewhere. As long as they were away from here.

His actions had lost Shye the right to argue for a change in destination and the right to hear the discussion that was had in the captain's quarters, but he hoped someone had at least tried. There was every possibility that the fight everyone wanted to avoid was waiting there for them. If they sailed right into it, everything that followed would be Shye's fault.

Strangely though, for a man who was a smuggler and sometimes an all-out pirate, the captain was a man of his word. They would make harbour in Corentin.

And then, Shye prayed, *get the hell out of Empire lands before I do something really stupid.*

CHAPTER 8

DORIAN RODE OVERLAND FOR THREE RISES STRAIGHT, USING AS MANY guild contacts along the way as they could swing on short notice to get fresh horses. They had to get to Corentin in time.

Talking to Leon had been both enlightening and helpful, as talking to Leon usually was. With one glance, Leon had factored the navel coordinates into the Empire maps he carried in his head and the resources Dorian would need to get there.

"Two spans," he had said. "Two spans if you want to ruin your horses, three and a half otherwise without respite."

Dorian was making good time on that prediction, but it might not be enough. They could see the dimness of the garden in their mind's eye with perfect clarity – the dark wood, the smell of perfumed smoke, and the hum of conversation. Leon taking a pull from his glass-wrung pint, the fingers of his free hand, one heavy with his family ring – moonstone twisting in circular scrollwork with a pearl skeletal hand piercing across it to grasp the scrollwork in its fist – occupied with sketching a crude map on a scrap of paper. Mistral to Corentin in three spans – it was possible, but only a hunter would ever have the need to test it.

Leon knew what Dorian was chasing – there was no way he didn't

– but the thing with Leon was that he also pointedly didn't care. He had always been more interested in miscellaneous scholarship than dedicating his entire career to hunting, and he hated going on assignment. He kept his place in the guild by virtue of his assisting the Huntsman and his hunters with all he kept inside his head, with a fee amounting to one-fourth of the bounty. He spent the rest of his time drinking and sparring with the guards, content to attempt the life of a soldier and scholar in an empire that had no guild and no trade for such a person.

Finishing his drink and signalling the bar for another, Leon marked the way stations with small, innocuous X's along the road where Dorian would be best served with fresh horses. He looked up, catching Dorian's gaze with eyes so sharp they might have belonged to any bird of prey.

"You know that navel coordinates mean they're most likely travelling by ship, otherwise why use them?" he said, though Dorian did, in fact, know. His hazel eyes sparked with all the thoughts flying through them.

Dorian nodded.

Leon continued, his teeth making a brief appearance in the burst of a smile. "It takes two spans for a ship to reach Corentin from Phirrun, so even if you kill your horses, you might not catch them in the harbour. If they're smart, they will have left Phirrun already, and if they're wise, they won't linger in Corentin."

Leon put down the small stick of charcoal he'd been using to illustrate his little map, fingers smudged with smoky black, and took Dorian's hand, swiping a friendly thumb over the hourglass on the back of it. The barmaid dropped by with two more full cups, and Leon turned with a cool glance over his shoulder to see her twitch a curtsy with an inviting smile. Leon's hand was warm on Dorian's and then it was gone, and he was pulling Dorian's drink over to himself.

"You'd best get going," he said, raising it in salute.

Dorian dibbed a parting kiss to his head, feeling a smirk pull at their mouth at the way Leon had swatted them away, and they thanked him by tossing a pouch of glass – jade fans and some eyes, maybe a disc or two inside it – onto the table. Dorian's grandfather hadn't been wrong about the quality of their friends.

And Leon hadn't been wrong about Corentin. Three spans and Dorian was trotting through the east gate of the new city. New, at least, compared to any made with folk-stone, like Mistral and Phirrun; its streets unmarked by Strange rivers of glass and bone, and somehow more mottled and colder for it, the air less electric, less alive, though the city had taken the space it needed and more besides, sprawling lazily over the land. Fresh air from the ocean weaved through the spaces between buildings, blustery and salt-rimed, while the streets were gridded as opposed to labyrinthine. Dorian could hear the call of gulls, even from the easternmost district.

In true Leon fashion, he had marked on his little map – crumpled as it was from sitting in the breast pocket of Dorian's shirt for three rises – the whereabouts of the guild stables, the name of the most popular sailors' hole on the docks, the Golden Fancy, and the name of a nondescript inn one street up and to the left called the Soft Needle. Dorian plied the landlady there with enough glass and compliments to obtain not only a room but also the name and description of the harbour master, and her cooperation in forgetting that Dorian was ever there in the first place.

It could only be called a rowdy night at the Golden Fancy by the volume of the game being played across the back tables, involving a fifty-sided die and a lot of lively sailors, and more than one double-gunning a mug of ale in each hand.

The other patrons had engaged themselves in much less-enthusiastic activity and were drinking in close groups, murmuring in merry but quiet tones. As luck would have it, or because Leon was an oracle as well as a genius, the harbour master was one of the few at the Golden Fancy having a drink when Dorian walked in.

Dorian swaggered up to the bar, with the obnoxious hat they carried everywhere dipped low over their face. With one hourglass-inked hand buried deep in a pocket, Dorian set their other hand down on the rough-grained wood of the bar top and nodded towards a shelf behind the bar and the bottle of liquor sitting there, amber and glittering. Sliding their hand away, Dorian left a disc gleaming sunnily behind.

The barkeep slid the glass into her palm and fetched a scooped tumbler to accompany the bottle, plinking it down at Dorian's elbow.

Dorian leant sideways on the bar and took obvious note of the harbour master two seats down and, once secured of his attention, sent him a wide smile and said, "Well met, Master Bosworth. It has been some time."

Julius Bosworth had learned on the job that turning a blind eye to trouble in return for reasonable glass was the secret to a longer, happier life, even on peaceable Empire docks. Those shrewd eyes, though one slightly misted, knew what trouble looked like in all forms, and Dorian hadn't paid overprice on their drinks on a whim. For Master Bosworth, Empire trouble required Empire glass, and now he knew what Dorian's trouble was worth.

The Harbour Master's cheek twitched, and his clear eye travelled from Dorian's head to their toes and back before he replied with casual ease, as though they were friends indeed, "Aye! It has . . ." He trailed off for a moment, lost as to what form of address to attach there.

Dorian smirked and did not help him to one. They gestured idly with the bottle to a more secluded table.

Quickly recovering, he snatched up his tankard and heaved off the stool. Waving a hand, he said, "Come, come. Let us catch up where it's quiet."

They found a table in the corner and Dorian set the bottle and tumbler down, sliding into the chair and kicking up a foot on the one next to it. The harbour master sat down heavily, his mug hitting the table with a bang and a slosh of liquid. Dorian withdrew their inked hand from their pocket to uncork the bottle and pour a splash of the sparkling amber liquid. The harbour master tracked it with his eyes, though no hint of surprise showed there. Dorian's hand disappeared back into their pocket.

Bosworth sipped his beer and asked, "So, Master Hunter, what can I do for you? And since we are so acquainted as all that, what may I call my good friend who I haven't seen for so long? It is hunter, yes? Not huntsman?"

He set down his mug and adjusted himself in his chair, folding his arms over his belly, settling in as Dorian raised their own glass.

The liquor was sweet and slightly sticky, ending with a burst of burning warmth that swirled over the tongue, licked down into the chest, and breathed fumes out through the nose like dragon flames. Dorian touched the rim of the glass to their lips and sipped a mouthful, pressing their lips together and pulling the fragrant spirit through their teeth, closing their eyes and savouring the first touch of it on their tongue. They swallowed and opened their eyes, downing the rest in a gulp.

They started talking as they refilled the glass. "It's Dorian Locke, but Master Hunter will do just fine. Only the head of the guild may be called the Huntsman."

Bosworth's shrewd eyes widened, and he took up his beer again.

Dorian grinned, skimming a finger around the top of their glass. "I see you know me."

Dorian gulped down another glass of the amber moonshine and refilled again, rubbing a thumb across their top lip to wipe away any lingering gleam of it.

They gestured with the full glass to the harbour master, without sloshing even a little over the rim. "And I want to know the names of any ships that made port here in the past four rises. I want to know which are still docked, which have made for other ports, and which ports they have made for. I want . . ." Dorian paused. A group of sailors were bundled around a booth across the tavern; two of them sitting forward in their chairs, their backs to Dorian, and two slouched in the booth, all with cards in their hands. Cards flicked from their hands into sliding piles on the table. It took Dorian a second to figure out why something about the group bothered them, during which a swift and sudden silence elapsed as Dorian's sentence trailed off.

Dorian frowned as they noticed the silence and continued,

collating the thoughts inside their head. "I want the names of the captains, the numbers in their crews, and anything else you might think pertinent about them."

Taking a sun disc from their pouch of glass, they tossed it to the harbour master. It plopped down into his drink, and Dorian failed to conceal a wince, but Bosworth just laughed and drained the rest.

"And you want me to get another drink?" he finished for them. But before he could get up, Dorian jerked their chin at the group as discreetly as possible, while rolling the tumbler between their hands.

"Who're they?"

The group was still playing cards, but something was wrong. Wrong enough to have sparked Dorian from across the room. They were absorbed in their game, though every so often someone would scoff, swear, or comment, and they would laugh and chatter and then return to playing, but none of them looked up. The rest of the room allowed themselves the curiosity of scanning the room to see who was in, of glancing at the harbour master and his friend. This group was resolute. No sailor cared for cards that much unless they were betting or avoiding something else, and Dorian couldn't see any glass on the table.

Bosworth picked the disc out of the bottom of his mug. "They came in first rise, not sure where they're heading. Ship's called the *Oathbreaker*."

"Sounds inauspicious."

Dorian's gaze slid away from the group, again finding it odd that none of them had acknowledged the weight of it upon them, and allowed the harbour master to stand. Dorian stood too. Bosworth held out his hand.

"Will that be all you require?"

Dorian placed their hand in his and squeezed mildly. "Yes, thank you."

They dropped a string of glass into the pocket of Bosworth's coat. Julius Bosworth nodded. "It was good to see you," he said, though none were close enough to have required the farce now.

Dorian smiled and returned, "And you."

The harbour master lumbered away towards the bar. Dorian corked the bottle of amber liquor with all intention of taking it back to their room and spending some time with it without interruption. Bottle in hand, they swept towards the doorway, sending a jaunty wave towards Bosworth in farewell.

Dorian shot a final glance at the group of sailors and, finally, one looked up. This one had a prickly look, which had written itself even into the pointed lines of his face. His gaze swept over the bar, lingering a little longer on Bosworth and his newfound glass, and then deliberately travelled Dorian's way. The sailor's face tightened, eyes pinching in the corners, and Dorian gathered he had thought they were already gone. Rather than withdrawing as though he'd been caught staring, which he had, the sailor leaned forward across his table and grinned. The edges of it were tipped with sharp-looking teeth, somehow sharper than ones Dorian had ever seen on a man.

Dorian exhaled through their nose and their lips pulled up into an answering smirk on one side. The sailor's turn came up in the cards and one of his fellows jabbed him on the shoulder, barking, "Edge!" and the sailor turned back to the game, his grin not fading in the slightest.

Dorian held their gaze on the group for a few moments and then strode out the door, bottle swinging.

Unlikely, but not impossible, Dorian thought. The *Oathbreaker* had come in two spans too late by all accounts, but it by far seemed the most interesting prospect.

Dorian took the long way back to their room, strolling down to the docks, peering at every ship in the violet night until they paused in front of the *Oathbreaker*. Taking a swig from the bottle and shuddering a little at the trail of warmth that burst along their throat, they pivoted and stopped.

There was a figure sitting over the side, still and silent as a statue and just as dark and featureless under the weak nightrun moon.

Dorian raised a hand and waved.

The figure startled, real and living once more, and then hesitantly waved back. Dorian laughed and half turned away, making to take another swig, when something flashed above them. A silver-white-lilac pulse of something, bright as lightning, for just a single second.

Dorian gasped and sputtered amber moonshine down their chin as they tried not to choke, whirling back to face the figure. But when they looked up to the *Oathbreaker*, the figure was gone. The wind picked up across the water, rattling through the furled sails, and it carried with it the smell of rain.

Well, Dorian thought, turning away from the harbour and wiping their chin with the back of their hand, *that is interesting indeed.*

CHAPTER 9

SHYE CLAMBERED DOWN THE RIGGING AND PLOPPED BACK ONTO THE railing. He could feel a storm brewing out on the water, lightning already flashing through the clouds, though no thunder rolled across the waves. He pulled at his hood self-consciously. His hands shook in his lap and his fingers felt tremulous, half real, like they weren't listening to the rest of his body. If he took off his hood, he knew his eyes would be gleaming like a folk-moon and his hair would be writhing with slicks of lightning.

He felt the knowledge of the approaching storm in his bones, an ocean of black- and light-split deepness there inside him. There hadn't been a storm on the way and yet one was coming in all the same. Coming for him.

He waited on the railing until the crew came ambling home, wondering with every second that the storm drew closer whether disappearing below might've been a better idea. Up the gangway they came, faces taut with anxiety, and one by one, they dropped with cat-like grace to the deck. He swung around and hopped down, stilling as they all turned to him, and a surge of panic raced up his legs as they left him feeling caught by their watchfulness.

Muse came last, looking out of the harbour, and Shye's worry turned to wariness.

"Storm's on the way," he remarked plainly, casting a glance and a quirked brow in Shye's direction.

Shye blushed under his hood and immediately felt a choking rush of chagrin, not sure what he was feeling it for, the storm or for blushing about it. Or perhaps it was the timing. Though he'd managed some fog, a bit of a gale, some water, or a splash against the hull, he'd had no evidence up till this point to suggest he could do more. If he could conjure storms from thin air, now was hardly the best time to be discovering it.

Perhaps it was the general discomfort of reconciling what he was to the world and to this crew; namely the biggest letdown in all of history, and what he felt within himself. Shye's being promised something to the Blooded, but as it stood, he had no power to help his people. He couldn't keep his head down long enough to help his crew. Whatever the light in his eyes promised, Shye was no Stormborn of Old, merely a shadow of their Blood. Yet, inside him there was a feeling of waking up and a well of deepness that was reaching out, racing through his blood, like something far beneath his bones had been dozing this whole time but now it was coming to. A useless feeling, if he couldn't do anything with it.

Thunder cracked at last and the sky lit up bright with spidering webs of lightning, radiant and clear, shearing everyone into glaring luminosity and then plunging them back into shadow as drops of rain began to fall.

Muse grimaced and shooed them all away from the open deck. They trudged out of the downpour into the warm recesses of the ship. Shye slipped coming in, nearly falling on Edge before Butler shoved him upright using Edge's body between them and his bony shoulder in Shye's chest as a wedge, waiting until he'd righted himself to let go. Shye ignored the swat Edge aimed at him and his slightly mean, "Thought yer weren't supposed to leave yer cabin, cabin boy."

Edge rolled his shoulder dramatically, a delicate sneer on his face, but listened to Shye's murmured, "No one was out."

Which wasn't technically true. Someone had been out, but the shadowy shape on the docks with a bottle of sparkling liquor in their hand was the least of Shye's problems and not worth the pain of mentioning.

"Besides," he continued, "I think 'cabin boy' is a promotion from kitchen wench."

Edge's reply was rough and teasing, "I'll give yer a promotion," followed by a yelp as someone pinched him.

When they didn't part ways as they usually did after some light cards and reconnaissance – Alice to report to the captain, Butler to his hammock, Edge to the galley and Muse to folk knows where – but carried on towards the captain's quarters, Shye knew they'd seen or heard something more than light cards and reconnaissance had intended.

He stole into the room with the rest of them, creeping into a quiet space in the darkest corner at the back of the room, hoping the captain wouldn't notice an extra body crowding up his office.

Alice moved forward, her red-dyed getup glowing in the light from the lantern on the desk, and the captain looked up.

His green eyes flicked one by one across the members gathered, as though ticking them off a list, and stopped at the small stretch of lantern light that reached over the edge of Shye's boots but no farther. The captain blinked and appeared to let it go unremarked for once.

He flicked over the page of his book. "How was the game?"

Edge grunted unhappily, and Alice quickly followed with, "Uneasy."

"But successful nonetheless?" the captain inquired, gesturing to them vaguely, attention still half-fixed on the book.

"They're already here. Someone imperial," Alice reported, sternly shutting the captain's book before fishing a deck of cards out of her pocket and stacking them on the table. She flicked them skilfully across the desk. All night they had been pulling the same cards: several varieties of star and the jack, the king of diamonds and the jack, and the queen of bones. Not in the same order, but all the same regardless, even when they were cheating.

The deck itself had been a gift from a boy they'd saved from the damned capricious Nain twelve long years ago. Shye had bought the cards from the moving market in the floating city of Aura to the north, the man-made city of waterways and ship wood grown upon the ocean itself; the first and last bastion of the Empire before the legendary territory of Yren Fe Ire Fell, where the first king's ancestors had reigned. Though with what money or token the gift had been bought she'd never figured out. Just as she'd never been satisfied that the Nain, who ruled the waters beneath the city, had just let them go after the captain had stolen Shye away, even after Shye had told her of their changeable moods.

The cards had developed a habit over the spans of telling small fortunes, which was no wonder to Alice, considering the boy who'd given them to her. Each crisp turn of a card echoed the turn of the stars that followed her at nightrun. Though, it wasn't in her to read either. Her line was the weakest among them, and the power of her gift had been lost long ago.

The captain moved the book aside, turning the cards over in his hands. His gaze caught Alice's and she gave a brief, warm smile. She wondered if Shye even remembered.

"Not the king," the captain murmured to himself, fingers catching at the edges of the last card that had been laid out. "The other jack."

He looked up, straight at Shye.

Edge cleared his throat, and said, "There was someone talking with the harbour master."

The captain's attention drifted away from the cards and his ward and back to the report his crew were giving. "And?"

Edge picked his teeth and made a low noise in his throat. "And they were different."

The captain inclined his head as if to say, "go on" in a mildly imperious manner. Edge clicked his tongue and did not add anything further.

"Imperial? Or Strange?" the captain prodded.

Edge gave a half-snorting laugh. "In a hat like that? Patched blue and silver—"

"Two feathered plumes sticking out of it," the captain finished, interrupting. He pulled open a draw on his desk and pulled out a pencil stick, drawing over something on his desk. He held up the jack of diamonds, a quick-sketched hat perched jauntily over its grinning head, wide-brimmed cobalt with silver patches and two wide, curved feathers at the back.

Shye's skin went cold.

The figure on the dock that waved up at him, bottle in hand, two plumed feathers bobbing in the air above their head and curving down over the back of their hat, swatches of silver catching in the little light.

"Aye, that's it," Edge agreed.

"Bounty hunter; well known, too," the captain said, flicking the card down again.

Shye snapped back into the room and felt blood thundering in his ears, searing through his veins. On the docks, that had been an imperial bounty hunter, and neither of them had noticed the other. "Well, can't be knowing everything then, can they?" he murmured to himself, jerking out of his daze as Muse turned, having heard him, drawing the captain's gaze with him.

The captain's face seemed to grow wearier as they watched; the room growing quiet and enclosing inwards, until his expression thinned, and he seemed to decide. He turned to Alice. "We're leaving," he ordered.

"No," Shye started, hand flying up to touch his traitorous mouth. He didn't know what moved him to say that, even less to say it out loud, but with it came the familiar taste of restless wildness and an odd strength of will. A gale wind cracked through the open window as the storm broke fully overhead, snapping at the shutters. Water sprayed across the hull, climbing higher.

"What do you mean, no?" the captain ground out, light and shadows playing across the aggrieved planes of his face. His eyes were sparking like a grass fire.

Lightning split and the thunder came growling.

"I can't leave," Shye said, some old whisper crawling, calling under his skin, his disposition flaring to the surface.

The captain pinched the bridge of his nose as the ship rolled on choppy waves, and when he opened his eyes, he fixed them resolutely on Shye.

"This . . . awakening, Shye, is no excuse for insubordination," he said, his voice rising to be heard over the thunder and the slop and spray of water. "If I could put you and your damned truth off this ship, I would, and may we both be happy about it, but alas you are my responsibility, and as such I say we go. Now."

Shye felt the restless longing like an ache in his chest, yawning wider, and the wildness in him rose with the tides outside. He spat, surprising himself with its ferocity, "No, there's something out there I need to do. How am I supposed to find it by smuggling and hiding and always looking down? What Stormborn has ever lived and died in insignificance, leaving the world to someone else?"

Shye stalked closer, breaking into the circle of light. "I will not be the first."

The captain eyed him harshly, hands flat on the desk. The room around them was silent, seeming to melt into the storm outside until it was just the two of them ensconced in the lantern light, glaring at each other, neither quite knowing how it had come to this so quickly.

The captain broke away first, leaving Shye with the sick rush of victory, but it sloshed into ice as the captain addressed Alice. "Get us underway as soon as it passes," he commanded, tones clipped.

A burst of cold, salted air blasted into the door before Alice had opened it even an inch, sealing it shut again.

"Stop it! Have you ever seen a storm run from the place it breaks upon? I won't—"

"SHYE!" the captain roared, standing up straight and making to march right around the desk into open confrontation.

Shye's face scrunched but he would not be cowed. His nostrils flared wide, his hidden eyes slit to a pinprick of black, taken over by the yawning, hungry glow that lived there. Another icy blast ricocheted through the room, scattering the cards laid out on the table. The king of diamonds flew into the glass of the lantern and began to blacken and curl with flame.

The captain and Shye both stopped to watch it. They all did, in fact, and Shye felt his breath come slower, the faint heat of the flame tickling his skin, and the wind in his ears calmed. The rain outside lightened. The window shutter snapped shut.

Shye blinked and seized upon the silence. His lungs took a moment to cooperate, suddenly starved for breath, and there was the slide of wetness on his face in contrast to the far away lick of fire, tacky and salt-rimed. His whole body felt scorched and raw, buzzing as though lit from within and, at the same time, bogged down and watery. He felt turned inside out and upside down, woozy, dizzy, and awake.

He gasped a breath and spoke, "I will not run away from it anymore."

The captain tore his eyes from the falling black ash and the smouldering edge of a diamond-inked corner.

"Fine," he said, and then with coldness spat, "Get out."

Shye swallowed and turned to the door. It opened easily. He crossed the threshold, wondering what to do now. It seemed the thing he'd tried and failed to keep consigned beneath his skin was determined to break free of its cage and Shye was afraid it would catch them all in its current. The mood had left him ragged and torn and had possibly ruined his entire relationship with his master and captain, but the nagging sense that there was something out there, beyond the ship, which whispered his name, had awakened in him and he could not ignore it. The world that always seemed to reach for him was pulling him forwards, determined to meet him.

The storm began to move off. No doubt the ship would soon be underway.

Shye winced as the door shut deliberately behind him and felt the last slips of the storm fade into the wind. Then the whisper sounded in his ears again, as if it was following him. *Shye.*

Looking to his boots, he saw the grinning face of the jack of diamonds wearing a broad-brimmed blue hat staring up at him from the floor.

CHAPTER 10

DORIAN DOZED, HAVING RECEDED OVER THE LAST COUPLE OF HOURS OUT of general drunkenness into regretfully hungover. Dorian was normally more careful, with well-trained restraint in regard to drink, but the amber moonshine had been good. Too good to let go to waste.

The aches and tingling pains, which came from locked joints and falling asleep in uncomfortable chairs, came rushing into Dorian's consciousness, but they didn't stretch, didn't move to ease the throbbing and niggling twinges. From under their hat, pulled down low to block out the light thrown by the fire only a few feet away, all they could see was black, but Dorian could hear the flames crackling and spitting. The thing that had awoken them was strangely soundless.

Dorian breathed deeply, evenly, their ears straining to hear even a hint of what it was, but the fire blanketed any softness of sound. There was a cold touch on their skin, at the back of their neck, from the movement of air, and with it was the dewy smell of rain. The window, which Dorian had closed before retiring, was open. Then, there! The quietest shift of breath . . . right in front of them.

Dorian waited till it came again, just the softest shift they could barely discern, and with it, Dorian sprang into movement. They whipped a small pistol out from the sash tied under their shirt, their elbow giving an almighty crack as they did so, and cocked the already loaded gun.

The almost silent breath hitched and froze.

Dorian tipped their hat back on the point of a finger and stood, heat lancing down their back as they did, only adding to the foul mood this awakening had brought them. A figure stood just to the side of the fire, cloaked and hooded, hands held peaceably in the air. Dorian did not lower the gun.

"Are you the bounty hunter?" came a bright voice from beneath the hood. The cloak the figure wore writhed in the slight wind from the open shutters, showing the barest outline of lithe but strong limbs. Dorian's room may have been on the third floor, but climbing was not out of the question for this visitor.

Dorian cocked a brow at the figure's calm and somewhat courteous manner, and deigned to answer with a similar mildness, "By the grace of this gun, I'll be asking you the questions."

Sizing the figure up, Dorian concluded they were of a size and maybe even an age as well, though Dorian was slightly taller and – despite being more noble-blooded – probably more inclined to be dishonourable, should the need arise.

Dorian could take them if they needed to.

The cloaked figure did not seem in the least intimidated by the pistol aimed at them, excepting the nervous, reckless air that clung to the breeze as it whispered around them. Their fingers, held aloft still, twitched restively every so often.

"By all means," the intruder said, and seemed to wave with their fingers in acquiescence.

Dorian did not need permission but was pleased with the cooperation provided, even if it was provided at the point of a gun.

"How did you get in here?" Dorian said; a brief flash of annoyance heating their breast at the obvious look the intruder cast towards the open window, which even the hood pulled low over the face could not completely disguise. The intruder did not seem to think much of Dorian's intelligence. Dorian rolled their eyes and tried not to be too offended.

Dorian continued. "Without my hearing?"

The figure paused and then answered with an honesty so ill-advised that Dorian found themself drifting out of irritated offence into amusement, which was more than the intruder deserved since Dorian had shot people before for much less than breaking into their room and insulting them.

"Well, from the whiff of you," the intruder said, "I imagine I had some liquorous help."

He stopped dead then. His mouth, quick with honesty and laid with a bewitching mood, stoppered shut with the sudden realisation of what he'd said to Dorian, who was still holding a gun level with his chest. He seemed to wait a moment to see if it would go off.

Dorian, however, conceded the point with a half-exhale, a shrug, and a smirk.

The intruder, which Dorian had taken to assuming was a young man from his turn of address, recovered with grace and continued, much undaunted, "That and natural talent, I guess."

Dorian gave a cursory nod of acceptance and settled back into the hard chair before the fire, their pistol still outstretched and primed. Settling the hat more comfortably on their auburn-doused head, Dorian said casually, "Then, if you wouldn't mind naturally talenting yourself back out again, if you please."

The figure froze in place while Dorian spoke. The breeze blew folds of the cloak around his form like a costumed sculpture, and then his shoulders dropped, his hands coming about halfway down but, remembering the gun, still high enough to convey harmlessness, which Dorian was more or less convinced of now.

"What?" came the intruder, dumbfounded.

Dorian yawned, their jaw cracking with the effort, and waved the gun meaningfully between the intruder and the window. The figure remained stubbornly in place, although his hands finally drifted down to his sides.

"Don't you want to know why I'm here?"

Dorian blinked, starting to idly fiddle with the pistol, lassitude settling a heavy blanket over their limbs. They held the notion that they really couldn't care less at the moment under their tongue. Their patience for lunacy and dockside mischiefs was thin and fraying every second that this cabin boy looking for a story to tell his mates remained without care in their presence. Once he was gone, they had every intention of going back to sleep immediately and waking only when the pounding in their head had ceased.

"Well, you're not here to murder me, or, if you are, you're not very good at it," Dorian started with the obvious. "If you're here to rob me, you've either already done so or I've cleverly woken up just in time to foil you, not that there's much worth taking."

Dorian took a breath, sighed, and kept going. "If you've ascended to the wrong room for a lay, or the right one, seeing as you wanted to know if I was the bounty hunter, then you have to admit I'm being very generous in letting you go without a new hole in you."

While Dorian listed, the intruder shifted and seemed eager to interject, but Dorian ploughed on. "And in all cases, you have no weapons, and I do." They gestured again to the window. "So off you pop."

The intruder stepped forward, shaking his head, saying, "You don't understand . . ."

Dorian slammed back onto their feet, impatience and lingering weariness erasing all trace of goodwill, and displeasure rolled across their features. They marched over to the intruder and jammed their gun point-blank into his ribcage, glaring into his shadowy cowl.

"Out, now."

Dorian backed the cloaked figure all the way to the window and jabbed at him ferociously when he didn't immediately exit, feeling the clack of metal against thin skin and bone, forcing him onto the rain-slick sill. The figure hopped out, balancing precariously. He turned back, and Dorian confirmed their assumption that it was indeed a young man under the hood. With their faces so close, Dorian could see the light splashing off the boy's jaw and the plush shape of his mouth, skating across fine, slanted cheekbones, while the rest was swallowed by dark mystery.

He leaned in and whispered, "Don't you know I'm right here."

Before Dorian could utter a bad-tempered retort of, "Well, of course you are," the figure followed quickly, in clarification, "I'm the one you're looking for."

Then, he raised his head a little and Dorian caught sight of his eyes. Burning, searing, glowing like a folk-moon. Lightning bright.

Dorian's breath caught and this time, it was they who froze.

The boy readjusted his grip on the sill, his cloak wafting around him, misted with rain. Tentatively, he reached for Dorian's gun and tried to manoeuvre it away, the barrel still aimed straight at him.

Dorian was still locked in place by the sight of him when they felt the gentle touch on their pistol. The boy's lips parted on some other utterance, a follow up to his revelation which Dorian didn't hear, his words tumbling under the spinning wheels of Dorian's mind. Feeling rushed back into their body with the cold pattering of rain, the world redesigning in their mind, shifting to encompass this moment and in that the only real, solid thing was the foreign hand upon Dorian's gun. Instinctively, Dorian fired.

The boy gasped.

Dorian heard it dimly and it sounded like shock and maybe pain, their thoughts tangled in the mesmerising impossible, improbable, hungry light of the boy's gleaming eyes. Dorian saw them falling away from the window. Dropping the pistol to the floor, hand stinging from a kick they hadn't braced for, they threw themself over the ledge of the sill to see.

The street below was clear, the shutters were closed, with no lights except the ones lining the street showing in the dark, and the boy was gone. A smear of red-golden blood on the edge of the sill and the discharged pistol were the only lingering proofs that he'd been there at all. Dorian fell back inside, staring at the shutters in bewilderment.

"Sweet Majesty," they breathed.

Then, abruptly, they began to laugh.

Mercy made her way out of the stuffy, oppressive heat of the galley, where the coals still glowed and the firebricks were warm from lunch, to the steadily fresher air drifting down from the deck. The ship had been quiet since lunch, and Mercy understood it was time to make herself known. She wasn't in the habit of appearing upstairs when there were happenings going on, preferring to keep the silence of the knowing and the speaking to herself, but there were limits to her uninvolvement, and the happenings of the nightrun before demanded she make some true noise, even if it was just a quick word with the quartermaster.

The hatch skywards was stuck in place but opened when she gave it a good shove, and she ascended through to the deck. Alice, her ship's sister and the only one she'd trust to speak to on this boat full of men who'd broken their oaths before, was alone on the upper deck. The murky silence of the ship was amplified here by the dark and resolute expression on Alice's face that gave the impression that she'd frightened the others away. From the silence, Mercy thought she'd done more than just that.

Mercy went over to her without fear and handed off the bottle she'd brought; a pungent gift of plum spiced wine, knowing it would be taken as the bribe it was the moment she broke her words.

Alice's expression shifted, and she seemed to put the resoluteness away, though no doubt it was still there on the underneath, and the darkness of it skulked elsewhere. She gave a grateful brush to Mercy's fingers as she took the bottle, uncorked it, and gulped down a swallow, wiping her mouth on the back of her hand.

Mercy waited till she was done and then asked, "Shouldn't we be gettin' under?" in a tone that spoke of disquiet.

Alice snapped the bottle back into Mercy's hands with a brusque but meaningful, "Belay that order."

Mercy noted the clang of metal on metal that followed Alice's movements. She found the source of the sound in the keys that Alice usually kept on a sash beneath her shirt or in the deep pockets she'd sewn into her clothes, which were instead hanging from her belt. The eddies of understanding that had been swirling in Mercy's wake solidified into a wave, and she breathed a little easier for the feeling of it. She raised her hand, the bottle in it, and curled her fingers into a fist around its neck in awe of the other woman's balls. The quiet of the ship had indeed been of purpose. Only they had the freedom of it and the captain would not be happy they had stolen it for a time, when he himself was free to walk up top again.

Likely that the captain would take those keys back from his quartermaster for the betrayal and the indignity of being locked below on his own ship, necessary though it was.

Alice returned her demonstration with a look that they had shared many a time, as women, as friends and as crew, and knocked Mercy's knuckles with her own, gesturing for the bottle. Mercy downed a swig and tossed it to her, wrinkling her nose at the aromatics as they swept across her tongue. She had always preferred her spirits smooth and with a kick.

"Been gone, has he?" she asked, though she'd known it the moment they had returned below come nightrun that he would.

Alice drank, looking out into the world, and then drank again.

"He was always meant to go, when has never been up to us."

"We did him right," Mercy assured her gently, seeing the ripple of her fingers clench around the bottleneck like that of many an unfortunate man. "Ez thinks he'll fail, too young, too soon. He won't. He hears the call, knows it is for him. It's Ez who ain't ready to return."

"The captain has every reason to never want to go back there, but Shye is different. As long as we can keep the crown's eyes off him a while longer," Alice agreed. "And if we leave now, we will regret it," she concluded, turning to meet Mercy's eyes; the resoluteness surging back into blooming. "This ship's not going anywhere."

Mercy took the bottle and sipped at it, handed it back and gave the other woman's wrist an acknowledging squeeze, her eyes narrowed in agreement.

"Good," she said and took up a post next to the other woman. "Now all's to do is wait and hope none do anything stupid."

CHAPTER 11

DORIAN CHECKED THE STREET FOR SMEARS OF BLOOD THE NEXT RISE, while it was still peaceful out, having spent the last few hours of the moon's nightrun staring blankly into the fire. A pair of lightning-speared eyes were etched into their memory, both too real and too Strange to be a dream. The rain had left only small splotches of rusted red on the stone and in the cracks between them. They led Dorian at odd paces around a corner street and into a squat alleyway where a puddle of muddy water mixed with ichor pooled lonely and Stormborn-less; a literal dead end.

Now lightrise had broken more fully and people were about their business, Dorian took a tour of the ships docked in the harbour one by one, saving the *Oathbreaker* for last, needing no guise as an agent of the Empire but playing a decent part as the Harbour Master's eager apprentice, partly for the discretion it offered and partly for their own amusement.

Apart from some minor contraband and the typical cargo carried by licensed merchant companies, Dorian uncovered less in each ship than they'd found in the alleyway, not that they'd expected much from these ships, but the chance had been there. But no, the boy –

the Stormborn, *majesty save them, he was truth* – had all but disappeared. Dorian could have kicked themself for their mistake.

Still, the *Oathbreaker* held some promise that Dorian could find
the boy again, holed up somewhere onboard. They would find the
boy again, regardless, just for the joy of seeing the look on their
father's face when they presented him as a coronation gift to the
crown prince; a gift the likes of which the Empire hadn't seen since it
was the empire of the Old World. The hunter who managed that
could claim anything, even the title of Huntsman, though whether
Dorian aspired to the role or not, they would never take that away
from their grandfather. There was a growing gnawing in their mind
that if Dorian brought the boy in, there would be no greater prize out
there. It would be victory in one fell swoop.

Dorian thought their stomach felt a little queasy at the idea, but
when they sidled past the Golden Fancy around noon, with little
evidence and no leads, and their stomach howled at the scent of hot,
salty food, they realised they were probably just hungry.

The *Oathbreaker* was still docked at the end of the harbour and
didn't appear to be going anywhere. The lack of activity onboard lent
credence to Dorian's vague suppositions on how sailing worked, and
they had been hunting long enough to know that while most runners
were inclined to skip town once they knew there was a bounty out
and a hunter on their trail, the Stormborn boy hadn't seemed the
type. No reason to skip a reasonable meal because of time
constraints, and maybe someone inside knew something useful.
Dorian's mouth flooded with saliva as the movement of the door
wafted that rise's lunch special right into their face.

The barkeep "hoyed" them from across the room when they
walked in and, apparently remembering the glass from before, whistled to the serving girl and gestured for her to go fetch a plate for
their hungry patron. Dorian smiled in gratitude and flipped a piece
of glass onto the bar – this time only the night's eye that lunch was
worth – and two more into the tipping tankard; a bronze-casted
goblet that rattled when patrons sat down and stacked their elbows
on the bar.

Taking a seat along the bar, sinking onto the stool with a small sigh, Dorian sunk into their food with chaotic enthusiasm as soon as the steaming plate was set in front of them. It was some kind of sweet and spicy stew, but Dorian wasn't paying much attention to it aside from it being delicious and getting it inside them as quickly as possible. It was served with bread warm from the oven to mop up the glistening juices and had a hearty heat to it; a good deal for only a single night's eye. It took two very different kinds of training to allow Dorian to all but inhale the meal while maintaining excellent enough table manners that no one took offence at the ravenous display, though the company here was a good deal less fastidious than Dorian's usual mealtime audience.

The barkeep, despite getting a front-row seat to the spectacle, only seemed amused and told Dorian she'd make sure to pass on their compliments to her cook, holding out a napkin over the bar.

Dorian laughed and took the proffered napkin from the woman's hand and wiped the grease from their mouth; their plate nearly licked clean. "I'm sorry, I'd forgotten that I had not had breakfast. Please do pass on the compliment."

The barkeep waved Dorian off. "No need to apologise, we've seen worse in here. How 'bout a drink to wash it down, perhaps a glass of the amber moonshine?"

Dorian coughed and pushed down the temptation, shaking their head and saying, "No, thank you."

The barkeep shrugged in a suit-yourself manner and made to move off, when Dorian asked, "Any news from the capital, or anywhere?"

The barkeep fiddled with her off-white cleaning cloth and thought. "None from the capital that I've heard, and believe me, I would've heard it. The sailors have been talking, though they usually are, so it's really not any different to the stuff they usually talk about."

Dorian leaned forward and folded their arms on top of the bar, the tipping tankard giving its customary jangle as they did. They really had no idea what sailors usually talked about, but they did know the barkeep would tell them without much prodding now she'd started.

She leaned towards them in confidence. "They've been saying that the north-east seas are getting rough and that storms have been blowing in from nowhere. Some of them think someone's gone and angered a marsh witch, though even if they were real, they'd be out north-west, not north-east, on the islands around Feng."

Dorian kept their expression mildly interested as the barkeep continued.

"Some say much the same, only it's the Nain that are angry. But I imagine it's only early frostfalls before the sun shines over, rather than some mythical water spirits throwing fits."

Dorian hummed noncommittally. They also had a feeling it wasn't mythical water spirits, though it wasn't an early frostfall in the middle of the sun span either, but perhaps something even more unlikely. Worth noting, all the same.

And come to think of it, where *had* the Stormborn come from? Before his appearance in Phirrun, how many spans had he gone undetected, and how had he managed such a feat? Perhaps the sailors, superstitious as they were, kept better records of the old stories than anyone knew.

The barkeep lapsed into silence and, finding no one in need of service, shunted Dorian's empty plate down the wood-grained bar top for the server to pick up on her way back to the kitchen.

Dorian hummed again and said, "You know, my grandfather used to tell me stories about all of them. The folk, y'know. But he never got around to what happened to them. I've always wondered . . ."

The barkeep gave a nod of acknowledgement and wiped down the bar with her grungy cloth, thinking again. "I don't think anyone knows for certain, except for maybe one of them dark wings, and how you would ask one, I don't know. They don't claim they sailed off, far away, and never came back. Although that would be a very sailor-y thing to claim, even these seasons there's too much Strangeness about to believe it."

She smiled self-deprecatingly at Dorian, and Dorian nodded for her to continue.

"I think," she began, "I think it usually ends with the crown. Camillus was the first king, but some folk majesty – a high lord or some such, though a queen we'd call her now, and there were many back then—"

Four, there were four high lords. One for each season, Dorian corrected in their mind, remembering Ever's stories, the guild children clustered round the assembly rooms to hear about the world before the Empire, of Kernon's chosen and their courts of sun and frost.

"—lost the Old World when Camillus stole the crown and declared that the world belonged equally to humans and we too should have the right to rule it. Then, I guess, they just faded away. Not all the way, of course, but all the stuff in them that was folk. True folk."

The barkeep paused to greet some new customers and then slid back over to Dorian, eager to tell her tale. "Now she must've fought, old queen Dana and the Blooded who followed her. High lord of a land that loved you, she must've. But Camillus had weapons the likes of which the folk had never seen and nothing to lose. A prince in his own right, but of a land that didn't know him and didn't love him. His crown which didn't want him, well, he stole himself another."

Her smile sparkled a little at the edges, and fondness washed into her expression. "Or at least that's the way Graysen tells it once you get her going. She tells it like she heard it, back from some master in the capital. Swears they was a dark wings, a Raven, but I doubt that's truth."

Dorian resisted the urge to mutter "not all of them just faded away", and instead put on a genial smile for the lady and thanked her for her time, before saying, "No other news then?"

If anyone had found a boy bleeding out from a gunshot wound somewhere around town, surely someone would've mentioned it by now. The Stormborn looked like a fairly inconspicuous ship's boy on the outside, provided he hid his face. Bright eyes flashed through their mind and Dorian shuddered a little.

The barkeep shook her head. "Not that comes to mind."

Dorian sighed and thanked her again, slipping off the stool; their boots hitting the floor with a dull clack.

"Though, perhaps . . ." the barkeep started.

Dorian looked to her and found her gaze flickering over them cautiously. She cleared her throat and said, "Perhaps, speaking of folk, you might be interested – that is to say, careful – of that there ship on the end. Some of the crew there . . . they got the Strangeness in 'em. We don't get a lot of them here, it's just stories usually."

Interested certainly covered Dorian's feelings concerning the *Oathbreaker*, although "careful" did not. Dorian pretended to take note of the advice, kindly meant as it was.

"Thank you for the meal," Dorian farewelled, and flicked another eye into the tipping tankard. "For the story," they said, and walked out of the tavern.

The *Oathbreaker* loomed over its little berth in the bay, its wood sleek, crafted and treated well. The flag it flew was an imperial one, though there was no doubt in Dorian's mind that there was a drawer somewhere on that ship full of flags and only one, and who knew which, was its truth.

Dorian loitered at the bottom of the gangway, frowning. It had been going around all sunning that the Harbour Master's apprentice was making the tours and checking inventories. The other captains had been careful to send someone, if not appearing themselves, to play guide and steer Dorian away from anything the Harbour Master was usually paid to overlook. The *Oathbreaker*, in comparison, was disconcertingly quiet, and no one was about on deck.

Swallowing their unease, Dorian stepped up onto the gangplank.

Behind them footsteps came pounding across the flagstones and then a body was colliding with theirs, heated, hot-breathed and heavy with momentum, with a hand fisting in their side, halting them.

A silvery voice said, "Wait!" in their ear.

Dorian turned into the grip and pushed themself and the owner of the offending hand back off the gangway with one vicious, violent thrust. Dorian's forearm pressed into the person's throat and a pistol pressed into their breast. The offending hand remained fixed in Dorian's side, and now they were face to face, Dorian saw the mouth under the curve of the hooded cloak twitch upwards in the beginnings of a sheepish smile.

Dorian swore under their breath. They shoved the offender away, catching the fleeting wince that flew across the Stormborn's face. There was no doubt it was him.

Dorian swore again and hauled him back in, pistol jamming in under his jaw. "What in all humanity—"

"Don't go on that ship," the boy interrupted quickly, casting a hasty, almost guilty, glance that skated along the ship, along its lines and rails as if in rapid farewell.

Dorian pulled their gun away from the boy, letting it hang by their side. They'd already shot the boy once, and once was probably enough.

"Well, I don't have to now, do I? Where . . . ?"

Dorian paused and sneezed on the next inhale, nose wrinkling. Wafts of musky, stale odours were rolling off the cloaked menace. Dorian almost took a step back into fresher air but managed to keep their ground by breathing through their mouth.

"Why do you smell like horses and dirty straw?" Dorian continued, their thoughts diverted by the pungent aroma arresting their nostrils.

The boy's cheekbones spotted red and his mouth twisted at them. He finally let go of Dorian's coat, his hand sliding away from their side to curl into loose fists.

"Well, I couldn't come back here after you shot me," he hissed, indignant, nearly spitting, picking up some of Dorian's own cadence in an odd mimic.

Dorian grimaced. "Sorry about that."

It was bad form for a hunter to harm the merchandise without explicit permission from the guild. Dorian did not like making mistakes and they liked unnecessary cruelty even less. They tried to be as merciful as their profession and pride allowed.

The Stormborn seemed to heave and then billow like a sail caught with wind, and his teeth came out in a half-snarl that was a little frightening. "You *shot* me."

Dorian opened their mouth to apologise again and possibly remark that he couldn't be this upset about everyone who'd done the same or tried to, considering the lines of work sailors sometimes found themselves in. He'd healed just fine, as far Dorian could see. If they wanted him hurt, they would've tried using black iron, whether the Old World poison worked these spans or not.

Dorian's thoughts were cut off before they could continue by a loud, female voice swooping in, following the distinct sound of a gun cocking above them.

"Let him go."

CHAPTER 12

THE WORDS RANG OUT, AND WHILE THEY WERE STILL HITTING AND hanging in the air, Dorian was moving. The Stormborn was still in arm's reach and had never truly left it even when they were arguing, and Dorian had him wrapped up in front of themself with their pistol pointed at the place the voice had echoed from before they had even tipped up their hat to see who it was.

Two women had appeared on the deck of the *Oathbreaker*. One of them stood at the lip of the walkway – the one with the gun pointed at them – while the other lingered a few paces behind her; a butcher's knife hanging from her belt. The one with the gun held it steady, and, with her free hand, unhooked a ring of keys from her belt and tossed them to the other woman.

"Get the captain," she ordered, not taking her eyes off Dorian and their captive.

"Mercy," the Stormborn gasped, with a little shake of his head.

"I'll try my best to provide," Dorian muttered against the Stormborn's ear, their mouth brushing fabric warmed by skin.

The woman with the keys slipped away behind the one holding the gun. That one had a dangerous look about her; lips painted, nails lacquered and a straight-shooting way, just like the gun she held.

"I said, let him go," she repeated coolly.

Dorian met her challenging stare without a flinch, and no one moved. She might be dangerous, but Dorian was a hunter, and they weren't going to give up this prize without drawing some blood first.

"She's a better shot than you," the Stormborn murmured, pressing back into Dorian slightly, and leaving Dorian aware that the side the boy was choosing was not the one Dorian had expected. There was no hint that the boy was hoping she'd shoot Dorian and take him up on the boat, but that if he'd rather anyone getting away from this, it was himself and Dorian.

"What would you know?" Dorian snarked back, a little off-balance.

"I know her," came the waspish reply, almost immediately. Dorian grinned despite it all; they'd never had a runner so interesting before.

"Then what do you propose we do?" Dorian asked, feeling the slide of rough-worn fabric against their lips, and then the soft give of skin as the Stormborn turned his head, assessing. And then he turned away.

"I'm not sure," he said, shifting in Dorian's grip.

Dorian frowned, narrowing their eyes at the woman who was watching them, only because they could not look at their captive and not get shot.

The woman's eyes were darting between them; her expression of previous confidence wobbling its way into confusion. Knowing she could not hear their conversation, but knowing they were having one, Dorian had to wonder what she thought their Stormborn ship's boy had to say to his captor. Probably, "Please let me go."

Hardly, Dorian thought to themself, with a muffled snort, and said, "Then we don't have much choice."

They sighed and cocked their gun, and the boy went stiff in Dorian's hold.

Clamour suddenly drifted out from the bowels of the ship and feet could be heard stamping upwards, along with yells and calls to the woman up top. For a second, her focus broke.

Dorian squeezed the trigger.

The woman's attention snapped back, and then Dorian heard the crack of the pistol. A fiery sensation surfaced in their hand, stinging shots of pain flashing up their arm from fingertips to elbow, and Dorian didn't need to look down to know what they'd see.

The woman was looking at them from above, smug, and backed by four men also wielding pistols, as well as the woman from before.

Dorian's pistol was useless on the ground, blood steadily dripping on it from where the bullet had grazed past Dorian's fingers.

"Told you so," the Stormborn breathed, and Dorian restrained the urge to growl at him.

"Fuck," they swore into the Stormborn's ear and tried to reach for the special pellets they kept in a pouch sewn into their coat. There wasn't much to salvage of this situation, except the Stormborn, and the choices from here seemed unpromising at best; lethal and humiliating at worst. Illegal on all counts as they were, the blue smoke grenades were all Dorian had.

"I believe the lady told you to let the boy go," said the only man who hadn't been at the card game the other night; the one draped in the silver-lined grey coat and levelling a fine piece of a pistol at Dorian's head. It looked custom. Dorian felt there was something familiar in the man, yet the longer they looked, the less they could place his face or the fading feeling.

Dorian gripped the Stormborn tighter, although he didn't seem particularly inclined towards going anywhere, though nor did he seem inclined towards helping Dorian either. That didn't mean he couldn't or wouldn't.

Dorian started talking.

"If you are what you're claiming you are, and those eyes are not just a trick or some worthless folkline, and you can do something here and now, then do it. Or I'll be dead, and they'll be taking you back, which I'm getting the idea isn't what you planned when you came to me in the dead of night and basically handed yourself over."

Dorian cut off their whispering and called to the man who'd spoken, hoping to stall just long enough for the boy to think it over,

"You must be the captain of this fine vessel? Pleased to make your acquaintance."

The man's smile was sharp.

Dorian's fingers were still digging for a pellet; the small oblong casings getting smeared and slippery with blood as Dorian discreetly tried to grab one and break it in half.

The captain spoke again, his voice travelling rich and smooth and threatening over the wind as he called down, "And I'll be pleased to end yours if you don't hand over our boy."

"Maybe he ain't your boy," Dorian shouted back, before muttering to the Stormborn, "Now's the time."

Another pellet eluded Dorian's grasp and their hope of coming out of this intact diminished with every quick slip and slide of the smooth shells through their fingers.

Four guns cocked and took aim. The Stormborn turned his head and whispered, "Close your eyes."

Dorian looked at him in surprise as brightness burst in front of them. Dorian slammed their eyes shut as the world beyond them was swallowed by light.

The grip holding Shye slackened and he stepped out of the bounty hunter's embrace, while grasping for their hand in the blind haze that surrounded them. Shye could see them there and the buildings too, the street and the ship, with the whole world overlayed with drifting fractals of light. The electric glide of lightning splintered and drifted like snow, shining like diamonds and night's eyes and the running rivers of folk-stone, and only Shye could see it. The deepness within slipped away beneath his skin with a hollow yawn, and his blood ran sluggishly where before it had raced and seemed to run with the light that was now drifting through the sky.

Shye caught his fingers in the bounty hunter's and laced them together until they were palm to palm. The hunter's intake of breath was audible and instinctively their eyes slitted open. Shye's hand slapped over them and held there.

"*Close your eyes,*" Shye repeated as gently and calmly as he could, though his own nerves felt frazzled with fear and awe at the thing he had done. His stomach clenched with nausea as he realised he had no idea how he'd done it.

"I can't see," the bounty hunter said, panicked, and Shye knew they didn't mean because he had covered their vision. He squeezed their hand reflexively, slowly removing the other from their face.

"I know. It'll pass, just keep 'em closed."

Shye could see the drifts of light and underneath the world untouched, but the bounty hunter had only seen blinding, lonely white and would again if they opened their eyes before they passed beyond the reach of this sudden, Strange display.

Shye pulled at their hand. "C'mon."

He led them away from the ship and the sweep of coalesced light, over the boundary, and the world solidified into itself again. He turned into an empty alley only a block away from the docks. The bounty hunter sauntered along behind, stopping a few paces behind when Shye dropped their hand.

"You can open your eyes now," he said softly, licking his lips in sudden nervousness.

The bounty hunter did so, blinking hurriedly, trying to pull everything back into focus after the white nothingness. They gave Shye a look of open astonishment.

Shye backed into the wall and looked away. There was a draining dizziness behind his eyes.

"You . . . that was . . ." the bounty hunter started and stopped, blinking a final time as their vision no doubt stabilised. They took a deep, relaxing breath. "I really didn't expect that."

A half-bewildered, half-disbelieving curl turned up their lip and they slipped over to the mouth of the alley. No one was around this part of town, not after the light show. They were all down at the docks.

Shye tried not to sink into the wall though the urge was strong. His legs, his fingers, his whole body was trembling, and his head was light and airy. "You asked me," he answered the bounty hunter testily, breathlessly, and swallowed to wet the dryness in his mouth, touching his hands against the solid brick at his back to hold himself upright.

"I didn't really think you could," the hunter replied, leaning just inside the mouth of the alley, looking over the rooftops towards the harbour.

Shye rasped a dry laugh, biting down the bubbling chuckle. He hadn't thought he could either; he didn't know the things that slipped under his skin half as well as he had known the wind, the sea, and the ship he was leaving behind. He turned to the side, checking that the hunter's eyes were away from him, and was quietly sick on the street.

"It's not fading," the hunter said, glancing back as Shye was wiping his mouth on a sleeve. Their eyes were ghostly aquamarine, encompassing and clear, but shallow almost, skating over the surface of things and in one glance seeing them in entirety. Except for him.

Shye pushed out of the shadows. "It will."

The bounty hunter stepped out of the light slanting down the mouth of the alley and stepped over to Shye with their chin raised, face coming over all determined with a little fascinated curiosity creeping in at the edges.

Shye waited with his arms crossed.

"Let me see," they said softly, not quite a demand.

Shye hissed and looked away, his arms tightening across his chest. The hunter reached out for the hood of his cloak and Shye's hand snapped out to stop them. Their wrist was warm beneath his fingers, their pulse strong and thumping through the skin. Shye watched their eyes go a little pleading without their permission.

"Just once" they said, "and I won't ask again."

Shye's hand, after a moment, slipped cautiously from around their wrist; his mouth set uneasily but soft. He reached up in his customary gesture of pulling the hood low over his face but stopped and made to thumb it back.

The hunter stopped him, hands on his.

"Together," they said.

The weighted fabric hit Shye's shoulders and he unconsciously looked down, before clenching his teeth and defiantly raising his gaze from the ground.

The hunter's lips parted, and they leaned in, passing beyond interested, like they had the previous night, into enthralled. Fascination bled across the hunter's face, dripping from their open mouth as they touched the corners of his eyes, close to his temples.

Shye could see the glow of his eyes reflected in theirs. It was a fight for Shye to keep his gaze steady, but he did.

They leaned back. "I guess you really are the real deal."

Shye snorted and detained the hunter's hands on the side of his face, pulling them off. "Do you still doubt it?"

The bounty hunter shrugged and stepped away. "I won't ask again," they said seriously.

Shye tugged his hood back up, touching the edge of the fabric hesitantly. "When we're out of the city . . ." he said and nearly lost his nerve. The hunter's eyes flashed to him and seemed to dare him to go on.

"When we're out of the city," he started again, growing more firm with every word, "then you won't have to. I'm done with running from the Empire, and with hiding."

The bounty hunter stilled, thinking his words over, turning them around and inside out, and then they nodded slowly. "If that's what you want."

Shye tilted his head in answer and a hint of a smile appeared in the corner of the hunter's mouth. Shye's mouth twitched in return, catching the look.

Then something slithered ominously between Shye's feet. He glanced down to see fractals of light skittering across the flagstones, whirling up between his ankles, blowing away and disintegrating before them. Shye's explosion of light on the docks was breaking.

He looked up. "We should go."

CHAPTER 13

SHYE RAN OUT OF THE SHADOWS OF THE ALLEY INTO WHERE LIGHTRISE broke across the buildings that sheltered their little hideaway. The bounty hunter was behind him as they both peered out; their chest bumping against his shoulder. Across the rooftops, Shye's break of light was drifting and decaying.

"We should go," the bounty hunter agreed. Their breath stirred Shye's cloak, an echo of their position back on the docks. Shye fished the hunter's pistol out of his belt, fairly confident that they weren't going to shoot him again and held it out over his shoulder.

"Picked this up for you."

He felt the hunter's grip take it. When he glanced at them, they were holding it loosely, and something in their face shifting and giving way had Shye's guts dropping to the floor.

"Not to be ungrateful for how easy you're making my job, but shouldn't you be running away from me?" the hunter said.

Shye wished he could interpret what was behind the puzzled stare the hunter gave the gun in their hand, but all he did was shrug and say, "Probably," before pulling them both out of the alley and into the street. Behind them, a crowd of people ringed around the fading light, and even though it seemed the whole city had come out to watch the show of light, it was very, very quiet. A chill wind blew through the harbour and the light spectacle shattered. The crowd gasped.

The hunter pulled Shye along in the opposite direction; the gun disappearing back inside their shirt.

"That weren't an answer," the hunter pointed out, hustling them through gridded streets.

Shye thought it was funny, the way the hunter spoke sometimes, like they were conjuring an illusion of themself with words to get what they wanted, and he supposed it must be a hunter thing. It was odd that they could borrow the tones of others so easily and speak them back to him like they were crew.

"Maybe I am running," Shye said back, the cadence of the hunter's speech echoing in his ears and winding about his tongue. It sounded like Muse or Edge, and in their candid tones demanded an answer. "And maybe it'll kill me quicker than you will."

It didn't seem like a lie when he said it, but it was at best only a half-truth. After all, it didn't feel like running away when it seemed to Shye he'd been running his whole life from port to port, away from the distant crack of thunder and his own reflection, hiding in his little world with its small expectations. He knew what running felt like, and this wasn't it.

"Maybe I'm not running away at all," Shye continued, confusing the hunter, whose expression pinched, their eyes narrowed at him. Shye laughed. "You must know, Master Hunter, that you can't outrun the storm."

The bounty hunter shook their head. "You are surprising."

Shye smiled and kept his final words tangled beneath his tongue. It didn't take a genius to figure out that the storms that broke across the sea were nothing compared to the one brewing within Shye, tired of waiting to run free.

They walked close together through the city, unnoticed by the people around them who were still exclaiming over the Strange happening down at the docks. They came upon the guild stables without needing to break into the maddening dash to escape that

Shye had been envisioning ever since he had decided on this course. The attendants at the stables had the hunter's horse prepped and saddled, ready to go by the time they'd breached the doors from where one of them had spotted them coming up the street.

The hunter snatched the horse's reins out of the stable hand's grip, giving an enthusiastic, low-voiced hello to the horse accompanied by excessive petting, nuzzling, and cooing.

Shye shifted restlessly, watching the hunter and horse with amusement until the hunter rounded on him and stood assessing him, leaving Shye feeling like he'd been caught doing something he shouldn't.

"Can you ride?"

Shye eyed the horse the same way the hunter was eyeing him, and shifted again, arms coming across his chest. He offered a slight shrug. Ships were one thing; he was a sailor and a Stormborn in his element, but equine travel was quite another.

The hunter smiled, their teeth tipped with a delighted ferocity. "Right then"—the hunter pointed at him and then jerked their thumb back at the horse—"you're riding with me and you can apologise to my horse when we get to Mistral."

Shye fought back a sigh, but the idea of struggling overland trying to control a horse and perhaps his miraculous "awakening" as well actually seemed far worse than being squashed onto one horse behind his eccentric captor.

"Yeah, all right." He gave in without a fight, stepping up beside the somewhat smug bounty hunter.

Grateful for the *Oathbreaker*'s lessons on balance, since that and one arm around the hunter's waist and one hand clinging to the saddle was all that stood between him and the jolting of the horse's back and the ground, Shye forced himself to wait until they were outside the gates of Corentin to look back to where to the ship masts rose above the tops of the buildings, the sea stretching out behind them. He closed his eyes as the last threads of the *Oathbreaker* slipped away from him. When he opened them again, the road towards the capital stretched out ahead, and there was warmth radiating from the rider in front.

They must have felt him press a little closer and assumed he was uncomfortable with the horse situation because they called out cheerfully, "It could be worse."

Shye sensed the hunter was grinning, though he couldn't see it; there was something about the set of their shoulders and the air around them that told him. When they turned slightly to see him, there it was. He watched their lips skate across the words and then pull wide in good humour.

"I usually make them walk."

Shye mirrored the smile, but his guts coiled and twisted until it dropped from his face. There was a choking heaviness writhing about in his chest. The *Oathbreaker*, the wind, the wood; all were gone from him.

So, instead, Shye reached for the sky and the land, the drifting breeze and the stone, the way *Oathbreaker* had listened to his call, pleading for something to replace the cold emptiness in his stomach. Aloneness dripped down his throat and his fist clenched in the rider's side, white-knuckling on the saddle. There was nothing there. Nothing underneath. Nothing so little in the vastness of this world that he could reach.

His skin was cold despite the sunning wind, and the world was untouchably far away from him now. The lines of his body and the hunter's rocked together in a fashion almost too intimate to bear. Shye shivered and pushed away the sweep of air against his skin.

"Hey." The hunter's voice broke through his reverie, thoughtful, and the squeezing fist about his lungs loosened. For a moment his mind stopped trying to find what wasn't there. "What's your name? I wasn't given one on the assignment."

A ghost of a smile pulled at Shye's mouth, and he began to thaw on the inside; warmth blooming and tingling on his lips.

The hunter waited.

Shye chewed his bottom lip, watching the sky stretch out above him. He wanted to feel it, but all he could feel was the rider and the horse and the skating touch of wind. It would have to be enough.

"My crew called me Shye," he answered softly.

The hunter's hat dipped in a nod, the plumed feathers bobbing against the side of Shye's cloak. The hunter, chin to shoulder, turned to give him a look. "Thought you were going to take that off?"

Shye's hand shot up to touch the rim of his hood.

The hunter made a harrumphing noise and turned away.

Shye cautiously pushed the hood back, swallowing, suddenly alert. The wind swept in from the sea behind them and stirred through his hair, chilling his cheeks, and his eyes blinked at the world unhindered by shadowed folds as golden, rosy stars came out in the evenspan. He shivered again, not from cold or the buried mourning of that deepness, but from the feeling of being bare, more naked than ever.

The hunter made another sound and reached up a graceful hand to flick their hat off their head and held it out for Shye to take. Waves of carnelian hair writhed free underneath, letting loose the scent of crushed pearl and sweat.

"Here," they said.

Shye took it gingerly and placed it on his head. It was lighter than the hood and easier to see out from behind with no way to hide his gaze. It smelled sweetly of the pearled soap the hunter washed with; a scent of perfumed silk and salt. With it on, Shye no longer felt so disconcertingly unhinged from and yet open to the world.

When Shye looked up, the hunter was once again examining him over their shoulder. They gave themself a little nod of satisfaction and a smile crawled across their mouth.

"You can call me Dorian."

The hunter faced away, and Shye felt the wind buffet him again. He closed his eyes and focused on the movement of the horse and the feeling of someone at his chest, sliding his body closer to the hunter's, his arm tightening around them. He settled against them, adjusting to the rhythm of their bodies until the heavy curl of his insides eased. His connection to the *Oathbreaker* was gone and he was on foreign soil with no touch of the world to guide him, his skin tight with the stillness beneath it, but at least he had this.

Nightrun was coming, the world was alive, and Shye was free. He smiled to himself, tipping the hat back to see the sky. The world had waited for him before, it would either do so now or he would find his way to it. Either way, Shye would be ready when it came to claim its Stormborn.

They stopped for what was left of the nightrun behind a copse of gangly shrubs and bushes a little way off the road. The bushes clustered around small spindly trees, which spouted delicately up and outwards, then bowed and waterfalled to the ground, tendrils dangling. They formed a half-circle of greenery on the field beside the road and then stopped, another cluster cropping up farther inland and another farther down the dirt path.

Dorian set their horse to graze, countering Shye's concerned look with an easy, "Don't worry, she's not going anywhere." Then threw the saddlebags to the ground and unfurled a length of coiled rope. Shye heard the unsaid *and neither are you.*

The hunter made a face and came over to him with the rope wrapped up in their hands.

"I have given you more freedoms than any other hunter would trust to you. I'm hoping you won't begrudge me this. For all you don't act like it, you're still my prize."

Shye held out his wrists sourly and said, "If you believe this would hold me if I didn't wish it to, you would either be very naive or very stupid."

Dorian dragged the rope around and between Shye's wrists, binding them gently but firmly.

"All the same," they said, and attached the other end of the rope to a metal ring hanging from the saddle of the horse. They returned and sat beside him, giving him a mildly sincere, satisfied nod. "Your cooperation is most appreciated."

Shye tested the bindings and found them sturdy and he left it at that.

The dinner they shared could hardly compare in Shye's mind to Mercy's expert handling of a meal. The grapes and cheese the hunter tossed to him, and the cold, long-wearing meat balanced on thin biscuits, with sides of dried fruit from a pouch, were fine and appealing but almost spare at the same time. There was a void in Shye's stomach and the food did not seem to be enough to fill it, but the hunter wasn't complaining, so neither would he.

Finishing the awkward meal with something sweet, they munched on honey-filled sun seeds, popping them open with their teeth and spitting out the husks.

There was not much talking. The hunter's watchful tension stained the air, and when they lay in the pale-gold grass after their meal, hidden from the road, with the spindly trees sweeping tendrils over them, the hunter pretended to be asleep until suddenly they were, so Shye pretended also.

Even in the dark of the nightrun, it was an act of no struggle at all to free himself from the rope bindings. If there was a time to escape and make his own way, this was it. No doubt it was what the hunter was waiting for, even with the chance that Shye was still tied down, but the thought lay stagnant and insignificant in Shye's mind and was swept away by the familiarity of the nightrun sky. Shye did not know the land, did not know why he had been called, but Mistral might have the answers for him if he was patient, and the prince's coronation promised to be a party not worth missing.

He looked over to the sleeping bounty hunter and then up at the twinkling violet night. Patience was not such a hardship now he had begun.

Moving away from these thoughts, he used his time alone to search for the deepness inside, trying in vain to move the wind, but once again felt nothing.

"Remember me," he whispered to the night, hoping it was the same one he had known on the *Oathbreaker*, but the wind did not whisper back and the feeling that he'd felt before the light and when he summoned the storm seemed far away. His blood ran quiet and his body yearned for sleep; the wakefulness of the world slipping away from him. He gave up reaching for the gleaming streams he remembered bolstering the *Oathbreaker*'s sails and let himself drift.

He watched the stars, with the grass underneath him tickling his neck, and the hunter's hat resting beside his head – a gift he hadn't expected. On the other side of the half-moon of shrubs, the horse was snuffling at the grass near her rider. At some point, his eyes slipped closed.

At some point, he dreamt that he was awake.

The grass was glittering, swaying with a wind that called his name, while firefly lights bobbed in and out of the waves, tinkling with the sound of small bells like Muse's hair, though there were no fireflies, and the lights were wispy like flame and golden-like globs of sunshine.

Inside Shye was the deepness.

Beyond the road, which he could not see through the copse of half-mooned bushes, but knew was there, was a forest, and the dancing lights led into its mouth. The wind called his name again.

Shye.

And then he was back on the gently sparkling grass, and he was alone, and he could hear the distant sound of the ocean over the chiming of the meadow, while in the skies rolled the sound of thunder. The deepness rang with the fizzled break of lightning, thrumming under his heart, beating against his navel, slicking his skin. Shye felt it prickle in his fingers, flash, and then ebb from him.

He stayed there for a while. Behind his eyes, the copse of half-mooned bushes burst into bloom.

At some point, the dream faded, and the hunter rolled over in their sleep to reach their fingers across the grass to brush his. The earth beneath Shye was tender and warm and he slept on, no longer so hungry as he had been before.

CHAPTER 14

SHYE WOKE TO UNCOUTH SNICKERING, WHILE SOMETHING WET AND large nuzzled his face, and foul gusts of tepid breath shot straight up his nostrils. He came awake suddenly with an involuntary shout, his skin tight, and nausea rolling through his stomach.

Dorian collapsed into open laughter on the grass.

Shye made a face and pushed the horse's snout away, wiping his cheeks and chin in disgust. The place looked different in the lightrise than from his dream, except for the bushes. The ring of trees was in early bloom, sprouting buds of violet, rose and deep blues that reminded Shye of the evenspan before nightrun falls. The petals and buds had burst forth in such numbers that they covered the ground and had drifted across the sleeping figures, threading all through Shye's tangled hair.

The hunter had already removed the offending flowers from their person, except for a singular ring placed lopsidedly on the crown of their head, which they had threaded together while waiting for him to awaken.

Shye brushed his clothes down, coiled the rope Dorian had used to bind him and dropped it onto the ground beside the hunter, sitting down beside both.

Dorian's grin died on their face, but if they were surprised he hadn't stolen away, they didn't show it.

Shye looked over the landscape and saw that the other half-mooned shrubberies that dotted the field were still barren and bare. His gaze wandered back to their little copse and the explosion of colour. He touched his hand to the ground and felt nothing. Idly, he pressed into the skin above his bellybutton and a wave of dizziness washed over him. Shaking the buds out of his hair, he put away the remnants of his dream from his thoughts.

"It'll take us the better part of five rises to get back to Mistral with only one horse. We can get another in a couple of spans if you're comfortable to ride by then," Dorian said, giving Shye a short, calculating look that said they still wondered why Shye had chosen to come willingly.

Shye tossed his head again to dislodge any lingering petals. He combed his hair with his fingers and retied it with the winterhide, before plopping Dorian's hat on his head to finish, ignoring the way the hunter's face turned interested while he groomed himself.

"We should get on then," is what Shye planned to say in response, the words perched on his tongue, but at the last moment they dissolved and what came out was, "You can ask."

Stepping over to where Dorian had their horse in hand, he repeated, "You can ask why I'm still here."

Dorian's expression was still stuck on bemusement, though something flickered through their eyes like they were tempted to do just that. Instead, they replied with a blatant lie. "I don't care why you are still here, as long as you remain here."

Shye wished they'd stop looking at him like that then but couldn't bring himself to make the request out loud. He nodded and let it go. "Of course, Master Hunter."

Shye waited but they made no move to get on the horse, staring over his shoulder with an expectant look.

After a moment, he crossed his arms and snapped, "What?"

Dorian's shapely brows twitched upwards and a smirk crept

across their face when they jerked their chin at the blooming bushes, their gaze flitting back to him.

Shye scowled.

"I'm not some sort of delightful genie," Shye started. "Not," he finished with meaning, "that you care."

"Oh, well, in that case," the hunter answered back, with a feigned and provoking courtesy.

Shye fought the temptation to gesture rudely and huffed instead, pointing gruffly behind the hunter. "Get on the horse."

They travelled farther inland throughout the sunning, passing between a tall set of boundary markers lining either side of the road, weathered and picked at by time, and crossing over creeks and streams as the lightrise sun grew hotter, the sea now at their backs.

Shye felt a wave of longing for it already.

With the monotony of the horse underneath them and the heat of the rider's back against his chest, Shye focused on keeping balanced and on the horse until the lightrise passed quickly into evenspan.

"We won't reach proper lodging for another rise," Dorian said, tossing the saddlebags and saddle onto the ground with some effort. "I don't suppose if I tie you, the bonds will keep till morning?"

Shye looked over from where he was dozing in the grass and smiled innocently. "You are welcome to try."

The hunter left the rope wrapped up in the bag.

Shye's smile widened. He rolled onto his side and propped his chin in his hand. "I'm happy enough sleeping rough, even if you feel you must bind me."

Dorian sat heavily on the ground with a relieved sigh. "Yes, but sleeping rough equals smelling rough, and you didn't smell so great before!" They untied the laces on their boots and toed them off, letting their feet stretch in the pale turf.

Shye had also noticed that the hunter had not stopped smelling so refreshingly of crushed pearls, so perhaps he was as offensive as they proposed, but not enough to prompt them to share their expensive soaps. He rolled onto his back. "There are creeks and streams."

The hunter tossed the same dried fruit and biscuits from breakfast at him, seeming to be more interested at pelting him on the chest than aiming so he could catch them in his hands.

"There's also real food and drink," Dorian shot back, amusement flooding their tone. "Not something I'd ever imagined I'd hear a sailor object to."

Shye chewed on the pieces of fruit, breaking the crackers between his fingers, and eating the shards, leaving a few scattered in the grass around him. At least Alice didn't have to worry about whether he'd cleaned his room recently.

"I'm not objecting," he said, turning his head to look at Dorian.

Their brilliant hair was splayed out across the grass, dimmed under the fading sun. They were looking back at him, jaw moving as they chewed their own dinner, the good humour still lively on their face.

Shye was hit with a sudden fizz of arousal and spent a moment in awe of the hunter and their crinkling eyes and their sensual chewing, and his body for being such a vicious traitor. For that moment, he wanted to groan aloud and die.

Dorian finished their mouthful and said drowsily, "Good, because you don't get a say anyhow."

Shye hummed noncommittally, while the fluttering feeling died out again as quickly as it had lit and watched Dorian as they watched him; their eyes glided over him, the thoughts behind them unreadable. Then, both of them turned to the evenspan above. It darkened into the nightrun around them.

Shye thought of the moon. It was a shadowy expanse across the nightrun, only in its first phase, and already the moonlight was weak. With the sunning heat there was no need for a fire. He thought of a moon so bright it made the violet night glow blue and outlined the earth in silver. A folk-moon. There hadn't been one in centuries and many assumed there never would be again.

"Do you have any matches?" he asked the hunter abruptly.

"Hmm?" Dorian grunted, and Shye felt something small and weighty ping off his arm and into the grass.

"There," they said blearily and rustled around in the dark.

Shye felt around for the slim box and smiled to himself, turning his face towards the slightly darker shape amidst already dark things, lumped in the grass to his left, and said, "Do you want to see something no other imperial has?"

The shape wriggled, and the hunter's voice clipped out low from it, "Is it delightfully genie-like?"

Shye sat up and unbound his hair, tossing his fingers through the curls and snarls, "Sure, I guess."

He lay back again, spreading his hair on the grass in a poor imitation of the hunter's untamed mane.

"Let's see then," came the voice, a little curious now.

Shye turned the slim box over in his fingers and pushed open the little drawer, fishing out a long, thin stick and striking the match into flame. He let it feast on the wood first.

"Oh wow, amazing," Dorian intoned, unconvinced, from the side.

The heat from the slow-growing flame glanced off Shye's face. He held it up with great ceremony and brought it down to meet the air above his forehead. He knew the light had taken in his hair by the quiet, involuntary puff of breath that followed, and a drip of violet-white appearing in the corner of his eye. He could taste satisfaction in his mouth as his hair turned and reflected the light, white fire creeping through the brown until there was only radiance left. Then he heard scrambling and Dorian's face loomed upside down over his.

"May I?" they asked, rather nicely.

Shye bit into his lip to keep his smile in check and the hunter read the acquiescence in his eyes, while theirs were wide and brimming with animation, comically upside down. He gave in to the urge to snicker, reining it in to a few stray chuckles at their expense, but they didn't seem to notice.

The match flame was burning steadily and would soon go out, but, for now, he could see the expressions flitting across Dorian's face, passing swiftly onto the next, as their fingers drew reverently through the lightning streaks: excitement, wonder, amusement and finally confusion tinged with concern.

"It makes my skin feel funny . . . like embers falling."

Dorian held up one hand in front of their face, turning it back and front, as though expecting it to be different somehow. The other remained buried amidst the waves and tumbles of dripping light. They moved the hand from in front of their face to in front of Shye's, wiggling their fingers above him.

"My hand's not going to fall off, is it?"

Shye let out a bark of laughter, a smile breaking through, caught off-guard by the playfulness of the gesture. He flicked the match out before it could burn his fingers, leaving his lightning trails as the only source of light, and they too would fade soon.

"You'll be fine."

The hunter continued to pick and poke above him, fiddling with the trails, starting and abandoning idle braids and combing it between their fingers.

Shye shivered and traced the dim stars. "Muse said it felt like embers too, and it turned his blood to gold, like it lit the thing within him that coloured him with Strangeness and set his hands to music. But he has a folkline and you don't."

Dorian's face peered over Shye's, their fingers twisted and tangled in his hair, tugging at it. An elated smile had come across their lips, and they wore it shamelessly.

"I'm both honoured and impressed, you delightful genie."

Dorian smouldered with pale-fire, rendered otherworldly, wreathed in the silver-white glow of his Stormborn Blood. Shye wanted to suffuse this moment into his soul as the space between them rippled with the possibility of something bigger than the deepness he had lost, but no less powerful.

Something sad flashed across Dorian's face as the moment stretched on, and they said softly to themself, "Cassius is going to love you."

The light started to shift back into the still nightrun. Shye frowned as the last look he got of Dorian's face saw something troubled there, and he said into the dark, "Is something wrong?"

The fingers untangled from his hair and the hunter evaded the question with a brusque, "Go to sleep."

He heard them shift away and he reached out, hitting their thigh with his hand, saying, "Stop."

They tensed under his touch, but they did pause in the shadows over him. Shye shifted upwards, trying to gain some understanding of the sudden shift in both figure and mood. Mystified, he said, "I'm sorry, am I not being difficult enough for you? Or are you disappointed in what you found and worried that you will not get your due?"

He heard them scoff out an incredulous, "Disappointed?"

Shye let his hand slide away to the ground. "You must hope to get something out of this; am I not treasure enough for the Empire?"

Dorian's breath whistled through the dark and their hands thumped down into the earth beside him, shaking into his ears like they had caused a tremor in it. They felt their way into his cloak and hauled him up, so Dorian's breath sailed across his face when they spoke.

"What the fuck do you know about the Empire?" They sneered and then stopped, and Shye heard the cold precision in their voice. "Treasure enough so I don't think they'll kill you. You're too valuable and that's value to me. But you don't have to be so congenial, so content. You don't have to please me with tricks. You don't have to ask if something's wrong. You're just a boy and they'll turn you into their Strange captive pet, and I'm going to let them."

"Evidently," Shye said.

Dorian let him thump back into the ground. "At least if you tried to fight, I wouldn't have to feel so guilty about what they'll do to you. At least if you tried to run, it might be like I'd earned it."

"I'm not doing this to be kind," Shye replied, catching himself on his elbows. "This isn't a favour, Master Hunter. I am aware that I will not be allowed to live free in the Empire, that an unfettered existence is a threat to the order of things and that your kind do not like that. I'm still here and I'm not going anywhere."

"Why?" Dorian hissed out through the shadows. Shye could feel their knees in the grass beside his arm, their weight in the shadows above him. If Shye had been powerless to stop himself speaking to his captain insolently and recklessly, he had no more power to deny the hunter an honest answer since they asked so earnestly. Reining in his tongue was not one of his greater talents.

"Because something called my name and it's waiting there. In a city that once belonged – and with it the crown and the first of empires – to the Blooded, and you were *our* guests. It doesn't belong to the prince, and who's to say I will either."

He paused and craned his neck, so he could see more of Dorian than he could feel in the shifts of air between them. He hoped a little viciously that his sincerity burned them, if only so they'd trust his word a little better for it.

"You will," they said eventually. "You'll learn how. Or you'll die."

Shye shrugged and thought he almost felt them seethe as he did it, though he could not see them or they him. "A few spans ago, it didn't seem worth the prize it was offering, dying. But staying behind and dying slowly on that ship with the world leaving me behind seems worse. What can they do to me that compares to that?"

The hunter's voice came whipping out of the violet night, "I wouldn't know. I was born to the hunt and its legacy. A hunter serves the crown. This is the only freedom I know, and if I were you, I would fight to keep it."

Shye sighed and closed his eyes, imagining a moon full and bright, lining the world in blue and silver.

"What waits for us is not your doom, Dorian, and it isn't mine either. It's something else, something like fate."

The hunter moved and lay down near him, close enough that he could feel their body heat and the brush of their limbs, and he heard their voice cut through the night like glinting steel. "No, something like fortune and something like boredom. Fate died with the folk."

Silence pursued their words into the nightrun. Shye listened to

Dorian's breathing, willing away that part of him that trembled at their words. Eventually, they fell asleep and so did he. In the violet night, a hushed voice whispered in the wind.

Not dead, merely sleeping.

CHAPTER 15

The next span's travel brought seasonal sun baths; intermittent, hot, damp and sticky. They had been lucky to escape them so far, but as they packed camp that morning, Dorian felt the rain begin to patter on the ground and heaved a sigh. The rains had been coming and going all sunning, as sun baths had an annoying tendency to do, and their shelter for the night, still the rest of lightrise away, was growing more appealing with every minute.

The road they travelled had forked early on in the rise into an old imperial trade route. Since the construction of the main paths near Eterentin, it had been ignored by most. The main paths travelled a longer route, but they had one advantage over a path like this. They avoided the Wild Mountains and the peak of Kernon's Seat, which loomed over the western farmlands of Mistral, barely glimpsing that place which best remembered the Blooded, a place which did not welcome the presence of humans. Only one guesthouse still remained standing at the midpoint of their journey, just before the road curved close to the dark dividing mountain range.

Leon had planned for everything in his maps, including Dorian's preference for a startling entrance. Here, there would be no one to spy on them as they went. Words would only be rumours and Dorian could stride through Mistral's gates, pretending it was any other lightrise, and see everyone's faces bloom and their father's break as they saw what Dorian dragged behind them. However, in this same breath that they praised Leon for his forethought, they also cursed him. Overgrown roads and overgrown fields with nothing but more of it in sight left little to distract from the feeling of the Stormborn boy's body fusing and peeling along all the points of Dorian's own, or from the encroaching thoughts of what had been said in the nightrun before.

Fate.

It was an ominous, ill-lucked word. It had no place in the Empire anymore. *How fitting*, Dorian mused, *that it should be uttered from the mouth of someone who also has no place in the Empire as it stands,* whose kin were often spat upon and whispered about for having the folk-touch that made them different and made them dangerous. The guilds had been useful for controlling those with folklines, but many found ways to slip under the Empire's waning interest. Peace and strength of numbers had made the Empire complacent, but fate was of the folk, and it was no friend to humans. If only Dorian could've kept the guilt cutting at their mouth to themself.

Dorian shuddered.

The rain was making their skin clammy; thoughts turning it cold. A hunter could not have anything to do with a word like that. A hunter made their own way, and Dorian needed to more than most. A hunter serves the crown.

Dorian squashed the urge to sneer at how secondary that seemed to some of their fellows. These seasons, most of them spoke of it as "a hunter serves the crown to serve themselves". Because who else would the guilds serve? How else would the nobles keep busy when the ideals of peace dictated they could not fight for glory or fight each other? Loyalty was a feeble thing, easy to claim and easy to break – a silent, untried thing in the capital. Trust a Stormborn to try Dorian's.

They would be the only hunter ever to claim such a prize. They should be radiating pride and accomplishment. Instead, Dorian only felt frustrated and vaguely ashamed. They knew better than most how well the capital constructed its gilded cages.

Dorian shifted uncomfortably in the saddle; the steady clomps of hooves the only sound that broke across the road. The Stormborn hadn't spoken yet, content to sit damp and silent, making Dorian grimace at the quiet and bump and ride of their limbs. Dorian had never known a hunt like this – hopefully never would again – and could only blame that for the way they had acted under the influence of the violet night. First, like a fool, and then with treacherous honesty; neither the things they needed to see this through.

The sun baths had come at first light and, ever since, even when it stopped and the sun dried them just enough for the rain to soak them again, Dorian had found themself huffing, pleading and praying, "Two more rises, just two more spans."

Two more rises and they'd be in Mistral and Dorian could finally untangle their head far away from the influence of any Stormborn or folk trickeries. Yet, when they closed their eyes, they were back on the pale grasses before the rains broke with the lightrise, and they could feel Shye's breathing across the space between their arm and his chest. The space that was barely any space at all.

Dorian had been thinking, *There's something in him that I'm missing, something which I know the shape of but cannot name*, and wishing it away as though it were a lie.

They felt soft and hated it.

Ahead, the guesthouse rose out of the earth on the side of a curve in the road, windows glowing with life. It loomed over the landscape before it in the same way the forest leading to the peak loomed over it, lanterns swinging from its eaves, splashing light through the puddles in the mud. There was a sign posted into the ground a few metres before it with Ashridge Below scrawled on it, and an arrow pointed towards the lively building.

"Finally," Dorian breathed, almost drooling at the prospect of hot food and maybe even a bath. Such luxuries were few and far between on a hunt, and Dorian tried to take advantage of them whenever they were able, to make up for the countless times when they weren't.

The body behind theirs shifted, and then their back was being pelted by rain where before it had been guarded, warm with sweat, by the boy who was now slipping off the horse, his boots spraying mud as he splashed down into a puddle.

"What are you doing?" Dorian asked, unamused.

Shye faced the forest, entranced by the dark trees leading up into the mountains. Finally, breaking his silence to answer, he said, "I want to see what's in there."

Dorian shivered, the sun bath turning unpleasant now that salvation from it was in sight. "I can tell you," they snapped. "Trees."

Shye stuck his hand into one of the saddlebags and retrieved his cloak. He'd taken it off only an hour into their first sun bath and Dorian had been trying to ignore the thinness of the shirt beneath ever since.

Wrapping himself in the dark green folds, he said distantly, "I want to stay there tonight."

"What? No," Dorian cried, slicking their hair off their face, and gesturing around them. "Can't you see it's raining?" Their voice became staccato, as if to further illustrate the obvious.

Shye's harsh expression fixed itself on Dorian and then on the glowing building. His lips pressed tightly, and his chin rose in Dorian's direction.

"I'm not going in there," he said and turned his back on Dorian and the guesthouse and started wading across the soggy ground towards the yawning gape of shadows between the tall trees.

Dorian's patience, worn fine over the long lightrise, snapped. The pressure of the task, the thoughts that would not quiet, the pull of the thrice-damned feelings and the fucking rain had not put them in the mood for some ridiculous Stormborn fancy of sleeping rough when a bath and bed were not ten metres away. They pulled on the horse's reins, wheeled it around and planted themself firmly between Shye and the forest.

"You go where I do," Dorian said, teeth gritted; an abrupt and overwhelming flash of rage bloomed in their breast. *Of all the wilful, unbelievable*, Dorian thought. Shye had been so easy, so amiable, and now what force did Dorian have to make him. None. They'd tossed their cards the minute they decided not to bind him. Time was not on their side – the secrets of this hunt would not hold for long – so they had him ride with them, but he was still a runner, a target hunted for imperial seizure. The assignment that would pay Dorian's way out of anyone's reach, that would make them close to untouchable, so that no one could threaten them again. It was Dorian's mistake. Shye was a prize, and Dorian should've treated him like one.

"If you go with me in there," Shye said smartly, pointing at the line of trees, "I will."

"No," Dorian said, springing lightly off the horse to grab Shye by the arm. "You will come with me now."

Shye's gaze was searing through the rain. Dorian's hand clenched Shye's forearm, ready to drag him underneath the inn's roof with their teeth bared like an animal's.

Thunder cracked through the sky. Dorian's head whipped up in alarm, then they noticed Shye's face had gone dark and cold, his eyes burning like glacial moons. Lightning split the gathering clouds and a storm broke from nowhere over Ashridge Below, spilling chilling frostfall rain down on them.

The horse shrieked, stamping its hooves and jumping. Another bolt sent it hurtling into the nearby trees.

"This isn't funny," Dorian snarled at Shye, their fingers white-knuckling into his skin, clawing at his arm. *Why won't he come with me?*

"I'm not joking," Shye replied, deadly serious.

Then, he pushed.

Dorian felt it flow under their skin, something they'd never felt before; a rushing, burning, scorching intensity, fathoms deep under the swell of blood. The wind came howling at them and Dorian slipped in the slickness of the earth, and then they were on their knees. Dorian's face was splashed with mud and their chest was burning with every breath.

Shye was out of reach, saying, "Someone best fetch the horse," with a mean sort of triumph that stung Dorian almost as much as the shove had.

Dorian stumbled to their feet and managed a few steps after him but was too far behind to catch up.

Shye disappeared between the trees.

The rage welled up in Dorian; a fount of frustration and doubt and fight. They screamed at the trees, "I'll find you. I will!"

They sank to their knees in the muddy turf with an angry cry, snarling at the rain. Then they took a deep, ragged breath, gagged and bound their emotions tightly in their chest. Dorian got up, their energy drained and the anger ebbing under the cooling downpour. The storm continued to rage.

Dorian trudged down to the inn, lamenting to the ugly sky, "You are terrible and fanciful, and I can't stand it."

But they did like it, despite how aggravating they found the Stormborn to be when he managed to knock them off-balance. His odd sincerity combined with an unpredictable disposition and at last a bit of *fight*, Dorian couldn't help but like that. The capital didn't make folk like that. Their father would laugh himself to death if he knew.

As Dorian pushed open the inn's door, light, heat, and sound hit them with resounding brightness, in painful contrast to the debacle they'd set in motion outside. Dorian heard the hubbub for only a moment before they found themself back outside, huddling under the eaves to stay out of the wet; eyes narrowed suspiciously at the door.

An inn this remote didn't even a have a porter, and its only staff would be the owner and their family, maybe a few hired hands, so there was no one to see Dorian as they crept around to the stables and counted the horses. Ten horses whickered and champed at the damp hay. Far too many for this road, even considering brave travellers like Dorian, and the foul weather that made sleeping rough impractical at best.

Dorian crept back and wavered in front of the inn's door. Pushing any wariness of the establishment aside, their thoughts flew back to the Stormborn, and their fists clenched, anger thrumming in their throat. If he wanted to soak and freeze that was his choice, it was only Dorian's concern *if he dies*, they thought waspishly. Finally, Dorian stepped inside, the door swinging shut with a *thunk* behind them.

James Locke glanced up from his meal in the main room. Any dreams Dorian had of sinking gratefully into a bath and having their supper sent up to their room stopped dead in their tracks. Five other hunters accompanied James; the ones Leon tended to term as James's "acolytes", which were vastly different to the other company he had also brought with him. Lords Ashea, Mysander and Veredan and ladies Fenrent and Bellhall were all accredited hunters with the guild, and each of them lethal in their own ways. They were a tough group to face down in the assembly rooms. Leon and Ever were the only ones who tried with any regularity. Dorian preferred to simply not be there.

Lady Tanith was something else entirely. Dorian had a healthy caution for any Master of Accomplishment who had a full set of ten gems imbedded in their knuckles, and they had no curiosity to know what ten things the Lady Tanith had become a true master of. Realistically, it was something like negotiation and political intelligence, but they idly hoped it was actually tea parties or flower arranging. If only to make the lady slightly less intimidating.

Dorian swallowed to see them all sitting there, with James Locke at the head, staring back. This picture they were painting was shaping up to be a bad one for Dorian, whose stance shifted into a guarded one. Perhaps, the Stormborn had had the right idea after all. Maybe it wasn't too late to go find him in the forest.

Except their father was standing and pulling the dining cloth from his shoulder. He wiped his mouth and discarded it, giving Dorian a pointed once-over.

"Dorian, arrived at last. Care to join us?"

As if on cue, a stout woman bustled down the stairs at the back of the hall and started talking the moment her eyes alighted on Dorian.

"My goodness, ye really are soaked to the bones. Weel, you're inside now and we've plenta of rooms. Not much company to be had out 'ere, 'cept for tonight, of course. Tonight, we're fair hoppin'. Ay, what can we do for ye, lovey?"

Dorian's father cut in smoothly, ahead of Dorian by a second. "Another plate, please, mistress—"

"Sent to my room, please, ma'am, and I would very much like a bath too, with that room and the plate, if it's not too much trouble," Dorian interrupted before James could get going or demand they sit with their fellows and the Lady Tanith.

Dorian sent James a tight, cloying smile over the woman's head, as she replied, "Orr no, so long as ye have the glass, ye can bathe and eat all ye want."

James's smile pinched, but he broke in with utmost gentility, the noblest of spite-tongued gentlemen, as he said, "Put the bills to my tab, this is my . . . uh . . ."

James paused, the flush rising to his aristocratic cheekbones, but obvious only to Dorian, and they let him wallow for a moment before they said with a wry tone and a challenging stare, "*Disaster.*"

"Thank you, Father, for the offer," Dorian continued without pause, "but I will pay for myself." Turning on their delightful charm for the woman, Dorian said, "Please have supper sent to my room."

James's flush deepened with the dismissal and his eyes flashed, purring malevolently, "Maybe you should accept a father's generosity while it lasts, as it is unlikely the crown will offer a reward for thin air."

Dorian fought back a scowl. This was why Dorian had wanted to take this road, to avoid an encounter like this, and yet if they had brought Shye in here, no doubt those hunters would be paying them blows and Shye would be limping back through the nightrun to the capital, tied to the saddle of their father's horse. But Shye wasn't with them, and James Locke had never tangled with the folk, let alone a

Stormborn, and he did not know the things that Dorian did. He couldn't know that Shye was here.

If he found out, it would ruin the big surprise.

Dorian breathed in, letting their lip twitch into a smirk as their father asked, "Where is your Stormborn?"

Because if he was real, James Locke wanted him. Wanted to parade him through Mistral so he could finally be hailed greater than the Huntsman and greater than the favoured hunter. If he was a lie, it was an opportunity for humiliation. James was ravenous and always would be until he was better than his own father and better than Dorian, and he could cast Dorian down, bend them, break them, into the heir he thought Dorian should be.

Dorian decided to let him have his moment now, if only because it would make theirs so much sweeter. When it came it would flow through them like wine across the tongue, and James could suck on the remnants of this bitter taste.

"Well, Father, he's in the forest," they answered simply, pasting on an impassive mask when they saw his eyes start glittering mockingly.

"In the forest," James repeated, as though blood was in the air and the kill was drawing near.

Dorian inclined their head gracefully to him, goading him. How he could call himself their father when he didn't know a single thing about them, not even when they were playing him. Ever would've known, but then Ever never would've stolen out of the capital to steal their prize from them. Sweet majesty, this man gave them a headache. And on a worse day, indigestion.

The innkeep bustled back with Dorian's room key, saying she had given instructions to the girls. The bath would be ready shortly and supper was on its way, adding, "Do ye need your horse stabled, dearie?"

Dorian saw a perfect moment unfold in front of them and they smiled, thanked her, and said, "No, thank you, ma'am. My horse has taken to grazing in the forest."

It took all their strength of will not to look at their father until she had bustled away.

"In the forest?" James did not wait long to remark. "With your Stormborn?"

There was a laughing rumble in his voice, vicious and smug, but Dorian had still won and that was the only reason they didn't hate it. They gave him a delicate, prideful shrug and said, "Yes."

They strode off to their room before any further questions could be hurled at them, head up and spine snapped straight, bidding everyone goodnight along the way. When they reached the landing of the stairs, out of view of the dining room, only then did a smile break across Dorian's face and a hum bubble out of their mouth. Guffaws came from below and with it an order for a round of drinks in celebration of Dorian's supposed failure. Dorian rolled their eyes.

Vipers.

Don't get cocky, Ever reprimanded in Dorian's mind, a lesson from several long spans ago. *You haven't won until the lightrise when your prize becomes property of the crown. Until then, you're still in the wilds, and the hunt isn't over yet.*

CHAPTER 16

THE HUNTERS WERE GATHERING OUTSIDE THE STABLES WITH THEIR horses in hand when Dorian appeared in the misty lightrise, fighting hard to keep the skip out of their step. The sun baths had passed for now and when the shines were out it was looking to be a pleasant rise.

Lady Amabilis Bellhall, affectionately called Billie by Dorian's father and the social circles she ran in, stepped aside from the group and swept over to Dorian. Her swaggering frame was sheathed in rich hunter's garb; a tucked burgundy shirt with a high-cinched skirt of deep purple, and tan trousers underneath, all exquisitely pressed despite the remote locale and lack of civilisation. Her umber skin glittered with accents of gold; from the sweep of powder on her cheeks and lining her piercing eyes to her chosen weapons – several swift daggers with neat lines of gilt seeped into the spines.

"Good rise, Huntress," Dorian greeted, their exuberance oozing into clear lightrise air.

Bellhall looked luring yet sombre, and she greeted back in a deep and serious voice, "And to you, Locke. Though I perceive from your cheer that you haven't heard."

Dorian froze, their good mood crystallising and shattering in an instant. A cold shiver ripping up their spine.

"Heard what?" They forced themself to ask calmly, almost coolly.

Their thoughts raced. James had figured out their play. Had he found Shye and gone to claim Dorian's prize, fame, and reward? Dorian had been barred from the guild for chasing storms and Leon had been charged for escaping service to the crown? Ever had retired and James was somehow, someway, the Huntsman now?

There was something sinister glittering in Bellhall's gold-rimmed eyes that had Dorian's stomach curling up inside their toes.

"The Huntsman is dead. Every hunter is being recalled."

She eyed Dorian up and down. "Even his favourite."

Dorian's mind went blank, like the endless white Shye had shown them in Corentin, and coldness crept over them. Bellhall went on, gesturing to the gathering of horses. Dorian noticed distantly that their father wasn't among them. Dull fears unwound and circled like birds of prey through the dazed fog in Dorian's head; things they had been afraid of and should be again. Things that James Locke had promised them he'd do one rise or run.

"Will you ride with us?" Bellhall asked, seeing their tracking gaze and smiling thinly at them. "Your father and the Lady Tanith left with the messenger. Someone must step up and lead the election."

Dorian swept their hands behind their back and rubbed their fingers together, another chill creeping up their spine and lancing through the fog clinging malignly to every thought in their mind.

James Locke had always wanted to be Huntsman. Dorian had dreaded the possibility. Now, he had a chance to destroy everything he hated about Dorian. The only saving grace was that they didn't have Shye. But if Ever was dead and James was standing Huntsman, and Shye wasn't Dorian's to fix the balance, that would be the worst of all of it; a blow like that Dorian could not recover from. They would be better off finding a cave or a hole and dying there than facing that.

"No," Dorian answered, keeping their voice level. "I have to go fetch my horse."

A mirthful smirk replaced Bellhall's thin one, and the sinister gleam seemed to spark with life. Dorian wished they could see into her head to know what was behind it, beyond the remembrance of Dorian's supposed failure.

"Yes, of course," she said, "and your Stormborn."

There was the sound of chuckling behind them and the tinkling laughter of Lady Fenrent. Dorian's shoulders stiffened at the ridicule, provoked as it was by their own foolishness. If James disgraced Dorian before they could offer Shye to the crown, all the factions of hunters, even the ones who would've voted fairly, would vote for James and Dorian would never hunt again. Their name in the ranks would be lost, their life would belong to their father's guiding hand, and they'd never be free again. Dorian would lose, right before they had the chance to win.

And Dorian had been tangling their head over the Stormborn's pretty face. James might've died of laughter or, more likely, of shame, but at least Ever would've been proud to know Dorian had actually thought of something else other than the guild, their next assignment and outsmarting their father before he passed.

"Good riding," Dorian farewelled stiffly, *and let my lady mother take you for a turnip.*

Dorian walked towards the forest, breaking into a run when the hunters passed out of sight. They burst through the edges of the forest and were enveloped in an eerie sense of hostility and ethereal plays of light from the branches above. Dorian gritted their teeth, following the tracks of horse hooves, and, after them, human feet, still imprinted in the mud. This was a folk forest. Unsurprising then that the Stormborn had been so eager to play in it, and it may have just saved Dorian's and Shye's necks.

Stalking through the greenery, Dorian tried not to upset the undergrowth or so much as step on a mushroom. While all their life Dorian had never considered how the Blooded felt about humans in their world, Shye had reminded Dorian that all that belonged to them once belonged to the folk, and now this was all that was left. Even these seasons, humans who strayed into what remained of folk lands too far or for too long rarely came back the same, if at all.

Those who made it out usually came back like the rumours of the good Lord Jensing's wife – mad and confused. The land hadn't taken well to human control and, it was often said, would strip it from them, if one offended in the wilds.

Dorian idly wished their father might wander into one and save them a great deal of grief.

Dorian followed the tracks through the odd splays of light to a glade, not too far into the forest. A willow myrtle grew tall and wide next to a spring across the opening of trees. Its long branches swayed rhythmically together in a wind that wasn't there; veins of labradorite, azurite, and jade ran through its bark and spider-webbed through the leaves. The spring formed in between two warped and overgrown roots, lighted with quartz geodes and streaks of glass and bone. Tiny white blooms blown from the willow littered the still water and the ground around it. Animals chittered out of sight and dragonflies skipped over the water, flashing and buzzing.

Dorian felt a warm breeze and the branches stirred out of rhythm, the sun shooting through to illuminate the clearing. The place lit up in hues of colour that Dorian would never be able to describe or remember with any clarity. The leaves of the willow glistened blue and green, and then green and black, shifting between glowing shades. The spring gleamed. The breeze swirled across the forest floor and into the depths of the trees.

Dorian took a step forward, heard a crunching sound, and glanced down. A line of mushrooms bobbed and twisted through the trees in a wide, arcing circle, just in front of their toes; the ruins of an unfortunate off-shoot crushed underfoot. Their heads were spun with coloured glass, moving between the glossy reds and dark bloody crimsons of rubies and garnets and pink floss quartz. Dorian didn't dare tread past their guardian line.

"Dusk Blooded," Dorian murmured to themself and then

corrected, unless this place should hear them, hear a human call on their name, "Strangeness."

Old places like this and the seals on the stones of Mistral were the few remaining that still rang with the name Kernon had given them. Dorian had not understood what it meant in truth, until now.

As if hearing them, Dorian saw Shye's face peer out between the willow's mineral-struck tendrils.

Dorian's chest constricted. They forced themself to swallow several times; a pretty face and beguiling eyes weren't worth the loss of their own freedom. They thought of Ever, without his warmth, without his spark, dead, and they thought of their father practically victorious. Their eyes turned slaty.

"Lady Lis preserve you," Dorian said in a flat tone and then ordered, "Come on."

The road the hunters and Dorian's father had taken was a wide beaten track, not well used but serviceable, and travelling on it would take at least a full rise, if not a rise and a half, to reach the capital again, even with the fastest-bred horses. The others could ride through the night to make up the difference. With Dorian's horse carrying two – even knowing that hunting horses were bred for strength and endurance – it was out of the question.

Giving a sigh and a low-voiced grumble, Dorian collected their horse from the shade beneath the willow and steered it out of the forest, before mounting and taking the Stormborn up behind them. With steady hands, Dorian manoeuvred down an overgrown winding path through the back sweep of Shye's folk forest to the hills rising beyond. The stiffness wracking the body behind them killed the air with thoughts unsaid, the grip at their waist as withdrawn and respectful as it could be without unbalancing them both.

Dorian had no words. And the Stormborn had none that would bring back Ever, so it suited Dorian that he didn't speak. They tucked their residual guilt away and shuttered their mind to it. The crown wanted him, they would have him, and he would learn, as they all had, how to serve. Maybe even in time for the coronation.

This is what he wants. This is what I need.

Their hands tightened briefly on the reins and the horse snuffled, bringing them over the rise where the path plateaued before climbing again, conifers and cherry trees and silver oak passing by on either side.

Better him than me, Dorian thought resolutely.

Shye's weight dropped back behind them, and Dorian grabbed for his hand on their waist, loping his arm around them till they cinched securely back together. Dorian fought back the slow tide of pleasure at the familiar feeling.

"Damn your modesty," they growled to him. "If you fall, we both do."

Their balance righted itself and Dorian let go hastily, as if they could cut off the feeling if they cut off its source. The Stormborn retained his defiant moue from the rise before, unaware of how it might save Dorian's life or how rapidly circumstances had changed for the two of them across the phases of a single nightrun.

"We'll reach Mistral by evenspan," Dorian said, staring straight ahead, picking the horse's way over the path without looking at it, distracting themself with thoughts of their arrival. They did not want to get lost on this road.

When their thoughts circled again to uncertainty, they found something else to focus on – brightly coloured bushes, the smooth movements of the horse's gait, the winding inclines – anything but the way directly ahead and the Stormborn pressed against them.

"What happened to two more spans?" Shye's voice broke in over their shoulder, unapologetically curious, remorseless for his part in turning Dorian over to the wind and the rain.

Dorian excused the lack of apology, not because they didn't deserve one but because the Stormborn was unlikely to give it. But he could pay them back for the nightrun before and the mess he'd made of their pride. Would, in fact. As a prize, he was worth that much.

The bitterness of their mood seeped unknowing into their mouth and made them frown at the world.

"The road we were on takes us around the mountains. Few people know of this way, and even if they did, almost none would take it."

Sending Leon a silent prayer, Dorian recounted every road in and out of the capital, including the ones that weren't on any map, like the one they travelled on now. It helped them focus again, thoughts carefully blank about the path ahead.

Shye's voice was surprised and uncertain when he asked them why.

They passed between two overarching ash trees, each trunk was wider and taller than any of the trees below and malformed around a third and fourth tree which had sprung up through the middle of each, the tops of which were decked with flame-coloured flowers, bright and bloody. Twisting and arching together, they formed a kind of monumental full-moon shape from their overlapping roots to their boughs overhead, blocking the view of the rest of the forest they were picking their way through. Unwelcome.

Dorian suppressed a shudder as they passed under them. They were unwelcome. They let out the breath they'd been holding when they breached the other side and steered the horse with a confidence they didn't feel.

Shye seemed unaffected by the transition into Kernon's Seat. Probably didn't even know they had entered it.

"This is folk territory. What's left of the wilds don't forget easily. Living in their cities is one thing; your kind are almost human in some respects—"

The Stormborn scoffed and snapped, "More than."

Dorian flushed. The views of the Empire on folklines had degraded further and further as the Blood waned. Spouting superiority over a victory none of them could remember, a fight the folk could no longer win. If so few could not change history, they could not change the future either. It was pervasive thinking. The type that Dorian had thought they'd shaken off.

"The cities are only stone, but some places don't welcome the presence of humans," Dorian continued. "They aren't safe for us."

Shye's weight shifted, but not enough to throw them off-balance and off the horse, and he lifted his hand from Dorian's waist to reach out and touch the branches overhead. "They just seem like trees to me."

Dorian strained to keep their limbs easy as the hostile airs coiled their stomach into knots, the trees clustering inwards, the path disappearing between them. Time stretched. Shye's arm slipped back around them, and Dorian breathed again in a rush.

"What keeps us safe?" Shye asked, seemingly over his mood.

Dorian grimaced and said, "You."

Dorian ignored the pleased hum that followed from the Stormborn's mouth. They didn't have much experience with yearning for things beyond the freedom to be as they pleased and to hunt as they pleased, and they were too aware of the dangers of wanting to entertain any sign from Shye that incited them to want at all. Unless it was wanting to get out of this place.

"So, humans built the roads because they couldn't trust ours?" Shye asked, diverted, his breath ghosting over Dorian's ear.

"Your kind had no roads. The cities were their strongholds, but as you've so defensively pointed out, the world was theirs and they walked it freely as they pleased. They had lords who ruled the seasons themselves, as well as the other Blooded, you don't think they had a thousand ways to cross the earth, with no need for roads the way we know them?" Dorian glanced over their shoulder and couldn't help adding, "You didn't know that?"

Shye's glowing eyes narrowed. His lips pressed together tightly but he was a shameless student. "What path are we taking then?"

Dorian concentrated on the feeling of the reins in their hands, the coarseness of the leather and the sweat of their palms and allowed themself an indulgent sneer. They pointed down at the path that would turn them about, strand them between the mountains and Mistral, without looking at it. Kernon's gaze was harsh upon them, and if Dorian was more unsure, if they looked to it for direction, the path might disappear entirely without an end in sight and no way anyone, not even Leon, could point them out on a map.

"Surprised you didn't notice," Dorian remarked, their stare fixed on the twist of trees around them, the capital lying at the end somewhere.

Shye's chin brushed their shoulder as he looked around and finally drew back, releasing a stunned, "Oh."

The path had stopped being the pale dirt track a long time ago, the wildlands having nothing so easy to follow. The horse trailed patches of dappled sunlight winding through the trees only in the likeness of such a thing. The shadows around the patches of light were dim, cool, and infinite, and hints of fast-moving pale sky speared through the thick branches. Brightly coloured, sweetly singing wrens winked and flittered in the dimness, but never came near the path.

"These trees remember," Dorian said, spurring the horse onwards as the ground seemed to shift and the horse shook nervously. "They remember you, but I am not wanted here."

The dapples were flowing silkily, slinking through the wood, and the horse began to pick up speed. Dorian closed their eyes as two more great ash trees appeared ahead, lost within the many until they were towering overhead, putting all else out of sight with their large, gnarled frames. Dorian choked back the building nausea.

Then, they were under the trees and the horse was slowing down, the ground straying from greenery back to dirt, the forest receding behind them, the trees losing stature and structure till they were barely shrubs. The west gate of Mistral lay across the cultivated land, down the rocky slope they were perched on the cusp of, the mountains and the craggy face of the mountain peak at their backs.

"Welcome home," Dorian murmured to themself.

The sky was streaked with pink waves, violet stars, and blinding golds as the evenspan descended. Lanterns bobbed ahead on the top of thin poles that wobbled back and forth in the breeze, lining the smooth dirt-packed roads, leading all the way into the heart of the Empire. It was a clear run back.

Dorian took a breath, fingers tightening on the reins, and then let their breath go. Seeing it again, in all its familiar glory, their features twisted wintry and ruthless. The task they had set themself solidifying under the weight of Mistral's gaze. They grabbed Shye's arm from their waist and threw him to the ground, snagging their hat on his way down.

"Welcome to the capital of our Empire, Master Stormborn," Dorian said, looking down on the boy in the dust and dirt. With merciless efficiency, Dorian dropped down beside him, lashing him to their horse with a grim, uncompromising smile. "Consider this your first lesson in the game it plays."

CHAPTER 17

THE WEST GATE OF MISTRAL LOOKED LIKE A MOUTH WITH A SET OF iron-tipped teeth. The original high-arched gates, with their decorative whorls of copper, rose gold, and sapphire steel, were pushed back against the inside passage, gleaming even in the dim and despite the years of disuse. Rising on either side of the gate, the border wall rose out of the ground, slick, black and shimmering under the evenspan skyline. Long, wide, and impossibly smooth. Inhuman.

The scholars Shye had studied out of his own curiosity more than at his captain's behest said that it was made of storm glass, though how one made or crafted storm glass, let alone did it proficiently enough to form it into a defensive wall, they had neglected to mention. With farmland and cultivated fields spreading outwards across the land, with tidy dirt tracks, it looked out of place, imposing its Strangeness upon a domesticated landscape.

Shye had tried to imagine it before, still as Strange and sure, but framed with trees and arbores latticing the streets and banners hanging over the side. The iron portcullis must have been a human addition, as it seemed to Shye that the Dusk Blooded would've found better ways to defend their strongholds without resorting to that particular measure. Another deterrent for those with the Blood to find a place within the Empire. Lucky for him, the folk's aversion to the black-forged metal had faded with the rest of their strength.

The guards patrolling along the top of the wall stopped as they approached and leant over the edge. Some paused for a quick look before moving on, but most made themselves easy somewhere along the rim to watch them. Shye forced his eyes up from the ground, bare without his cloak or Dorian's reappropriated hat.

"Is that—" one of the guards above said, loud enough to carry, but was cut off by a round of orders shouted out. The guards saluted lazily to their commander but did not change their posts just yet.

Dorian stopped the horse just outside the entrance and Shye trailed one of the sentries over to Dorian, where they spoke cordially. Formalities persisted, though they hardly needed to confirm who Dorian was and what they were doing.

The sentry felt Shye's curious gaze and glanced over.

"Sweet majesty," Shye heard them breathe.

The satisfaction set about Dorian's shoulders.

"It is!" the guard above called.

"No way," the guard next him jeered. They jostled each other on the shoulders and others sauntered along to join the show.

The sentry stood unmoving, staring at Shye, open-mouthed. He stared back defiantly.

Dorian shuffled the horse onwards, assuming leave from the shock-stilled and speechless sentry, calling a cocky, "Good evenspan to you, masters," to the rapt collection of guards.

"Fair damnation," the sentry finally found it within herself to breathe as Shye moved past, chin raised even if he was loping behind the horse, fastened to Dorian's saddle. If this was the spectacle Dorian wanted, Shye would not embarrass himself or the crew who had raised him. If there were any of his kind still in Mistral, he hoped they were watching. They would not see him bow.

"It is. The rumours were true. Locke's brought home a Stormborn."

"Pssh," replied the other guard, "they ain't real. It's just a boy, another runner. Bet he's done some thievery or somethin'."

Shye listened to the two guards talk, accidentally catching the believer's gaze as his eyes wandered across the crowd atop the wall. The believer jabbed his friend harshly in the ribs and pointed down at Shye. "Did you see his eyes?"

The guard's sceptical friend jabbed back and shook his head, his arms defensively crossed, his eyes sliding off Shye without really looking. "I don't care what they say, even Locke can't catch the storm."

"If anyone could do it, it'd be Locke," retorted the first guard hotly.

The commotion got louder and more heated – the sounds of the city joining in the fray – and as they came through the entryway, feet pounded across the wall above. The guards had come over the other side to see them pass into the city, still arguing and jostling, ignoring orders, like they hadn't had this much entertainment in a long time.

Shye craned his head back to look at them. Catching the eye of that same guard, he breathed in slowly, counting heartbeats. Flexing his fingers and feeling the blood coursing in them, he breathed out. It welled up within him, black and split with light. Waking up. Thundering.

He wasn't sure what he expected to happen until heat twisted through him, the blistering light swelling from the fathoms of a hungry, longing deepness that had almost forgotten him, so fierce he felt like he was glowing. Dry lightning spidered across the sky above them, cracking through the pink and gold and violet stars. It hung there, suspended and fulminous like bursts of trailing sparks, as the lanterns on the side of the road caught in his hair and set it to burning, white fire in challenge to Dorian's red.

A cheer went up from Dorian's faithful among the guards, ringing across the city, while the disbelievers could only curse quietly in shock.

Shye suppressed a smile and a shiver of pleasure, while a tendril of lightning-trailed hair caught in the corner of his eye. He flicked it away, head held high, and winked at the guard's disbelieving friend. He spun back around to see Dorian watching him with badly concealed surprise, half-twisted in the saddle. The expression slowly passed and their back pulled up straight as they faced ahead, relaxing back into their conquering smirk.

A pang lanced through Shye's chest at the way it was different, less genuine than the ones he'd seen before; the freedoms they'd shared a distant, dying past. Dorian's satisfaction was now edged with pain and something crueller. Something like glory. Something untouchable.

Shye forced himself to look away.

People crowded onto the streets, flowing out of buildings, court-yards and storefronts to see Dorian pass, but they jerked away when they saw Shye being towed along behind. They avoided his eyes and spat at the ground; some held onto pendants made of iron while sticking close to the sides of the avenues, allowing them to pass unac-costed and with great ceremony. It might have been the norm for Dorian's return from the hunt, but more than one mother stopped a curious child from venturing too close.

Some, not many and not obviously, sank to one knee and bowed.

They made Shye uncomfortable. He did not like the gesture or what it might mean. He was a sailor, sometimes a pirate – always a Stormborn – brought up to never bow before any man but to respect the authority of all things that lived in the balance of this world, and such deference to anyone made his skin crawl. He tried not to notice them among the crowd.

The streets Dorian led them confidently down felt slick and smooth beneath his feet. The stones shimmered with violets, greys, blues, and were etched with many more seals of glass spindling through the walkways. He saw the sun, the moon, the stars, and the seasons of sun and frost, all within them. They ran into the buildings as well, climbing into the air where they cracked through corner-stones, spiralled through columns, and lit up under windows and balconies. Trellises and flower boxes bloomed above, leaving petals scattered and crushed underfoot, their beauty and brightness marred by their cultivated, uncelebrated presence. They did not know his kind the way the sky and the wind sometimes did.

The city had retained his kin's particular aesthetics for open rooms with wide balconies and flowing draperies to give a shallow sense of privacy. Pavilions and courtyards were frequent, merriness tumbling out of them, and small groves and orchards, meticulously cared for and dense with vibrant fruit, dotted the outer districts. Yet any sense of the wildlands, the deepness of his Blood, that he'd felt in the forest or crossing the mountain path was scrubbed clean from the veneer of the city. The only wildness here was in the sky above. He had brought it inside himself, and the humans were feeling it for the first time since the folk had left.

Shye tracked a boy scurrying between people, flashing in and out of sight, following them through the streets. Dressed in a manner befitting a minor noble, Shye tried to get a glimpse of his inking, but he bore no emblem that he could discern, not even an apprentice mark. Perhaps he was too young to apprentice to a guild, Shye mused – though he seemed old enough, certainly at least fourteen. Or perhaps, he was just low born enough to be barred from the Guild Circle and high guilds, and worked the lower trades instead. Perhaps he was a Raven. Shye had to stop himself from laughing aloud at that thought. Even if Ravens were so young, he was of little interest to them now. The boy was a good tail though, and he watched Shye boldly, without fear.

Shye found himself seeking him out as they drew nearer to the palace. More than once, the boy appeared on the edges of the crowd before slipping back into the crush, his face marred with an expressive attentiveness towards the goings on, but no shock, no awe. Shye smiled at the certain pragmatism he saw in that, like a brief reflection of Alice or his captain.

They circled closer to the palace's approaching reach through winding streets. The sweet fragrances of tea streamed into the air, nearly to the Guild Circle if they were passing so close to the tea houses. The Circle broke through a clearing in the buildings ahead, each singular hall hung with banners, which shifted in the wind, crouching on diagonals across the four roads that led directly to the Brightspir.

If Phirrun was cosy, verging on stacked, and Corentin was spaciously controlled, then Mistral was perfectly formed. For the Dusk Blooded. But for those that now claimed the land, it was a maze that had barely been tamed. They swanned the meandering labyrinth of main avenues, even though Shye had spotted several different shortcuts which ran through the heart of the city. The folkways of twisting stone boughs that appeared in the space between shadow and shadow's edge were a well-documented phenomenon of sealed cities like Mistral, but although humans had attempted to study them in more detail, they were invisible to all except the Blooded. The tunnels, which seemed to bend space, running into darkness, were made for the folk to walk the city in secrecy, allowing them to disappear into walls and slide into shadow like ghosts haunting the city streets at evenspan.

The Brightspir hung a sunburned shadow over the city. It was carved out of a towering pillar of stone; the high-wrought stalagmite spearing incongruously up from the ground. The stone was cut away into walkways, atriums, and terraces, wrapping around and running in and out of the natural mountainous feature. At the summit shimmered rivered veins of spectrolite, crowning the structure with iridescence. The rock itself, magnificent in presence and in architectural beauty, wasn't the usual grey, brown, or black, but a pale yellow-gold, like honey and fine sand. The banners that hung from its outside flaunted a crown, like rays of a sun, above two vertical and intersected spheres, one simple and one a wreath of flowering wheat, on standards of royal purple and others of bloody maroon. The antechamber at its base, huge and asymmetric, opened onto the compass-rose of the streets. Arched columns half-circled the outer ceiling on either side of its cavernous entryway, where braziers burned within, and grand staircases danced in and out of shadow ascending to the far hollows of the lofty Brightspir's reach.

Dorian slowed to a stop before the hunters' banner, fluttering on the guild house fixed before a small square, where the crowd had begun to gather. Two guards marched over, and a groom appeared from around the corner of a large tea house to take the horse's reins. Dorian dismounted gracefully, despite the heady weight of their growing vanity.

Shye bit his lip and went back to watching the boy flitting between the pooling spectators. Dorian's sugar-spun conquest tasted wrong in the evenspan – all of Mistral did – and Shye found himself needing distraction from the nervous thrum that was starting to gather under his skin.

The boy slipped behind a man and woman who crowded close to the front – a front that started only a good few metres away from Shye. Shye could tell one was a hunter by the inking on his hand, the same as Dorian's, but the other . . . her knuckles claimed a full set of ten bloody rubies. The boy peered through the gap between their figures and Shye saw him smile, right before he sank onto one knee in that same disturbing bow.

Frowning, Shye jerked his gaze away, just as the guards heaved his body forward, untied Dorian's merciless knots, and forced him to his knees.

No one seemed to see the boy's perplexing gesture. When Shye risked a look back, the boy was across the pool of people, spectating next to a man in noble dress with the hands of a high guild glass-blower and the roving, sparked eyes of an inventor.

Lightning hissed through Shye's hair in conversation with the wind that blew in it, and the webs of lightning still blazed above, dying, splintering, and breaking again across the skies, but no storm had broken, so it was weak and died more quickly every time.

The guards held him by the arms, afraid to touch flesh or his waves of light-run hair, in fear he'd curse or kill them, of which Shye could do neither. Their gloved hands had banded tightly around his upper arms, but their reluctance to do more left his head raised as high as any prince's, and it would take much more to cow him than being forced to kneel on cold stone. Even if it was to Dorian.

The hunter had left their horse to be carted off by the groom, and they made their leisurely way over to the guards presiding over Shye's

captive form. Dorian looked down at him, the pleasant and sometimes unpleasant company they'd shared was wiped out by
triumphant pride. They stepped around him to address the gathered
audience, while the glitter in their eyes flickered across the distance.

Dorian called out, "I invite any hunters present to step forward in
accordance with traditions long ignored"—their gaze shifted back to
Shye briefly, the edges of their smile savagely cut—"to acknowledge
the end of this momentous hunt and the prize which it has brought."

The hunter Shye had seen before stepped forwards, as did four
others, who materialised towards the front of the gathered people.
They all wore varying expressions as they stood there, some grim-
faced, others shifting between emotions of cautious awe and resentment, but underneath there was a current of magnitude about what
Dorian had done and they all observed it dutifully. As one, they
clasped their hands, one over the other, their hunters' marks facing
Dorian, and raised them to their heads.

A wicked, victorious grin bared Dorian's teeth to the world as the
hands came down.

Shye tried not to shift on his blunted knees, even as his muscles
began to lock in place.

"Thank you," Dorian said to the hunters, who inclined their
heads with respect and, with lingering glances towards Shye, stepped
back into the crowd.

The guards pressed Shye farther into the hard stones as Dorian
wandered over again; their weight on his arms and shoulders
bending him down. His teeth sank into his mouth at the flares of
pain, and he fought to contain the swirl of heat that followed them
and the continuous drip of lightning in the periphery of his eyes.
When he remembered Dorian was watching, he stopped and fixed
his lips tightly shut.

"Shall we take him to lockup, Master Hunter?" one of the guards
asked gruffly, now that Dorian's ceremony seemed to be wrapping up.

Dorian's smile drooped in the corners when they faced the
guards, becoming provocative.

"You don't have to be so afraid of him," Dorian challenged.

Shye shivered at the tone of Dorian's voice, and the sense of impending disaster coiled in his joints, and colour flooded his face as Dorian sashayed over till their boots knocked his frozen knees. They carded a hand through his hair to the sounds of horror and outcry from their onlookers, then wrenched his head back, exposing the line of his throat. Shye swallowed as dread filled his stomach with lead. There was a reckless energy he recognised in Dorian's eyes as they leant over him – frenetic and full of inglorious notions.

"He's nothing to be scared of," Dorian said, standing over him, body bent in pleasing lines, hair pinned by their reclaimed hat, hand tight in the roots of his curls. And kissed him. Smiling into the rush of chaos that followed.

Shye bit them. Sinking his teeth into their bottom lip, he cursed their name with all the air he had left, humiliation sparking in his pulse, sending his blood thumping through his veins. Dorian stepped back, laughing, swiping at their bottom lip with two fingers to remove the taste of blood.

"Heh," Dorian huffed absently, cheekbones a little flushed, and then withdrew into a swaggering composure, before saying to the guards, "He's only a Stormborn."

The roar of the crowd had come and gone, and now they stood muttering to each other and themselves, fixated on the exhibition, and wondering what Dorian would do next. Shye wasn't sure himself and, licking his lips distastefully, he hoped they'd move along before anyone found out. Fixating on the banner for the Hunters' Guild House, he pushed away the pressure lingering on his mouth. The hourglass on the banner distorted and rippled, the waves of its surface deep enough to mask the heat and shame that welled up when he thought of catching eyes with Dorian.

"The lockup, Master Hunter?" the other guard interrupted, sounding strained. Dorian's prideful delight was seeping from their pores, thick enough to charge the air.

Shye felt sick. This had been a terrible idea.

"Oh no," Dorian said, sweeping around on their heel. "We take this one to see the prince."

Shye breathed a sigh. His nausea abated with a rolling surge of determination.

Finally.

I'm here, he thought, straining to hear the whisper of his name reverberating on the wind, below his blood and beneath his skinning and through his very bones, *now what do you want?*

CHAPTER 18

THE BRIGHTSPIR HAD A VIEW OF THE CITY LIKE NO OTHER, AND ascending through the smooth rock walkways and hollowed halls with rare mineral-mosaic ceilings, Dorian could see all of Mistral stretching out below them. Beyond, the farms and fields that fed the city, and beyond them the roads that led out of the capital and into the Mountain and River Lands, where imperial peace was a straightforward set of rules and negotiations. But in Mistral, peace was defined in murkier lines. The restrictions of the ideal floating on the surface of the city hid the mire of personal and professional politics several layers underneath, which were made shrewder by the deftness with which such things must be handled in a capital whose core ideal opposed them.

Dorian had taken pains to avoid this place, despite the nobility that kept them leashed to it – a founding aspect of their friendship with Leon.

It had suited the old king, gone now for years and a known tyrant for years before that, and had suited many kings since Camillus – all as immemorable as the last – as it now suited the crown prince, to have a somewhat revolving guest list within the palace to keep the nobility from getting too comfortable within the walls of the capital. To keep infighting to a minimum and politics fresh, the guilds formed a perfect solution to keep restless nobles in line and parties lively.

Dorian had always preferred assignment or drinking in the gardens with Leon over the decadent frostfall masques and balls, fire festivals, and glacial spas, because while their attendance to either had aggravated their father in vastly different ways, at least when they were out, he and his aggravation were farther away.

The lingering sun season had less time for frivolity while the lightrise lasted, and Dorian had spent it cultivating hunts enough to bag them a Stormborn, as opposed to courting scandal to mortify their father. That particular flair for the unwise was no doubt adding some charming details to their character as much as it had now caused Shye to avoid anything within the vicinity of their form.

Caught between two guards at Dorian's back, Shye had slipped into a composed, curious state, and fixated on the details of the Brightspir as they moved through it. He was defiantly beautiful in every line and angle of his body, and alight too. The sky just outside the carved railings had returned to quickening evenspan, but the folk Strangeness was still aglow in the Stormborn, and something a little pleased disturbed the serenity of his gaze. Anticipation lurked in his bright, inhuman eyes.

Dorian was trying to forget his words, but they could not stop the fleeting thought that perhaps what had called Shye here sought to destroy them all from within. Fate, if it was still out there, owed no favours to humankind.

Smothering that whispering doubt and kicking it into a box in the back of their mind, Dorian marched Shye and the two uncomfortable guards up from the lower levels into the interior, away from the open walkways and garden balconies of the exterior and the shining spread of Mistral below. The open-air halls transformed into light-specked rock walls as they continued inwards and upwards through the central wing and into the crown's wing. The space was wide enough to fit four across, alleviating any sudden onsets of claustrophobia. The doors to the throne room were standing open for them.

Polished labradorite had been set in a glass-like surface across the entire floor, sparkling in shades of blue or grey, except that it had been manipulated into form without a crack or line to mar it. A flowering tree with a mountain rising behind it had been carved out of glass-scarred stone behind the throne, along the back wall of the large, square room. All of it naturally sheared by the Strange ones with their influence over raw material. The throne was carved from the same yellow-gold stone as the outside of the Brightspir and was draped in silks. It stood empty.

There had been another room like this in the higher reaches of the palace. There, the lords who had used it could look out onto the expanse of their beloved domain of Dusk, when the Brightspir still belonged to the Strange ones who had crafted it. But since the rise of the Empire, some lingering Strangeness had barred it from Mistral's kings and no might of man had gotten them inside. Imperial kings used the lower throne room.

Although their duty demanded they secure the prisoner, when it came to Shye and being near him, the guards would only do as their duty demanded and no more. They wouldn't stay inside the room with him. The shock and awe, a hint of revulsion, that lingered in their eyes was all for Dorian, for daring to touch Shye so casually, without fear or disgust for the enemy they had brought to Mistral. The guards begged off at the outer doors as soon as Shye and Dorian had firm footing inside the room.

Shye wandered around as Dorian waited, posture lax, near the middle of the room. He touched his fingers to the tree rippling across the wall and toed the floor with his boots. Perhaps he was wondering at the architecture, perhaps trying to establish a Strange connection known only to him. He ended up before the throne, his head cocked in consideration.

After a moment, he wandered back to Dorian's side, still carrying some of that unearnt and undeserved trust he'd shown Dorian since the first, if a little roughed up around the edges with exasperation, humiliation, and tender bruises. He should've realised by now that Dorian was unworthy of it.

"You'd warn me if this was a prelude to my beheading, the showmanship for your fans notwithstanding?" he asked, deigning to throw Dorian a caustic glance, looking so very different in his folk Strangeness, his hair not yet dimmed, his eyes on show for all to see. Yet not Strange enough to be a stranger.

Dorian cut him a look in return, the remembrance of those spans previous coming again to the forefront of their mind; Shye sprawled in the grass, radiant and bold. *There is something in him that I am missing . . .*

They tamped down on the image and willed it away. This was it; this was their moment. They would not ruin it for the sake of this boy.

"What would be the point of bringing you all this way just to behead you now?" Wryness crept into Dorian's tone, although they had meant it to come out as acerbic as the look Shye had cut them. At least, the familiar barb directed at Shye was a weakness that they would soon be rid of. They might savour the flavour while they could.

Shye graced them with such a perfectly blank expression that it travelled the whole spectrum of emotion and ended up being vaguely judgemental for all its effort. "Unnecessary drama," he suggested.

Dorian laughed and then felt guilty for it. They watched Shye's mouth lift in an involuntary smile of his own and wondered at their priorities and how this place could set its decorous ideals upon them so insidiously. If they didn't feel guilty for kissing him, laughing at him was a negligible offence. If only, they merely felt guilty for laughing.

Dorian bit their lip to stop the rising tide of sorry words that started up their throat, the apology that would ruin them in the eyes of their Empire, when they were so close to victory. This boy knew nothing and had done nothing, but he trusted Dorian.

A wrench of pain burst under their teeth, but a careful touch showed no blood. Only when they saw that Shye was looking at them properly again, lingering with a questioning expression, did they realise they must have made a sound.

A slow, pointed grin broke through Shye's clouded features as understanding bloomed. A grin with teeth and teeth with points. Teeth making points. Pointed teeth. It was insufferably all that and more.

Dorian touched their mouth again and wondered if that thoughtless trust was his mistake or theirs. Humanity, where was Cassius, so they could stop thinking?

Footsteps flowed across the polished mineral floors as though Dorian had summoned them, and they heard the guards' leather bracers clink in salute. Composing themself before the crown prince swept into the room, Dorian gleaned the briefest glimpse of Lord James's condescending, delighted face before he made an ugly sound; his face going pale at the sight of Dorian standing next to the glowing aura of Shye.

He stiffened in the entryway, a mere step behind Cassius, the whole line of his shoulders knotting tensely.

Dorian sank to one knee.

Shye did not.

"Father, arrived at last. Care to join us," Dorian greeted wickedly and remembered, a wide smile breaking across their face. This was what they had done this for.

"You brought him here?" Dorian's father hissed, as though he did not feel the prince's eyes on him, on them all.

The animosity was palpable. Shye could feel his body responding to it, pulling up straighter, eyes narrowing, despite the fact he had stood easy as the crown prince of the Empire had stalked between him and Dorian, as Dorian had sunk fluidly to one knee.

The man trailing behind, now identified as Dorian's *father* – and with that Shye could note the lay of their mouths and the curves of their ears and a general sort of relation that was well hidden by their stark differences, especially their attitudes – was all puffed-up pride and young nobility cunning. The type his captain had detested most.

"At least the old crowd had some honour and better taste in brandy," Captain had said, as they'd sailed out of Emin Rif with several cases of the Ashea family's stocks of night-thorn wine.

Until he saw Shye, and then his face drained. Awful as it was, Shye didn't hate the way it made his insides bloom to know the man was afraid. Like Shye was half the legend his eyes claimed, and these men were right to fear him. The tortured sound that accompanied it, his eyes flicking between Shye and Dorian incomprehensibly, caused Dorian to smile like a beast would stalk before a kill, and Shye felt the prince's eyes upon them.

"Where else should I have brought him?" Dorian replied, too gracious to be sincere instead of incendiary, as pale sparks of victory danced in their eyes.

"It is one thing to bring him, another to not have him bound. Better you didn't bring him at all."

"Better for you," Dorian sniped, tone knife-edged, their face turning ever so slightly from the floor to glare darkly at the man.

Dorian's father sputtered and two red spots made themselves known on his wan cheeks. "What do you mean by that?"

Dorian's teeth glinted in the hint of a smile decorating their still bowed head. They were kneeling before the prince of the Empire, but Shye had never seen them so unattainable, so unrepentant. "Only the best, that's what you wanted for me, right? Well, I am the best, always was. *You* are the disgrace to our family name, and *you* could never be Huntsman."

"How dare you—" Dorian's father replied, low and mean with promises in his words that Shye had no knowledge to comprehend.

The prince ignored them. Splaying himself over the throne and affecting boredom, it was he who finally captured Shye's attention. With one leg kicked up over the armrest, his opposite wrist dangling off the end of the other, his hazel-eyed gaze roved the father–hunter pair and then landed on Shye. The prince was wearing the Horned Crown.

Shye had seen a drawing of it in a book once. Crafted from wood and sapphire steel, it was bent along thick lines, which arced and curved together till they reached three points. Two curled over the back of the prince's dark hair like horns, and the third – widest and smallest – speared straight up from the centre. In the drawing it had several ornamentations that a mortal prince could not produce. Firefly lights, blossoms, strings of jewels that no longer thrived in Mistral's mines. Once, it had been worn on the head of Dana, the Blooded Prince of the Mountain and River Lands. Before the first king brought down her court, the rest of old Emin Rif following soon after.

The prince of it now watched him curiously.

Shye did not know much about him, only that he was king in all things except name, and only his coronation kept that at bay, which was now speedily approaching in the season of his twenty-fifth span; the same age as when the first king came to his throne. It was his lack of knowledge on the prince's character that left him to hope that maybe this was still a good idea. If it went wrong, he could at least blame that this was all he knew. This and the prince's name – Cassius Sands.

Shye was taken aback by the resolve of the prince's gaze. The sharp sweep of his brows lent authority to a face not much older than his own, the angles of it intensified by the high collar of the short-cut jacket of black he was wearing. Nothing like the layered frock coats, cloaks, and ankle-length billowers worn by the noblemen, or even Dorian. The shoulders of it were decorated in whorls of embroidery and glass in bright purples, deep blues, and turquoises, with actual lapis and pearl. For all of that, the prince wore no extra ornamentation other than the stolen crown and a ring of whole lapis. Streaks of what must be real frost stone sliced down its middle, gleaming like frozen water moving through the deep-blue base.

"Lord James," the prince interrupted after a while of watching Shye.

Dorian's father immediately paused, faced the prince, and bowed.

He cast one furious glance at Dorian before backing off to the end of the hall, though he did not leave.

Dorian rose sinuously, without leave. "Your Highness."

The prince inclined his head and said distractedly, "I've been told that impertinence should not win you favours, Locke, but I'm not sure I'd have you any other way."

The pair of chains belted at his waist, draped over the deep-lilac vest underneath, clinked as he shifted. A symbol of the crown's service to the people, which made Shye twitch with the brief flash of bitter resentment it induced.

His attention did not shift from Shye. He stared at him, into him, and said, "What is this?"

There was an eagerness in his features that told Shye he already knew and just wanted it said aloud so that he might revel in it.

"The Stormborn, Your Highness," Dorian responded in kind; smug vanity dripping from every word. The temperature dropped at the back of the room as Dorian sent a cheeky flash to where their father had been exiled.

The prince's lips lifted in a mockery of amusement.

"He does not kneel?"

It wasn't a question meant for Shye, or really a question at all, but he answered it anyway, with a little warning truth stinging his tongue, "You may wear our crown, but you are not my prince, certainly not my king. I do not kneel, I burn."

The prince's leg slipped off the arm of the carved throne, and he leant forward as a flash of surprise angled across his face. He slid off the seat, swaggering off the dais. He shared a knife-sharp smile with Dorian and said, as though ignoring Shye, "He has learned your every flavour of insolence, I see. Ever and I have always liked that about you."

Shye saw Dorian's face shutter and go still at the name, and Cassius, as if sensing it, spared them a rueful glance before clearing his throat and moving on, slipping back into conceited princeling, the sudden sensitivity gone from his expression.

He approached Shye, stopping just out of reach but close enough to be felt, almost as if a force on the air. His eyes darkened as Shye lifted his chin and looked him in the eye, refusing to shrink.

"It is all right if you do not kneel," the prince purred. "We can teach you."

"What is his name?" the prince spoke again, this time to Dorian, not bothering to face them as he did. Looming over Shye, a head taller or so than him and well aware of it, he continued to inspect him with an interest that was only slightly less aggressively ambitious than the touch Master Fox had left upon him what seemed like a lifetime ago.

Dorian made to answer but Shye cut them off, pivoting to block Cassius when he said, "Not to put you out, Dorian, but I have a tongue, as you well know, and I can speak for myself."

Dorian's mouth snapped shut without a fuss and they made an elaborate "go on" gesture with what should have just been their hand but somehow involved their entire body.

Out of the corner of his eye, Shye saw the prince's demeanour become a little less patient. Where Dorian's father harrumphed in the background at their antics, Cassius seemed at least tolerant, slipping into impatience but not outright anger. He even seemed cautiously entertained underneath it all. It was unlikely that as the prince of a "peaceful" empire, he had much else to divert him, aside from capital politics.

"Speak then," he invited.

Shye's eyes narrowed at the half-order, and he crossed his arms behind his back, pulling his shoulders straight and not backing down. He even tried to be downright amiable as he said, "My friends call me Shye."

Cassius, for all he was vain and arrogant and princely, nodded with respect. The dark of his eyes seemed to dance, and he stepped around to reach out for Shye's lightning-slicked hair, tracing the space around it. His hand drifted down and settled on Shye's shoulder.

"And are we friends?" he asked.

Shye dipped out of his grasp, telling himself it wasn't a retreat, and flicked a little glance at Dorian, who leaned against a wall, opposite their father. They watched the scene, their face impassive, their eyes on the prince instead of Shye, no doubt waiting for the reward they had been promised.

Shye frowned and said to Cassius, unblinking, "That remains to be seen."

Cassius hummed and returned to his throne, gesturing to Dorian's father with a finger to move forward.

Dorian leant forward to hear what was being said and they all seemed to forget Shye standing there.

"I have considered your proposal, cousin, and I agree to waive the election."

While Cassius spoke, his gaze strayed from Lord James to Shye; his dancing peridot-specked hazel eyes swallowing the whole room. He smiled and cleared his throat, holding up a hand for silence when it seemed Lord James might speak.

"I have made my decision," he said, brooking no argument from any quarter. His smile widened to show teeth, and he slid off the throne to commandeer Shye, spinning him to face the doors, slinging his arm over Shye's shoulder.

He pointed to Dorian and ordered, "Dorian is Huntsman."

Dorian jolted, their face a conflicting tapestry, but upon seeing their father's cold and suffering expression, they kneeled obediently before Cassius and smiled a savage smile.

Cassius fluttered a dismissive wave at Lord James and said, "You may leave."

With Lord James stalking away down the hall, Cassius clicked his tongue and addressed the kneeling hunter as he paced deliberately around the room, "Your father was adamant that on your return I should bar you from the guild for crimes that I don't particularly care about or wish to punish you for, but he was not the only one. I'm glad I didn't listen." He gave a small smile, pleasant and honourable. "It wouldn't do to lose my best hunter, who brings me gifts such as this."

He stopped in front of Shye and touched his cheek, tilting his chin up to stare into his face possessively. He paced back to Dorian and gestured for them to rise.

"You will begin your office immediately. I trust you to honour it as your grandfather did," he paused, his eyes sweeping over Dorian with a care that surprised Shye, before he nodded slightly to himself. "Dismissed."

Dorian rose and bowed, pausing just barely for the prince to read the question making itself known in the lines of their limbs and smile delicately, nodding at Shye.

"He will stay."

Dorian left. Their roguish smile was back in place and was making peace with the rioting glory in their eyes, a spring forming in their step. They did not once look back.

Shye tracked them till they passed from sight and wondered if this had paid his debt to them in full. Was there more? Would he ever see them again?

Shye's expression pinched, and he squashed that thought and all its swirling diversions before they could form fully in his mind. They weren't each other's problems anymore, and he shouldn't expect their lives to come together again after this day. He wouldn't hope they would seek him out, even quietly.

Once they were alone, Cassius strode over to his side, fastening a strong, elegant hand around his arm. The break of his mouth took on more bite but also seemed more genuine too.

Shye found it hard to focus between the eager sparkling of his eyes, the bareness of his teeth, and the sharp, pleasing lines of his face. He was bizarrely dazzling for a human. Different in magnetism from Dorian, but he could see how these two people with such something about them might be related in some way.

"I've been waiting for this from the moment I'd heard you'd surfaced."

He squeezed Shye's arm and looked at him so earnestly that Shye thought this couldn't simply be the delight of a new amusement. The prince was looking for something in him. Now, all Shye needed was for him to tell him what it was.

What do you want?

The call could be linked to Cassius. The heat of his hand on Shye had an answering heat rising beneath Shye's skin, burning like the glow of deepness. He had been right to come here.

Cassius's lips shaped and moved, and Shye waited for him to speak, but he stopped and said nothing. His mouth pursed, looking thoughtfully at Shye, and then a good-natured smile bled onto his features and all intention seemed to clear from his expression.

"Let's walk," he ordered, and dragged Shye from the room.

CHAPTER 19

THE BALCONY WAS HIGH ABOVE THE CITY, SPILLING OUT FROM THE Brightspir into the open air like many other identical spherical plates far above and far below. This one was well into the upper levels of the rock structure, with a long drop to the next one directly below or a no-less-dizzying far leap and plunge to the right to the one adjacent. Draperies billowed inwards into a room that gleamed in yellow-golds, from the walls cut with seals of glass like the city stones below to the curtains and bedclothes, ranging in shades from caramel and bronze to those pale enough to be silver.

Cassius was sprawled in an armchair that had spiralled silver decorations dripped into the timber. He lounged across from an empty fireplace, the plush rug beneath his boots muted red like a precise patch of silky blood. Most humans would get lost in the décor. Cassius was outlined in stark contrast to it – dark against the pale, bigger than all the little details, ordered and serene – where the room was emulated wildness, riotous, and colourful.

Shye tried hard to stop laughing.

"I'm sorry," he apologised, insincere with mirth, his laugh petering off into intermittent giggles. "It's just I would've expected a prince to know *not* to ask the prisoners and enemies of their Empire to hold their crown at their highly imperial coronation and place it carefully on your very precious head to mark you king of the Empire that eradicated their kind."

Shye's giggles attacked again, and tears clung to the corners of his eyes. It wasn't how he'd expected his first private meeting with an imperial prince to go, but he was glad it wasn't worse.

"You're not my prisoner," Cassius said coolly, his brows creeping up at Shye's unabashed display as he waited patiently for it to conclude.

"Please," Shye said, coming in from the balcony, looking windswept and lightning-branded, to sit in the chair across from Cassius. "You will leash me, you will trophy me, and clearly you will exploit me for what I am. A willing prisoner is still a prisoner. Besides, I'm sure your council has some reservations. Shouldn't this dubious honour be awarded to someone loyal and *human*? Why even consider having it be me?"

Shye doubted that his awakening had begun so he could attend the imperial coronation that had the palace steadily abuzz and betray his kind by crowning the prince their king, but he could hear the echoes of his name in the walls and the deepness had yet to sink into sleep, so there must be something here. It was the only reason he could speak of his lack of freedom so straightforwardly and even with a smile, though a part of him burned at the thought.

"Even if it was me, what would you gain by it?"

"You, here, where the world can see you," the prince countered. "You disturb the order of things, which could jeopardise the peace that I maintain. A reconciliation between our peoples could be good, as long as you serve just like everyone else."

Shye made a helpless gesture with his hands and shrugged. "And if I don't want to serve?"

Cassius sat back in his chair. A persuasive smile turned up his mouth, making him look younger, like the prince he probably should be. "I don't know much about the potent Blood of Stormborns or the folk. I don't know how storm glass is made or how your kind influences the earth to create rare minerals and metal, or the sky to make storms and unseasonal falls. I don't know how some of you can steal the secrets from our eyes and I wonder if it is true that your blood runs golden instead of red. I don't know if you'll be content to stay here for a day, a month, a year or more, and if I could stop you if you chose to leave."

His smile had the same daring quality as Dorian's, and he turned it on Shye. A stack of books piled on the little table next to the chair he sprawled in gave the impression that Cassius had done his reading and found the records unsatisfactory, if not wholly incomplete.

"But now that you're here, I'm pleased to have this chance to learn. Though some questions," he said, pausing, "I would prefer to leave unanswered. I could be asking for worse, but I'm not interested in worse. I'm interested in you."

Owning you, Shye added to himself.

He kept that thought behind his lips and vaulted from the chair, wandering over to the prince's large, stocked bookshelf, before trailing his fingers over the lavish spines of several editions his captain had also owned. It seemed sometimes that his master was still looking out for him, reminding him to use his head.

The terms weren't bad. The prince was offering Shye a chance to learn about his own history, which might help him discover the whisper that called to him, and if he did that quickly enough, he might be gone before the coronation even happened. Even if he was still around, what difference would one more king make? The Empire had stood for a long time, and he had no ambitions of toppling it, though he wasn't so happy about serving it either. An agreement on his part would earn some goodwill, maybe enough to get something in return. Shye's captivity would not come without conditions.

His hand dropped from the shelf, and he said to Cassius, "I didn't realise you were a scholar. What did you tell your council for them to allow this?"

His attention caught on a book that he recognised, the last book the captain had given to him as punishment. He hadn't gotten around to reading it before jumping ship with Dorian. His fingers came up to trace its spine idly.

Cassius's eyes tracked his movements.

"A peaceful Empire provides ample time for reading . . ."

"A peace predicated on the stolen lands of an entire people, their descendants' lives once heavily policed by the guilds within your capital, now so far gone you think there's nothing to fear. Peace and order in a world of humans, which brought me here, the dead winds calling my name to remember what your people have done. If it is peace, it is a false one, but don't let our problems cut into your reading time."

Shye walked across the room and sat down again. He sent Cassius a falsely charming grin. "Still want me to crown you?"

Cassius's eyes flashed at his challenge, and he responded in kind.

"You disturb my Empire just by existing and there is much I could do to correct that. This is not a land where the Blooded can just roam free, without consequence. But I don't want another suppression and as long as you are here and you behave, the people can be assured that the status quo remains intact without one. Runners from justice will think twice now one of my hunters has caught the Storm. You have the chance to become a symbol of peace for us – real, lasting peace. You should think on this thoroughly before you condemn my offer."

Especially since Feng and now Aura are petitioning for independence, and Mistral needs the strength of such a symbol to threaten them into silence without promising anything or provoking all-out conflict, Shye mused.

The confidence and command did not fade from his voice as the prince followed his speech with a look that advised discretion and said, "Your understanding of the folk and the crowning are, at the moment, my private request. I do have significant forces at hand that I could use to make my case, and do not think I would not exhaust them all to find one that would be more compelling to you. Considering that, you must admit, I am asking very nicely."

Shye nodded. His brows furrowed as he turned the situation over in his mind, but he didn't see much choice. He had to be here. His freedom was always going to be the price to set foot upon imperial lands without a cloak to hide behind. He wasn't going to get better terms, so only one thing remained.

"What do I get for my efforts in fulfilling your private *request*?"

The prince took off his crown, running his fingers through his jet hair, ruffling the smooth set it had fallen into over the day and set the crown back in place like it weighed nothing at all.

"Freedom," Cassius answered sincerely, "and as much of it as I can grant. You will be given leave within the palace to go and do as you wish, within reason and barring any time set aside for myself. You may even enter the city under escort, though who knows what you'll find there. And we will endeavour to treat you as a person, instead of a performing centrepiece. Will that be enough for you, Master Stormborn?"

Cassius shrugged. "Or we do we need to explore some of those significant forces and the concept of worse?"

Shye couldn't help but admire the obvious thought Cassius had poured into this, but he hid it well, narrowing his eyes and staring the prince down. This was a negotiation after all, and Shye needed all the advantages he could win and the rules to be laid out clear between them, so he could choose if and how he would break them.

"And what if I should wish to leave?" he asked without pause.

Cassius's mouth twitched, not up into a smile or down into a frown but somewhere neither, and it was not so comfortable as the rest of his form made out to be. "Then, as my subject and prize, you will ask, and as your sovereign, I shall consider."

The prince got up from the chair and fetched a glass from a stash on the mantle of the fireplace. He popped the silver top off a decanter sitting among a clustered circle of bottles on a spinning bronze disc in the middle of the small dining table.

"Do you think you will?" he asked, while occupied with flicking the lid of the decanter closed with his thumb, the pearl-rimmed, clear glass now half-full of something darker than spiced wine and faintly sparkling.

Shye had a sinking feeling it was night-thorn wine. Incredibly hard to smuggle as it only grew in the orchards within Mistral, and every cask was sealed with a royal stamp. The first choice of the harvest was always the right of the king, while the next pick went to the noble families before it even reached the hands of merchants. Casks rarely left the city after that. That hadn't stopped his captain though. The glass it went for outside the city was good enough to keep the *Oathbreaker* sailing for three or four seasons, and though the captain had kept a sample, Shye had never tasted it himself.

Cassius continued, glancing up as he put the decanter down again. "Wish to leave, that is? They're saying Dorian conquered you and that is why you're here . . ."

He took a sip from the glass and then offered it to Shye. "You don't seem very conquered to me."

Shye took it.

"Things are happening here. Perhaps good things, perhaps great things. I am here to find out," he said as he tracked Cassius, who plopped back into the armchair. Shye's fingers traced the rim of the glass and his interest moved to the dark depths of the wine. "After that, who can say?" He looked up and continued ominously, "You might not be sovereign, and I might not ask for permission."

Shye swirled the alcohol with his finger and sucked it into his mouth. Flavour cascaded on his tongue. Vivid and then arcane. He tipped the glass to his lips, downing it in one. Closing his eyes to knock the drink back, he heard Cassius laugh and answer, "Or you might kneel before me, as with everyone else. You might choose to."

Shye coughed as the drink slipped over his mouth and down his throat, leaving a slicked trail of heat and an aftertaste of something dark-rose and bubbly. He coughed again when he was done and wiped his mouth.

Cassius was laughing at him over the arm of the chair, looking as young as he should be, and carefree in his delight of Shye. He gestured for the glass, his fingers making grabby motions in the air.

"Another then," he commanded and refilled the glass, sharp-eyed gaze on Shye's reaction, "to seal our pact."

Shye wasn't sure when the room had started spinning or how he'd ended up lying on something vaguely furry but rather soft. Something smudgy and black moved next to his head, and with great effort, he held the room in focus long enough to see Cassius, who still sat in his preferred armchair, a book in hand. His attention fixed on Shye.

"I don't know why but I expected you to be better able to hold your drink."

"Sorry," Shye apologised. His tongue felt thick in his mouth and his throat was dry and jammy. "We didn't drink that much, did we? One would think a night spent with a ruling prince would be a responsible one."

Cassius threw Shye a funny look, bookmarked the page he was reading and snapped the book shut, putting it down on the little table with the others. "You'll be fine by morning."

Shye tilted his head to eye the prince more precisely. "Will you? What will your council say when they hear I spent the night in your rooms? Scandal? Murder?" he teased, a little reckless and a little plain with liquor.

Cassius shook his head, unworried. "These aren't my rooms. They're yours."

The prince seemed much better off, but then Shye had never had night-thorn wine before. He couldn't even recall how much they'd had . . . if Cassius had even had any at all.

"Even worse!" he cried, wincing as his head pounded in response. "What if I don't like the colour palette?"

Cassius laughed at him and, as with every time he had that night, he looked more real than before.

"You are not what I expected, Master Stormborn. But I wanted you honest and I wanted you unguarded, and now I want to ask you again, why are you here?"

Shye giggled, a more embarrassing sound having never left his mouth. "You brought me, I came, and I am always honest."

"But why – how do you exist?" Cassius pressed.

Shye's breath whooshed out of him at the end of an inaudible laugh. "Things. Words. Whispers," he answered breathlessly.

"But why a Stormborn, a piece of folk legend, when their time has passed? This is not your land, not your kingdom, not your city. What should we be preparing for? What is here for you if all that of true Dusk is dead?"

"I'm not dead," Shye said, "merely sleeping." He forced his eyes to open and focus again. He felt a wash of emotion at the sight of Cassius's pursed lips, his agitations singing out of him. Shye's tongue ran away with him again.

"I suspect you are lonely, Imperial Prince. This Strangeness will not fix that."

He held his breath as Cassius's face pinched. He was older again, cursed with honesty he didn't ask for, and Shye could not pluck it out of the air or out of his head to take it back.

Cassius sighed and pushed a hand over his face. "Perhaps you are right, Master Stormborn, or perhaps your disposition for truth has betrayed you," he said with a bluntness that implied he did not expect Shye to remember it come morning.

Shye's mouth burned. Stained with wine, his tongue turned with truths that tasted of dark-rose drinking and begged for candour, and he was not good with silence or restraint. He could not stop what Cassius had started. What Cassius had asked him for. And the prince clearly knew something about the Blood Manifest after all.

"If I am right, then you should have gotten a dog, Lord Prince."

He'd been focused on the silver swirls of the chair instead of the prince's dark, blurry form. Cassius was suddenly by the door and Shye's head spun trying to process the movement.

"A dog cannot teach me about the folk, and a dog does not talk back," he replied, a glitter of challenge in his voice and in his eyes when Shye could hold them in place long enough to see.

"I would rather not talk to you," Shye said and stuck his tongue between his teeth and bit down gently, to better express a meaning, which was slowing trickling away from him. Somehow, Cassius was laughing at him again, his eyes dark, as his answer seemed to come from far away. "Unfortunately, what you would rather matters very little compared to what I want. You are mine now, Master Stormborn."

When Cassius withdrew, Shye couldn't say. It seemed between one blink and the next he was gone, and the room was filled with firefly lights, gently wafting through the open drapes. They were the only light in the room, but the tiny glowings were so many that they speckled everything with flickering luminescence. He didn't remember rising to follow them out of the door.

They led him through the Brightspir, up – always up – until he was outside the arched doors to a room. A dark ballroom, a dark throne at its end, its floor a sheath of black stone cut with rivers of spectrolite, glittering under sheaves of dead leaves from the four dead trees that lined the edges of the room. The empty throne of stone, carved to look like branches of wood, sat on the other side, across from the doorway Shye could not move from. The firefly lights hung in the air and the wind began to whisper.

Cassius's crown, the Horned Crown, rested on the seat of the throne. It glinted sleekly at him.

Shye heard a great cracking and groaning as the trees began to shiver. They came alive and began to bloom. A rush of elation caught Shye's breath. The firefly lights flickered and went out.

Shye tumbled into bed, not sure if he'd gotten off the floor or off the top floor, and as he drifted, the last thing he remembered was toasting his agreement to crown the prince of the Empire king.

CHAPTER 20

SHYE STOOD ON THE HIGHEST TERRACE OF THE GARDENS ON THE SOUTH side of the palace, before the levels returned to assembly rooms, parlours, and libraries, or turned inwards towards the imperial wing or the central and crown's wing on the other side. A waterfall ran off the side of the terrace to a pool. Greenery ate into several different levels in the exterior, with a view of the mountains and the back districts of the city before them, curling around railings and creeping along walls, sprouting up from rock-carved basins and draping down from balcony to balcony all around the Brightspir. The air was fresh with mist and the smell of earth, and the sun warmed Shye's face where he stood on the edge of the balcony, attempting to call a storm across the mountains.

By the time he willed himself out of bed that morning – temples pounding distantly – he licked his teeth and resolved to leave night-thorn wine to the nobles who knew how to drink it. Someone had discreetly laid a breakfast spread out on the dining table while he'd been sleeping. A delicious mix of breads, fruits, and jams, which Shye tasted with spoons or fingers, smearing the preserves over warm bread, and licking up fruit juices as they ran down his wrist. The only thing he couldn't bring himself to touch, let alone taste, was the pastries. The idea of that betrayal coated his mouth in ash and coiled his stomach in knots.

On the *Oathbreaker*, pastries were a special treat to mark the day they'd picked him up from the floating encampment of Aura, where he'd been raised on the dockside by the ocean tide, playing with the Nain, from his earliest memories. Before they tried to drown him the day the captain made shore there.

Despite the bargain he had struck, there were places and parts of him that Cassius and his kingdom could not have and, ridiculous as it seemed, not having one now made bitter sweetness roll through him.

Shye cringed at the cloying feeling it brought to his chest.

Night-thorn wine might have the smoothness of silk, the charms of a rose, the wiles of a rake, and the bite of the briar, but, apparently, its hangovers made you maudlin.

Abandoning the food along with that train of thought, he picked up the top book off the pile Cassius had left behind on the side table and skimmed through it. A third of the way into his light perusal, he found that anything concerning the folk from the human perspective was almost entirely theoretical, and unless the prince had been hiding some books actually written by the Blooded, the ones he had left were not going to be much help.

Shye's education had been cursory, his element a slumbering whisper, his disposition for truth hated by the crew. The Blood Manifest was a dream, broken by thin folkness. He was as informed about his kind as the useless book. And considering the esteem under which the prince seemed to hold them, he could only assume the other stacked books were more of the same. He could only hope the prince would be too busy to notice that Shye was no better informed.

Licking his fingers free of juices and jam, Shye had quietly put the books away.

Searching the reaches of his rooms, he found little more than he'd expected or already known was there, although he did find a washroom in an alcove off the bedroom with a large pool dug out of the rock. It swirled with running water, which drained away unseen so that it never had the danger of overflowing.

Shye undressed and washed away what was left of his journey, and the rest of his hangover as well. Ducking underwater, he ran his fingers through his hair, clearing it of bristles and debris. He stayed under until his lungs started to strain so that he could see the way his hair lit the water around it with a gentle glow.

Surging up for air at last, lungs burning, he wiped the water from his eyes, then jerked back against the far wall of the pool, staring wide-eyed at the youth standing at its edge. The same boy who'd followed him through the crowd the day before and then bowed to him with that uncomforting gesture.

He grinned toothily at Shye.

"They've sent me with clothes for you." The boy pointed back towards the bedroom. "I left them on the bed, would you like to see?"

Shye shook his head, floating defensively away from the wall. "Who are you?"

The boy did not deign to reply and fetched the clothing anyway. He held up for Shye's inspection a pair of loose-hipped trousers with a tight 'V' at the waist and buttons on the sides, followed by a deep-cut vest in a rich pattern of bronze and white, and a sleeveless coat of black with a high collar decorated with embroidery and glittering stones. The prince, evidently, did not want him mistaken for just another young noble, as if that would ever happen while his hair still writhed in white flame.

"The prince said you should have an attendant, and since nobody was interested in volunteering and I was already in the palace . . ." The boy shrugged and laid the clothes back on the bed.

"I meant your name, and I don't need an attendant."

The boy retrieved a towelling cloth from over the top of a dressing screen shunted off to the side. "Oh."

He deposited the cloth within Shye's reach.

"Thank you," Shye said and reached for it.

"They don't think you need attending because you actually need it – they need someone to watch you, to report on what you do, because they're afraid of you and what you might mean, but they're hardly going to let you go now," the boy explained, as he crouched down and lay a hand over Shye's, which gripped the towelling cloth tightly in response.

A wash of warmth suffused through Shye's hand. His fist unclenched, relaxing as the veins in the boy's wrist slipped into a telling gold.

"I'm with you though, so you don't have to worry," he continued and took his hand back, slipping out of the room with a clever grin, leaving Shye to change.

A folklined boy, with a knack for some weak sphere of lingering influence. From the feel of his gaze on him, Shye was guessing it was something of the mind, maybe a disposition of persuasion – like Muse.

Not a bad ally to have if I ever needed one, Shye thought, slipping on the high-collared coat, the last piece of what the prince thought constituted an appropriate outfit. At least, despite the ostentatious nature of the ensemble compared to what Shye was used to wearing, he was relieved to find it easy to get into.

"So, what is your name?" Shye called into the other room, where he could hear movement and the clinking of plates. Tying the last ridiculous ribbon on the bottom of the pants, he crossed through the silk-lined doorway, towelling off his hair, which had yet to fade back to its light-lacked brown.

The boy had heaped the leftovers from breakfast onto a plate. A dripping piece of jammy bread sunk between his fingers, and he spoke as he chewed, "I figured since you don't know what's what around here, you wouldn't mind if I helped myself."

Shye waved his hand in invitation, sitting down at the table. He watched the boy inhaling food, waiting for a break in the ravenous feast so he could prompt, "Name?"

The boy sucked juices from his thumb and cleaned his face and hands primly with a napkin. "Jin. Jin Jensing, one day Lord Jensing, today your attendant. And what do I call you? You look noble like a 'Lord' except for your colouring." He gestured mainly to Shye's hair and eyes. Shye sighed out loud. "But everyone else has been calling you 'Master Stormborn', as if they can't get over it, so it's best to ask."

He eventually cracked a smile at Jin's practical, calculated bluntness.

"Just Shye is fine."

"Shye?" The youth made a face. "Sounds Feng, like one of their face names. Definitely not a folk name. What about Donin or Dorrev or Daymos?"

"Because all Blooded hails start with D?" Shye challenged.

The boy continued, his voice rising as he took up the contest without hesitation. "Or Neirin, Shaesa, Serin, Phebe, Idrith . . ."

Shye held up a hand to stem the flow. "Just Shye, please, Jin. These spans, it is good fortune for true imperial names to end with an 's' like the first king and 'n' like his queen. But the old cries are ill-lucked."

Jin stopped and considered, eventually nodding. "Right, just Shye it is then."

Jin showed Shye some of the libraries and the gardens. Shye quickly became overwhelmed by the sheer number of books in the former, though Jin apologetically mentioned that he'd need permission to take any away with him.

"It's fine. Unless this library has a vaulted section, I doubt it's stocking the books I need to borrow."

Jin considered this before putting out a suggestive, "What sort of books do you need?"

Shye had shook his head. "Later."

Now, he sighed over the view from the terrace and brushed a hand through his hair. Jin had explained that it was not the fashion to leave it unbound or wear it long, but Shye had retorted that if Cassius could do it so could he. Shye was sure Jin had only relented because of the lightning brands that still coursed through it, and the image that would give the court when they saw him walk by.

Jin sidled up to him as if hearing his name called in Shye's thoughts. He wore an expression that was more mischief than was probably good for him, and asked, "Something wrong with the view?" in a way that implied at least a double meaning, if not infinite ones, and gave Shye both the chills and the impression that persuasion was often preceded by perception.

Shye tried to only answer the surface question, looking out to the end of the capital of the Empire, the mountains that banded it at one end, the sea at his back on the other. It was as peaceful as Cassius claimed, ordered and controlled, built on the void left in the Blooded's wake. And Shye sensed it would ruin anyone who threatened that.

"It's not what I expected," he answered honestly.

"Maybe you're looking at it the wrong way?" Jin suggested, slipping away before Shye got the chance to wave him off.

Maybe he was.

Blinking at the sky, Shye cleared his mind of the blinding surge and nauseous, bleached aftermath of the deepness, and breathed fully again. He remembered counting the beats of his heart, the feel of his body as a deliberateness that held something true and alive. There was a trickle in the back of his mind, a pull under his skin. A gentle breeze stirred through the gardens.

Shye.

His eyes shot open. Something snagged in the rush of his insides and then the flood of it spilled up to his fingertips from the abyssal spring within. His blood was swallowed up again in light.

Out, he demanded of it, holding the call of the whisper close, the clouds moving faster over the rising mountains. Thunder ate through the clouds ahead of the city and lightning crawled after it. The wrong way of looking at it, outside instead of in. It was deceptively simple. There was no reach out there that did not start within. Perhaps, that was also the secret to Mistral.

When he breathed again, he stumbled back from the edge and tried to stay on his feet, struggling to calm his thundering pulse, breaking free of the backlash of release. The remaining fizzle of energy bled from him and into the rock beneath his feet. The deepness withdrew.

He felt the weight of eyes on his back. He had gained an audience. A small mob of nobles had gathered in a misshapen circle, watching him with the tenacious eyes of birds of prey, wondering if what they'd spotted was predator or lunch. They ambled away as soon as he turned to face them, with hands tucked over their mouths to disguise their whispers.

One stayed.

A noblewoman, dark-haired and dark-eyed, dressed in so burnt an orange it was almost copper. A full set of rubies decorated her knuckles, like the sapphire-women of Phirrun. She had been in the crowd when he had been taken into the Brightspir. She smiled at Shye, luring with her dainty white teeth.

"Careful," she said, "it's a long way to fall."

Shye was saved having to choke past the haze in his mouth to give a reply when an attendant rushed their way, coming out of the maze of open-air passageways and warren-like inner halls, calling, "Master, the council—"

She was interrupted both in speech and in being overtaken by the purposeful strides of Lord James before she could even approach the lady.

"Tanith, they're waiting for us."

The lady held up a fine, ringed and rubied hand for Lord James to take. He kissed it briefly in greeting and then folded it through his arm. She inclined her head at Shye with the slightest of curtsies. Shye held back a shudder despite her polite manner and wished she'd leave all the quicker.

"Good rise, Master Stormborn," she farewelled, sweeping off with Lord James, giggling when he bent low to speak into her ear.

Shye's skin tightened and prickled. He waited till they were gone and then went out onto the balcony again, away from the edge. He took one last look at the view, the waves of cloud undulating over the mountains, brewing wind, and spitting rain, and left the terrace.

Jin popped back up at his side to guide him wherever he desired.

"So, about those books?" he started, and Jin's face lit up with impish eagerness.

◐

Dorian crouched in the wreckage of their grandfather's sunroom; the small library in ruin around them. They itched to put it to rights. The only thing that stopped them was the small stain of dried blood near the toe of their shoe and the growing ache in their chest.

Wood creaked behind them. Unsheathing a dagger from their boot, Dorian hoped their eyes would stop watering before they had to turn and aim. Their breath caught. They strained their ears to hear the intruder. Poised, waiting.

The groaning wood stopped at the door and Leon said, "The heads of the guilds usually sit on the prince's council, but since no one could find you, your father all but jumped at the chance to take your place."

Dorian let out shaky breath and sheathed the dagger, wiping their lashes across the backs of their hands. They continued to contemplate the red stain on the floor.

"Well, let him have it," Dorian replied, their voice muffled and thick. They cleared their throat to disguise it. "I have no interest."

Their entire being felt weighed down to be in this room, and they kept having to surreptitiously wipe the wetness from their face before it began to drip on things. Tearing their gaze from the red patch of blood, Dorian stood up, knee joints cracking, and appreciated that Leon was still waiting by the door for them to speak when they glanced over at him.

"I don't understand," Dorian said, eyes roving over the room.

"They said it was jail-broken thugs from the outer-northern districts. Thieves or brawlers who'd run once and paid the price and were looking to pay it back."

"I know what they said!" Dorian screwed up their fists to keep from trembling head to toe. "Executed already and Ever dead. No ashes, no pyre, no honour, and no body, either."

Dorian squeezed their eyes shut, willing the roiling in their head to stop. They pressed their fists to their eyes and pressed in till they saw red and dancing spots of light.

"No!" Dorian snarled, their voice breaking across the word,

peeling their hands from their face and snapping, "Humanity, for the smartest man alive you can be so stupid."

Leon, to his credit, did not even pretend to be offended, though perhaps if this had been any other conversation he might have, and Dorian would have laughed. He stepped back, just outside the threshold, and said, "Tell me."

Dorian sighed and spat, "I see no scuffs, no more blood, nothing. Ever was old but he was strong, and he always had at least one dagger to hand. They're saying he didn't get a hand on one of them before they took him down. No. I'm seeing one measly patch of blood but not enough for a fatal wound, and they're saying they killed him. No."

"It could be the intruder's blood," Leon reasoned in a tone that provoked Dorian to prove him wrong. Dorian's mouth lifted just a little. Leon's echoed in agreement.

Dorian followed on with more analysis. The cold rational mind of the hunter giving them clarity, even as their chest wound tighter and tighter.

"Then why did no one see anything, hear anything?" Dorian gestured to the books scattered on the floor, the bottles shattered, and the paper strewn across the room. "How do you take Ever by surprise but not kill him here, trash the room but leave no marks on the walls or floor in the struggle, no blood except for that, then leave, and no one sees or hears any of it?"

Dorian shook their head vehemently. "No. There are too many things wrong here."

The room seemed to tilt as their eyes caught on the maroon smear again. Dorian hissed in a breath and pressed their lips together, the ache in their chest splintered the more they spoke. Ever really was gone. His sunroom was a damaged echo of the comforting, curious place it had been.

"And they are caught and executed the next day, but how, when no one saw or heard anything, and they left no trace to follow, no evidence?" Leon finished, completing Dorian's thoughts aloud when they could not.

After a moment, Dorian turned to Leon. "Word is, they didn't even try to run."

"Why would you? When you have nothing to run from," he replied, concurring. "When you're set up."

Dorian stacked up some of the books tossed on the floor and put them on the ledge of the bookshelf. "But we can't prove it. They left nothing to trace. Though I bet the families got a pretty pension for the sacrifice, if there was one at all. No one was there when the pyres went up for those boys."

Dorian pushed the books off the shelf with a careless hand. They fell to the ground with thumps and lay among the mess, as though Dorian had never picked them up in the first place. The whole room had been staged.

"And with such scheming, they maintain the peace."

Dorian followed Leon out of the sunroom, taking his proffered handkerchief with a grimace and scrubbing the vileness of their emotions off their face.

Leon demurred when they made to hand it back and nodded to the room behind them, offering an encouraging look and a shoulder to stand beside. "You've used your first morning as Head Huntsman well. What now?"

"They must have known the game, the way it is done in the capital, the play between politics and peace. Well enough to know that if you say someone died of natural causes you have to produce a body."

Dorian's disgust curled over their heart and dripped from their pores. There was something terrible in their bones and it had never hated like this before.

"Isn't that how we do it here? Make it neat and undetectable, quick and quiet, sorted and solved, and the peace will simply go on and the crown will forget one or two minor indiscretions. But not a Guild Head, not a noble, not Ever. So, they *have* to make this stick."

"Which means," Leon prompted, leading Dorian to a conclusion only they could decide. Leon's own conclusions were well-guarded, evident in understanding but unspoken. Dorian had neither the heart nor the precision for more reason and logic, for more dragging over the facts of Ever's death.

Dorian shrugged on their coat, tucking Leon's hanky into their pocket. They went to a cupboard hidden in the hall's shoe rack and pulled free three bottles of night-thorn wine and two bottles of House Iosse brandy. Dorian barely remembered their mother, but Lady Lis was a name still uttered with the power of a curse and her house was well known for the quality of their distilleries, and Ever had always been a fan of an afternoon tipple. He used to invite Dorian's mother along, even before Lady Sybilis Iosse became Lady Locke, and when Dorian was old enough, they too received an invitation to the sunroom and a sampling of the secret liquor cabinet.

Sticking two of the bottles in their coat pockets, they tucked one under their arm and handed the rest to Leon.

"Which means you have to be some sort of person to make this city believe this load of horseshit," Dorian's voice growled, emphatic, angry to its depths and cracking on the pain that slipped from their breast. Their mouth twisted, their eyes red, running, burning at the world.

"Malicious, ambitious, of good standing and well connected. And I'm very glad Shye stood between him and the title of Huntsman."

Leon hissed and shook his head. "We can't prove—"

"No, we can't."

They slammed the hidden cupboard closed, breath coming deeply through their nose as they fought to control themself in front of Leon. *You are Huntsman now. Ever would have that mean something.*

"And without proof, knowing means nothing."

Dorian stuck their arm through Leon's, warmth sneaking up their side as they leaned into him. *It will mean something*, Dorian thought, *I will do something.*

They led him out of their grandfather's house. "We can't do anything without evidence. That's what makes my father brilliant, instead of brilliantly stupid. Let's get drunk."

I will hunt them. I will hurt them for this. But the rites of sorrow and honour come first.

CHAPTER 21

"To Ever," Dorian drawled, their face flushed with drink, mouth shining with wine. Warm tears leaked down their face, and every so often they would brush them away with Leon's hanky. Leon collected his sorrows with a cloth he'd grabbed on the way through the public tearooms.

"To Ever"—Dorian cleared their throat and began again, glass raised in the air, full to the brim with near-black wine—"who was the best."

Draining the glass to all but a mouthful, they tossed what was left on the fire, which spat and crackled at the offering.

"To Ever"—Leon declared from the chair he was loosely sprawled in, pulled close to the fire, giving half a toast to it and half a toast to Dorian—"who raised the best."

He drank and offered it to the fire.

They had been honouring Ever's spirit for a while now, but the toasts were not winding down. The time for honouring had not yet passed into the time for sorrow, though Dorian could feel it creeping on them. Soon, it would arrive.

The tearoom they had commandeered was a private one. As no body had been recovered, there would be no pyre for Ever, and private rites were all Dorian could offer to his memory. But it wouldn't be the first time the Hunters' Guild tearooms had been used for such a thing. The table was stocked with the bottles they were using to toast Ever's honours; first the night-thorn and then the brandy. It was a preferable wake to any Dorian's father, the guild or anyone else could devise, and possibly the only one Ever would get.

Which should shame them all, Dorian thought bitterly.

Both Dorian and Leon had divested themselves of their coats. The privacy, the heat of the fire and the suffusing affection of the heavy liquor allowed them to undress to their satisfaction, their faces shining by the firelight with unhidden salt-tracked tears. Dorian poured them both another drink and raised their glass again.

"To Ever, who remade our noble name, made it worth something."

They drank and made their offering to the fire, their throat moving to swallow the thick, fragrant wine. Their breath smelled of dark-rose when they exhaled the fumes.

"To Ever," Leon said, his face breaking into a smile despite the tears they'd shared, "who married a princess. May they meet again."

Dorian hummed in approval of the toast and then fell silent. The moment stretched on, and both began to think that the time of sorrow had begun and tried to find the words they would need to say, but the time wasn't right, and they would not come. Then, Dorian spoke.

"To Ever," they murmured, and fresh tear tracks spilled on their cheeks. "A good man. My grandfather."

They toasted and drank and with it the time of sorrows arrived at last.

"A great man. My friend," Leon echoed and toasted the near-last drink.

"Whose only mistake was the traitorous devil I have the misfortune to call my father," Dorian whispered. Staring deep into the embers, the heat drying the tears on their face, Dorian began to speak their words of sorrow.

"You were right, old man. I wish you were here, so I could tell you.

I wish you were here, so you could see him. Shye," they drew out the word fondly. "In different circumstances, I might have called him my triumph, but every time I think I've won . . ."

Dorian sighed and touched their mouth. "And Shye, he is like nothing else. He will not be owned, and I wish you were here to tell me why I can't forget him."

They huffed and allowed a sad smile to break across their face, wiping their face clean with the borrowed handkerchief. They balled it up in their hand.

"Ever, I give you the honour of your life and the sorrow of your death. Know you were loved."

Dorian tossed it among the embers, where it smouldered and burned. Taking a deep breath, halting their tears, they refilled the glasses with liquor as Leon said his words and gave his sorrows over to the fire. They handed him a glass when he was done.

"To us, the ones who love," Dorian said and clinked their glass with Leon's, their eyes dry and scratchy but their soul less weighted, the ache in their chest loosening till it was nearly gone.

"To us, the ones who live," Leon answered and clinked his glass in return, the shadows in his eyes clearing with the release of the rite. They both tossed back the glasses and doused the weak fire with what was left in the bottles.

Dorian swept the ashes into a small wooden box with their family crest on it. Usually, the rite ashes were mixed with the ashes left from the funeral pyre and then given to some place significant, to earth or fire again, wind or water, or more commonly folded into metal or jewels. Dorian hoped Ever would not judge them for planning to put the box on the mantel of their rented room and forget for a little while that the mantel in their family home belonged, like all other things inside, to Lord James.

By the time they'd rebuilt the fire, barely lit this time, barely a wisp without heat, Leon had returned with a steaming pot of tea. After the funeral and the rite, there was normally time given to rest and recovery, but their private ceremony had no such observances, and they both had roles to go back to, regardless of the things they did in undisclosed tearooms.

The tea was poured out of its gleaming wood-glass pot into its matching dainty cups, and, in spite of the steam rising from them, Dorian and Leon threw back the first one to cleanse themselves of the lingering effects of the drinks and tribute. They slowed down to sip politely at the second.

"So," Leon began, sounding only slightly haggard, "do we feel better now?"

Dorian inhaled the delicately fragrant steam from over the top of their cup, soothing their ragged, torn edges and managed a weary smile. "We could feel worse."

Leon gave an eloquent shrug, topped up their cups and said, "Good enough."

They tossed back once more, refilling and refilling again, returned to mannerly sipping, each new cup leaving them feeling more human and better prepared to face the world outside their tearoom oasis.

"Now," Leon exclaimed, regaining some scholarly excitement along with his humanity, "I'll apprise you of the gossip. Surprisingly, no one's talking much about the prince's crowning, and by the quality of the decoration going up, I suspect it'll be a right bore inside the Brightspir, but hopefully short. It's still on the last nightrun of the season after all, and if he wanted a party he would've waited one more span until frostfall. And now, you'll tell me about your adventure while you finish your tea. After that, the only thing left to do is address the guild."

Leon laughed gently as Dorian slumped forward onto the table, sloshing tea everywhere, and a pitiful sound crossing their lips at the idea.

Of all the hunters that had responded to Dorian's summons, most were not thrilled to be called upon. Many didn't even deign to show up and those that did were uneasy, if not entirely hostile. Dorian couldn't entirely blame them, considering they had no real interest in making the address either.

They hadn't even started to speak, hadn't even sat on the Huntsman's bench, when one of their father's followers pushed to the front of the meagre gathering and spat, "What right do you have to lead us? You are a child, talented though you may be, and it is well known you give no respect to this office, your actions, or your family name. That display in the city, consorting with the enemy. You are a disgrace!"

The fact that their father wasn't here was a blessing, as Dorian wasn't sure what they'd be compelled to do to him if he was, but the fact that Lord Veredan was screeching at them in his place, using Lord James as a rallying banner against Dorian wasn't making their first day as Huntsman an encouraging one.

Dorian felt the heavy slide of rage heat in their chest and breathed in slowly to cool it, stepping down from the Huntsman's raised bench to meet Veredan before replying, "I have the mandate of the prince, Lord Veredan, and it is within *his* right to grant guild titles to whoever he wishes."

There was some murmur in support of Dorian among them, but it was quickly drowned out by the voice of Lord Veredan.

"The prince is blind if he cannot see what you are. Just like the former Huntsman. They can't see the disease in their family tree. Lord James didn't deserve a traitor like you to take his name."

Dorian didn't fight the burning madness this time. It wasn't Dorian who was the disgrace, it wasn't Dorian who was the disease. What had Dorian done to deserve a father like Lord James? Who had *Dorian* killed to deserve losing Ever? They didn't think, didn't breathe, as their hands clenched until their knuckles cracked and they rocked their weight backwards before swinging their fist into Lord Veredan's face. He dropped to one knee with a satisfying crack. It wasn't Dorian who was the traitor.

"Get out," Dorian snarled to the lord at their feet.

Lord Veredan stood, cupping his cheek, a promise of retribution in his eyes. He spat on the floor and left, a number of the gathered hunters following in his wake.

Dorian crossed their arms over their chest, taking in the remaining hunters watching them with more agitation and even less trust than before, Leon the only one standing at Dorian's side. Dorian opened their mouth, they still needed to give the address. Then they stopped and shook their head, this demonstration had already done its work. They couldn't salvage it now.

"Go," Dorian ordered the rest, pointing to the door, "Everyone go."

The room emptied quickly, and Dorian slumped down on the nearest bench, the burning in their heart subsiding and sorrow rushing in to fill it instead. So much for honouring the position as Ever had.

"Well, that could've gone better."

Dorian's head was in their hands, but they didn't need to see Leon to know he was standing over them, hips cocked, arms crossed, face sympathetic.

"He provoked me."

"No, you punched Lord Veredan because he mentioned your father, who you recently believe arranged the murder of your grand-father. And if you were a better politician, you wouldn't have made it so obvious."

Dorian grumbled and pushed themself off the bench they'd collapsed onto. "His cronies will never be for me being Huntsman, and now none of the rest of them will either."

Leon grabbed their arm as they started to pace. "But you *are* Huntsman."

"I never wanted it like this!"

Dorian tore free and stomped to where their family banner hung behind the Huntsman's bench, as it had for all Ever's years under the title. "I didn't even want to be a hunter until I learned I had a talent for it. By then the talk of legacy and family and convention began and I thought I could change his mind about me. And after that, all I've really done is serve our name, our legacy, as though one rise things might still change."

Leon had heard it before and didn't let Dorian's ranting stop him from moving forward with the problem at hand. "I'll give you a list of hunters who'll support you if you talk to them individually first, even after this. Humanity, some *especially* after this."

Dorian shook their head. The Huntsman was not a title or job they had intended to deal with, and they didn't want to deal with it now. They reached up and grasped the banner, tearing it down and tossing it at Leon. They had just wanted to stop Lord James.

Leon caught it, fingers sinking into the rich fabric.

"And what of that?" Dorian asked. "I tried to stop them taking my freedom and it was taken anyway, shackling me to a position nobody wants me to have. I can't win! Because of him. All I do, all I've done, because of him. It isn't enough."

Dorian marched over and grabbed the banner from Leon's hands and threw it to the floor. "What is this worth without Ever? How do I make my life mine again? Forget about winning, how do I stop playing?"

Leon caught Dorian gently by the shoulders and pulled them close, holding them as they began to shake. His voice was warm and true in their ear. "I'm sure Ever was waiting your whole life for you to ask him that."

Dorian leant into the grounding embrace and then pushed away, picking up the fallen banner. Backing up to the bench, they sat down, twisting the material between their hands.

"Ever isn't here."

Dorian watched the banner stretch and distort between their fingers. "But if he was, what do you think he'd say?"

Leon's boots appeared across from their own and he loomed over them, arms crossed, a smile playing across his mouth, ready with wise and fitting words. Dorian knew better than most that this ruined city did not deserve a man like Leon Payne.

"He would say that if you feel your life is not your own, you must start by making yourself your own. Choose what is worthy of you,

and damn everybody else," he answered and paused, a cheeky indulgent twinkle passing across his face. "Then, after you talk to Ever, you
come up with a plan and talk to me."

He gave them a meaningful look, rocking back and forth on his
heels. Dorian huffed with amusement, shaking their head at him.

"I don't have a plan."

Leon mocked with an astonished, "A Locke without a plan? Well,
glory be."

Dorian threw the balled-up banner at him, hard. As hard as a wad
of fabric could be thrown, which wasn't very. Leon chuckled and
caught it as it unfurled. Dorian felt a rueful smile settle into the
corners of their mouth.

"I'm a Locke without much of anything at the moment, not that
the name is worth much with what's left of it," they replied wryly and
then stopped, staring at the banner cradled in Leon's arms; slate and
shadow, its standard a disc speared through the centre by stalks of
flowering wheat. Like the simple circle of steel that Ever had said
represented a world in balance. If this place was in balance, then it
was a balance as skewed as its ideals of peace.

Dorian shot to their feet, posture suddenly straight and eager,
their eyes shot through with light.

"I have an idea."

Leon flung the banner carelessly onto a bench and threw an arm
around Dorian's shoulders, leading them out of the guild house with
a lifted stride, long and loping and ready for a fight.

"Good enough."

*Five Lords in Mistral's keep, One to lie and four to sleep, No more sons will
Dana bear, Till marked time meets Stormborn fair, The Horned Crown on
head, the kingly sit, Blood to Blood of gold is Dusky lit, Under the watch of
those Ravens keeping, the secrets of the ones not dead but merely
sleeping . . .*

Shye sighed and slammed the open book in his lap shut, ignoring Jin's admonishing, "Careful."

He tossed the book onto the side table. "I asked for books about folk history, politics, knowledge . . . not for ones of obscure poetry. *Let us not die in burning bright, but lie and dream of better delights. Frost wakens in the turnings deep, and storms come in to break our sleep.* Does anyone know what that means?" He kicked his feet together restlessly where he'd thrown them over the arm of the chair.

Jin didn't look up from the deck of cards he had laid out on the carpet in some complicated stacking game that might as well have been divining the future for all Shye could understand of it. Shye saw no reason to question the fact that Jin preferred to play card games on the floor of Shye's rooms rather than do whatever it was he was supposed to be doing, and worried that if he did, he would lose the easy company.

"Any books about the folk by the folk, scholarly beggars cannot be choosers. You're lucky I found you those five. Our histories are not listed in the libraries of Mistral, and if you're going to complain, you might as well sail out to Feng and check the vaulted section in the Library of the Dead. If you can find it."

Shye found it disconcerting that Jin seemed to know much more than he ever said, but he couldn't deny that he appreciated the companionship, unused to being alone. Even if it put him on edge when Jin mentioned things a boy, even one of his status, couldn't possibly know. With Jin, it was easier not to think about Dorian and if he wasn't thinking about them, he certainly wasn't missing their company.

"Four," he corrected smartly, with no bite, nudging the book of poetry with his toe. "Pretty words in rhymes and verses aren't going to illuminate the mechanics of the Blood Manifest or the fall of our empire or why I'm here now."

Jin spared him a look that said they might if he'd just give them a chance, then went back to playing his game, flipping over several cards at once, looking confused and somewhat concerned, and then gathering them together to start again. "If that's your criteria, you should try the one on the bottom."

Shye raised a brow but dug around the small pile of books near the floor of the chair, letting out a small *a-ha* of triumph as he fished out the one on the bottom. It was a large book and what might have once been a glossy crimson cover made of rubied steel and wood was now rusty red, and patched with whorls of yellow and brown. He flicked through it first, before looking down to Jin.

"Wow," he said insincerely.

Flipping the book over, he held it up for Jin, displaying the mess of symbols and Strange, sharp lettering, that decorated every page, spreading out past the margin in intricate blocks of text, similar to the lettering of Ancient Feng that the captain hadn't seen fit to teach him.

"I can't read this!"

"Some folk hero you are," Jin grumbled, his mouth turning up when he heard Shye huff and turn the book back over with a thump.

Flicking back through the book, mostly to see if there were any passages he could recognise and a little because he thought the Blooded might just be arseholes enough to make a book you couldn't read unless you read it backwards, Shye almost crushed the aged bookmark that fell out from between the pages. He caught it just in time as it slipped into his lap before he managed to smush it with the book that had been protecting it.

He picked it up gingerly. The leather and paper slip was thin and delicate with the odd ochre that Shye associated with the very old.

It too was covered in old scratchings, no more useful than the book, but his attention caught on the small, cramped handwriting that flowed along the borders of the bookmark, like someone had been taking notes.

"The Horned Crown holds the past of an empire. Upon its will, turns the world. Ask the Ravens of the whispered winds," he read aloud. "Helpful. Is this book recommending that I talk to a raven or a Raven? And how in Strangeness could I possibly do that?"

The bookmark, as if sensing his disrespect, cracked into fine flakes when he shoved it back between the pages and was fine dust by the time it slid down the centre binding and onto his pants.

"I'm sorry," he tried to apologise, but didn't quite manage it. He dumped the book with the others and stood up, brushing the dust to the floor.

"You could always try standing in a field and screaming, something will find you, but I doubt Cassius actually cares for his request aside from the image it'll give when you stand in front of the Empire and crown a human king of our lands," Jin suggested, laying out his cards again.

Shye watched him do it this time, thinking he had been rather lucky that Cassius was so distracted with the coronation and his imperial duties that he'd more or less left Shye alone. Cassius's scholarly request of learning more about the folk was tidily shelved away until he had the time. Shye prayed he never had the time, and if by some miracle he did, that Shye would miraculously be somewhere else.

Jin pulled some cards, placed them in a row and then, as he flipped their faces up, he stacked them in order. Shye counted them as Jin turned them over. Several stars, two jacks, one king, and a queen. Jin stopped and frowned.

"What?" Shye asked.

A brisk wind blew in from the balcony, scattering the cards. Shye grabbed the jack of diamonds as it fluttered past his feet, and a second gust of wind slammed into the room, sending the king of diamonds and the jack of stars and the rest of his suit skidding into the fire. Jin gasped and tried to fetch the king out. Shye shot over to stop him before his fingers touched the flames.

Snatching up the fire poke, Shye knocked the king onto the floor, where it continued to blacken and burn. Shye could almost taste the distress in the back of his mouth that seemed to feed into the room from Jin. He covered the sudden chill that raced down his spine as he watched the king of diamonds burn a second time, remembering Alice turning over those same cards in the captain's quarters on the *Oathbreaker*, the king floating onto the lantern and burning, and the grinning jack of diamonds with Dorian's hat perched on its head waiting for him on the other side of the door as he left. His guts twisted into knots.

Shye couldn't read the cards any better than Alice, but there was no mistaking that they were the same. He shoved the thought of Dorian aside and handed the untouched jack of diamonds to Jin, joking, "Did you win?"

Jin gathered up the cards into a pile, gingerly placing the blacked king on top.

"That doesn't seem good," he said. "We should—"

He was interrupted by a knock on the outer door. Shye dragged his eyes warily from the pile of playing cards and hopped up to answer it. The unsettled coil of his insides grew in every heavy step.

Lady Tanith, in a burnished silken dress flickering with strings of gilt, smiled at him from the other side, her gold-painted lips full and pleasing. The queen of bones card stared up at Shye, trapped under the hem of her dress.

"Master Stormborn, we didn't get to finish our conversation," she greeted. "Walk with me."

It wasn't a request and despite the wariness that pricked his eyeballs and made havoc with his organs, clutching at his heart and clawing at his guts, sending his blood to darkened slush, Shye complied.

Jin let him go in silence, watched him leave with Tanith, until Shye's rooms were swallowed up by the halls of the Brightspir that Tanith led him down.

CHAPTER 22

SHYE WALKED THE UPPER REACHES OF THE PALACE WITH LADY TANITH on his arm, though she never spoke to him. Instead, she gave low satisfied simpers as she pulled him around, seemingly with no aim until they reached a corner of the palace Shye had never encountered, nor did it look like anyone had for a long time.

Shye.

Shye jumped as the whispers returned. Barrelling past him down the hall, louder than they'd been in Phirrun, more insistent than they'd been in his dreaming.

Shye, they called again, waning, turning thin, and once again leaving him.

Tanith continued to lead him forward, towards a spill of light across an open chamber. Ivy writhed across its walls, hanging down from the banisters of a second level. Flowers burst and died, leaving sprays of colour and withered husks on the floor, once immaculate but now rustling with forgotten flora, obsidian cut through with folk seals. The air was thick, hanging low to the ground like fog, and the thumping of Shye's blood yearned to leave as he walked on at Tanith's side, leading him deeper into this pocket of wildland. There was something wild about Tanith herself, something not quite Strange, and it made him stay even as his nerve endings screamed at him to go.

She led him to the bottom of a curving staircase slashed with tracks of sunlight at the far end of the chamber, its fluid lines ascending into the dark, the untouched summit of the Brightspir. The deepness rushed under to slick his skin. From above there came whispers, a call he'd come all this way to find. They commanded him to answer.

Shye, said the whispers, the only word they seemed to know, and this time it was faint and longing, worried at the same time.

"Go on," Tanith encouraged, and the whispers hissed away. She pushed him towards the stairs.

He felt a wash of memory overtake him and he stumbled upwards. One step and then another, the tension winding tighter, his blood loud under his skin and exuding deepness, a relief in the back of his mind that Tanith did not follow him into the darkness. In his mind, he could see it.

The vision of a throne room, old and flanked by trees, four trees shivering into bloom, shaking alive, the air thrumming with new life and the crown of the Empire lying there for its heir to take. He could feel it guiding him, inside him, the deepness reaching out beyond his control. He could not turn and go back down the stairs, though he did try, just once. Surely, this was what he had come here for.

His feet walked as his mind dreamed. Beyond the top of the stairs was a beautiful landing. Glass-set arches threw glittering shapes out of the darkness and between them rose a colossal door, one thick slab of stone and steel and glass, glinting, with no way inside. The air was almost choking with the weight of it, each step taking an eternity to land. In this place of time and age and Old World things, Shye could barely breathe to save his life. With every tearing of his lungs, he felt the haze of the dreaming tug at his mind. The deepness that thrummed in him battered at his chest, drumming an order to open the door. It twitched him closer and closer, until his hands closed around the Horned Crown in his head.

His hands went cold. He blinked.

His fingers were caught on the indentations of the door at the other end of the landing from where he'd thought he'd been, on the edge of the steps. Four blooming trees sprouted from the edges of the door, their roots turning inwards, twining together in a ring in the centre. A line, sharp and shaped like a light-trailed star, speared through the middle of the ring. A mountain loomed in the background, the craggy face of a watchful old man carved into its peak.

Tracing the lines and ridges of the image, he gave the door an experimental push. Nothing moved. He pushed harder, straining. The deepness rushed out of his fingertips, sinking into the stone and steel and glass, and the door shuddered against them but did not open. He pushed himself away and cursed.

"Come on," he whispered to the stone. "All this and you won't even open. What are you waiting for?"

The door stared him down, old, unmovable, judging, weighing. Shye swallowed. If the door could look at him, it would find him wanting. He knew nothing, came from nothing, was nothing. This call demanded more than he had to offer, and he had less now than he'd ever had before. No crew, no friends, no freedom. He'd lost it, traded it, like he knew what it was all worth. He had not.

"I hate you," he spat at it, suddenly angry. It was only a door, and there had to be a way to open it. He shoved his shoulder against it once, twice and then slapped his hands against it when it did not budge. "You brought me here!" he yelled in frustration. "All I had to give, I gave for you. For this. Let me tell you, it was not worth it."

The door did not care.

His fingers scrabbled through his hair, fisting, pulling as snarls rose up inside his chest, dark and angry and tasting of dark-rose on his tongue. It filled his lungs like drowning wine, slicking his mouth to reckless honesty. He had no element, no Blood Manifest, but he did have this, the one thing that no one ever asked for that he could still give.

The door seemed to mock his weakness as he felt tears prick his eyes. He beat his fist against the stone. Again, again, again, willing it to hear him. Nails cut into his palms and blood started to trickle down his wrists and the beat shook its way into his bones.

"Open," he chanted quietly, between him and the door. It would not.

He spun away from it with a cry of dismay, fire licking at his mouth, demanding he speak the words he held on his tongue, words worthy of any Blooded curse or lashing. Growling, he incited, "Oh, fine then! Have it your way, but here is where you brought me, so here I am."

He struggled to get his breathing under control between the surging deepness, the weighty air, and the blood in his mouth. Images flooded his mind and the call squeezed in his chest. He choked and coughed on the glowings that had sprung into the air, wispy and humming faintly. He lay his wild, bright-eyed gaze on the ring and the lightning line in its centre.

"No, I know you like bargains, so let's make a deal instead. Worthy or not, I am the only one here and no one, not even old doors, old thrones, imperial princes, or fate, will tell me what to do or where to go. Not anymore. I have let you own me, use me, and this is the only chance you have before I walk away forever and never come back, so you'd best hear me."

Shye chuckled harshly at the wilful door and somehow, he knew that if the door had eyes to see him, it would glimpse a man kissed by lightning, glowing like a folk-moon, a Stormborn of Old. And Shye was wild in that knowledge.

"All I've ever wanted was to be free in this world without hiding and to know the reason I was called into it. I will not let you stop me," he threatened, voice deepening. "I will crown Cassius your king, while you wait here. A hundred years, a thousand, who knows how long you'll wait. There may never be another like me."

He placed both his hands on the centre of the ring, blood smearing the streaking line, and stared into the heart of the guardian of the Old World.

"Open and set us both free."

"Set us all free," came Tanith's voice from behind him, swathed in the dark.

Shye took his hands away, his bloody handprint red-gold, shot through with unearthly radiance, and the door groaned and split down the centre, swinging inwards. A gust of wind blew outwards, scattering dead leaves at his feet. Sweet air came upon the landing, the heaviness blowing away with the wind.

Elation shot through him, cracking down his spine, and his blood spiked. His face split into an open smile and he laughed as he caught sight of the throne and the tree behind it in full bloom, dropping petals on the dais. The wind ruffled through his hair.

It whispered to him in a voice he now recognised.

Stranger.

Then, a sharp pain speared into his side and the taste of rust rose quickly to the back of his mouth. Something hard and fever-giving slipped free of his body. His knees gave way beneath him. The jarring pain of hitting the obsidian-plated floor like shooting stars; the pain in his side liquid fire and salt.

Something whooshed past him again, this one like his deepness only larger, longer, older. It kissed him on the way past, gliding away from the slow drip of blood that seeped from him to muddy the floor. He could feel his body trying to mend itself, but it could not.

Skirts rustled among the leaves and obsidian-slick stone, then dainty footsteps flowed past him over the threshold. Shye forced his bowed head up, his twice-bloody hands covering the wound leaking life from his side. The dagger glistened red and gold and black, and wet in Tanith's hand.

"Thanks for sweet talking the door, hun," she purred, "but no son of Blood, no prince of Dusk, will sit on this throne again. This throne was made for stronger things than you."

"What the fuck," Shye gasped, clutching his side to slow the

bleeding, but it did little to stop the running trails of ichor from re-
painting the dead leaves, dully glowing on the floor.

"Oh, my dear boy, if only you knew how long I've waited for this."

I've been waiting for this from the moment I'd heard you'd surfaced.
Shye recalled Cassius's words and shook his voice from his mind,
then repeated, more quietly, "What the fuck?"

Tanith shone like rosy evenspan before him; the rest of the room
waved and rolled away at the corners of his vision. The world
blurred. Behind his eyes, the Horned Crown glinted at him, just out
of reach.

"I was called here," he breathed, uncomprehending, distant, as
fiery pain burned up red-gold clouds of smoke in his mind. Tanith
scorched like a beacon between the feverish pain and confusion.

"Of course you were," she answered kindly.

She crouched in front of him, setting her dagger inside her
bodice, still slimy with spilled blood. She held his face between her
lacquered claws, while her sharp mouth lovingly tilted at him. Shye's
eyes slipped away, and she pinched his face.

"Who are you?" he asked, through the growing poisonous flavour
of rust and iron. His eyes tried to hold hers, but they wandered,
growing dark without his permission. The skin of her wrist was soft
and rich, falling away from the cuff of her sleeve. His eyelids fluttered,
caught on the stretch of unmarred skin, something . . . he forced
himself to focus on Tanith's face.

She was smiling at him.

"Blood pays for blood," she murmured to him. "I had to wait until
you were old enough, until you had awakened as you awakened me
all those years ago. You will understand soon."

Shye felt liquid dribble over his lips. Black spots tore into his
vision, and his entire body cupped by burning hands. He leant into
her face and snarled, "I have never met you before in my life."

She laughed with delight, as one of her rubied knuckles brushed
his jaw, cold and hard against his skin. "Don't be silly, baby," she said
with shining teeth. "I bore you."

Shye tried to pull away from her, but she held him tight. Fingers traced his face with nails sharpened to points, her eyes boring into him; tawny discs mixed with lethal green. She leaned down and slotted her mouth over his; her perfectly painted golden lips tasting his stained ones. She whispered to him on his smeared-slick mouth, "Blood of my blood."

Then she let him go with a girlish giggle and patted his cheek affectionately.

Shye gagged and spat ichor onto the floor, hating himself when a line of wetness dribbled down his cheek. Tanith thumbed the tear away.

"So noble-hearted, so beautiful, my baby," Tanith mused. "A shame," she said, turning firm. "In the new world, there will be no place for pure beauties like you."

The tiniest of breezes ruffled through the leaves between Shye's fingertips. He felt some of the deepness spring like smoke from a doused candle to clear the ashes in his mouth and the spots from his vision, sucking at droplets left on his skin.

"And what of the current world? I may not know it as well as some, but I'd rather not see it end," Shye replied.

She laughed her tinkling laugh and stood up, towering over him. She hefted him to his feet and jabbed her petite fingers between his blood-smudged hands into the deep slice her stiletto had left in his flesh; pain rocketing through him with the thump of his pulse. He fell onto her, his weight bearing down on her shoulder. Tanith half-carried him from the room, her grip as strong as steel, dragging him away from the old throne room.

"Oh, my darling boy, there was only one door our power could not open. It's near over now. The game's done, the Dusk Lords have failed again, and the crowning is nearly upon us. Then it will finally be done."

She kissed his forehead and left him at the top of the stairs, before picking her way down with silent steps, wiping his blood on her underskirts. Her voice danced back to him as she left him there, "You could burn the whole city down, but you cannot stop it."

Shye, the small wind trilled mournfully when they were alone.

His element. His guide. The other half of his Blood Manifest and the voice that had called him here.

"You were warning me. And this is what I get," he gasped to the spinning chamber, "for not recognising you sooner."

Shye felt the trickle of his blood slow, he was definitely going to pass out soon. The black was encroaching, and his side had gone oddly numb. He reached within, but the pulse of his blood was all around him, and he quickly lost focus. The glowings were flickering out.

The splay of evenspan speared the chamber and echoed the glare of auburn hair. He felt the sway of unconsciousness like the rocking of a horse, and a body sliding against him. There was warmth and pain and the taste of wonder on his tongue.

Shye, the small wind entreated loudly, cutting through the empty space, like someone had shouted it from the end of the hall.

The sense-memories blacked out with the slow fall of his eyelids.

Dorian.

Something called his name. He was cold, and then he was nothing at all.

"Wake up, you bastard," Dorian's voice rasped in Shye's ear. Forceful, threatening, and not the first time they'd requested this. Dorian went quiet as a warm whoosh of breath rushed against his ear as they spoke.

His eyelids fluttered, crusted together with salt, but Dorian's voice had done a thorough job of dredging him up from the elsewhere of unconsciousness, and he peered through his eyelashes to the blurry world beyond, pulsing with swathes of black and copper. His body, from what little he could feel of his extremities, was nicely dreamlike, lax and warm, weighted down. A mouth brushed his ear. Pleasure began to slowly unfurl through him, and he inhaled deeply, filling his lungs with cool air.

"You awake yet?" came Dorian's voice again.

The mouth retreated, and Shye felt the pull of the deepness inside rising to slip him back into blackness. Dorian was faster though.

A cautious hand graced his side, running along the bandages that wrapped his wound. Pain exploded back into his body, shooting down to his fingers and toes, tearing through the dreamy haze he'd so welcomed.

He gasped, breath stuck, eyes shooting open. His body jerked up to stop a second attack. The figure above him lurched back to avoid a collision, barely visible through the burst of black and grey through Shye's vision. The pain stopped him halfway, along with a pair of hands reaching out, arms wrapping him up, easing him the rest of the way.

He blinked the room back into focus and blushed from the roots of his hair to his toes, while breathing heavily through his nose until the pain faded into a forgettable throb.

Dorian leant across him, holding him up, saying, "Whoa, there."

Dorian's eyes were sparkling a little and they shuffled back once Shye was steady, but their arm was still pressed into the linens near his thighs, their body still close.

"A gunshot wound heals in two seconds, but apparently a pot shot under the ribs takes you down," Dorian said lightly, and then their shallow blue eyes lost some of their shine and turned icy. "Who was it?"

Shye scooted backwards into the pillows, and Dorian reached behind him to stack them so he could sit upright. A cursory glance around the room suggested someone had collected him from atop the black stairs and brought him to his room, as well as tended and dressed his wound. If he was careful, he couldn't even feel it beyond the constrictions binding him together.

"Lady Lis preserve you," he answered impolitely, repeating something he'd heard Dorian say once. He watched their face, unable to look anywhere else lest he be reminded of how closely they were perched. He saw it shutter for a moment and then it cleared. Dorian licked their lips and rubbed their brow, a newfound vulnerability settling between the lines and angles of their face.

Shye sucked in a breath with the way they looked at him, his chest tightening into an aching squeeze.

"I'm tired of courting peace, playing the game, and playing by its rules," Dorian started. Their fingers skirted the bandages on his chest, pensive and restless. "And I can see someone tried to teach it to you."

Shye's breath hitched as their fingers stilled, spilling over the bandages to his skin. A quirk turned up their mouth. "And I'll thank you not to invoke my mother without knowing what you call upon. We're too shiny to have her barbed eye upon us."

Shye flushed and dropped his gaze away.

"Almost no one knows that I've removed myself from the family line."

Shye looked up at that, and Dorian's eyes moved away from his face. They drew away, their fingers questing to pick at the covers of the bed.

Shye pushed forward, his hand skidding across the blankets to grasp at their arm, and they paused, looking at him again. Startled by the fierceness growing in their eyes and the weight of meaning they placed behind their words, Shye forced his lips to move.

"Dorian . . ."

He wasn't sure if this confession was meant for him to hear or if he'd forced it unwittingly. He didn't want to disturb this tentative moment, but he had a sinking feeling this moment wasn't his.

Dorian shook their head and shoved their palm over his mouth to quieten him.

Continuing in low tones, earnest for reasons Shye wasn't sure he wanted to examine, they said, "I've disinherited, disowned, and de-named myself. And the first thing I did after freeing myself from obligation, entitlement, expectation . . . was to listen when you called me."

Is that enough? Their eyes seemed to ask.

Shye didn't remember doing that, only the sound of the whisper in his ears, calling his name.

He reached out to trace the bare-faced honesty in the shadows of Dorian's mouth and the corners of their eyes that for once rivalled his own. They shifted forward to lean into his touch, their hand slipping off his mouth. He couldn't resist pushing his thumb into the crook of their lips to turn them upwards, which made them huff a laugh and their teeth poke through in an uncertain smile. His fingers trailed down to their jaw.

Their hand came up to hesitantly touch his.

He let it fall into their grasp.

Dorian twined their fingers together with Shye's, creeping cautiously forward until they were knotted together.

"I'm just Dorian now," they told him. The tense openness that sent a frisson off them caused their gaze to dive away before they wrenched it back. Their thumb swept innocuously over his skin.

"Just Dorian," Shye repeated, a smile pulling at his mouth, and pleasure flooding his mouth as he tasted the words on his tongue. It suited them.

Dorian tightened their fingers and didn't even look embarrassed as they hummed and said, "I was inspired by someone I know."

"Oh?" Shye responded. Pleased heat thawed his blood as Dorian inched closer, and their uncaptured hand reached out to cup his neck and jaw. He tensed, his heart jumping beneath his ribs. He felt their hand pull back, their eyes wide in panic, and he shook his head quickly, leaning into the touch, trying to assure, "No, don't—"

Dorian stopped pulling away and laughed as Shye stammered, the sound vibrating against his mouth, as they leant down to kiss him gently and thoroughly. He felt the brief press of their teeth against his lip and a familiar fizz of arousal spike inside him. He made a sound that could not be blamed on pain and they both knew it, blazing up red with embarrassment.

Their fingers pressed in briefly on his skin as Shye licked his lips and said, "I was just surprised."

Heat suffused his face, but Dorian did not seem to mind as they laughed softly at him, a wicked glint coming across their expression as they nosed along his skin until their lips found his again.

Is this enough? Their lips asked.

For now, he answered back.

CHAPTER 23

Kiss me. That's what Shye's face was saying. Although, it had been saying that a lot since Dorian had followed the call of the little wind. It had screamed *Shye* and *Stranger* with enough folkness that even Dorian could hear it long enough to find the Stormborn bleeding a pool onto the floor in an ancient area of the palace, before the ancient throne that no man had been able to find, let alone open, and which told Dorian that *something* had happened there. So, perhaps Dorian was just projecting.

Shye's mouth cracked into a smile above them. "Kiss me," he said, as if reading their thoughts.

Leaning up, Dorian obliged, smoothing careful hands down his ribs, over his waist and down to his hips; the rough bandages spanning his torso the only thing he was currently wearing, the feel of them entirely different to the surprising softness of his well-sunned skin. Dorian kissed his mouth and then his jaw, his neck, and his collar. One hand came up to thumb at the wrap of bandages. The pain of Shye's wound was fading as it healed, but Dorian could not forget the blood, shimmering red-gold on the landing, dripping down the stairs. Someone had been playing the politics and peace of the court far too well for Dorian's taste. First Ever, then Shye.

"Tell me who and I won't ask again," Dorian offered, catching Shye's face in their hand when he tried to look away. His eyes were big and luminous, his vulnerable mouth twisted in keeping the silence. How far and how long could Dorian push him before he caved, or worse, before he pulled away?

"You're never the one with nothing to say," Dorian prompted, pulling him by the chin so they could ghost a kiss to his cheek. They felt his lashes flutter against their skin.

Shye's reticence, evident in the tension striking a line across his shoulders and the way his jaw clenched and jumped, had Dorian pulling back. All the closeness in their journey could not have prepared them for truly feeling him against them. His skin, his desire, his heart, it was a yearning they'd locked away in fear until now. An indulgence in sentiment like this was a distraction, but one that Dorian was determined to keep. Dorian's obligations, after all, had been damned with their family name.

Shye made a displeased sound when Dorian jerked away, and he slumped onto them, his stomach pressed against theirs, their legs tangled together, a splay of white-fire curls spread out on the sheets and pillows. Something of that night had struck Shye together with the wound that had struck him down, and Dorian was learning it was not so easily broached, let alone healed. Through their naked skin, Dorian could feel the thump of Shye's heart. They could see in pinpoint detail when his eyes turned from vulnerable to resolved and then darkened to something else entirely.

"I don't know what they want," he said, pushing up on his elbows, his chin jutting out defiantly, "but I'm going to find out and I won't risk other people's lives, livelihoods, or reputations to do it."

He said that pointedly and Dorian had nothing they could say sincerely to counter it. They wanted to say damn their life, livelihood, and reputation, it was all on the line anyway, but they had a feeling that wasn't what Shye wanted, as charming as it sounded.

They tried to hide their concern, but Shye was perceptive, and it was hard to hide from someone who was more or less lounging on top of you. It hadn't stopped Shye trying before though, in some of their more amorous moments, blushing easily at Dorian's touch.

"What?" Shye asked warily.

Dorian's finger brushed with astounding gentleness over Shye's wound again, before sliding around to link at the small of his back.

"Leon says the reason you're healing so slowly is because they used fever iron, forged by humans. Despite your previous imperviousness, the folk's susceptibility to the black metal has started to affect you. Even if they didn't kill you, they wanted to hurt you."

Shye stopped them with a hand over their mouth, shaking his head. "Don't," he said, distress coiling like a serpent across his face and in his limbs, tightening its grip. "I don't want to. Please, Dorian, you will never convince me on this, so just stop digging."

His eyes shut for a moment, scrunching, brow wrinkling. Dorian could feel the tremors of his fingers on their lips, emotion rioting in quiet movements, confined to the smallest spaces he could force them to. It shook something loose in their chest. They pulled his hand away.

"You stole my move," they remarked softly, guiding Shye's face till their foreheads were brushing. "Okay," they said. Shye wouldn't talk and they wouldn't ask again as they had promised, but Dorian had been navigating the politics of Mistral their whole life. Eventually, someone or something would slip. Dorian would let it go for now.

"Shall I make you moan instead?"

They felt the relieved upturn of his mouth, the feather-soft movements of his lips as he said, "Yeah, that sounds nice."

Shye waited until Dorian was asleep – until long after they had eaten and bathed, and Dorian had touched and loved him to both their satisfaction – to ease himself out of bed. His side flared as he stood, and he had to grab onto the bed frame to keep himself upright with the sudden bright slice of it before the pain retreated. Dorian turned over in their sleep to face him and he stopped breathing for a minute, trapped by the serene expression smoothing out their features and the alarming spike of being caught, but Dorian didn't stir, and the pain faded away after a moment.

After twisting and shuffling his way into a pair of pants, Shye crept out into the main chamber, calling "Jin?" as loudly as he dared.

Jin was curled up on the carpet in front of the low-banked fire, with a pillow under his head and a blanket tangled around him, the season's end bringing less and less warmth into the room.

"Jin?" Shye whispered, crouching down and shaking him gently awake. "Jin."

The boy woke abruptly, his hand whipping out from under the pillow, a small sapphire steel dagger clutched in it.

Shye flinched and jerked back. "Whoa, whoa, it's just me, put that away."

Jin blinked and gave a muffled, "Sorry," before slipping the dagger out of sight.

Shye sat back on his heels, ran a hand through his hair and eyed the boy with care. "Where did you even get that?"

Jin eyed him back, fidgeted for a moment without replying and then launched at him, knocking them both backwards and Shye off of his heels, onto the floor. Shye returned his embrace, his arms coming up around his back to hold the boy. Shye's breath whooshed out of him and he gave a wheezing chuckle, until the pressure of the position set off a twinge in his side and he had to push Jin away. He held the sound he couldn't make in his throat, feeling the first slick of sweat stain the underside of his bandages and the back of his neck.

Jin grabbed his hands, pulling him upright till they were both kneeling, facing the other.

"Sorry," Jin apologised in a whisper.

Shye nodded slightly, detangling a hand from Jin's and pressing it to his ribs. Heat poured through the thin gauze and the pulse of his heart thumped against his palm. Slowly, the acidic and injured mewl in his throat slipped back towards his stomach. The phantom taste of blood remained. It grew strong as he asked, "Jin, who is Lady Tanith?"

Jin skipped his gaze and shook his head, wiping the back of his mouth on his hand. "I don't know."

Shye narrowed his eyes.

Jin could lie. He obviously didn't want to though, if he was doing such a poor job of it. Added with the fact that when he did flick a look towards Shye, it was practically begging him not to ask again. Shye hoped that some of his honesty had rubbed off on Jin, as well as Dorian. Then, maybe, he could finally get some answers.

He tried again.

"How about you try looking at me and saying that?"

When Jin did not, Shye gently pinched his chin, holding the pointed curve tightly when Jin tried to jerk away, sensing the gamble Shye was about to make. Shye held him in place, their faces aligned, until Jin's eyes curved towards his. Shye offered him all his secrets in return for just this one.

The veins in Jin's neck and chin sparked aurelian and warmth bled into Shye's fingertips. Time slowed. Shye's breathing followed. Jin's pupils expanded. They were very black. He felt like they covered him, like a nightrun with no stars, unwinding through his mind, unspooling it to see what was there. The blackness of them filled his lungs and his nose, his chest starting to burn. He stopped breathing.

Then Jin blinked.

"Oh! She's your—"

Shye wrenched away, shuddering.

His head throbbed dizzily, the blackness still inside him and he couldn't cough it out. The room swayed and his fingers clawed into the rug for balance and at his throat, at his chest and face. He didn't see Jin move but suddenly he was there in his face, his hands on either side of his cheeks.

"Breathe," he ordered.

The blackness climbed up to his mouth, drooling over his tongue and out over his lips. He pushed past it to gasp a painfully clear breath. The feeling went away, but a headache bloomed behind his eyes as the dizziness melted away.

Worth it, he thought, if what Tanith had told him, if his secret, gained him some ground with his young friend.

"I was hoping for something I didn't know but at least I'm pretty sure I know what you are, secret stealer," he grouched, panting a little. He took in Jin's worried face and wondered if he should just leave it alone for now. He was hurt and he missed the soothing reassurance of Dorian's body against his. He sniffed and regained control of his body.

Jin's expression was clearly asking him if he was going to ask again. Shye sighed and shoved out a hand to push himself to his feet.

Jin's hand slid on top of his.

"I'm glad you're okay," he said, squeezing his fingers into Shye's skin.

Shye's mouth tucked and quivered. He took his hand from under Jin's and grasped the boy's shoulder. "I'm not okay, Jin. And if you don't tell me who Tanith is, so I can figure out what she wants and what she's planning." He paused, shakily inhaling, tugging at his hair. He grimaced and let Jin go, tone falling. "I'm not sure I can be."

Jin's mouth wobbled, his eyes shining, lit by the dying embers of the fire. He brushed his fist into them, whisking the frailty away. A hot slash of regret and panic fumbled through Shye and he tried to give Jin an encouraging look.

"I'm afraid of her," Jin admitted, his voice cracking.

"So am I," Shye admitted, patting Jin awkwardly on the arm. He saw Jin's eyes flick to the gauze wrapped around him. Shye stood and walked over to the fire, fumbling with the logs and kindling and tossing them into the fire. He faced Jin, the boy watching him, waiting for whatever would come next – an interrogation or something he couldn't predict.

"I'm afraid," he repeated, "but that doesn't mean I'm just going to let her do what she wants."

Shye's arms wrapped unconsciously around his bandaged ribs, and then he crossed his arms, rocking back on his heels, feeling the weight of the quiet. He shook his head and turned away. Jin made a sound and he half-turned back.

The boy's face shuttered, and he avoided Shye's gaze. His fingers picked fibres from the rug on the floor. Shye waited a moment, uncrossing his arms, but when nothing more was forthcoming, he rubbed his eyes and said, "Goodnight, Jin," before starting to walk away.

"Tanith's a Raven."

Shye stopped. A cold shudder skimmed up his spine.

"Many, if not most, Masters of Accomplishment who wear more than eight jewelled knuckles are. But it's not just those masters. Some are courtesans, guild scriveners, couriers and lower guild maids. The oddities of folklines make them both valuable and vulnerable, surrounded by secrets," Jin continued. A pop and crackle from the fire almost drowned him out. His voice was hushed as though he feared who might hear him. "Though some are chosen from other places if they show the right talent. The right Blood ancestry."

Shye's skin prickled as his chest constricted beneath the coarse gauze, and he slowly turned around. "An ancestry that produces someone like me," he stated warily.

Jin's eyes were huge and bright in the light from the hungry flames. "More like someone like me."

Shye padded back into the warmth of them and sat in one of the plush chairs. Jin huddled in his blanket to the side of it.

"Secrets like the ones you are uncovering here are best kept by those who make secrets and spies their business."

"So folk knowledge survives, even if there are no Blooded," Shye said plainly. "And Cassius doesn't know?"

Jin shrugged. "There's you and whatever follows that. Someone or something remembered, long before Tanith, and thought the Blood would call us back. They made sure all Ravens would remember too."

The Dusk Lords have failed. Shye grimaced at Tanith's name – his mother if he could believe it – and tried to put her voice out of his head, bitterness rising in his gut as he remembered her words. He could not thank them, whoever they were, for all they may have preserved the secrets of his kind. They had gifted knowledge to the Ravens but left him in the dark. *Ask the Ravens of the whispered winds, the note in that book really did want me to ask a Raven*, Shye thought to himself. *But of course, without Jin, how would I have ever found one? Though, Jin found me and gave me the book, which was probably the point. I just had to ask the right questions; still why can nothing ever be simple?*

"And Cassius," Jin continued, skating over Shye's inner turmoil, "is a mortal prince, soon to be king, and would never question a Raven's loyalty to the crown, even if he mistakes the crown and the king as synonymous. He would never think to ask."

"I imagine," Shye began, "that they find your abilities very useful, Jin."

The boy nodded once, his face placid, marred by the smallest quirk in his brow. It told Shye that Jin could be a good Raven if he chose, and he was choosing not to with him.

"So why have you decided to share what is meant to be secret with me?"

There was a moment before Jin answered where Shye felt the kiss of an old, slow wind that whistled conversations to once night-dark Ravens, who flew whispers to the ears of their princes and lords. The father of his familiar little wind. This wind did not speak to him, but, for the first time in a long time, it was there. Because of him.

"Your secrets are mine because you gave them to me. These secrets are yours as well, because they were given to me for you."

Jin said the words slowly, with enough purpose that it seemed like he felt it too. That the wind was marking them, holding them, and Jin, in turn, would be held by these words because of it.

"I'm with you."

The curtains fluttered and billowed, and the moment was gone. The breeze that followed through the room was fresh and came with the scent of rain upon it. Jin's tilted mouth fell to the creeping concern of his teeth as he mumbled, "But Tanith scares me."

Shye sighed, and a phantom twinge laced up his chest. "Yeah."

A small hand smacked suddenly onto his knee and Shye jolted, hissing through his teeth as real pain shot through him. He shot a small glare in Jin's direction, watching as the boy's teeth stopped worrying at his bottom lip and his wide eyes verged on feverish.

"You should meet my mother."

Shye's face took on a dubious cast.

Jin hurried on, earnestly speaking, "Ravens are apprenticed and trained in secret. My mother trained me, was like me, and she was, I think, an old friend of Tanith's. If you want to know the secrets of Mistral and perhaps Tanith's as well, we should talk to my mother."

Shye's chin dipped briefly in acknowledgement, before his expression smoothed out and he squinted sleepily against the fire-light. "At nightrun," he agreed and stood. "I'm sorry, Jin, but I just can't help but feel we're running out of time. For what though, I have no idea."

Jin nodded and lay down upon his pillows in front of the fire.

Shye slipped back into bed, careful not to jostle or wake the other body curled up under the covers. An arm slid laxly over his waist and he shivered as heat shifted into place along his spine. Lips moved drowsily on his neck.

"Who are you and what have you done to me."

It wasn't phrased as an awake question, or even a question at all, and the curve of those lips against his skin didn't seem interested in acquiring an answer. Astute and contrary even in sleep, Shye felt a sinking flare of fondness for the hunter invading his bed and his life.

I don't know yet, he thought to himself and resolutely closed his eyes, *but, either way, I'm going to find out.*

CHAPTER 24

DORIAN CAUGHT JIN IN THE HALL OUTSIDE SHYE'S ROOM. THEY grabbed him scuttling out the door, off to get breakfast or to see his father or perhaps to have more whispered conversations from nightrun to lightrise that kept Shye out of bed and Dorian dimly, regretfully, awake.

Sidling up to him, Dorian gently waylaid him into a corner, grip settled firmly around his upper arm. Once they had him trapped, looming over him, they announced, "I want in."

Jin met their eyes without a flicker, no fear and no hesitation on his composed face. He waited without a word, seemingly unbothered by their attempt to detain him. A voice growled enviously in the back of Dorian's mind over his lack of surprise. They had never been this cool, confident, or impassive, not now and certainly not at his age.

"Whatever is going on with Shye," Dorian continued, "whatever Strangeness, whatever plans, plots or happenings, I would like to be there."

Jin blinked at that and shrugged Dorian off with a blithe smile, and an unsettling perkiness flooding into his youthful form. He leant back into the wall, two heads shorter than Dorian, and tilted his chin up to look them in the face. Something about his eyes seemed different to Dorian now, or maybe something about Jin himself wasn't the same as it was before.

"Hunters serve the crown, Locke," Jin answered cleverly.

"A crown that once, like all things, belonged to the folk. Shye's a living reminder of that. And it's not Locke, just Dorian."

Dorian crossed their arms, unimpressed, as Jin shifted easily out of their shadow, saying, "Then, Dorian, which crown do you choose? Which crown does our Huntsman serve? A forgotten crown or a stolen one? The invitations have been sent, the tailors engaged, the streets bannered, the season nearly ended, so surely you must decide before attending the coronation?"

Dorian's eyes narrowed on the small boy, whose expression remained as placid as ever and left Dorian feeling as if they were the one under investigation; Jin distinguished and unflappable, and Dorian the unruly child instead of the adult. It was a feeling Dorian did not appreciate.

"I don't know," they answered truthfully. "Maybe—"

"Maybe you serve no crown at all," Jin cut in sharply, all the soft curves of his boyish expression bearing a harsh and unexpected maturity. "In which case you betray your guild and are a traitor." Jin canted his head cockily and continued, "I'm sure your father would love that."

"Jin, you little—" Dorian started with a hint of a snarl. This was getting them nowhere and Jin had a prickling intensity to him today that unnerved them, his arguments so carefully prodding with enough truth to make them fume.

Jin held up a hand to stop them. "You aren't prepared for this, Dorian."

"No one is!" Dorian protested in a hiss. "That's what *happens* when a Stormborn washes up."

Dorian's voice died, as though there had been more they had meant to say but they suddenly couldn't find the words. Jin allowed a shadow of curiosity to creep across his face.

Dorian lowered their voice to a threatening level. "Except someone was, weren't they, Jin? And I can only imagine that they slipped an iron dagger into Shye and left him before that forsaken throne for a reason. Politics or peace or something worse, don't you want to find them?"

Jin reached out, seeing the steely resolve forming under Dorian's skin and patted them lightly on the arm, but he shook his head. "You are the Huntsman now, Dorian. Only the Huntsman. Can you afford more enemies than you already have?"

The small hand slipped from Dorian's arm and Jin padded away, composed as though they'd only idly spoken of the weather or the current rounds of gossip, none of which included any of Dorian's recent indiscretions, though no doubt word would soon get around.

Dorian resisted the urge to give in to complete childishness and stamp their foot. Instead, they rubbed a hand over their face until the frustration of talking to Jin had receded enough that they could push it aside. They turned on their heel, arms folded, and loped in the opposite direction, hoping to get clear of the Brightspir without anyone waylaying them. Leon would help them figure out what to do.

They had barely crossed into the sparkling and foliage-drenched walkway around the corner from Shye's suite before footsteps climbed towards them.

Slinking to the side, Dorian sighed when Cassius's tall frame honoured the folk-sealed floors. The intricacies of his short coat sent whirls of filmy sunspots across the walls, and his crown jutted proudly from tousled hair.

Lord James grew dour, several steps behind, and Dorian felt rage bubble in their heart.

"Cousin," Cassius greeted Dorian, distracting them from the presence of their father. Good humour was etched across his fine-boned face. He looked, and always had, in all things a prince. But today Dorian thought that, like Jin, perhaps he was starting to look like something else.

A *king*, Dorian's mind suggested, but they quickly discarded the thought. To be a king you had to have a coronation, and while Cassius's was . . . soon – the preparations had been going on forever and Jin had said invitations had been sent, so it had to be soon – he wasn't their king yet.

"Dread Lord," Dorian responded, deadpanned.

James glowered so darkly he was beginning to appear in physical pain, but Cassius only chuckled and said, "Now that, I like."

With a brief nod towards the way Dorian had come, he continued, "How's the weather this rise?"

He meant Shye. He did not know yet that someone had injured his Stormborn prize and Dorian intended to keep it that way. He'd only make it harder for Dorian to find the culprit. They inclined their head respectfully to him and said, "Fair as ever," before attempting to move off.

Their lip twitched at the fight breaking across their father's face the longer this ridiculous encounter went on. Loathe as they were to cut it short and end his suffering, there were things they had to find out and no answers to be had here.

Cassius laughed and then stopped them as they turned away, his lively hazel eyes raking over Dorian.

"Please visit a tailor before my coronation, Dorian. Wear something nice – don't care what. You are a royal cousin after all," he said and let them go, commanding Lord James in the next breath to wait for him as he was going to check the weather for himself.

Dorian bit back a grin at Cassius's excitable humour – resolving to find out when the damn crowning actually was – and the terrible agony it must be causing their treacherous father, before raising their head to leave. Before they could do so, a hand caught them from behind, gripping tight and spinning them around.

Lord James's hand resettled sternly on his hip to match his even sterner expression.

Dorian's mood soured further, and they barely held their ground, wanting to take a defensive step away but knowing they couldn't give ground without seeming weak. Their mouth scrunched but they inclined a raised brow in question, attempting to appear as unbothered in a way that Jin had mastered and they had not.

"I want to speak with you," James gritted out, part clipped tones and frostiness, part demand.

Dorian clenched a fist, eyes slitting, as a tart and biting response rose unbidden to their lips; a spitting jab at his morals that was blunter than the politics of the cosy capital demanded between nobles. And that was what they were now, warring nobles instead of blood-bittered family.

"What could you possibly have to say to me?" They hissed and slapped away the hand that reached out to take hold of their elbow, to drag them away as he had been doing since Dorian was a child, whenever he determined they were no longer fit for polite company or when he felt they weren't listening.

"I could save you, Dorian, if you would just listen," Lord James snapped back at them, and Dorian nearly laughed. There it was.

"Save yourself the pain, Lord James," they answered in dark tones, as footfalls clattered towards them from the opposite wing of the Brightspir, coming down from the central interior, and Dorian's name was called out as Leon loped over, sticking an arm through theirs like a true gentleman. He gave Lord James an assessing glance.

"I'm sorry, your lordship, but if you want to speak with the Huntsman, you'll have to make an appointment," he cut in and started back the way he'd come, with Dorian hanging off his arm. "You need to see this," he whispered, ascending back within the solid stone walls.

James watched them go and strode off in a temper towards the place he'd left Cassius.

"You have excellent timing as always, Leon," Dorian said in thanks, their stomach heaving with the acidic flux of suppressed anger. Ever's memory cast a long, murderous shadow, and the touch of Lord James stung their soul, burning them hot and cold.

Leon squeezed their arm, looking extremely pleased, and led them up through the reaches of the Brightspir, beyond the levels that they or anyone else regularly frequented and even beyond the imperial wing, where the king's chambers lay, away from the suites and parlours, ballrooms and libraries, council rooms and gardens, as the breeze swept down with the heady scent of flowers in bloom. The floor beneath them became brushed in a thin swathe of blown-away petals. Vines wrapped around pillars and railings, bunched with clusters of tiny jade and moonstone grapes. Perfume rolled off them.

Coloured glass danced on the floor and the great obsidian stair was clean of Shye's blood. Dorian remembered him sprawled at the top and running, racing through this forgotten hall, ignoring the throne that no doubt stood empty at the end of the landing and the chamber above. They gave Leon a look and started up the stairs.

"Until we know what currents are moving around us, I didn't want you to do something ill-advised," Leon answered, climbing up behind them.

"Who advised you that what I was thinking would be ill-advised?" Dorian bit out, with a harsh edge of amusement. They could admit that Leon was probably right.

Leon stopped them near the top, sincerity and caution stalling them. "You know much less than you thought."

Dorian frowned, and a voice echoed out from the throne room, crackled with age but warm and hale.

"Now that is fascinating."

Dorian's feet dragged them forward. A shaky, unwanted blur welled up across their vision as they stumbled towards it.

The splayed doors opened into the chamber, light reverberating across the space, and standing within it, straight-backed and strong despite his apparent retirement and supposed death, was an old man. A hunter disguised as a guard with eyes only a few shades brighter than Dorian's.

Ever leant back from his appraisal of the flowering tree behind the old throne, clasping his hands behind his back and flashing Dorian an affectionate smile.

"Ah, my dear, I fear I must apologise for deceiving you. For all his perceived sins, this is one crime your father did not commit."

"You're alive."

Dorian felt their legs give under them and they slid heavily to meet the floor; flickers of pain registering in their knees. Their eyelashes flickered against the threat of tears but couldn't hold them from dripping past their nose. Brushing a hand over their wet cheeks, they swiped away the snot gathering on their top lip. Their body started to shake, trembling hands wiping away the muck onto their clothes. Covering their face as a sob made its way up their throat, they hoped that even if they couldn't stop it, they could at least hide from the embarrassing display.

Ever crouched and flopped a handkerchief in front of their face, while a calloused hand stroked their hair away from their face. Dorian slid their hands away from their pinking face and grabbed the cloth. Ever's reassuring grasp latched onto their shoulders.

"And thus, we remember our lesson on the value of carrying a handkerchief at all times," he teased, "as you never know when a family member might unexpectedly return from the dead."

Struggling not to sob – their throat trapping the little whispering hitches that threatened to spill over their lips – Dorian blew their nose into the hanky, their eyes flowing water. Leon's hand clapped down on their head. Warmth spread out from the spot, and Dorian blinked quickly, pulling themself together with a self-conscious cough.

"I wanted to tell you earlier," Leon admitted, crouching carefully next to them, as if waiting for Dorian's anger. All Dorian could manage was a quick fist to his shoulder, but there was no anger in it. It thumped against the armoured filament in his coat. Even if Leon had figured it out first, even if he'd known all along, the only thing Dorian felt was relief.

Ever chuckled a little and pulled Dorian, with Leon's help, to their feet. He valiantly rejected their gestured offer to return the hand-kerchief.

Patting their hand with a barely disguised look of disgust, Ever said, "You keep it," which made Dorian laugh, and they swept away the remaining salt tracks on their face, shoving the hanky into a pocket.

Ever eyed them both, a hand coming to rest on each of their shoulders. He patted Dorian's cheek on the way with a smile.

"Good to see you, my dear," he said, tone dry and laced with happy humour, running true and unyielding underneath. Dorian sucked in a breath as they felt the weight of his gaze on them. Steeling them. And the well of emotion inside dried up under it like it had heard the drums of a hunt on the horizon, or the drums of something else entirely. His hand squeezed on their shoulder, their family ring catching and pinching into their skin, suddenly serious. "And if we're all done with that, there are things we must prepare for. I rather think . . ." He took his grip away and looked to the old throne. "Yes, I rather think that there are storms on the way and the crowning is near indeed."

Captain Ezra Creed moved by nightrun. After so many years spent at sea, it was odd to be in Emin Rif again. This was the capital of his birth, where the house he'd been born into no longer existed, the Creed name as blistered and scorched as the fires the king had lit on their estates. His family had never hidden who they were, and worse than being openly folk, they'd been folk who'd challenged the king's right to rule them. After all, Ezra's blood had been passed down from one of the four original lords of these lands, the Dusk Lords who'd chosen to serve the first king and a stolen crown in exchange for their lives. Lives they'd spent trying to protect their own kind and win back what had been taken from them.

And even now, Ezra had a Dusk Lord's seal to prove it. There were only four true seals in existence, one for each of those first among the Dusk Blooded.

He twisted the ring on his thumb three times around. It was a habit he hadn't been able to shake since it'd first been placed on his hand, though he felt no nerves and held no superstitions that were not true, though the world might not agree. He'd had it reforged before he'd left this place. Now, a jade mast drifted within a spherical compass-rose of misted glass, flanked by a set of fan-like sails. Even newly shaped, there was no escaping from the history it held. The history of his world and his family.

A history written in Blood by those four who fell to Camillus's *generosity*; their stolen crown firmly upon his brow as he issued forth an empire that waxed humanity as theirs waned into trickling folk-lines and nothing more. The seals – Ezra's seal – were a promise that they were not gone for good. That they could one day return.

The world was wrong and the folklines were fading. Camillus had made it so. His manipulation of the Dusk Lords, his desperate longing to avoid shedding their blood because it was part of his own, his determination to avoid it, meant they were still here to undo that mistake. And if they managed to stumble on a true peace at the same time or they started a real war, well, Ezra was ready.

And that seal of the first king's, a fifth ring forged for a false Dusk Lord, for a king with a stolen crown, had fallen to a human as it must. Not to the imperial prince as expected, but an ally. A human who saw the world for what it was, the Strangeness of it slowly dying.

In gaining that when he'd been so much younger, he'd lost – along with his family, title, and home when he'd left – trust in those Lords who were left behind. The blackening of his family, the razing of their estates, the guards with their spears tipped with black iron, and the following suppression, had sent a clear message to all other folklined nobles within the capital, and many had sought refuge else-where or took to seclusion in fear of a cull.

He did not know if anyone else had escaped the fires, but he had heard nothing of his family since. The Creed name had been given by the first king and the last had washed it away, leaving only Ezra to carry it defiantly onward. It had only taken one of them to fall, and the previous king needed do nothing more to assert his power over the Blooded remnants in his dominion. Titles and the promises of a long-dead ancestor meant nothing to a human king.

Through lightrise, Ezra had sailed the *Oathbreaker* up the Amor-sithe River; dark like night-thorn wine, and running inland from behind Corentin, flowing through the Starless Caverns beneath the Wild Mountains, where Ezra and his trusted partners snuck into the capital at evenspan. They left the *Oathbreaker* and the rest of their crew in the deep estuary before the mouth of the cavern stream, among the wreckage of lesser smuggling ships, their rotted bones the only remains of the unfortunate humans who couldn't tell up from down in the bottomless, sparkling waters.

They had not come for Shye.

That was what he'd told Alice, regardless of its truth. The Empire would betray the Stormborn eventually, would betray them all, as it had been doing for centuries. It could not be trusted with Shye, not since it had abandoned him in the floating city as a child to die at the hands of the vicious Blood that ran in the outer seas, feral and forgotten.

They were in Mistral to meet Ezra's associate and to meet with the other seal bearers still in the city to see if they would help. They would need it, if they were going to break the coronation before Cassius could be crowned.

Ezra had led his main crew through Mistral's wandering streets, using the ancient folkways to pass unseen, settling, at last, to wait for the appointed time in a ruined courtyard behind the closed, battered gates of Ezra's family home, in the southern districts of the Bright-spir's vast shadow. Blackened and browned vines stretched out across the estate at their backs. Orchards and a vineyard within the landed interior were once a respectable inheritance, and then their gains were given away by sovereigns past, and their fields burned for insolence. No one owned these lands now, left desolate on the edge of the city.

Edge squatted, using a circular whorl of blackened bricks to build a fire pit, while Butler trawled through the wreckage, yanking bits of timber out from the ruin for Edge to add to the licking flames.

Ezra watched Muse closely, his violin left safely onboard the ship for now, his face darkly contemplative.

Alice handed Muse a drink from her flask. They had grown close since Shye had left; the two people who could and would talk about him still, even as everyone else, himself included, stayed silent on the subject of their wayward Stormborn. And, despite its vacancy, Alice had not reclaimed her quarters from their runaway.

Ezra might not be here for Shye, but those on his crew, even Edge and quiet Butler, they were. He let them hope, perhaps vainly and far down, that they would get the chance to drag their boy back home. Providing Lord James's whelp, Dorian, didn't do a flattering job of convincing him to stay first. Ever had much to answer for when it came to his family, for all he'd done Ezra the *kindness* of filling all his recent letters with the rumours he'd heard of Shye and Dorian's exploits since their arrival, which had all but convinced Ezra that his ward had been seduced and not by the wonders of Mistral. Where the young hunter had landed upon a countenance so incredibly adverse to their stern-faced sire, a man whose fine exterior, in Ezra's opinion, was neither backed up by wit or geniality, and therefore lacking in true charm, only Kernon knew.

And even then, that was supposing that there was anywhere for people of their blood and reputation to stay after this. If this little rebellion didn't succeed, then the Dusk Lords would have failed a second time, and all their planning and preparation would be wasted. The Blooded would never rise again. Their family lines would decay until there was nothing of them left at all and even the Wild Mountains forgot the folk who had walked among the trees. His family had raised their voices and been crushed, so Ezra would take back the crown without a sound and the line of the first king would finally be broken. His Empire, his tyranny over the Dusk Blooded, breaking with it.

He tipped his head back to track the violet stars as Muse started humming, accompanied by the popping of wood and the crackle and spit of embers. The smell of smoke tainted the air, but Ezra supposed in a dark way that it had never truly left this place.

Alice knocked his arm and proffered her flask with a small smile, before sitting down at his side. He took the canteen from her fingers and gulped down a swig. The refreshing taste of plum spice slinked warmly through his gut. Across the firelight, Muse began to sing.

Ezra sighed and handed back the flask.

Alice took it gently, her round lips forming the words to sing along; her voice sounding sweet and even.

Edge picked up in the chorus.

Butler shared him a look of bemusement but slipped into keeping time with punctuated claps and alternated slaps onto the brick ground. His low, rumbling voice complementing Edge's husky rasp.

Ezra closed his eyes on the nightrun and the shadow-flecked faces of his companions. The slow melody of the song seeped through the wind and pushed a little smile onto his mouth. In time, he started to sing, picking up the counterpoint, while the light in Muse's eyes across the circle became a wild and sparkling thing.

Silence pulled in around the city as the nightrun grew longer and darker at their backs, but it found no welcome in their circle; their voices rising as they reeled through verses, one song becoming another and then another. The moon would soon be dark before its second run from its highest ascent to travel the second half of the sky's domain. Under that second run, there would be a meeting, the purpose of which was an end to the Empire.

An end that, Ezra could only hope, would set the world to rights.

CHAPTER 25

WITH EVENSPAN FADING AROUND THEM, EVER SETTLED GINGERLY NEXT to Dorian, bunching his old joints together at their side. The old throne room, like most along any walls of the palace, cut away to display the far-off horizon and the city before it, where the glowing moon was ascending into its first run; a watchful spy in the violet night.

Dorian drew their legs up to their chest, arms wrapping around them. The lights of Mistral waved to and fro beneath them. Leon had left hours ago, hurriedly taking some rudimentary sketches in a small notebook before rushing off, scribbling notes and muttering to himself, with a pencil stuck behind one ear and another sliding between his fingers. He would be noticed, unlike Dorian, if he went about skipping appointments.

Dorian had not yet called in on any council meetings, and presiding over the guild had taken a backseat since the incident with Veredan. Any urgent business had been dealt with by the couriers, who ran themselves out between the guild house and wherever Dorian was – usually wherever Shye was.

Leon was probably out making himself useful, drinking with

Lorqin, and he would probably return with the patrol routes for the nightrun and the current number of the guard.

Dorian would leave him to it. Their presence tended to have unexpected reactions as of late, somehow both more and less popular than ever.

The hunter who brought home a Stormborn garnered drinks and toasts, while the Huntsman who divided a guild got polite, perfunctory remarks and cool, hostile glares. Dorian didn't mind overly much, but they'd never be able to charm like Leon could, especially with their reputation so thoroughly garbaged by their own hand.

A laugh burbled in their throat and a flush of mirthful warmth swelled, but they held it inside. Ruined with no regrets. They weren't sure how Ever had managed to avoid detection thus far, but they should ask. A quiet life with Shye became more appealing by the day as the coronation heralded its imminent arrival across the city with bountiful strings of glass and wreaths of fragrant blooms.

When was that again?

A frown drew down their mouth and they sighed. Ever glanced over, his crinkled face lifting. Their family ring winked on his third finger, resting on top of his knees.

Dorian recalled Leon's own ring. Worn since his parents had passed several seasons ago, the circular scrollwork flashing with every pass of lantern light as he had taken notes: the skeletal hand at its centre fierce and strong. A circle speared in half.

Their frown deepened. They had admired both before, as though their eye was continually drawn to them — just like in the guild hall before their hunt for Shye had begun and in the wine garden as Leon had sketched them a map to Corentin — but had not perceived the similarities. Another thing they should be asking Ever about. Their tongue felt heavy in their mouth.

Well, they didn't have all nightrun to get answers.

"Why'd you do it? Pretend to die and let us all believe it," Dorian broke the silence.

Ever looked at them out the corner of his eyes, their family ring seeming to glimmer at them. "In some ways," he answered, "it's difficult to explain, and in others, suspiciously easy."

Dorian grunted and Ever spread his hand to plead for their patience.

"Easy first, my dear. No doubt the difficult will come soon enough."

He took a breath. "I did it because it had to be done. I did it so they wouldn't do it for me and wouldn't look once it was done. I can't continue my work in the capital if I am truly dead and so the secret of my living is yours and Leon's to keep, the only people who can still move within the city who'd I'd dare trust with my life. Well, two of the three."

His old face crinkled, and his hand came down on their shoulder, catching in their hair, and he kept speaking even as Dorian's confusion played out across their face, pinching their brows, and wrinkling their forehead. "And now, I must tell you the difficult bit. The why. Why everything, including why things are changing now and only now, why they must be allowed to do so and why we must defend that change when it is opposed, when no one else will, and damn anyone who tries to stop us. The time for it has come. I made our move and, soon, they will make theirs."

Dorian shivered as a surge of dread shattered through their bones, recalling Jin and Cassius, and how they'd seemed like something else earlier, something different. And Shye. He had to be a part of this.

But who were they? And what did they want?

"You know this," Ever acknowledged solidly.

Dorian met his eyes and slowly nodded. They did. Here was their chance to understand it.

"Tell me."

The sound of the knife thunking into the wall blocked out the sick feeling in Dorian's stomach. Flipping another dagger deftly through their fingers, they sent it sailing across the room to embed next to the first, pointedly trying not to brood, and failing. Though their eyes were dry, there was an anxious watery sensation clenching their stomach, but it seemed like a waste of energy to fret over history long since erased from the world. Except that it was Shye's history, the history of his people, and it mattered to Dorian.

Their fingers twitched, their eyes growing dark. They were out of knives.

The Dusk Lords, the ones Ever had spoken of in stories, the high lords of old and their glory years ruling the seasons, the ones who bore their blood, were in Mistral. Some had never left. Dorian had never heard their true title before tonight and never of the betrayal of their people. Never of the true power of a crown and how it brought down the Blooded. Dorian could hear it again in their mind. *Tell me*, they had said, and now they understood.

The Dusk Lords had been waiting a long time to undo their past.

They hadn't fought Camillus, the Empire's glorious first king. They chose to survive and for that choice, others of the folk had lost their wills and their ways and each subsequent act of rebellion from their descendants could never change that. No war, not even a fight to go down swinging. Dorian clenched their hands into fists. That was intolerable.

Their hand crept up to the ring that Ever had pushed onto their finger before shooing them off.

"Did you know? What your ring, your seal, meant? That you were one of them, a prince among the folk, born to rule the seasons like one of the high lords from Ever's stories because they weren't just stories. A Dusk Lord living in the land of your enemies, pretending to be one of them, helping me hunt your Stormborn."

They glared at their knives, so far away now, longing to feel the swift deadliness, the satisfying glide of them through the air. Dorian's question was met with careful silence and they sighed, standing, their joints popping as they went over to collect their daggers from the wall.

"Did you know what we did to you?" they asked and heard Leon shift uncomfortably out of the shadows near the doorway, mute in face of the knowledge that was now swirling around Dorian's mind, filling in the gaps of a story that had only been told in pieces, in whispers, and lies. "Did you know that the Dusk Lords didn't really leave until the king's suppression. Until Cassius's father, my great uncle, destroyed his own court over what you were, the fact that you even existed in his sight and dared to claim a title that made him recognise you? Even though you had so little left to take or claim."

Ever's voice was still repeating over and over in their ears.

"Some left the city for the safety of the outer lands. The other Dusk Lords went quiet and still, they hid themselves away, their folklines already dim with time. The seal that marked them as princes among mere men were left to them by their ancestors."

Shye's rooms were filled with the same prodding emptiness that they had been when Dorian came home to them, and it filled them up with something unimaginably cold. They ripped knife after knife from the stone.

"Have you always known?" they asked quietly.

Leon stepped into the soft light of the room and touched them lightly on the shoulder. They turned slowly to face him, daggers threaded between their fingers.

Leon squeezed their shoulder slightly. "I have always known who I am. Just as I know who you are. You are one of the good ones, Dorian, I have never doubted that. We cannot linger on the mistakes we made, only take care not to make them again."

Dorian squeezed their lips together tightly. They brushed his hand lightly away and bent to shuck their collection back into their sheathes.

"Long ago there was a high lord, Dana of the Frost, chosen to rule," Leon started with a flourish, staring down at them. Turning away, his feet took him about the room as he recounted from memory. "And there was a man, a prince of Yren Fe Ire Fell, who had been banished from his lands."

Leon paused and looked back at Dorian, who crossed their arms over their chest as it grew tight. Still, they nodded at him to continue. Leon shared a small smile with them and returned to the recitation.

"When the frost took hold, the people chose Dana to carry the burden of the crown. She would keep the land in balance, moderate the fancies of the folk, and keep the order of their people. At the end of her season, Dana removed the crown willingly. The banished prince took it and placed it on the head of his son, Camillus. He said—"

"He said, 'Do with this what you will. It is your birthright, but though you are a prince of both lands, none shall have you. You are owed a crown, but they will not give it. So, we must take it from them,'" Dorian hissed the words spinning round and round in their head.

Leon came to stand in front of them again, the truth of what Camillus had stolen falling from his mouth. "And from Yren Fe Ire Fell, he brought black iron. There was no resistance, no rebellion. The Lords bowed to the will of Camillus, your first king, season after season, never again to have our turn to rule."

They hadn't just taken land. They'd brought poison to the folk and barred them from their own cities. But Dorian shouldn't have been surprised; the Horned Crown was and always had been everything to those that served it. And the crown served the king.

The folk had wrought it to serve their world. Camillus had only used it to serve himself, as had every king that followed.

"But even if we do not rule, at least we bow no longer," Leon finished; a heated determination lighting in his eyes.

Dorian turned their back on it.

Looking out to the balcony told them it was still nightrun, though nearly the second phase of it. They'd been here longer than they'd realised.

Ever would be expecting them and . . . wherever Shye was, it wasn't here.

Dorian's unease unfolded through their limbs, and they prowled out of the room and onto the balcony, but Shye had left better traces on Dorian than he had in the chambers he'd been living in for over half a season now.

Wherever he is, Dorian tried to reason, *he can take care of himself.* Worrying would get them nowhere. Unfortunately, that did little to stop the unoccupied parts of Dorian's mind, the ones less inclined to brood and not worry about the fate of the world, small though they were, from doing so. They flushed hot in embarrassment for themself, cringing at the damage Shye had done to them. Dorian had felt desire before, but this was wholly something else.

Even Ever had been able to see it.

"*Do not think*," he had said, after he had finished slipping their family ring onto Dorian's finger, "*that just because I've been dead, I've remained uninformed of your exploits.*"

The phantom squeeze of his hand wrapped around their arm, and Dorian closed their eyes, hearing his voice in their head.

"*I asked you to consider what was truly worthy of your talents. Perhaps, I should have asked you who instead. You are the only one who can carry this honour for our family, and you should carry it, if you can, for the boy as well. A world you can both live in is a worthy goal, Dorian.*"

Ever's eyes had twinkled at them as he lay his bare hands over theirs; the cool sapphire steel band digging into Dorian's skin. "*When all is said and done, I'd like to take the time to meet him.*"

Leon's delicate cough and the dimming heat of his keen eyes on them seared through their remembrance, and Dorian blinked to find themself standing numbly above the city, gazing into the distance.

"I'm sorry for what was done. I'm sorry that Camillus made you choose between your lives and everything else that you were. I'm sorry we seem to keep doing it."

Leon's reply came from behind them, hushed in a way that was unusual for the well-spoken man. "Thank you, but it wasn't us. We didn't do this. Not that anyone could have known what would happen to the Blooded. But it is our choice now to make something better and give back what has been taken."

Dorian heaved a breath of nightrun air and then came back into the room. They started forward hesitantly and caught Leon as they went. Side by side, they trudged with him down through the Brightspir and out into the darkened streets.

Through the centre of the city, they avoided the patrolling guards with an ease that attested to Leon's charm and excellent memory. When they were out of danger of being spotted or followed, trailing the dusty paths of the outer districts, Leon finally said, in a low, unquestioning voice, "Still, you have reservations?"

Dorian rolled their eyes at him, their oracle, and answered softly, "I do."

"You are unsure about committing to this? You are worried about Shye and concerned about what this might mean for Cassius?"

"I am."

Leon grabbed their arm to halt them as a pair of flickering torches, and the only pair of guard boots to walk this route, trooped by. He flicked Dorian a quick glance and led them on, speaking again when he felt they were unlikely to be overheard.

"But you wish to know who is involved so you can decide whether you'd rather be a traitor to the crown and your cousin or a traitor to your heart."

In a perfect world, I'd be neither.

Dorian huffed and said nothing. This was not, after all – with everything Ever had told them – a perfect world.

Leon took that as permission to continue. "Although the answer is already obviously clear. Yes, one side can give you titles and land and is the only family aside from Ever that you actually like, never mind that the Empire itself is as closed-minded as your father. However, the other you'd like to bed for the rest of your life, so—"

Dorian choked on air and punched Leon, not gently, in the kidneys. He let out a surprised *oof* and covered the mild pain with a mirthful laugh; the heaviness that had trailed them from Shye's room slinking away at last. They pointed their finger menacingly at his nose.

"That . . . that is not anyone's damn business."

Leon rubbed his back and shot them a fond look. "Stop pretending you have to decide, Dorian. You're going to pick him."

His smile shifted viciously. "Because he—*ugh*."

Dorian elbowed him in the stomach.

"Finished?" they clarified politely, spying the estate up ahead, its charred outsides lit by the orange glow of a fire. Dorian's chest seemed to seize with the weight of knowing.

Leon nodded, quelling a smug smile to one corner of his upturned mouth.

"Not everybody's loyalty lies between their sheets," Dorian grumbled, ignoring the heaviness that threatened to retake them, and making Leon laugh when he heard them.

"Naps are very important for the soul," Leon replied, a certain wickedness glinting in his eyes.

Slipping through the battered doors, they rounded the small foyer and stumbled through the blackened and breached wall to the courtyard. A small fire hosted several figures around it, with Ever perched among them on an upturned bucket. The chatter stopped as they stole into the fire's splay, and a pair of darkening green eyes met Dorian's before the sound of five pistols cocking broke across the air and the captain's low, rich voice rumbled at Dorian, "I hope you've been taking good care of my ward, Master Hunter."

Dorian watched in horror as Leon's eyes narrowed.

"Oh, you have no idea," he drawled, and Dorian snapped over with a swift and subtle kick to Leon's shin, murder flashing in the shadows of their face.

"No one needs you to clarify what type of care I am taking, right now," Dorian hissed.

One by one the pistols uncocked and disappeared back into belts or inside shirts. The captain's brows rose across the flames at Dorian. They pinched Leon in retribution for his smart comment, his yelp echoing through the nearly empty grounds, and walked closer to the huddled group.

"Can't say I'm filled with confidence, Grandfather," Dorian said, glancing around the spill of firelight. "Leon may be a Dusk Lord in disguise, but I doubt that carrying this ring of yours makes me worthy of the title."

Dorian tapped their finger, where the black opal and sunstone was radiant like the moonstone and pearl in Leon's, and the jade and smoky glass Dorian had never seen before in the captain's.

Something moved out of the corner of Dorian's vision; a shadow, small and swift. They barely saw it move before it was gone. Their eyes narrowed. They watched the spot it had been in while trying to listen as Ever started speaking.

"We cannot allow the coronation to succeed. Cassius cannot wear that crown if the Blooded are to live, the first king's line must be broken for the world to change. If another king wears that crown – now when there is a chance we can do this and we fail, then there is no coming back from what is. When Cassius removes the crown before the ceremony, he will have surrendered it willingly, then it can be taken."

"Who will take it?" Leon asked next to them. "And why can we not simply destroy it?"

The shadows remained still on the other side of the wall and Dorian relaxed, allowing their attention to rest with the group.

Ever reached out to the fire, stretching his pale fingers to the flames, saying, "The Stormborn is the only one with Blood pure enough to unravel the will of Camillus and undo the damage of his reign. He will be its wielder. Only he can bear it into the wilds, only he can beg the mountain lord for its cleansing and keeping under his eyes."

"We'd destroy it completely if we knew how," the captain answered from the other side of the fire, glaring into the flames. Dorian was once again struck that there was something familiar about him, about the grey and silver coat that complemented the hat they'd once worn but which now sat next to a green cloak thrown carelessly over a dressing divider in Shye's rooms. They should retrieve it at some point; it was their favourite.

Dorian shook the distracting thoughts from their head, butting in. "Who's to say he'll accept?" Their eyes flicked back to where the shadow had been and then roved back when they saw that again there was nothing there. "So, I got him to the capital where he needs

to be, but you can't guarantee he'll say yes. If he wields that curse"—
Dorian shot a glance around the circle—"who knows what happens?"

Ever looked back at them sharply.

Dorian drew up straight with a slight shake of their head, then
said to Ever with determination, "I won't speak for him. My words
won't stand for his. You can't guarantee that he'll agree with this."

The captain watched Dorian from across the fire, with something
oddly admiring in his eyes once you looked past the Strangeness of
them. When Ever called on him, he named him Ezra Creed. Dorian
remembered that name. It was a name that was etched into the walls
of the burnt-out husk they were gathered in and below a portrait of a
much younger man in their grandfather's old assignment papers. So
this was the man who had started Dorian's hunt for Shye with just a
slim scrap of paper signed EC and a set of navel coordinates.

Dorian stared back at the captain challengingly. Ever called on
Creed again and the captain waved a vague hand but would not
speak for Shye.

Dorian saw the shadows move again.

After a moment of silent discussion between the two men, Ever
said, "The Horned Crown called him here. His blood cannot ignore it
when it is so close. Choice does not come into it."

He glanced around the highly Strange group and at Dorian. "For
anyone here."

Dorian grunted, not desiring to argue, and watched the shadow
resolve itself into the shape of a curious youth spying on them. Dorian
couldn't say if this was right, or that Shye had been called by the
Horned Crown like they said, or that he would accept it when the time
came, but they would bet their life that that shadow belonged to Jin.

And anyway, they had heard enough. Dorian walked away from
the fire, with the eyes of the figures at their back heavy upon them.
Leon jerked towards them, but they waved at him to stay.

"You carry the seal of the first king, a false Lord," Ezra called to
their back, not raising his voice but it reached their ears all the same,
"but we're running out of time. The last seal bearer is lost to us, she

chose a different path. Have you considered that if you walk away now, you also walk away from Shye and the reason he exists?"

Dorian lingered near the edge of the courtyard, the group of figures watching for their reaction. The captain's crew challenged them with their steely eyes flickering in time with the jump of the flames.

"How can we change anything if all you do is steal back a stolen crown, repeating to us what our ancestors did to you? That isn't peace. Shye is more than just a Stormborn; he is change itself. It's not that I won't help you, but surely Cassius deserves the same consideration you're giving me. Tell him what you know and let him make the right choice," Dorian said.

"Cassius is weak. Camillus rules him," Ever said.

Dorian started at the cold tone of Ever's voice. They trembled to see the hard-edged expression on the face of a man who'd always been warm to them, who'd respected his prince, who'd served the crown and served it still, if not for the reasons Dorian had thought. A flash of something spiralled through them. Dorian had been weak, too, blind and entitled; Ever hadn't condemned them. Couldn't a world that both Dorian and Shye could live in include even flawed men like Cassius too?

Ignoring Ever's grim pronouncement, Dorian jerked their chin towards the group and asked of Ezra, "You going to tell Shye before you do this?"

Ezra nodded; a laughing manner come to life in his eyes. "If he listens."

Dorian felt the twitch of a smile in answer.

"Unlikely."

But he'll do what he can, what he thinks is right. In that, I trust, even if I don't trust you. Dorian stepped into the darkened atrium, looking for the boy with a roving shadow. They walked out of the estate, following the scuttling darkness just beyond the gate. Jin's face peeked out from an alley across the way. The hair on their arms prickled as Jin rushed out. Had he been waiting for them?

Jin's nervous face stared up at them and he grabbed for them in a desperate grip, pleading, "Dorian, you have to speak to Cassius."

"Jin, what—"

Jin's eyes were void-like under the second phase of the moon.

"Shye's gone. Cassius sent guards to arrest him, but no one knows why."

Pain flared in Dorian's arms from Jin's grip, his nails raking skin and shirt. They shook him free, his voice turning to so much noise in their ears, their feet moved and then they were running, sprinting towards the shining rise of the Brightspir.

Ever's voice sang through their thoughts.

He is weak.

CHAPTER 26

SHYE STUMBLED DOWN DIM AND DANK STAIRS, HIS NOSE WRINKLING AT the pervasive smell of rotted flowers. The walls were close, extending out towards the bottom, and his hands skidded across the smooth stone, staining them with dust and grime. He came to an unsteady stop at the base, his chest heaving with panted breaths, as a radiating pain pinched in his side where a guard had struck his still-healing wound. A motley of bruises were rising on his wrists and arms from where they'd tried to grab him.

Sliding down the slimy wall, knees pushing up to his chest, he tried to catch his breath. There was no sky above him, and the walls of stone seemed to stretch into forever. Craning his head back, he wondered where he'd ended up. At least he was no longer in the palace in any way he could measure.

The guards had done their best to grab him before he slipped away and before Jin could return, but Cassius had been right about their inability to stop him if he chose to leave. If he'd been human, the calloused grips that cinched around his arms as he rounded a fountain in the gardens, trying in vain to get out of the Brightspir, would've pushed him to the ground. The twisting, blue-ish contours of the cultivated greenery at nightrun had hidden the flash of oiled leather and steel.

Shye touched his elbow. It twinged at the memory of him throwing it into one of his captor's breastplates in a desperate effort to shake himself free. He hadn't had a chance to appreciate his Blood Manifest for what it was before it had lashed out of him. The burn of white lightning had surprised them.

The guards had held on well, even blinded.

Then, as if hearing his distress, the wind had come howling at them through the open level. Light started to crawl up his throat and leak from his skin to shatter across the ground at their feet and break across the ceiling above their heads, and their knees brushed against his legs as they slid to the ground. The rush of force which crested the waves of the deepness inside him exploded outwards, the blackening kiss of breaking storms, rain, and thunder pushing them away.

At least this time he hadn't vomited, and nobody had stabbed him. Lightheaded and trembling, he'd lurched away, tripping over their winded, light-struck forms. The opening of a dark tunnel in the shadow of the garden stonework glided apart between the gloom and its blueish edges, twisting vines of stone lining the midnight ways and stinking of rotted blooms, and he'd wedged himself inside.

"What was that?" one of the guards said, groaning. The sound of bodies scraping themselves off the floor reached Shye's ears as he crabbed backwards into the tunnel.

"Find him," came the stern order.

The guards regrouped with surging, angry voices as they recovered, combing through the garden, eventually giving up, uttering curses and damnations. The light had broken up, but they were still blind to the entrances and warrens of the folkways, though Shye could see them and the flash of their lanterns as they passed from where he huddled inside one.

The flickering warm light faded from the serenity of the garden, and they left to report his loss to Cassius.

Cassius, who had finally found the time to visit his prize without an audience – no courtiers, not even Jin, who he'd sent away – and whose veins had turned gold under Shye's hands, and who had tried to have Shye arrested when he realised what it meant. That a human prince who'd worked hard to maintain order and peace for his people, placing them above all others and building upon the remnants of those that came before, wasn't human at all. He was one of them.

Echoes from the city filtered from somewhere in the distance, the sound of people and life, glints of moonlight tunnelling down from above and off towards drifting noise. The yawning maw beside him led back up into the bowels of the palace, and the guard patrols that were looking for him.

Slowly, his lungs stopped burning. He brought his grime-smudged hands up to rub his tired eyes.

Shye.

His little wind called him, urging him to get up.

"Go away," he slurred.

Humanity. He was tired. Tired of this. Was it possible to sleep for a thousand years and wake up when it was all over? His little wind nudged him again, cool breezes smacking against his cheek.

"All, they sleep. Long, they sleep. Not me," said a voice.

Shye's eyes shot open from where they'd been listing towards closed. Looking around the narrow folkway, he saw nothing beyond the dim glitter of stone. The breeze stirred the leaves and muck at his feet.

"That wasn't you," he said to it. Warily, he pushed himself to his feet. Skimming along the wall towards what promised to be an opening into the city, he heard it again. A strangled, warbling voice that seemed to come from a diverging path, a cut crevice just before the spindling drift of filtered light. "Not me."

A face peered out to blink at him. One Strange void-and-starlit eye – the pupil spilling into the iris – and half a pair of painted lips, the other half of the face hidden by the musty stone of the ways and the buildings they ran through. Then, she was gone.

Shye crept around the corner, away from the calls of Mistral and the twisting ropes of stone that beckoned a way out. He saw her moving down the narrow lane, dancing around slopes of tilted stone, spectral with her bare feet with sooty soles and her filmy dress that moved in the hypnotic way Tanith's did, but older, greyed and frayed around her thin ankles.

The little wind blew past Shye, tumbling his hair in his face, and chased after her.

Shye, it called his name.

The lady's voice floated back, "Not me. Not him. No, you can't have him."

Shye swallowed and followed after her.

She wandered through the folkways, never once stepping past a gate into a proper street, still mumbling as she went. He slowed as the woman stopped in the middle of the path, crashing into the wet and rough walls to make sure he wouldn't be see behind her and looked up for the first time up to see the stone around them ascending dizzily into the open sky. He had no idea where in Mistral he'd end up if he left the ways now. The breeze tugged at him as the lady lifted her foot, her skirts swaying, and giggled as she felt the wind's caress. Then she put her foot down and took off running. Twisting, turning through the maze of hidden lanes, the tight ways seeming to pull away from her skin even as she hiked up her skirts and twirled down them.

Shye sprinted after her.

The wind soared between them, the echo of her laughter ringing off the walls, and then she was gone. Shye skidded to a stop. The way seemed to converge on him, pressing inwards; the way ahead was clear and dark, bare shimmers of light bouncing off the rock from intersecting paths. A small, fragile hand touched him on the back.

He spun around, feet moving backwards until the cool slimness of the tunnels replaced the suddenness of her touch. She stood serenely in the middle of the way again, skirts still swaying with the memory of her wild dash. Her hand was still raised innocently in the air.

"Don't go chasing storms they say. Not me. The wind and storm chase me," she said in a high, inquisitive voice, not quite like she was talking to him. Her eyes looked right through him, the void in them leaving a bare sliver of colour and the rest of the cold nightrun and secrets glittering like stars inside them. She giggled girlishly again.

Then her face fell, and Shye saw something like tears in her eyes, the void inside them expanding. She looked at him, seeing him there before her, and the blackness rose up over him. Time slowed in a familiar way, lengthening like a rope being pulled taut between them.

"Someone stole the storm away. Bellows and blusters, whispers and thunder, they went away. To sleep they went, then wake to go away. Not me."

The nonsense spilled into Shye's ears, whispered in earnest, and the words tumbled incoherently from the void crushing his head between velvet-wrapped fingers. Then, loud and definite, he heard it, cutting through the unspooled nothing and faraway stars. He blinked dizzily in a dank, cramped folkway, a lady's gloved hand biting into the skin of his jaw.

She wobbled closer, hollow eyes sliding away, her voice silken clarity, "It wasn't the first time Tanith tried to kill you. Sacrificed to the Nain. Blood pays for Blood."

She smiled at him, nails unpinching to slide down his cheek lovingly. Slipping past him, light as a feather carried by the wind, which swirled around her skirts, she floated down through the rippling maze under and between the city streets. Ignorant of him, she began to hum.

Shye gasped a breath, eyes dry, the blood in his head pounding like he'd been under water. Reaching out to the wall to steady himself, he turned and resolutely trudged after her, trailing after the reverberation of her lilting voice.

"Coming home for supper," she called airily back to him after a time.

They turned through the ways until nightrun began to spill down on them and the walls pulled back into twisted branches of chipped stone.

"Guess what, Jin, darling, Mama's brought a friend"—she giggled at the dapples of moonlight—"Mama's met the wind. Mama's found the king."

She sat Shye down in a small parlour and smiled gently in his direction, halfway between seeing him and seeing nothing at all. Bringing out fragrant tea, served in dainty jade and glass-blown cups, she poured his to the brim. Then she sank into the only other chair in the empty, lamplight-soaked room, her feet dangling off the floor.

The house she had led him into was in the outer districts. It was cosy but obviously abandoned, with cracked seals webbing across the building, throwing wispy lines of coloured glass through every room inside. The parlour she sat him in was the only one not covered in a thick coating of dust; her nest of domesticity bundled between close walls, chairs and curtains liberated from who knows where, and a working stove in the corner, built into the interior of the cracked façade. Books lay scattered around the chair legs, and sketches, varying from deep black to shades of purple and ochre, were struck across the warm stone floor.

More than one, Shye noted with a dull throb, bore a harsh resemblance to Tanith. Jin and a man Shye had only glimpsed once also dominated the area.

Unsure of what to do, he held the chipped cup in his hands and sipped at the mild tea. The warmth settled inside him like a calming balm patching over his weariness, and a headache fizzled behind his eyes.

Jin's mother looked cautiously pleased as he relaxed. She nodded to herself as he took another sip.

"Ayslin knows. Though, a long time since she's served the king."

Shye's brows furrowed, cup on its way to his lips. He set it down on an upturned crate with a clatter. His eyes found their way back to hers, his stomach roiling.

She seemed unbothered by the noise or the paleness of his face and stared at him as though she had imparted something absolutely understandable and not at all confusing and probably treasonous. She nodded at him again.

"I'm not the king," he said.

She hummed in response.

Slipping off her stool, she came haltingly forward, reaching for his face.

Shye let her.

She traced softly over his cheeks and brows, skimming down his nose, and cupped at his jaw. Breaking away, she knelt on the ground and began to trace him onto the stone floor to join the other renderings. Her fingers slid near a sharply drawn likeness of a younger Tanith.

"Not him?" she said to it, inquisitively.

Her voice grew dangerous, and her clean, pinked nail dragged down Tanith's rendered cheek. "Not you," she bit out.

Shye watched as deft fingers sketched out his features. He slid off his chair to join the lady on the floor. Silently, he reached out to touch his mother's rendering. He'd never devoted much thought to his parentage; it hadn't mattered before. It didn't even really matter now, except that Tanith had tried to kill him, apparently more than once, and although he owed nothing to the Empire, the crown or the man who wore it, the thing that called him still whispered that it'd be his failure if it happened to anyone else.

Ayslin stopped, her hollow eyes tracking his movements, roving over the lines of the sketch.

"Who is she?" he asked, tapping the inky lines, aged enough to start to redden and brown.

Ayslin tilted her head, birdlike, and her mouth opened and then abruptly shut. She hissed through her teeth and then hummed but couldn't seem to find the words to express the fear and fury bubbling up in her blackened eyes. With sudden fervour, she picked up her paintbrush and began to draw again.

On a clear tile, she brought together twisting, curvaceous lines until the Horned Crown was wrought into the floor in running ink. She tapped it with her nail.

"One of us," she said urgently.

Shye stared blankly at her and then at the sketch. He tried to puzzle out how the crown fit into his question, but without a more specific answer, the possibilities seemed endless and overwhelming. The history that Ayslin apparently expected him to know made little sense in connection with the question he had asked of her.

Under his silence, Ayslin groaned and slapped her ink-stained hand to her breast and then pointed it at Shye's own.

"One of us. The first king stole the crown away. No more is it."

Shye found this no more enlightening than the rest, but still she continued, pointing a condemning finger at Tanith, with ink dripping down to splatter and stain her curved beauty. "Someone stole the storm away, but first the storm king stole from her. No more is she, no more. Blood pays for Blood."

Shye felt his headache throb to life as riddles and nonsense writhed from Ayslin's mouth, and he tried to shake them from his head, his hair falling in his face. His fists clenched, and he pushed to his feet, rooted to the spot because he knew he couldn't leave. Jin had said Ayslin would know and Shye believed she did, if he could hear it through the maze of madness in her speech. Slowly, he sank back down.

"I'm not the king," he repeated, lost as to what else to say. "Cassius—"

She interrupted with a giggle and assured, "Yes, one of us."

Shye looked at her in surprise, but before he could gather his thoughts or even begin to process how to proceed, with a startling cry, she drew his attention away and he was knocked back as she lunged forward to strike a violent line through the Horned Crown; ink bleeding into messy, indistinct lines.

"No more. Not him," she repeated heatedly. "Not her. Not me."

Onto the floor she scribbled a full circle with the curve of a black bone-thin wing slicing through its centre. "The crown serves the king. Not him, not her, not me. Long they sleep, all they sleep, but not us. Not yet."

She made motions in the air over the spreading ink, gazing up at him with broken eyes, the secrets in them spilling over in her shimmering pupils but unable to make themselves heard.

Slowly, she tried to speak them, as though she had trouble interpreting his confusion.

"With Cassius, we sleep. With Tanith, no more. Destroy the crown, destroy the sleep."

The tang of acid rose to Shye's tongue with the phantom slide of an iron dagger and Tanith's voice whispering that he would understand soon. *The crowning is near*, he could hear her in his memories, but he still didn't understand what Tanith meant. He swallowed and responded, his voice rough. "Whatever Tanith is going to do, I really doubt destroying the crown is part of it."

Ayslin crept forward, then grabbed him as she rose to her feet, black smears on her hands and skirts. "None can, no more is it," she said. "Not him, not her, not me."

Shye backed away, his thoughts whirling furiously, but Ayslin dragged him back, knocking her fist into his chest and demanding, "Listen!"

Shye stopped backtracking through the parlour and strained to muddle through as she dictated slowly, "Destroy the crown, destroy—"

"The sleep, yes, but I don't understand why! Or how!"

Frustration bled from him, even though he was trying to stop it. He tried to listen, like Ayslin told him. She clucked at him till he breathed in sharply, hissing him into silence with the sheer impatience that lit up her face. He was not impressing her with his understanding or his manner.

Shye held his churning mind at bay long enough to listen carefully to Ayslin's words, wondering if he'd ever hear them as clearly as he had when she'd told him about Tanith. If he'd understand her again long enough to *do* something about it.

"With Cassius, we sleep," she repeated again. "With Tanith . . ." She paused and poked her finger into his chest, finding the words.

"No more," Shye answered.

Ayslin nodded. "We are no more," she drew the circle and line with her finger. "One of us. No more. The end."

She saw comprehension dawn in Shye's eyes, as the hot slash of fever iron in his side surfaced once more. Heat rose above the deepness and he had to turn away from Ayslin's pale, even face.

"The storm stole it from her." His mouth struggled to form the words. His lips felt numb as he uttered Ayslin's damning secrets. "Cassius is Dusk and Tanith . . . is human. But then, why can't Cassius inherit the crown, why can't he fix it?"

Ayslin's face shifted, delighted that she had finally been understood, that the secrets that sparked through her mind could even be shared, rather than raging within her, so numerous and lost that they burned on her tongue, decaying her words to simple noise.

"None can," she repeated and then struggled to add, "No more is it. Corrupt. Broken. Dead. Dying."

She nodded her head at Shye and put her fingers to her head in an imitation of the famed Horned Crown, still terribly happy that Shye could understand, intoning earnestly, "With Cassius we sleep, dying. With Tanith, no more, dead. None can. Only the storm, awake, alive. Destroy the crown."

She shook him on the arm and repeated it, her hollow eyes gazing up at him, secret stars blazing. He felt the brush of wind through the room as though it was a thundering gale. He touched Ayslin's face gently and she returned the gesture with a beaming smile, letting him lead her back to her chair.

"Destroy the crown," she echoed and then giggled, patting his arm in a motherly way that was unknown to him. "End the sleep," she continued. "Save the world."

Shye's mind raced again, now with a mix of trepidation shivering across his skin and determination fuelled by this final comprehension. He couldn't hold back the slightly mad laugh that bubbled to his lips.

"Yeah," he said with a sigh, a Strange relief flooding through him, "that sounds about right."

CHAPTER 27

As he stood before the throne that he had never doubted was his by right, Cassius wondered which Cassius Sands, if any at all, Mistral would have rule it in spans to come – the Cassius of that truth or the one with the gold that now twisted under his skin.

By next lightrise, he would be king.

Seasons, even years, of preparations had come and gone for the results of that final nightrun, the last of the season after his twenty-fifth span. His minority had ended long ago, but tradition had said he should wait. Had he been waiting so long for this? For wondering if it would be better, in the end, to step away.

In doing so, he'd be leaving his Empire open to civil war as the line of succession would be broken for the first time in written history. His father's family had built this Empire, starting with Camillus, and after him no other outside their family had born the crown he'd given them. They made and upheld peace. Cassius's duty hadn't changed just because his blood had.

Yet under the rushing of it, something shivered awake, and it rang with Dusk. The chill of a coming frostfall curled deep inside his bones.

His father's line was already broken if he could be Dusk. And the people of Mistral, the whole of the Empire, weren't his people anymore. A select few among the population but no more than that, and they lived in this place that wasn't made for them, which had been taken away from them.

It had made sense. There were more of them – more humans than folk. Their dispositions, influences, and manifestations were chaotic and terrible. They resisted order, resisted humanity itself. He was one of them.

This Empire, this throne – they belonged to someone else.

Which Cassius would sit here, if any? He held up his hand, trying to see the glow that Shye had coaxed from within it, but it remained invisible to him. The throne seemed to dare him to return to it. He remained still.

It mocked him for not knowing.

With a sigh, he lifted the Horned Crown from his head and rubbed his temples; the weight that rested there seeming to grow the closer his coronation loomed. With the crown dangling from his hand, Cassius stepped up to the throne.

Inside him, there was something swirling, like snow falling upwards. The new throne room gleamed all around him.

During the rise, it would be decked in flowers and wreaths of silk and glass. People would arrive within the public wings of the palace to wait for nightrun to fall. His fingers skimmed along the sleek, chiselled lines of the stonework and a shudder tripped down his spine.

Cold burst at his fingertips.

He couldn't help but suck in a breath, and from it flowed calm precision. With some fatigue, he placed the crown back over his brow, welcoming the cooling rush of sharpness. The guards at the entrance admitted Lord James to see him, and Cassius straightened his shoulders, re-collecting some command and ignoring the pain that lanced down his neck to settle tensely in his shoulders.

His father had never betrayed the weight of kingship; he could only try to do the same.

"Your Highness," Lord James greeted with an abnormal geniality for the early rise. He knelt quickly as Cassius returned his greeting and did not wait for leave to rise and grip him considerately on the shoulder.

"You look tired," he stated, as kindly as he could manage.

True and genuine dispositions were a talent reserved for the folk and a few gracious humans, while the rest of them affected when they could and lied for the rest. Cassius included. He had been the prince long enough to know how quickly sincerity died in Mistral, and in that the Stormborn had been a refreshing change. He'd had an obvious disposition for truth.

Cassius already knew it would not be the same for him. That talent was not in him, but he had liked it in the Stormborn. Even if his element, his Blood, his very being, had proved too forceful to cage, striking all too easily and disappearing without a trace. It might be a while before Cassius could play on that field, as finding his element and disposition and manifesting them would not only take time but required he accept that he could even have them.

Lord James cleared his throat respectfully, pulling Cassius from his thoughts. He shrugged away James's grip and responded with a half a lie. "I suppose I'm nervous."

Lord James smiled and nodded. "To be expected, Your Highness. You, we, your kingdom, have been waiting for this moment for a long time."

Cassius gathered his thoughts into line, barricading himself from the curl of his insides, and urged Lord James towards the doors, saying, "Come, the council will begin soon."

"Of course," said Lord James and followed him from the room.

Cassius walked tall and proud as he knew he must, finding security in the limited paths that led forward from this rise to the next. In the end, it didn't matter which Cassius sat upon the throne, as long as the crown was his. He could never give it up to another. Never watch another place it on their head and know he had failed in the one thing he had been born to be. Whether it was right or whether it was wrong, at nightrun, he would take off his crown one last time as the prince, and by next rise, he'd be king of an empire. Human or Dusk, whatever the truth of it, whatever the lie, they were someone else's to

own. He was done with both. He would be king come lightrise or he
would be dead.

The Empire could take him as he was, whatever he was. Or it
could have one less king, civil war, and a dead prince.

Cassius scowled to himself. And that, he simply could not allow.

Ayslin made Shye rest before she let him leave her. She had plied him
with tea to bring warmth back into his bones, the deepness singing
within, rising with patience to see its task through. When he woke
the deepness would slick his skin, sweat fixing tacky at the back of his
neck.

Ayslin hummed while puttering around her little hideaway until
his eyes slipped closed. His limbs soaked in the fading heat and early
light that bled through the cracked walls to warm the ink-marked
stone floor.

He dreamt of the old throne room, the Horned Crown on its seat.

Lights danced in the corners of his vision and the sound of trees
cracking back to life from hard stone rung in his ears. Sapphire steel
winked at him, gleaming wood worn to a lasting polish, the horns of
it strong and unforgiving. He reached for them, his fingers curled
around the crown's grooves and graceful arches. Cold burst in them.

The sleek wood turned sharp, sliding through his skin, and
drawing blood that ran gold with every drop. Shye saw the darkness
coming for him, yawning open from the ancient thing between his
hands, swallowing the room and everything else, and seeping into
him like poison from the shining crown. Burrowing within, spreading
without. Dark and burning cold. Like black iron.

He screamed as it tore and blistered within him, the blood rising
in his mouth again, the taste bitter and vile. It dribbled down to leave
smearing crimson and gold on the crown, all-consuming in his
hands. A pool of it spread beneath his feet, the leaves already dusty
with blood from Tanith's ministrations.

The deepness abandoned him to its mercies, shrinking away from sheer will and centuries-old Strangeness. Shye bit his lip till it split and then it made him scream again.

He jolted back into wakefulness, curling into a ball on the floor, with a sharp ache behind his eyes. He rolled to the side and heaved. Bile splashed into a puddle in the corner of the parlour. Distantly, he heard Ayslin hiss at him.

The scream lingered in his throat, sour on his lips, and the deepness rushed back to comfort him. He rolled back over and lay there. Ayslin's hands came to rest gently in his hair. He could feel wetness under his eyelids and prayed it'd stay there.

A light breeze pulled at his clothes, diving over his form, ruffling the hair between Ayslin's careful fingers. It used no voice to call his name, but he knew what it was here to say. He could stay a little longer, but soon he'd have to go.

Destroy the crown, end the sleep, save the world.

CHAPTER 28

THE PATROLS WITHIN THE BRIGHTSPIR SEEMED TO TRIPLE OVER THE course of the lengthy nightrun. Dorian had pounded into the lower atrium just come lightrise and ran straight into Lorqin Mansel, the Captain of the Border Guard, heading upwards with a team of weary-looking troops behind him. The man also seemed to sag with the weight of little sleep and the return to sunning with no reprieve from work, but he lifted a hand to steady Dorian as they knocked sloppily into his shoulder.

"Whoa," he said with a grim half-smile, "long run?"

Dorian nodded, swallowing past the feelings swirling in their mouth, replying, "You have no idea."

Then, shaking off the well-meaning grip, Dorian hurried off again, moving through the common levels of the Brightspir towards the imperial wing.

There were no guards in that section, though they'd passed several patrols on the lower levels. Cassius's quarters were also unguarded, secure within the interior. Glass lamps were set into the walls to replace the minimal natural light and the stonework glimmered with seals. Half library, half personal office, Cassius's main rooms were a cluttered mess of papers and books, shining discarded clothes, and empty carafes of wine. His private room was often unslept in, with a long couch with battered pillows the substitute for a proper bed.

Dorian shoved open the doors only to find the chambers empty. They turned fluidly on their heel and strode out again. Coming out of the imperial wing, they seized upon the first patrol that crossed them, halting them with a scowl and a pointed look at their leader as they marched by.

"Where's the prince?" Dorian asked, a small bite to the end of their words.

The guards stopped and seemed inclined to stare, but their leader read from Dorian's face that they were not in the mood for patience and snapped the hunter a clean salute.

Dorian resisted an eye roll, their feet itching to tap on the polished stone.

The guard ordered them on, pausing to say as the line of soldiers passed, "Early council, Huntsman," with a tone and a hidden glare that suggested Dorian would not have to ask and waylay them if Dorian bothered to do their job and took their place on said council.

Dorian let it go, nodding sharply to the gruff leader and abandoning him there, staring after them and muttering under his breath before moving on with the rest of his patrol.

The main council room was on the crown's exterior wing, just above the common levels near the central wing; it was a large austere room with two grand fireplaces at either end to combat frostfall winds and heavy rain, and to stand empty during sun seasons. A map of the old empire was tiled into the floor, left from the centuries of the Blooded, and, like them, the kings kept no throne within it, only ornately moveable chairs set into a close circular formation.

Cassius's father had notoriously hated the room. The lack of desks and writing boards for the council members meant trusting the guild scriveners to record what was said, regardless of how sensitive. He'd conducted meetings in his offices or within the guild assembly rooms themselves. Whereas Cassius actually liked the old council room, the freshness of the elements and the visual of the lands they worked so hard to keep in line.

Dorian had no intention of ever attending a council meeting, regardless of where it took place, and, despite the heavy doors they hastily approached, they did not intend to start now.

Lorqin Mansel winked at Dorian. His hands were clasped patiently in front of himself, blocking access to the council, probably on someone's orders. Or he had deduced that Dorian would be coming, and it might get messy in a way that, even after a long night, Dorian figured Lorqin could still find amusing. His mouth twitched as Dorian charged down the hall towards him.

"Announce me," Dorian demanded, shooting the man a quick look out of the corner of their eyes as they came to a stop before the doors.

Lorqin's grim half-smile took on a genuine cheer as he huffed and pushed open a single door, sticking his head into the room beyond, courtly etiquette barely maintained.

"Huntsman to see you, Your Highness."

Dorian heard the hum of discussion halt.

Lorqin pulled back through the door and gestured for Dorian to go in. A twinkle lit up in his eyes that betrayed his enthusiasm for being outside the room when whatever would happen next happened.

Dorian narrowed their eyes at Lorqin and straightened their shoulders, pushing through the doors and into the council room, which was silent as they came in. Dorian ignored the council and moved over to the cutaways to find a column to keep them company until Cassius acknowledged them.

The prince was another – apparently among many – who had seen better nightruns than the one just passed. He headed the circle of chairs that supposedly made them all equal – guild heads and noble houses alike – but which was undermined entirely by the crooked shoulders of a prince who was trying not to slouch, Cassius's attention anywhere but with the council, his eyes staring vacantly across the tiled map beneath their feet, even as they talked in his direction.

He looked up as Dorian came in, shifted in his seat as the silence reached him, and then looked away again, signalling with an absent finger for the council to continue.

The council anxiously threw glances Dorian's way, ones of particular menace coming from the seat that was supposed to be theirs, before haltingly taking up the conversation again.

Dorian watched as Cassius shifted again. They fought back a smile. Did he feel their eyes on him?

Someone cleared their throat, catching Cassius's attention for a bare second, and the Head of the Guild of Glass began to speak numbers for the coronation, the state of their mining operations and the treasury. Then, the Head of Trade, who was formidable for using her Feng–Taren ancestry to run the capital's markets, despite the Feng's quiet detachment from the Empire, butted in and spoke of glass and deliveries, the logistics of supplying the coronation and the short feast to follow.

Lord James cut them both off somewhere around discussions with the representative from House Ashea over which vineyards would be providing the spice, and hushed them all with an authoritative, "Yes, thank you, Aulus, Shallow, my lady." He nodded to Lady Ashea. "Let's not pretend that this is the business we are here for. We're gathered to know who will be given the honour of crowning the prince. Anything else can be taken care of in private meetings."

Cassius remained silent, even as the council members waited on his answer. Slowly, his focus moved from the room to the people inside it.

"Dorian," he intoned, as though he was only just remembering that Dorian had come in. Mouths dropped open in shock, before closing again just as quickly when he finished, "You wished to speak with me."

With a sigh, he stood and everyone else stood with him. The scrivener on duty scurried to the back of the room. Addressing the members of the council, he continued, "I have yet to make a formal decision on the subject of my crowning, but I am aware that I lack the time to delay any further. Lord James, the task is yours."

Dorian's stomach turned over at the triumphant curl that came upon their father's smile and didn't miss the way it was briefly levelled right at them.

"Now, if you please," Cassius continued, gesturing to the door, "I have business with my cousin."

Dorian watched their father saunter out and wondered if this was going to put a big kink in Ever's plan. Whatever the plan was for retrieving the crown, whether Dorian was necessary or not, they'd have a hard time prying it loose from James's hands once he got a hold of it.

And whether or not Dorian would be doing the prying depended on Cassius.

One by one, the council members filed out. Cassius slumped at last into his chair, lifting his crown and pushing his hair back wearily. He set the crown back down with a certain heaviness that Dorian had rarely seen in him. The difference of last rise sat tensely in his shoulders, lacking all buoyancy and power, twitching him into restiveness.

"What can I do for you, Dorian?" He mustered up his spiralling focus to actually look at them. He had always been a curious mix of thoughtful and carefree, but the troubles crowding his mind were beginning to write lines on his face, and he had none of his usual temperament.

Dorian stalked forward into the centre of the room, cutting off one of the smaller islands of Feng on the map at their feet, their shadow shading the isles like the presence of a dark sun.

"Where's Shye?" Dorian jumped in, without any particular finesse.

Cassius's fingers tapped on the arms of his chair, his expression flashing through several emotions, all of them with that pensive, pinched undercurrent that had infected his youthful aspect with something old. And Dorian had assumed they were the only one in the family that was bad at managing their face.

Eventually, he settled into simple coolness. "I don't know. He is a threat, Dorian. If he is gone, let him go."

Dorian felt the acid drip, a contempt rising that was usually reserved for their father alone. It was unexpected to be so disappointed by someone else.

"A threat? If your rule is so weak that one folk boy can bring it down, perhaps we should consider that it is because you shouldn't be ruling in the first place."

Cassius's eyes flashed and the space between them shivered, the nipping bite of frostfall creeping in and chapping Dorian's lips, but then he sighed and the feeling pressing in on them splintered. The shivers in the air faded to an odd remembrance that no longer seemed real, only a trick of the old room.

"It is done, Dorian," he said finally. "The guards have their instructions. He is to be arrested, questioned, and then removed from my sight, my capital, and from any place within Emin Rif. He is not to enter it again on pain of death. Should he find respite in either Feng or Aura, I will command that they contain him so he cannot leave. If you see him again, you will fulfill your duty as a hunter once more, give the runner over to the guard to be dealt with, and forget your association. These are my orders. I'm sorry."

They bit their cheek to stop the rolling bitterness that spat in their gut, spilling into fumes in their lungs where it bloomed in their heart's blood. Sadness, shame, and grief for him. It shook through them.

Cassius's tired eyes landed somewhere to the left of Dorian.

Their chest burst and set in bloody pieces. *You are weak*, Dorian thought, and the sadness rose up again, *and Ever was right.*

Dorian nodded sharply at Cassius and closed their watering lids to save face. "Yeah," they choked and then held their breath till they were cast in iron once again. Shaking their head to themself, they turned their back, bitterness clogging the painful laugh on their tongue. "Me too."

CHAPTER 29

As soon as Dorian had compelled their way into the council's meeting, Jin took up a position out of sight at the end of the passageway. No one saw Jin, those coming or going passed him by without a glance, they didn't seem to notice or care that he was lurking in the area. When Dorian returned from their personal council with the future king, theirs were the only eyes that quickly caught on him.

They paused at the corner that protected Jin from stark visibility and scowled at him.

"What news, oh spy?" they asked archly, pursuing a determined pace as they set off, Jin loping alongside. He could tell their patience was wearing thin, their time so rarely spent within these walls, and their tolerance for the lordly machinations had never been high in the first place. Then add Cassius's mess and Shye into it . . . Jin decided to keep his mouth shut.

"Damn him," Dorian muttered, without provocation, sinking their teeth into the flesh of their mouth, eyes glaring ahead. They said nothing further, though their posture straightened, the tension sliding away into something more considered rather than doggedly wretched, their thoughts extending within.

Though Dorian hadn't known about his training or his small role in the web of Blooded schemes and crown politics, Jin had always found their peculiar friendship a comfort. The young hunter with a penchant for performance and Ever's merry twinkle in their shallow eyes did not choose their friends without care. When someone was dead set on carving a life that careened recklessly around the perceptions and expectations laid out for them by others, they had to choose their allies carefully. Cassius had failed Dorian in that room.

Jin could see the light of that revelation between the casts of shadow on Dorian's face as their trust in Cassius shifted. Dorian had hung between having every faith and having none when they entered. Hanging between Huntsman and traitor as Cassius spoke. Whatever he had said, in that slide of his breath, he had lost his loyal hunter.

"So, you've decided which crown you serve just in time," Jin said, adding lightness and flippancy to his tone, hoping they'd remember what it was like to tease and spar, to make bargains and smirking offence. Instead, Dorian gave him an unimpressed look, pushing their mouth into a spiteful sneer.

Jin flitted a small, satisfied smile anyway. After all, he already knew their answer and they hadn't managed to disguise the edge of goading that undermined the severity of their expression. "And damn the rest," Jin said.

He suppressed a wider grin at Dorian's surprise and said coyly, "That is your noble motto of late, correct?"

The look of surprise collapsed into mellow consideration, or at least the mask of one, as Dorian answered, "You're cute. And I'll allow your meddling, cryptic remarks and knowledge, but your fight for the crown ends there."

They brought their voice down and then fell into a deliberate hush as the way ahead broke out into the glossy, sun-speckled floor of an exterior walkway, where leaves shivered across the cutaways. Dorian pasted boredom across their face and walked on.

A smile, not exactly genuine and not exactly nice, pulled at the pleasant curl of Jin's mouth. "If it isn't my fight, it certainly isn't yours," Jin eventually deigned to respond once they were all out of earshot.

"I'm choosing this one, Jin," they said quietly after a time, and then with a bite of challenge and the savoury relish of it, "and damn the rest. Damn Cassius, damn them all, and damn me too for a traitor."

In the growing forthrightness of Dorian's step as they weaved the way ahead for Jin to follow, and the vanishing heaviness that traced them back to Cassius and the conversation behind those closed council doors, Jin could see they meant it.

Damn them all.

Patrols of guards jogged past, tracking repetitive routes across the grounds of the Brightspir. No success to be had capturing the missing Stormborn. *Good*, Dorian thought, *that means I still have a chance to get there first. To make sure he's okay.*

They halted Jin with a rough touch on his shoulder, the taste of a threat already on their lips, the burning need to finally have an answer. "Who hurt Shye, Jin? I need to know. Before whatever happens happens, I need to know who."

For once Jin did not try to disobey, disappear or derail.

"You have no idea who you're dealing with, Dorian. There are two sides to every fight and they're not going to let the Horned Crown go without one. You damn them and they damn you, and Mistral is damned as well, while Shye is forever caught in the middle."

"Cassius would never—" Dorian began.

"I'm not talking about Cassius."

Dorian's pale brows shot up and their focus narrowed on Jin.

Beneath the steely determination that had served them so well, borne about like armour, and the inclination to disbelief, which Shye's efforts had done a good job of cracking if not totally dismantling, they still felt relieved to hear that.

"Who then?" Dorian asked, crossing their arms restlessly over their chest as fire sparked in their chest. Inside Dorian, a persistent hammering battered at their determination to condemn Cassius entirely. Wasn't there a way, it screamed, to save something of them all, deserving or not?

Jin's fingers pulled at their wrist, leading them down and then hauling them into the break of the shadows in the corner the grand stairs, away from the atrium spinning out beneath their feet, strewn with dried flora for the crowds, incense wafting from unlit braziers.

Dorian took a quick catalogue of the branches of rock and glass that twisted above them, the tunnel which stretched out into darkness beyond Jin's small frame, a brief cloud of puzzlement passing over them. They shook themself out of it and said, "Later."

Like the snap of a fuse, they were back on Jin, pinning him to the wall with the intensity of their gaze. "Speak now."

Jin grimaced. "Lady Tanith—"

Dorian's brows cocked in surprise. "And here I thought you were going to say my father. It'd make sense that they'd be involved in this, him and his cronies. Especially Bellhall—"

"Lady Tanith—" Jin tried again but Dorian cut him off with a sharp sweep of their eyes, speaking over him.

"Is a voracious, untrustworthy Master of Accomplishment and companion of my father, who probably drinks diamonds instead of wine, but she hardly works for my father."

"She is a Dusk Lord," Jin snapped over them and continued before Dorian could open their mouth or do more than widen their eyes and hiss in their next breath, "or she was when my mother knew her. With an iron dagger. She does not work for your father; your father works for her."

"Tanith." Dorian drew the word over their teeth with feeling, shaking their head with a disturbed hum. A hand came up to sweep across their eyes, and when they brought it down, their composure hardened into stone. "And Shye?" they asked at last, hoping Jin had some clue, something more that might help them.

Jin shrugged. "I'm no oracle, Dorian. I can't tell you things I don't know."

Dorian breathed in and schooled their expression until it was still and smooth as polished glass. The boughs above them seemed to shift as their human eyes trailed over them. The way out glittered like an iced-over mirror, and the way ahead flitted into nothing except more shadow. Dorian turned and strode towards it.

"Coronation's at nightrun," Jin said to their back, with a note of warning. In the atrium, the rise was reaching its second span. Those who gathered in the city for the celebrations did not have a long rise to wait.

"I can't say I'll be ready, but I'll be there," they replied with a sharp look at Jin. "And you"—Dorian pointed finger at his chest—"will be well away."

They reached out to pat his head in an echo of the people they had been before Dorian's hunt and Shye's capture, when the secrets of the capital had been just that and the crown had seemed absolute and unchangeable, the Blooded doomed. Their hand faltered halfway and dropped.

"Until next rise," they farewelled, with enough implication to reinforce that they had meant it when they said *well away*. With that, they slipped into the sprawl of the city and didn't look back.

The Hunters' Guild House was quiet when Dorian approached; the obligation not being to work while the rise lasted but to get ready for the ceremony like it was the frost season already. The city was just starting its celebrations and getting back to the guild house had proved arduous as they had been stuck dodging shoulders and coasting through long-winded backstreets to avoid the crowds that clogged all the main thoroughfares. Dorian stopped only briefly to send away the messenger that waited for them there. Whether from Cassius or their father, they had no interest in further conversation with either man. If Tanith was involved – a Dusk Lord and a defector – and on a side that was neither Ever's nor Cassius's, then there was no point in wasting time with soon-to-be-meaningless summons.

No other hunters were in sight when Dorian swept through the entryway. They crept across to the assembly rooms and pulled the doors open a crack. There was a chance, if only a very small one, that Shye was hiding inside, waiting for Dorian.

But only Ever sat alone inside.

The old man's face was lost in contemplation. His warm, wrinkled hands were folded restfully across his knees, and the lighter skin where his ring had sat glared at Dorian from his seat in the place that Dorian wished they could return to him. Between them both, chills struck up Dorian's spine, settling behind their eyes, making them sting.

But he was alive. A liar and a special kind of traitor for what must have been most of his life, a man who'd claimed the title of Huntsman and risen to the noble elite through marriage to the then-king's sister, all the while working with the Empire's enemies to save the Blooded. Another inheritance that had skipped Lord James to come straight to them. But he was alive, and for all of that, Dorian could forgive him as long as he remained that way.

They twisted the Dusk Lord's ring on their finger – their family ring from Dorian's grandmother – and pushed away the guilty, wavering voice exemplified in it that said they'd never be free until this legacy was gone. A stronger voice – honest like Shye's – chimed in that that was exactly why Ever had done it in the first place.

Because humanity knows they couldn't trust Dorian's father to save Shye and his Blooded kin from the crown.

Through the gap in the door, Dorian saw Ever look up.

Their eyes met, and Dorian's breath caught, trapped like they'd been caught out, while a slow and crooked smile cracked across Ever's face. Then he gave them a look, barely a dip of the chin and a message within his penetrating gaze, and Dorian understood the meaning without a word.

He's not here. Go. Find him.

Dorian shut the door to the assembly rooms. As they stepped back out into the bustling city, they found the rise disappearing into evenspan around them. Stars began to shine violet, rose and gold across the changing sky. A surreptitious breeze swirled around their ankles, and they remembered the night it had led them to Shye's side, chasing them through the Brightspir's reaches.

Shye, it whispered eagerly, caressing their clothes and skin.

It tugged at them, playing at the laces of their boots, and rippling through their coat, pushing them towards the outer districts to the south-west, through the main market. Dorian hoped they could find Shye before the evenspan got any later, before the guard shifts changed and the Stormborn got the idea that it would be better if he left the city. The wind didn't help expel their worries as it whistled at them to hurry up.

"If only I had you on all my hunts," Dorian muttered to it grudgingly, setting off in the direction dictated by the wind pressing against their back.

Sshh, it hissed – just air – and then, like an echo, said, *Find him.*

CHAPTER 30

IF THE CROWDS OF PEOPLE WERE BAD BEFORE, COME THE FIRST GLIMMER of evenspan they were even worse. Everyone in the city seemed to have some last-minute appointment, and they flitted in and out of dress shops, gem artists, cosmeticians, and clogged all variety of market stalls for small bits of finery, newly blown or cut glass to drip down their gowns or over the backs of their suits, and appropriately jubilant spreads, trying to put on their best for the prince's coronation.

Children ran and played in the streets; noble younglings free from tutors and those from the lower districts free from their apprenticeships. They spread garlands of cheap lapis and artificial frost stone, matching the new king's family ring, across Mistral's sealed streets.

Blossoms of night-thorn and wreaths of edible buds, and quartz imitations of expensive pearls, fought for dominance all over the city. Strings and weaves of them dangled from balconies and light posts, stretching in lines dotted with round candle lamps across the tops of buildings and overhead, and trodden underfoot by eager children where they were strewn on the ground.

Dorian blinked as a familiar face ran past – cheerful laughter bubbling up from the group as they passed – and the ghost of a smile sprang to their face. *Good,* they thought, *Jin decided to listen.* They didn't notice the way the group thinned as they continued on or the careful figure that broke away as they did, following the hunter from a safe, respectable distance, preoccupied as they were by the gentle push of wind leading them through the crowd.

Coming upon the business district, which was more refined than the main market or Phirrun's snaking alley of stalls, Dorian stuck to the centre of the wide avenue, out of the eyelines of several familiar faces that they were in no mood to encounter. Council and guild members were taking advantage of their affluence in enjoying the celebration, several of them drinking together in a wine garden across the way, crammed on the edge of one or other of their housing estates. The company included Lady Ashea and Lord James's favourite, Lady Bellhall.

Lord James himself glided out of a respectable tailor's shop, Lord Veredan at his side, carrying what must be a fine suit, wrapped carefully in cloth. Dorian took a sharp turn in the opposite direction, shoving through the crowd only for them to shove back until they stumbled over a stoop and ended up crouched behind the door of the shop they'd slipped into to escape.

The shop assistant greeted them uneasily, asking, "Are you here to pick up your order for the ceremony?"

Dorian turned with a raised brow and then shook their head, turning back and peeking out through the woven crystalline windows. They relaxed as no one moved towards the shop and their father strode off with lackey in tow. Dorian hadn't been seen.

The assistant *tsked* at them and said, "Well, it's a little late to make a custom wardrobe, but I'm sure we could sort something out."

Checking the street again and seeing no familiar and unwanted faces in the passers-by, Dorian rose to their full height and said, "Thank you, but no."

They stepped out onto the busy avenue again, and the breeze

immediately swept along low to the ground and then rose up, catching in their hair. It hefted its airy weight against their shoulders. They hurried through the buzzing people, anticipation of a new king flying thickly on the air, while it hissed and snapped at them, nipping at their heels like an invisible, overeager puppy, urging them towards the outermost districts.

It abandoned them suddenly outside a glass-stained cottage, which was tucked away at the end of an orange grove. A small yard stretched across the ground under their feet, backed by crumbling walls. It was empty without the breeze to fill it, which had scattered and skittered away as soon it had led Dorian into it. The highs of the city were lost between the busier streets, and the ruckus of the celebration barely reached out to even be heard in this small, deserted space so close to the border wall and the farms sitting just outside.

Dorian had never really visited the small pockets of the agricultural district that had sprung up within the city, close to the border wall and so far from the heart of the Empire that few in Mistral had any desire to live there. There was something of the wild in this one, and perhaps that was why people were so keen to stay away; a touch of menace under the heavy scent of fruit. Dorian was surprised to find they found it comforting.

Turning a slow circle of their surroundings, they froze at the gentle sound of humming. Backing up to the high, crumbling wall behind them, they slipped into a defensive stance, their pistol sliding into their hand. The humming here grew louder, accompanying a lady with hollow eyes, who floated out of the abandoned cottage towards them, with a tray of tea steaming in her pale, soft hands.

Shye's wind stirred up at Dorian's feet, suddenly having returned, and Dorian cautiously put away their gun.

The lady stopped a few feet away and cocked her head curiously. Her features were familiar. The sweep of her cheeks and the sliver of colour left in her blown eyes and the manner – Dorian swallowed and avoided looking too deeply into her wrecked eyes – the manner she gave of knowing forgotten, secret things, just like . . .

Dorian pointed at her in surprise, feeling glad they'd taken the
encouragement to put their pistol away. With another glance around,
Dorian understood. This land belonged to the Jin Estates. Dorian
could see the main house looming above the stretch of the orange
trees in the distance.

"You're—"

She shushed them gently, setting the tea tray on the ground.
Wisps of steam collected in the air. With a slight dip of her chin, she
gave a parting sigh to the air and padded softly into the rows of
oranges. Her hand reached out in front of her to touch the sound of a
man calling out her name somewhere beyond, her form floating
away in the direction of the manor house. She left the cottage and the
tea tray behind, as though she had forgotten about them and Dorian.

Lady Lis the scornful and Lady Ayslin the mad, Dorian thought. *Look
at what this place made of you when you weren't looking.*

A hand clasped intimately on Dorian's waist, making their skin
jump at the sudden touch of fingers pulling at their shirt, and
someone heaved them backwards, jerking them into the shadows
inside the broken stone wall. Dorian stumbled through from the
outside into another Strange tunnel like the one Jin had pulled them
into, branches of twisted stone and glass running above them into
darkness, what little light there was drifted through the turns of a
labyrinth of paths carved into the heart of Mistral. The wind whistled
in their ear and went barrelling past them into nothing.

They whipped around, half in darkness and half in light, and
grabbed Shye's wrist before he could retract it from their waist. Their
fingers danced up his arm to his shoulder. His eyes went wide,
glowing in the dim, and Dorian felt a smirk threaten. They reached
out for his other hand, not wasting his surprise, and quickly hauled
him in, throwing their arms around his shoulders, their chests
beating together with enough strength to force Shye's breath out of
him with an audible grunt. Dorian felt Shye blink against their neck,
and his arms, slow to slide forward, wound around them in return,
and then he relaxed into them, breath sighing against their skin.

They smiled over his shoulder and brushed a furtive press of the mouth to his jaw, near the junction of his ear.

"I figured you'd have torn into me by now for leaving the bed cold," Shye muttered in apology, his grip loosening. He followed it with a quiet, "You didn't have to come find me."

Dorian was not quite ready to let him step away.

"Oh, I'm furious," they admitted, a little more roughly than they were comfortable with, "but not at you. None of the things I am at the moment change you."

Dorian felt the dip of his chin over their collar, and they moved with him back into the Strange grim stone that ran between the streets, hidden from sight. Their bodies swayed together as they shuffled farther into the dark. With a sharp smile pressed into his sun-dark skin, they promised without bite, "And I'll always find you."

A huffed laugh bubbled out of Shye, and he pressed a grateful dib of a kiss to their jaw as tingles of lightning scraped over them from the sweep of his glow-struck hair. They swatted it away, which only made Shye laugh quietly again. He pulled back, tucking his hair behind his ears, and Dorian reached for the curve of his mouth, tracing the uplift they found there. His expression turned sheepish.

Pulling away, they placed their offending hand over their chest and sank to one knee, announcing, "Is now a good time to pledge my loyalty to the king?"

Their fun quickly died as a haunted look flashed over Shye's face – a swirl of clouds across his glowing eyes – and with strength gained from hauling sails and climbing ratlines, he reached down and yanked them back to their feet. Steadying them, he dropped his hands away, only for Dorian to snatch them back. His fingers curled into theirs, squeezing.

"I don't want to be anybody's king," Shye said, the troubled distance crashing through the clouds in his gaze. Focusing on them again, his expression turned pleading. "Don't give up on Cassius yet. Yours and mine aren't the only destinies that turn on the whim of the Horned Crown."

His feet came to rest between theirs as he stepped closer; beautifully terrible and earnest in his plea. "Whatever happens, please just trust that I wasn't called to be a king. I wouldn't know how to be king, and I have zero interest in learning."

Dorian's hand crept to Shye's waist, moulding to the curve and twist of his firm form, slinging easily over his back. His fingers detangled from theirs to slide up Dorian's arm. Dorian's opposite hand clung stubbornly to Shye's fingers, dangling between their bodies.

"As long as you do the same for me," Dorian agreed, wondering how much, if any, Creed had told him before he'd left their company, and how much Shye had learned on his own. They could only hope and try to trust, as he had asked them, that Shye knew what he was doing, regardless of Creed and Ever's scheming.

To be fair to Shye, he had managed well enough so far, with a little help from Dorian and Jin. Dorian would follow his lead. Whatever games the others were playing, Shye wasn't going to be their tool to use. Dorian had learnt that for themself and learnt it well enough to see the truth of it reflected in Shye's radiant, inhuman eyes. He'd save them all.

His fingers skimmed up to their shoulder.

Reading the look in each other's eyes, they both moved forward at the same time, their mouths meeting in an enthusiastic clash from which they quickly broke, stifling laughter, and then Dorian chased his mouth again. It parted warmly under them, and they slipped closer, hands sliding up Shye's back and then down to grasp his hips.

Sweet and terrible desire ripped through Dorian's body as he pushed back against them. Shye conquered them with his lips, sweet and slow, with the delightful press of his smile, the brief surprise and flash of heat that followed a nipping bite. He left starbursts pulsing in Dorian's chest and their hands tightened to ruck up his clothes and run across hidden skin.

Dorian thought he tasted of salt and rain. The storm inside him roiled through him to scorch their body with a desire neither of them had any care to resist. With the fervour and honesty that Dorian saw in Shye, it consumed them, and Dorian made sure Shye was the first to feel its truth reciprocated. And that he was the first to moan it out loud.

He wanted their trust; he'd have it.

He wanted their loyalty; he had it.

Dorian pushed him to the cool stone beneath them, divesting him of his clothes. Each new revealed part added to the blaze of heat in their chest and stomach, their lips tingling and setting them to mark his skin with a brand of their own making. Shye lit up the folk-made walkway like a strike of lightning frozen in time, the workings of his throat like the rumbling of distant thunder.

Dorian swore their life to him in the press of their mouth, swore it again in the rock of their bodies together, their hands clutching him close, and swore it a final time as heat welled up and their heartbeat accelerated, their mouth seeking his as he gave a gasp and they swallowed it, hazy pleasure unravelling under their sweat-slicked skin, and Shye's fingers digging into their lower back.

They'd never let anyone else have this beautiful, Strange boy. Not Cassius, not their father, not Tanith, not Ever, not Creed.

Shye panted against them, a smile and a stuttering laugh breezing against their clammy skin. They felt his tongue trace a line of sweat up their collar and then up their neck, before he lay back, satisfied.

"I trust you, Dorian," he said in the quiet, taking a moment to calm his breathing. "I always have."

Dorian leaned down and kissed him again, pressing their bodies closer as they started to cool and became aware of other things in the fading dazzle of pleasure.

"Don't go just yet. Stay," Dorian commanded in a whisper, stroking his hair back from his face, tickles of power striking up in their questing fingers.

Bright teeth flashed at them, and his calloused hands trailed hungrily up and down their back. He made no move to retrieve his clothes or get out from under their weight. His expression slipped into gentle smugness.

Kiss me again and I will, it said.

Dorian obeyed. They deepened their touch until he broke away in surprise as their hand slipped between them, and then he huffed and sighed, choking the rumble of a moan in his chest, his head knocking back into the stone, eyes tightly shut. Dorian grinned smugly, placing a hand on his body, fingers splayed at his throat, to feel the shift and shatter of his heart against his ribs. The quiet was once again broken by the sounds of pleasure.

When it was over, far too soon for Dorian's liking, Dorian picked up Shye's shirt from where they'd thrown it into the gutter of the folkway, handing it back to watch it slip with regret over his strong, smooth skin. The ornamental imperial jacket settled into place over the top of it.

He leaned in and pressed a gentle kiss to their cheek, while a hidden, half-tempted uplift pinched in the corner of his mouth, the tips of his fingers lightly floating over their jaw. Looking into his eyes, they saw their own determination reflected back.

Letting him go, Dorian stepped out of the dark tunnel into the break of evenspan across the courtyard.

"I trust you too," they affirmed clunkily, wincing at how the words sounded out loud, minutes later than they should have said them. Embarrassed, they hurried on, "So what's the plan?"

"Does not running away count?" Shye's dip of a smile was shaky but genuine before it faltered and slipped downwards into the hint of a grimace. His expression turned serious. "I want to talk to Cassius. Alone."

"You're just going to ask him to give up the crown, then?" Dorian questioned in dubious tones. Shye raised one shoulder in a bashful shrug and the feeling of dread in their bones abated for a moment as Dorian let out a burst of unexpected, incredulous laughter. Almost immediately, they felt bad about it. Giving a crooked smirk, they attempted more positively, "Well, I do love a simple plan."

But their smirk wilted rather than bloomed, unable to withstand even an attempt at levity, their positive façade fragmenting under the weight of the nightrun that lay ahead. They exhaled a regretful breath and felt compelled to warn him, "Cassius gave me orders to hand you over to the guard if I found you. Said it was my duty as a hunter. I want to believe in him, I really do. But . . . please be careful."

Shye frowned and picked up on the completely wrong point of what they had said, the hesitancy in his eyes swallowed up by concern for Dorian. "If you're letting me go, what does that mean for you?"

Dorian shook their head at his earnest, uneasy face and ridiculous question. Whistling out another breath, they tried on another smile for him. It was small, but truthful this time and that made all the difference. "It means I'm resigning. And I'll do it now, so I'm free for . . . when its finished."

Shye's eyes widened a little in shock, his lips parting alluringly.

Dorian tried to focus on his words and not on other things.

"But you're Huntsman?" Shye protested and Dorian's heart warmed. "You're THE hunter. The head of the guild."

Dorian gave up resisting and pecked him lightly on his tempting mouth, pulling away with a tiny but satisfied warmth in their eyes. They shrugged. "Maybe, but it's not all I am. And if Cassius is making me choose, then I want to be yours first, I guess."

Shye's eyes went suspiciously dewy, and his mouth tucked, no doubt in a repressed need to protest. Dorian interrupted him before he could or before he could say anything that, while no doubt true, would embarrass both of them. Shoving him gently by the shoulder towards the folkway, they ordered, "Okay, no more feelings."

Shye stumbled back a step, pulling Dorian with him. He paused to lean in, resting his forehead against theirs, his breath sailing over their lips. It was Dorian who closed the distance to kiss him and then gently pushed his chest with both hands, "You have to go."

Dorian felt their heart pulse as he looked at them, his eyes bright and roiling with purpose, desire and something more.

Finally, he nodded.

"I'll see you when it's finished," he said, sending a sincere and fleeting half-smile in their direction, so alight with the Blood and the heart of the storm that he'd never seemed more untouchable — in defiance of the fact that they had just been touching him — or more beautiful. And then the brightness of his eyes was hidden by the sweep of his eyelashes as he turned away and disappeared into the stretch of the folkway.

Dorian wavered as the courtyard grew silent around them and then drew themself together. There was no guarantee of the world his words would come true in. But they'd fight and die before proving them false.

CHAPTER 31

THE FOLKWAYS WERE STILL A MYSTERY TO SHYE. HE COULD IMAGINE living in Mistral for years and never running out of paths to follow in the labyrinth, but that particular musing wasn't important right now and he pushed the thoughts of it far from his mind as his little wind plucked around his ankles.

Growing impatient, it howled ahead of him, sweeping around corners into consecutive dim tunnels that all looked the same to Shye; twisting stone and seals and the funk of Old Things, but a small part of it lingered with him, driving him relentlessly back towards the Brightspir.

Turning again through the seemingly endless ways, he almost tripped, catching himself just in time as the wind bellowed one last roar and his feet found the edge of the stairs he had stumbled down in the early rise, the opening ready to swallow him back up after spitting him out. Masking his trepidation and calming his jittering nerves proved difficult as his hands shook and his throat closed, even after Dorian's tender attentions. Taking a resolute breath, he ascended the steps back into the bowels of the Brightspir, pushing those clenching, clawing feelings down inside himself. Even so far below the clatter and clamour of the people gathering for the ceremony, he could hear them.

Closing his eyes and delving deep within himself, he dove into the rising, vivid waves that crashed through the deepness and felt it surge under his blood; bold and light-split. He would need the slick, shifting proof of his Blood to make it through the nightrun. In his mind's eye, again he saw the doors to the old throne, with the Horned Crown glowing gently within. This time, the deepness did not shrink away.

A Strange thrum seemed to be in the air as the season waned. Whether from the Horned Crown as its time drew near or from else-where, it reached for Shye like a single note from an instrument that only he could hear. It left a kind of golden humming in the air, and Shye followed it, the lingering feel of it like the whispers of the wind that led him to the old throne and, before that, to Dorian. Calling to him with the shivering rhythms of Dusk.

His hands slid and skittered on the walls, wincing at the rough-hewn stone as he blindly chased the pull of it in his chest. At the other end of the deepness, something waited with a sigh of frost, the first of the season.

Shye's eyes came open and he nearly lost the feeling as strains of real music surged over the thump of Blood and deepness. The eerie lilt of a violin floated through the walls to reach him, seeming to swell from every direction, its source impossible to locate. It pressed sooth-ingly against his consciousness, playing a familiar lullaby.

Shye batted away the haze it brought with it; the work of no human musician. There was only one person who possessed that skill and talent, only one person Shye knew of with the necessary disposition of persuasion and the lingering element to sail a siren song on the air. What Muse was doing here, Shye lacked the time and space to contemplate, though an apprehensive rush shot through him at the thought of his crew and captain.

He hurried on, sensing that the small time granted to him before the world turned again to the will of the Horned Crown was draining from his grasp. Holding onto the faint cry within and without, he chased it until it beat in time with the batter of his heart against the cage of his bones. If his crew and captain were here, it could only be for the crown.

The tunnels seemed to stretch and narrow all at once as he drew closer to the drumming of Dusk in his veins, and suddenly the frosted gates of an entrance into the folkways loomed from the boughs overhead, glimmering in the darkness like ice-rimed water, forcing Shye to a sudden stop.

A figure moved in the room beyond, his dark form distinguished by the curl of wrought horns from the crown on his head.

Shye choked back a sigh.

Of course, the call had come from Cassius, maybe even the crown itself. After all, Blood led to Blood, if Tanith was to be believed.

Destroy the crown, end the sleep, save the world.

The words rang in Shye's ears, and whether he was ready for that confrontation or not, he couldn't let them go unanswered. This was his opening.

"If only the task were as simple as the instructions," he muttered to himself, so much aware that first he had to do things like get the crown before he could even attempt the rest.

Through the gateway of frosted glass, Shye saw Cassius moved towards the door. The vast rooms he moved through were cut off and disfigured by the narrow scope Shye was gazing through, the prince's form blurring and getting smaller.

He could end everything now, as long as his chance to do so did not walk out that door.

Without thinking, Shye pushed his arm through the gateway and demanded, in a clear, unsparing voice, "Your crown, Imperial Prince."

If Cassius was surprised to see an arm extend from one dark crevice between two bookshelves, ancient stone glittering within the dimness, Shye could not see it.

The prince stalked over without pause.

Sweeping in close to Shye's fingers, imperiously thrust in demand and belying a confidence that he was barely holding onto, Cassius's eyes roved curiously over them. Slowly, he looked up, looking Shye in the eye as if he had found him in the space between, and shook his head.

Shye cautiously took his hand back – it had been a hasty, ill-thought production on his part anyway – only for Cassius to lash out with blurred speed and grab a forbidding hold on him.

The prince hauled him into the half-light between the gateway and the prince's quarters, his expression sneering. He raked Shye up and down with damning hazel eyes, unimpressed.

Shye wasn't too impressed with his attempt either but tried to keep his own expression arch and imperious, staring back with equal fervour as Cassius's veins sluiced auriferous under his touch. His deepness ran over his skin to spark across the space between them, reaching out for the Blood beneath.

It was met with the bite of frostfall's chill, as Cassius's fingers burned ice-white bruises into Shye's skin, their edges glittering dully like flaking crumbs of glass.

"Not on your life, Master Stormborn," he bit out in reply and sent Shye tumbling back beyond the gateway with a hefty shove, falling to the ground in a heap.

He scrambled back up, kneeling before the entry to see Cassius walk smoothly from the rooms, with the Horned Crown jutting above his brow.

Soon, Cassius would have to concede to Mistral's rituals, and remove the crown before beginning the ceremony that would make him king in name as well as deed. Except Tanith would never let him get that far. Shye had to get to him before then.

"Wait!" he called out, his voice far losing sureness but carrying farther as he tried to get Cassius to stay. Shoving his way through the frosted gateway, Shye stumbled into the prince's rooms, just as the doors slammed shut on him.

"Fuck," he said emphatically to the swirl of wind at his feet.

Shye, it said in response, flowing gently towards the door. Shye's brow furrowed, and he nudged the coalescence of air with a brief tendril of deepness. He felt it rise and puff at his attention and it brought a small, lost smile to his face.

"You tell him," Shye commanded, an idea taking root in his mind, just to get Cassius to stop and listen long enough to give him a chance.

"You tell him we had a deal and that despite unforeseen circumstances I truly intend to uphold my end of the bargain. I'll crown him, and if by lightrise he still wants all this, tell him I'll make him a new one."

The little wind whistled in response and howled through the doors, blowing them open and leaving them rent in their sockets.

Brightspir servants – garbed for the occasion in bloody maroon tunics, the crest of the prince stitched on their backs – and people attending the celebration, dressed in finery of all colours and strewn with minor gems and fragrant blooms, looked his way, taking in the splintered doors and the Stormborn that the guards had been searching for. As one, they all turned away as if they'd seen nothing Strange at all.

Shye blinked and then, following the trailing hiss of the wind, took off in pursuit of Cassius. Slipping farther from view, the prince walked through the imperial wing and out again as he headed for the crown's exterior wing and the lower throne room on its inside, enclosed within the heart of the Brightspir.

Shye ran through the interior after him, knocking harshly into a lady as he came into the thicker crowds of the central palace. She looked at him with glazed eyes and said distantly, "Isn't that music lovely?"

She offered him a vapid smile in exchange for his hurried apology and he took off again, thundering after Cassius.

The central atrium was clogged with people. The galleries above were strewn with minor nobles and not much else, and Shye could see flickering firelight ahead across the archway to the exterior and down the stairs into the milling crowd, as the last moon of the season started to make its final nightrun. He could see Cassius as he walked the long cutaway between the exterior and the half of the interior that made up the crown's wing, the lower throne room within it.

If he could stop him now, he could still end it before it started. Before Tanith could do a damn thing about it.

Someone grabbed Shye from behind, and with a firm grip they pulled him around.

Cassius turned as Shye let out an involuntary cry and was flung towards the nearest wall, the impact ricocheting along all the points of his spine.

He couldn't see Cassius stop and pause, watching the scene and perhaps thinking on the whispers of a quiet wind. He couldn't see much at all beyond the hulking mass of the captain of the Border Guards, who looked down on him through glassy eyes. But the hold of Muse's lullaby must have been slipping because the captain, though Shye had only ever known him in passing, seemed far more lucid than the gathered masses below.

Cassius had likely already realised there was something more going on, especially after Shye, and especially if the little wind had caught up with him as Shye had asked.

The captain's fingers pinched into Shye's skin, pressing him into unforgiving stone.

"Aren't you—" he began groggily, half drunk on siren song.

Shye, in a panicked half-formed thought, wrenched the deepness back inside his bones and shut his eyes. Without the glow of his eyes and the shock of his hair, maybe the captain would forget that he was holding onto a Stormborn. Under the influence of Muse's song, maybe he'd forget that Shye's tangled brown hair had just been furious white and that his eyes weren't shut from fear.

He heard the captain almost sniff, his fingers loosening just a touch, and he gave a gruff cough. A finger pawed ungracefully at the bottom of his eyelid, and Shye prayed that meant his little trick had worked. He felt the weight of the captain move. He whispered an apology to the man before cracking an eye open and sending a rush of force pushing under their skins to bring him to the ground at Shye's feet. The captain slipped and fell, knees cracking into the polished floor, where he remained with his head bowed.

Clattering through the cutaway, the captain groaning on the floor behind him, Shye saw Cassius almost frozen up ahead, with the fire-light washing his face in lines of red and gold.

Slowly, the prince turned to face the city and the swathes of greenery that fell over the side of exterior walkways, and something else hidden behind the bulk of a pillar. Shye heard a voice growl something and he recognised the acerbic tone Cassius used to answer it. Over the thundering splits of light that rushed through his blood and bone, Shye caught a flash of cold metal and gunpowder on the cooling air, followed by the unmistakable sound of the cock of a gun.

Cursing, he called out, "Wait, Cassius, please," damning himself for taking the risk of not knowing who held the gun.

Without looking away from the person holding him hostage, Cassius held up an imperious hand in Shye's direction and said, "Don't come any closer."

Shye wondered for a brief moment if Cassius was worried about Shye or himself. Hope welled hot and insidious in his chest. He slid quietly to the far side of the walkway but didn't advance farther towards the prince and his gun-toting captor.

The long barrel of the gun glinted silver and pearl in the firelight. Custom work. Its reach extended down to a hand as Shye drew closer to the wall. It jerked upwards towards the crown, and Shye skated carefully along the shadowed stone until the man who held it, his green eyes lancing through the running night, came into view. His finger curled around the trigger. Shye couldn't restrain himself from calling out again, darting forward to intercept.

"Master, stop!"

Ezra Creed's green eyes went light and wide as Shye flashed over, putting himself firmly to the side, just in front of Cassius.

"Get out of the way," Ezra ordered. "We have histories to make right."

"You cannot have my kingdom," Cassius replied, a pulse of chilling slush cracking across the deepness in Shye like ice over the ocean. Shye breathed out and tasted Cassius and salted frost on his tongue.

Turning to the awakened prince, Shye reassured in equal measure, "We don't want your kingdom."

"No, just my crown," he retorted, eyes suspicious.

Something shifted in the aether of the palace, like a stone had been dropped into the well of deepness or a wrong note had sounded in the symphony of nightrun, but Shye couldn't put his finger on what had changed, and his master did not give him the chance to figure it out.

"Yes," Ezra said smoothly, playing the part of the Blooded bandit and obviously enjoying it, "before you destroy us for good. Now, be a good boy and hand it over to my apprentice here."

Shye rolled his eyes and snapped, "Master, please. He's one of us. If he destroys the Blooded this night, he destroys himself."

Shye felt a bloom of satisfaction at Ezra's stunned silence, catching his darting glance to the ring on Cassius's finger.

"Then it worked. So, she was right," he murmured to himself in a grave tone. Shye didn't know the significance of his look or words, but put it aside for the moment. The tang of metal had not budged from the air and Shye knew he didn't have their attention for long. He did the only thing he had ever proved good at; he spoke a reckless truth out of turn and begged them to hear him.

"I promised to crown you, Cassius, and I mean to keep my word," Shye said, looking at Cassius and reading the hesitation in his eyes. He ploughed ahead with a confidence he didn't feel, saying, "But I cannot crown you with that."

He pointed gently at the Horned Crown. The prince's eyes turned dark, and his hand reached for the metal and wood over his brow.

"Even if it wasn't a curse upon our kind, they wouldn't let you make it to the throne. The world they want to rise doesn't have a place for us."

Cassius's expression was crafted, though his gaze moved between Shye and his master's polished pistol. Shye grimaced and stepped in front of it, blocking Cassius's sights, forcing his attention on him.

"Please," he pleaded. "You're not the first king, so don't make his mistakes. Don't betray the world you live in, in the name of his peace. Camillus barely knew the word, let alone its meaning."

Cassius's expression flickered, and Shye saw doubt there, making war with suspicion. The prince sighed and hesitantly removed the crown from his head to hold it between his hands. Shye felt the hope in his chest flutter, but Cassius did not hand over the crown.

Instead, something to the side of Shye's shoulder caught his notice. Cassius stepped back, expression freezing, the doubt fading. His eyes narrowed on the captain's pistol, the crown still resting in his hands.

Too late, Shye heard the drum of footsteps from the entrance to the cutaway.

"Your Highness," came the call, before there was the sound of a pistol firing and a blast of cold, slow fire shot through Shye's body, as shatters of metal liquidised into iron-born poison. His mind slowly turned over that the thing that had changed was Muse's music – dark warning notes weaved underneath his siren song.

The books called the age-old weakness of the folk *fever iron*. The natural metal from Yren Fe Ire Fell, deadened further by the fires of the forge, was immune to the Blooded's pleas, turning hard and cold and black. Even after Tanith, he hadn't known it could feel like this.

Muse's music wavered in his ears, and he swayed to his knees, his blood burning and his tongue thick in his mouth with the taste of blood and rust. He forced his head up from where it had sunk close to the floor to see his captain fire at Cassius.

He missed, the bullet indenting in the woven band of Cassius's crown, and Shye's vision blinked out on the shock, fear, and fury in Cassius's face. Another gun fired behind Shye and his vision whited as he tried to open his heavy eyes, and then the world returned to hazy colour. He watched dizzily as the glinting bullet whizzed overhead and punctured through Ezra's coat and, before his blood could stain the fabric, he fell backwards, off the side of the cutaway.

Shye might have tried to scream. His throat burned, with the taste of blood and the bitter smell of hot metal all around him. The fire in his veins was dimming to a blistering cold that seized through every heartbeat. It slipped, needle-sharp, into the deepness and shut it back beneath his bones.

Booted footfalls landed at his back. Through bleary eyes, his ears ringing with the sound of bells somewhere far away, he saw three men walk up to Cassius. They had neat black ink on the backs of their hands in the shape of an hourglass. Shye turned to the side and quietly spat some foul-tasting bile onto the floor.

Hunters. Lord James's, no doubt. Meaning they were Tanith's men too.

Cassius drew himself up and thrust out the crown. "Give this to Lord James," he ordered, and waited for one of the men to take it.

"They'll kill you, Cassius, don't you fucking dare—"

Shye cried out as a hand settled in his hair to drag him back, and a boot crashed heavily across the side of his face. They let him fall to the ground. Rattling joined the symphony of bells in Shye's ears, and then, with a click, pain laced into his wrists and up his arms as they shackled him in more iron. He sagged under the weight of it on his arms and in his veins. He cursed as blood dribbled from his mouth to the floor.

Forcing his eyes up, he watched the lead hunter order, "Take them both," while his hands securely grasped the Horned Crown.

They grabbed Cassius, even as he swore and threatened. The black metal came down to bite against Cassius's skin, and Shye smiled because he had only a moment to feel the screaming wash of fear, and then he was spared from feeling at all by the descent of iron-clad blackness.

CHAPTER 32

THE FEELING OF ENCROACHING DREAD DID NOT GO AWAY AS EVENSPAN progressed. The curling in Dorian's gut was out of place with the luminous joy that surrounded them on all sides as they travelled Mistral's streets once again.

They had fulfilled their mission in their own way. They had found Shye and then let him go again. It had never been said that they should return with him. If Ever or Creed had a problem with that, it was one of their own making for fundamentally underestimating a Stormborn.

Dorian wished their insides could stop making the same mistake, though their mouth managed a smile as they skirted the edge of a courtyard, which had turned into an impromptu ballroom as couples careened across the space in time to the music rising in the avenues around the Brightspir. The frostfall spirit was descending with the waning season and the wine gardens were filled to overflowing; people spilling down from the palace to take over the streets in celebration, which had started early and would end late.

Amidst the revelry, Dorian could almost laugh at Creed and Ever's misfortune in choosing the two most ill-equipped beings with their historic mission; an unruly Stormborn and the unconventional hunter. Someone should've foreseen the mess they'd make of it, but apparently even Ever couldn't account for that. But when they stepped out of the courtyard, their tenuous amusement vanished; the celebrations carrying on and leaving the Guild Circle almost untouched between the riot above in the tall spire of the Brightspir and out across the city floor, and the Guild Circle a quiet disconnect between.

And the future, though it seemed certain to Mistral's people, was anything but. Humanity, Ever, and Creed didn't even know who they were fighting.

It was that thought and the information lurking behind it that spurred Dorian into the emptiness wreathing the guild house.

The lantern lights blazed within the foyers, and the hanging banners were freshly dyed for the occasion; the oaths sworn to be sworn again come lightrise. Dorian paused on the steps, breathing past the embers of unease coalescing in their chest and the ominous taste of ash that hammered their senses as soon as they approached the doors. This was the Hunters' Guild, but Dorian felt the tremor of prey hanging over them.

They shook themself lightly and pulled their shoulders back. The tension in their chest strained against their will to dislodge it. Every person of note was within the palace for the ceremony, and all the danger of the nightrun with them. Still, Dorian's hair stood on end as they stepped into the foyer and rushed over to the assembly doors.

Sliding open the doors, they knew why as soon as they saw Ever's crumpled body on the ground before the Huntsman's bench. They heard their own shaky inhale as they took a step inside the room. Blood seeped from the wound in Ever's belly, and a red-stained hand desperately clutched over it, but the barely-there rise and fall of his chest told Dorian that he was still hanging on.

Something heavy, cold and metal landed against the back of their neck and they tensed as the cock of a pistol sounded loud in their ears. Slowly, Dorian turned away from Ever, with the dark stain of his blood branded in their mind. Their father's pistol glinted several inches from their face, while the man himself smirked behind the elegant piece.

Unabashed rage swirled through Dorian.

"Dorian," Lord James greeted, "shame on you. It's your cousin's crowning and here you are cavorting with the enemy."

"You're the enemy here," Dorian said, restraining a flinch as James's face darkened and he jabbed the pistol into their chest, sending them back-stepping into the assembly room.

"He's got you twisted all around his finger, Dorian. Him and that Stormborn," he sneered. "But they're not worth dying over."

Lord James backed Dorian towards Ever's prone body, gesturing with the pistol. "It doesn't have to be you. I could still save you; you could still save yourself."

Dorian couldn't help but snort at that. In the corner of their periphery, Ever's fingers twitched and between them flashed a sliver of metal.

Recklessly, Dorian goaded him. "Please, Father, here's the chance you've been waiting for all your life. The chance to finally define our family name. Don't lie by pretending you don't want to take it."

The gun seemed to wink coldly at them while Lord James considered and then started to smirk. Dorian fought back a shudder and the spit of hot anger and fear.

"Just remember you asked for this," he agreed.

Dorian took a protective step back, in front of Ever, and angled their shoulder towards the gun. They didn't heal like Shye did, but as long as they were alive to heal, they'd take it. Their fingers caught hold of the knife that Ever slipped into their hand, hidden from view by the angle of their body. Dorian's focus narrowed, their grip clenching on the hilt of the knife.

James's finger twitched on the trigger.

Dorian snarled at him and dove as it fired. The bullet whizzed overhead and shattered into the wall behind them, tearing a hole in the Huntsman's banner. With a flick of their hand, Dorian sent the knife across the room. It cleaved into Lord James's shoulder with startling accuracy. They charged at him before he could recover and fire again and hit them, or, worse, Ever.

Despite the stiffness and altered mobility, and a delicate spread of crimson on his fine coat, Lord James lifted the pistol again.

Dorian slipped to the side just as he pulled the trigger, and then careened back to knock the gun out of his hands. It skittered across the ground, and Dorian lost sight of it as the back of Lord James's hand whipped their head to the side; the force of the strike breaking across their jaw and rattling through their teeth.

Dorian stumbled, overturning a bench.

Lord James yanked the blade from his shoulder, and a patch of red immediately seeped from the wound. His arm hung limply from the shoulder. Dorian knew it was too much to hope he'd pass out from blood loss before he could do more damage to them or Ever.

Dorian reached for their pistol, slung inside their shirt, only to abandon it as Lord James let out a vicious cry and slashed at them with the knife. Throwing up their forearms in front of their face, a thin slice whipped across their skin and they jumped back as he advanced. Boxed in by rows of benches, they circled around the centre of the assembly room dodging blows like a fighter in one of Phirrun's dockside matches.

Their heel clipped the discarded pistol with a jangling clink.

Lord James licked his lips in anticipation. He charged.

Dorian kicked the pistol up with their toes and sent it across the room barely managing to dodge their father's oncoming attack, their arms stinging as the knife sliced through the flesh of their forearms. Over his shoulder, Dorian watched as Ever's fingers crept towards the gun they'd hurled towards him.

Then they saw the glint of the knife as it neared, and the cruel twinkle in their father's eyes as he leered at them, and they let out a roar that made their father flinch. Sweeping in towards their guts, the blade glittered red and silver. Their eyes widened as they heard the click of a pistol arming and, without thinking anything except that they couldn't sustain a wound like that and still help Shye, they split their hand down the knife and pushed it away from their body.

The report of the gun went off.

Lord James jerked, the knife driving deeper into Dorian's hand. And then he fell back a few paces, his face turning pale even as his eyes narrowed in spite. He did not turn away from Dorian, and the fingers of his working hand idly grabbed as though he still held the knife. The wound in his shoulder had spread a dangerous patch of red down the sleeve of his coat. He swayed, a half-snarl pulling at his mouth as he fought to remain standing.

Dorian stepped towards James, their legs feeling oddly disconnected from the rest of them, slow but steady where the rest of them was wobbly at best, bleeding and aching at worst. Lord James's eyes sluggishly followed them, blinking closed as they drove their uninjured fist into his jaw, and he collapsed to the floor.

"Lady Lis preserve you," they said to his unconscious form, their breathing becoming heavy from the exertion and the strain of remaining on their feet.

With a grimace, Dorian looked to Ever. His old face was lined with pain as his shaking hands lowered the pistol as he placed it gently, regretfully, on the floor.

They pried the knife loose from the flesh of their hand, applying pressure to the wound, which began to bleed immediately. Ever signalled with two weary fingers at them.

"Come here," he croaked, awkwardly patting the spot next to him on the hard assembly floor, one hand returning to clutch his wounded belly.

Dorian shuffled over. The numb itch in their hand was building into a sharp sting and from there, they imagined, into a cry of shattered flesh and muscle. They dropped heavily beside their grandfather, hand held out for him to inspect.

He poked and prodded a little, ignoring Dorian's attempts to hide a wince. His expression dimmed but he said gently, "Well, you'll live."

Dorian tried to muster the strength for a reply, taking their hand back, but their tongue stuck obstinately to the roof of their mouth, sealed shut with the taste of gunpowder. They reached for the hem of their shirt and split the seams up the side, tearing strips to bandage up their useless hand. It would need proper medical attention to save it.

They tried silently to flex their fingers and garnered only a twitch and a flare of pain.

Ever's warm hand, the one not holding his insides together, descended soothingly on their back.

"You'll live," he said again, and Dorian forced a nod. They'd live, they could adapt to fight one-handed, to ride, fire a gun, throw a blade . . .

The doors to the assembly rooms slid open and all thoughts cleared from Dorian's mind. They leapt up, the blade still clutched in their good hand, as Ever weakly reached for the pistol again. A small, childish face popped through the gap and Dorian sighed, tossing the knife to the ground in relief, ignoring the twinges that sounded through them as they forced their body not to slump back down next to Ever.

Jin pushed the doors open, looking over his shoulder and calling, "In here."

Walking over to the doorway, Dorian swore as Leon stumbled through it, supporting the weight of Captain Creed, with the hulking form of one of his crewmen bringing up the rear of the group led by Jin. Stepping out of the way, they helped Leon deposit the captain in a spot of bare floor in the centre.

Leon's eyes caught on the slumped figure of Lord James, also taking up space, and he flicked a quick look at Dorian, then at their hand, and then at Ever. After a moment, he gestured to the crewman that Dorian remembered being a bare, huge shadow around a small fire and said, "We brought a surgeon."

Dorian hummed noncommittally and sank down next to Ever again; the medicas already crouched and tending, with a pouch of supplies, to their grandfather's injuries. Dorian turned away after he had cleaned the wound and brought out a length of gossamer silver threaded through a sapphire-steel needle, picking at the bandages on their hand. They saw movement in their periphery and pointed with their good hand at the small figure of Jin, who crouched near the door.

"I thought I told you to stay away from all this," Dorian said, distracting themself from the unsettling throb thrumming through a hand that wouldn't work even as they tried to make it move.

Jin rubbed his cheeks and shrugged. "I stayed away from the palace and stayed out of sight, and I brought you the surgeon, so . . ."

Whatever argument Jin was about to make was cut off as the captain groaned and cracked a bleary eye.

"Butler," came his cracked voice in a hiss, and the medicas, having finished with Ever gave Dorian a quick, questioning once-over. The colour was returning to Ever's lined face and some of the vitality returned to his form now that he'd been sewn up and bandaged, and a poultice spread over the wound.

"There is not much we can do for your hand as we are. I can pack it with herbs and bandage it, sew the flesh together, stave off an infection, but . . ." he murmured to them kindly.

But he couldn't heal broken tendons and muscle. They flexed their hand again, but it remained limply still – raw and numb in turns – so they sniffed and shooed him away, and he scooted over to the captain without another word.

Dorian stood. Ever reassured them with a slight pat to the calf, and Dorian moved over to their father's prone form. Blank faced, Dorian rolled him over; his pale visage was marred by a streak of blood, which bubbled to his lips, while his shoulder slowly leaked more blood to stain his shirt and neck. A nasty bruise was blooming on his cheek.

Dorian held their ruined hand as it began to ache, pressing their thumb into the wound until tears pricked their eyes, as if that could overwhelm the dark revulsion that overcame them and the pitiful hate beneath it.

Next to them, the captain groaned from Butler's administrations, his green eyes wheeling and then focusing on Dorian. "Your ring," he rasped, startling them.

Dorian looked over their shoulder in surprise to see him watching them.

His hand was raised elegantly, fingers twirling to point at Ever's ring, which gleamed between their knuckles, their fingers limp and useless where they cradled them to their chest. Creed's hand then fell, as though suddenly too heavy to hold in the air.

"Use the seal," he continued, hissing as Butler pulled a bullet from his skin and then stripped him to clean the wound. Bruises littered the captain's torso and Dorian could see the uneven jut of broken and dislocated bones.

"Heal it enough. There should be enough Blood inside us yet, if you beg Kernon for mercy," he commanded them, while his fingers crept across the ground to grab and twitch insistently at Dorian's coat with what little strength remained in him. "They have Shye, and we are out of time."

Dorian's stomach dropped and the captain's eyes turned pleading, before they closed to let Butler continue his work in peace.

Fumbling for the ring and managing to slide it free, Dorian pushed at the sunstone and black opal glass. The sapphire-steel fitting held firm as their fingers tried to break the seal from it. Frustration boiled in their stomach like acid as their fingers slipped, and the weight in their chest grabbed a hold of their lungs until everything inside them seemed to burn.

A large, cool hand, dark as a frostfall nightrun, lay over theirs.

The captain's eyes blinked open to watch on as Butler took the ring from Dorian's hands and gripped it between thumb and forefinger, crushing the fixture between glass and steel. Unwrapping the bandages from their hand, he pressed the stone into the slice in Dorian's palm.

Pain surged as their flesh tore, giving way to the unyielding shape of the priceless gems – cold, twinkling glass batting away the burn and numbness and slotting hard and inhuman into their hand. A small sound escaped their tightly pressed lips, and then it was over.

The pain seemed to pull inwards through their skin, as though soaking into the stones, and then vanished altogether. Tiny veins of glass, black opal, and sunstone grew like the roots of the tree they'd been forged into across the bloody slash.

Butler dabbed another poultice over the wound and rebandaged their hand, hiding the glimmer of it from sight.

Dorian tried again to flex their fingers, but their hand remained limp, though all the pain of it was gone.

The captain acknowledged them with a bare, white-lipped smile. "Go," he said.

They looked to Ever, who nodded, while resting against the bench, wrapped in pristine bandages, and smelling of crushed jade and honeyed yarrow from Butler's good work. They hesitated, and Leon's hand clapped down on their shoulder, sending a trickle of warmth through them in appreciation for the other hunter.

"Don't worry about us. I'll handle it," he said, casting a look towards Lord James's still form. "That too."

Dorian's stomach swooped as they came closer to their father's body, before reaching out a hand to touch the fineness of his ceremonial coat, a beautiful cluster of embroidered gems creeping over the shoulder blades and down the back.

"To end this, I need to get to Tanith," Dorian murmured. Their fingers brushed down their rumpled, bloodstained appearance, their shirt hanging with rips up both seams and their face and arms a mess of bruises and cuts. "They'll never let me in the palace like this."

They gave their father another long, probing look.

Then, their mouth quirked, and they snapped a finger at Jin, who was still crouched by the door, waiting for something to happen.

The boy jerked and looked at Dorian with wide, waiting eyes. The brief impression of his mother's hollow gaze swept through Dorian's mind before they pushed it away. They shared with him a growing, feral smile, their eyes lit with abrupt inspiration.

Fishing the blade from the floor, Dorian twisted the spill of their auburn hair around their knuckles and sawed swiftly through it. Drifts of long red locks fell in pieces to the floor until the length matched that of Lord James's cropped cut.

Is this not what you always wanted, father? An heir who was just like you, Dorian thought with sour amusement. All that remained was the colour, the styling and the clothes.

"Jin, I need you to find me a tailor and a cosmetician, and be quick."

They flipped the knife confidently and jammed it into a holster in their boot. Dropping their voice with a frozen edge in imitation of Lord James, they said, "For I am not known for my patience."

CHAPTER 33

PAIN HAD A GRIP ON SHYE AND IT WOULD NOT LET HIM GO. IT WAS A line tethering him to a body weakening by the minute. Full of the bitter taste of the forgotten fever, it had him hoisted between the world of darkness and the one where Tanith twittered at him through his shadowy vision; the men who marched him to the old throne dropping him to his knees before her.

Lights burst and danced across the room and the smell of rotted blooms was overpowering in Shye's nose. Every movement sent a screech of hollow aching through his shoulders, his arms – otherwise terrifyingly numb – and then piercing through his eyes as the chance to blissfully fade away was dragged back by the poison shivering through him.

Cassius, who came to rest on his knees beside him after being similarly thrown before Tanith, hardly looked in better shape. Still, he looked defiantly up at Tanith and the men who'd arrested him with a fury undaunted by the clasps of black iron holding him in place.

Despite the effort it was to do so, Shye managed to spare him a suitably condemning look, and the expression of regret the prince threw him in return was not enough to ease the burn of his betrayal, the burn of fever in Shye's blood. But even still, Shye admired his display. The imperial prince evidently had a little more bite in him than Shye had thought.

Then, Tanith's hunters brought in the unconscious form of Muse, tossing the battered remains of his violin next to him. A flash of heat that had nothing to do with the fever raging in his bones shot through Shye, and his hands clenched into fists, straining against the cuffs binding him. It only served to make the pain incandescent and the room begin to tilt beneath his knees.

The hunters removed wads of cotton from their ears and one of them – a vicious woman decked in gold and rich garnet – said, "The guests will be waking up." Cutting a glance at the lordly figure holding the Horned Crown, she smiled, her teeth pearled, expression pleased. "Ready to receive a new world."

The huntress kicked Muse with her pointed boot and said to the man holding the crown, "This one wasn't particularly hard to track down. And I see you got your quarry too, Veredan."

Shye's gorge rose as she turned her hungry gaze on him and Cassius, his knuckles going white with tension.

"And one for Ashea and Mysander too," she huffed in amusement. "The only one who's missing—"

A smooth, charming voice cut through as someone new entered the room, the grand stair echoing with his haughty approach.

"No need to miss me, Huntress," Lord James said, striding imperiously to join them, taking up residence behind Shye to become his watchful guardian, relieving Lord Ashea, who then retreated from Shye's awareness.

Shye suppressed a shiver from working down his neck as the Lord's fingers brushed his wound gently and then tangled harshly in his hair to wrench his head back. Pain tumbled down his spine and he clenched his teeth to choke the cry that rose to his lips. Feverish tears pricked the corners of his eyes and he struggled to catch his breath, each tug jerking through his shoulder blades.

"I was just sorting some family business," he continued, brushing his sweep of dark hair behind his ear in an elegant movement.

Cassius failed to hide a wince as Lord James wrenched Shye's neck again, and Shye felt a flush of resentment settle in his stomach. If only Cassius had given up the damn crown.

"Well," Tanith purred, "now that we're all here, I see no reason to delay any longer."

She clicked her ring-laden fingers together and Lord Veredan brought over the crown.

"I hope it eats you," Shye hissed at her, earning himself another sharp wrench through the roots of his hair. A breathless sound passed his lips as it shot down through his body.

Tanith's mouth curled in a slow smile. "Hush, child."

She took the crown into her hands and gazed at the smooth wrought lines, the curl of the horns that gave its name. Lust shone in her gaze, and she spoke softly to the room, "It's almost anticlimactic."

Soft malice laced the lines of her face and she turned to Shye, her tunic shifting and shimmering in colours of violet night and bleached bone run through with glittering filaments of iron. Her cloak spread out behind her, in that same gauzy bone white, and was drenched in strings of pearls. She looked terribly human in her iron-shot armour; the desire to own the whole world hungry within her.

Shye knew he had little chance of stopping her now.

"To think it is so easy to destroy you," she said, her face narrowing into bare apprehension, "as you destroyed me. And everything will be the better for it. No Strangeness, no disorder, no Dusk Lords, just a world with no wildness in it. Camillus had it right, after all."

Shye tried to move his arms, tried to force his legs beneath him to stand, but the aching numbness had clambered into every limb, and the bullet lodged in his shoulder was a mess of piercing fragments and splintered metal. A heavy, liquid feeling was crawling up his throat and though he caught Cassius's pleading, panicked stare, he could do nothing but lean forward and hack up golden-edged bile onto the floor by Lord James's feet.

It burned past his lips, and blood joined the mess on the floor. He swayed towards the polished expanse and was yanked back by Lord

James, who, even as Shye was too cloudy to feel it, bent down close to his ear.

Tanith was still talking to them. Sweeping through pools of light, she appeared to glide between the long blinks of Shye's eyelids, raising the crown to the light, its twistedness wrought in broken oaths.

"I had such plans. To restore the Dusk Lords and our kingdom, to take this crown . . ."

She held her ringed hand out to Shye, so that he could see the bone-hewed seal resting on it, the gem fitted within matching the veins in the polished floor he'd just blemished with iron sickness. Labradorite, a Blooded gem.

"I had this made when my brother fled the king's wrath. I stayed when he fled, I served while he hid, while our estates and our standing burned down around us. I was the true Dusk Lord of our family. His seal should have been mine. His title would have been mine. But then I realised, what use are the Dusk Lords when you are not Dusk Blooded? All the power of my Blood, in you, and not even the Nain could give it back. That Blood is what you took from me, sucked it from me to feed your own, and with it my family, my loyalty, and my purpose. It's almost flattering to know that this is how Camillus and our last dear king must have felt when they saw what we could be. It's just a shame neither of them had enough backbone to finish it for good."

Her lips twisted viciously with the force of her memories. "Ezra would never have found you if it weren't for those wretched Nain. He wasn't even looking." Then, slowly, her face relaxed and she sighed and said in a milder tone, "But then, he wouldn't have returned if it weren't for you, which means he'd still be out there somewhere with his own ideas of rebellion and not bleeding and broken somewhere below the Brightspir."

She hummed in pleasure at the image.

Shye's mind reeled from her words, scrambling to pull past the pain and fatigue, trying to understand, but his mind failed to fit the pieces of her words into the world he knew before this day and the people he'd lived nearly his whole life.

"You're lying. I don't have a family – the crew, the captain, we made a deal. They were my family but not – not – not my blood, not like that," Shye choked, spinning nonsense of his tongue as though somehow he might stumble his way onto a truth that didn't hurt so much. Until he did.

"Not like you," he continued, before raising his head to glare at Tanith, leaning forward with a ferocity as though ready to lunge at her although his body could not follow through, "He was better than you could ever hope, or wish, or dream."

"And yet, I must point out he never gave you the Creed name. Our name. As his nephew and my son, you are entitled to it." Tanith tilted her head mockingly at Shye, her smile returning as Shye said nothing and she shrugged at his condemning silence. "Ah, I suppose, you can't win them all, my love. I don't expect your admiration but at least I've never lied to you. For the sake of humanity, this must be done. It's the only way that's fair."

She lifted the crown above her head, awaiting no ceremony.

"Wait," came the voice from behind Shye's ear. Craning his neck back, Shye could see the cool calculation in Lord James's pale, shallow eyes. They flicked to him, just for a second, and Shye's breath caught. He looked away, bowing his head, mind spinning over again, shaken by a whole new revelation.

They were the wrong colour. Lord James had eyes of a darker, harder blue.

Lord James pointed to Cassius. "Why not make him do it?"

Cassius choked and sent a murderous glare towards his cousin, growling out, "You traitor—"

Lord James interrupted silkily, and Shye found himself second-guessing what he thought he had seen in that gaze. "I think you'll find that the traitor here is you."

If Lord James was truly Dorian in disguise, then they had already surmised how Tanith had got her claws on the key to their undoing.

But their words seemed to please her and she purred, "What an excellent idea. Perhaps we should have some ceremony. After all, I am finishing what his father started, what dear little prince tried so hard to avoid, playing at peace with your pet Stormborn."

Tanith dangled the crown in front of Cassius, knowing he could not take it with his hands bound. "I will do this in your place, and they are proof so I will show you that the true face of peace can only come from one last suppression."

Her cloak swished across the floor as she turned her back on them all, handing the crown off to one of the hunters, and she went to her knees before the throne, spreading out her cloak behind her. Lord James leaned in, lips brushing Shye's ear, which only made him shiver all the more.

"Fight it," they commanded, Dorian's façade failing slightly as they whispered into his ear. "Iron is an old weakness from an old world. That is not the world we live in. If you don't want to see it end, you have to fight for it. You have to burn for it."

"Why can't *you* just take off the bindings?" Shye hissed over a wave of rolling acid and the vile taste of ember and ash.

"I can't, not without them noticing. You've got to bring the storm." Dorian was apologetic, Lord James's tone creeping back in. But then they said in words that were all theirs, a memory threaded about their mouth, "Bring them to their knees."

Shye closed his eyes and wondered, past the oily tastes clogging his mouth, the spears of pain lancing occasionally through the numbness and the creep of flagging deepness past the pores of his bones, if it would be easier to just give in.

A little wind fluttered around his knees and he sighed.

Shye, it whispered his name, and he drank in the furtive touch that Dorian left on his shoulder before he shut out the world and dove into the well of viscous dark within. He heard them haul Cassius to his feet, heard the prince's vehement protestations, and the snap and clink of his bindings being loosened and retightened. His snarl as the Horned Crown was shoved into his hands.

Shye could only breathe.

Feeling dripped slowly back into his arms with burning ferocity.

Blackness swirled around him. He felt Dorian move away from him, leaving him to the swallowing ache of iron all alone, and his eyes snapped open, searching for a tether to bring the deepness out. He saw Cassius raise the Horned Crown.

The deepness rose to the call, crashing over the yawning void offered by the fever iron twisting through his blood. Light pricked at his fingers and the weight of the poison rose up and up, through his stomach to his lungs, his throat . . .

The deepness splintered under his flesh.

He screamed as light – pure and searing, singed at the edges – poured from within him and thunder rolled above the palace and in the beats of his heart. Lightning and rain ran from the violet night around them, like the light and tears dripping from Shye's skin.

In a flash, the light withdrew, and Shye shakily got to his feet.

The hunters stood there, stunned, though Dorian had enough sense to cover their eyes. One of their number, Lord Ashea, stumbled towards him and Shye grabbed him close, sending a burst of condensed light through his body until it sparked in his eyes, and he fell to the ground – dead or unconscious, Shye didn't care.

Tanith rose from kneeling and swirled around; aggravation washed across her expression. She held out her hand to Cassius. "Give it to me."

Shye stepped forward and Cassius snarled at her, his bindings curving red trails of blood poisoning up his arms.

"No," he said vehemently and backed away from her.

Shye felt the air shift behind him, the storm running wild inside him, and dodged out of the way as Mysander tried to grab him from behind, a second pair of bindings clutched in his rough hands. Shye pivoted and pushed on the hunter's fine coat to the body that lay beneath it and sent the fathoms, which echoed in the howls of the storm outside, rolling through the hunter. He dropped like the other to the floor, reddened water leaking from his mouth and nose.

Across the room, Tanith slid an arsenal of thin, needled blades into her palms. Cassius was batting them away, using the Horned Crown as a shield. Sensing an opening, Cassius disarmed her, sending one of her blades flying to clatter to the floor, and followed it up by swinging the weight of the crown across her cheek, blood rising to mar her skin.

She reached a hand to touch it and let out a beastly cry when it came away stained with red. As she lunged for him, her last blade in hand, Cassius saw Lord James standing wearily near the throne.

Shye read the decision on Cassius's face as the prince tossed the crown in the air and sent it flying towards James. Towards Dorian.

Cold, unforgiving, screaming metal fastened around Shye's neck in a collar from behind, a blow to the back of his head following it. The room tilted as his skin tightened and the taste of old blood and tar surfaced in the back of his mouth. The void burst open beneath his feet.

Shye, called the little wind, seeming very far away.

He blinked and stars rained down across his vision.

The Horned Crown glittered before him, merciless and cruel, with the room around him blackened and bare, and the scorched floors and dust hanging heavy in the air.

Shye.

Ash scattered on the ground. The air was hot. The stench of rotten blooms and age was all around him, and the wind that moved them sweet but silent. There was no sound in the room at all.

Shye!

The trees in the corners of the room were broken and bent; decaying statues from ages long past. Whatever force had kept them preserved for so long dying along with everything else. The throne too was desiccated stone, the remnants of gleaming mineral washed to dull white-ish-grey. Everything in this room was dead. Everything in this room, including Shye.

Outside, the city lived and thrived in its own ordered, rewritten way. In the name of humanity. And Shye was a ghost, like this room was a ghost, like the rest of his long-dead kind. He blazed alone, cold and white.

The Horned Crown glittered before him. With an anguished cry, the memory of it sizzling in his veins, he reached out ... and took it.

SHYE!

Something heavy landed in Shye's arms as his vision swam between Dorian, struggling to keep their composure as Lord James, shouting orders for the remaining hunters to 'Stand DOWN' and Tanith laughing, and an empty, desolate throne room.

Gradually, Shye strung himself back together, with his fingers catching around the arches of the Horned Crown that Dorian had thrown to him. The last two remaining hunters had pistols levelled at Shye, and Tanith had Cassius wrapped up in her arms; the only blade left in her arsenal pointed into the soft flesh of his throat.

The prince's hazel eyes watched Shye with regretful vigilance. "Do it."

Tanith pressed her knife deeper, drawing a trickle of blood to the surface. The cut on her cheek was starting to clot, long after it had permanently stained her white pearled cloak. She laughed at Cassius.

"You think he can?" She eyed Shye up and down and giggled again. "It's a miracle he's still standing with all those bindings blocking his Manifest. I mean," she lowered her voice to a husky tenor, painted lips curving, "look at you. You're as helpless as a babe."

She turned her sharp smile on the two hunters still standing and nodded at Shye and Dorian. "Kill them."

Pistols cocked. Dorian armed theirs in return, steadying it with one hand and sliding back the hammer with the other. The bandages wrapped around their palm, which cradled the familiar piece, slipped to reveal a synergy of glass and flesh, dazzling and inhuman.

Shye swallowed and hoped he'd have the chance to ask about it later.

"Do it," they echoed, aiming their pistol at Tanith, while Cassius remained unflinching in her clutches.

"Shoot him," Tanith said, looking at Shye, "and bring me the crown."

"Go ahead and try," Dorian challenged, bringing out a second pistol and arming it.

Shye clutched the Horned Crown tight and felt the chill of its power. The remnants of a will so old pressed on him, and underneath it ran a current of Blooded strength; corrupted and neglected. It surged up, hissing.

Shye reached in for the deepness, feeling it coil and caress his senses, and then he reluctantly let it go. It settled in his centre, the fathoms keening, rolling thick and black and mournful, as he searched instead for the deadly touch of poison that coursed through him. It thrashed and seared his blood, rising like bile in his throat. His nails dug into his palms as it battered against him. The deepness wrapped his heart, and splits of light lashed through its infinite waves.

Dimly, he heard the report of guns. He opened his glowing eyes to see Dorian looking back at him, with a bloom of red ruining their fine coat. He whispered to the wind his words for them. The breeze fluttered away, and Shye let the fever iron in.

He raised the crown, with the taste of that other world on his lips, the fever blistering behind his eyes, under his blood, between his insides and out. It blazed and roared, cracking his bones in its teeth.

"Blood pays for Blood," he spat at Tanith and watched her eyes go wide as he brought the crown down onto his head. When the crown touched his skin, he let it burn and his body burned with it.

Dorian screamed his name, but Shye could barely gasp a breath as light cracked and spiralled from the clash of the feverdeep, the crown pressing in on his head, his nose filled with the burnt smell of metal, cleared by the wash of rain. His insides unravelled and in the middle of the light something screamed.

It might've been him.

Dorian felt their heart freeze as Shye put the Horned Crown on his head and regarded them for a moment with his beautiful, glowing eyes, before erupting suddenly into a pillar of blinding light. Warring flashes of cold silver-black and sickening red streaked through it, and they heard themself screaming his name.

Tanith screeched, louder than the wind that seemed to echo from the pulse of light, and Dorian tore their eyes away from where Shye had been to see Cassius's bindings melting off his wrists, and the red-and-black stain of iron sickness going with them.

Cassius granted Tanith a cold half-smile, and Dorian felt the air shiver as Tanith's knife turned to glass and shattered in her hand.

Tanith cried out and backed away.

Lord Veredan and Lady Bellhall, the only two hunters left after Shye's attack, were busy being subdued by the late arrival of two of Creed's crew, Alice and Edge – right after they'd managed to put a bullet through Dorian's coat, grazing their side.

Glass glittered beneath Cassius's feet, lashing towards Tanith like ice crawls its way over water, seething like a living frost.

Dorian's side twinged a little and their breath choked in their lungs as the wind continued to repeat Shye's last words to them. With an ache in their chest that had nothing to do with injury, they clenched their eyes resolutely shut and started towards the pillar of light.

"What are you doing?" Cassius called.

Glass crept up Tanith's cloak and turned it to cool, black stone, creeping up her legs and over her waist. She screamed as it locked her in place and kept climbing higher, the tips of her fingers turning black, her flesh turning to glass-run marble. It climbed from her elbows to her shoulders, and then to her neck. Glossy, black eyes stared into the distance from her frozen face, immortal terror in her gaze, her mouth still open in a now silent scream.

Alice and Edge finished their business with the hunters, leaving two more prone bodies on the floor. Alice stood guard over the hunter's bodies, as Edge moved to tend to the fallen Muse.

Dorian felt the force of the light numbing their cheeks, and the insides of their closed eyelids splashed with its brightness.

"Saving him."

Sucking in a breath, Dorian ran forward and pitched themself into the pillar of light, colliding with it, through it and immediately felt its presence all around them. A rumbling hum vibrated through them, and a numb shock slithered from their head to their feet. They reached out their hands.

Their fingers grazed something solid. Shye.

He was emitting so much light and storm's force that it made it seem like a bellow was blowing and pushing Dorian away, and rain seemed to be falling from above, splashing on their skin. Their fingers slipped on the slickness that coated Shye, before they dug their nails in deep and grabbed a hold. Circling their arms around him, they whispered into the light that pulsed around them, the voice of the little wind ringing in their head, "I burn for you too . . . now try not to die."

And Dorian shoved them both from the storm of living feverdeep light as it started to spin and coalesce around the Horned Crown, which hung in the air and then clattered with a splintering crack to the tiled floor as they tumbled to the ground beyond it.

The light rumbled and flashed, sliding through the fissures in its dented form – the Horned Crown becoming a part of it – its ghostly feverish brilliance breaking and reforming again and again until, in a final unbounded flicker, it burst, and a wave of melted heat and wind crashed through the room.

The Horned Crown shattered with the fractured light.

Shye's bindings melted away; the iron sickness passing from his skin, leaving it hale and sun-loved, and the rest of his form still and silent where he lay in Dorian's arms. They thumped their head on his chest, ignoring the prick of tears behind their still-closed lids, and prayed for a heartbeat.

CHAPTER 34

THE RAINS HAD STARTED ON THE NIGHTRUN OF THE CORONATION AND its failed revolt, and they continued over the spans as the frost took hold. The people of Mistral spent the cool, fleeting rises under the cover of estates and glass-hewn conservatories, moving quickly between private and public residences, venturing into the chill only if they had to and always with thick fur-lined cloaks or thin glass-shuttered parasols.

Businesses opened late and closed early. The Guild Circle and high guilds handed out limited rosters, and even the palace slowed some of its operations to plan a season's worth of parties and firelit festivals. The braziers had been struck on the nightrun of the coronation and would continue to burn brightly in the dark and through the meagre hours of rise for the rest of the frost.

Those same braziers glowed across the city at Dorian's back as they trudged towards the teahouses, a number of lanterns hanging happily from their eaves with strings of glass strung between them from the celebrations, which instead of being ignored in the wake of the coronation assault simply slipped quietly into the usual frostfall gaiety. The hunters stained by James and Tanith's treason were crossed from the guild records, and their inkings stripped from their skin. There wasn't much sense left in Lord Ashea – his eyes had faded into blindness since the assault on the old throne, and the dark had taken his words with it. Mysander suffered a traitor's death; his flesh numb and unfeeling since the crash of Shye upon him, and on paper so had Veredan and Bellhall.

But Veredan and Bellhall had not gone quietly from the throne room, despite being trussed and frog marched by Alice and Edge. As they had passed Cassius, Bellhall's face had twisted defiantly and she spat at him with hateful vehemence, as Veredan called him 'bastard' and other crueller names for his tainted blood. Dorian remembered the way Cassius had flinched, his power suddenly spilling from him like ocean spray, flowing across the floor. How it had turned her and Veredan to petrified statues of pale jade. They remembered the shock and the fear on Cassius's face, his eyes going wide and horrified, as he realised what his Manifest could do. And so, Kernon and his powers of Dusk had declared their sentence: immortality in service to those old doors. Their smooth, insolent faces were to remain there, glaring out from the shadows of the grand stair, set to guard the room they'd failed in, and daring people to look upon them and not feel a quiver.

Lady Fenrent retired from service to crown and from society and did so in silence, fortunate to have not been involved in the assault directly.

The few remaining people even aware of that nightrun's proceedings, and the reason for the prince's sudden decision to remain uncrowned, were also the only few willing to brave the frostfall inclemency for a meeting that Dorian was not only attending but had also called for.

Heavy, near-frozen drops spilled incessantly from the skies, and Dorian cursed that they had only their old favourite hat and coat to protect them from the first falls of the season. They left the sodden things hanging on a coat stand near the door, next to a line of glass parasols set on hooks for forgetful patrons to borrow, which Dorian made a note to remember as they turned their sluggish feet towards the private room Leon had recommended they rent for the occasion.

The teahouse was emptier during the falls, but even then, Dorian still didn't expect to see Cassius lounging in a chair pulled before the fire, especially after everything that had happened. He gave them a thin, wry smile, looking bare and boyish without the weight of the crown.

"Cousin."

Dorian slid the door shut behind them, placing the pilfered bottle of Corentinian wine, the cheapest they could find in the cabinet of their Brightspir chambers, down on the low table in the middle of the room. A set of tea and little jade cups waited there for the rest of those to arrive who'd been involved that night.

Cassius eyed their offering, rather than the hand that deposited it – the woven mess of glass and flesh glinting prettily and horribly in the firelight – and, in turn, hauled up a bottle of night-thorn and placed it on the table next to theirs.

Dorian snorted ungraciously. "Put that down. He doesn't deserve it," they said.

Cassius idly picked up the fire poker and jabbed at the coals until a comfortable heat suffused the room. He replied, "He wasn't a good man, but he was still your father and a hunter of some renown, and no one – not even him – deserves jade wine at their funeral. How much glass did you pay for it? Two fans and called it a day."

Dorian slumped into one of the comfortable chairs positioned around the low table, rumbling a laugh when Leon's voice sounded from the door, "Would ten fans be more acceptable? I'm all out of the good stuff."

He traipsed over to sit across from Dorian, followed by Ever, who walked gingerly and was only just allowed out of bed, then Ezra, much in the same position, though healing fast, and then Jin. Dorian was surprised how glad they were that they were all here.

One by one, each took their seat around the table and thumped down a bottle. As promised, Leon's offering was almost no better than Dorian's, and Ever's was not much better than that.

Cassius *tsked* them gently, though Dorian noted a smile settling in the corner of his mouth.

Ezra had brought something green and hazardous looking,

supposedly from a small boutique in the Feng capital, and it was less a funerary offering than an offering to himself. Jin brought a tiny bottle of sherry that Dorian could only assume he'd nicked from his father's liquor cabinet.

The captain looked at the tiny bottle with a raised brow and then shot Cassius's offering a disappointed glance.

"Really?" he asked dryly.

To which Cassius levelled archness like a weapon and said, "Oh, were you hoping you could steal some more?"

Ezra's eyes deepened in colour, returning without pause, "You know, I almost didn't recognise you without a crown."

"I'll wear another when your apprentice – a shame you still haven't acknowledge your connection to him – keeps his promise and makes one for me," he snapped back, and then caught himself, flashing a glance at Dorian, who grimaced and reached for the teapot, busying themself by pouring the clear, aromatic liquid into their cup.

Cassius's expression dimmed with guilt.

Creed sighed and reached over to Dorian, before sliding the handle of the teapot from Dorian's fingers and filling the rest of the jade cups to the brim with steaming tea.

Ever spoke up gently in the silence that followed, "The boy hasn't recovered, then?"

Dorian nodded, cupping the little mug between their palms.

"He'll wake up," they said and lifted the cup to their mouth, thin, fragrant tea burning over their tongue.

"Let us not die in burning bright, but lie and dream of better delights," Creed recited, levelling it at the table at large with an expectant air and a pause.

Cassius snorted. "That was lovely, Captain. The gulls must be charmed by your work."

Ever hummed peaceably and finished for Ezra, "There is no death for the Blooded bold, for every breath returns to Kernon's hold, so dream and fear none as the wild winds sigh, the blood of Dusk cannot die."

Ever's eyes crinkled at the tempered surprise on Jin's face and the sharpened interest on Cassius's. "From *The Rise of Dusk*. It is rare to find a prayer that not even Feng could record its origin."

Dorian's grip tightened on the cup and for a moment they feared it might crack. They raised the cup and downed the tea, clacking it down on the table and reaching again for the teapot.

"He'll wake up," they repeated softly and didn't wait for further words before raising the cup to their lips again.

Silence followed and, for a while, they were all occupied in draining the teapot dry. When there was nothing left to pour, Leon reached beneath his chair and placed a plain wood-grained box on the table.

Dorian took it and stalked over to the fire. Without a second glance, they tossed it into the flames and watched as it caught alight.

With great ceremony, everyone uncapped their bottles and poured a glass of their chosen liquor.

Leaving their bottle untouched, Dorian glared at the table and dared anyone to say something, but in silence, they only toasted and drank according to the least amount of observance to the rites. Leon grimaced visibly at the taste, though Ever downed his without a flinch, despite the lacking quality of the wine.

Jin pushed his over to Creed, who was smacking his lips in satisfaction of his green abomination, and he took it with a shake of his head, avoiding Jin's eyes and the cheeky look on his face. He knocked back the sherry and pointed an elegant finger at Jin's pearly, impish grin, saying, "Don't look at me, Raven boy. I knew your mother and my secrets lie with the Sereni, so don't even think about taking a peek inside my head."

They filled their cups again and tossed them respectfully into the fire. Whatever they had thought of Lord James, his death deserved some recognition and the rites that accompanied that.

Privately, Dorian was glad that none of them seemed keen to do the same – even like this, which was hardly the ceremony James would have thought he deserved – for the shining glass statue that Cassius had made out of Tanith.

Their finger dragged across the glass of the bottle, but they made no move to open it.

"Well," Cassius said when it was done, shorter and more stilted than most rites for a dear departed, "that should lay his ghost to rest."

He tapped his finger against his cup in an echo of Dorian, turning segments of jade into spiralling pearl.

Cassius jerked away, and Creed clicked his tongue. "You need to learn some control, Imperial Prince, for all you're a quick study."

Cassius dropped the cup to the table with narrowed eyes. "I did not mean to do that."

Ezra just smiled, his green eyes shifting from dimness to light. "A manifest is born of blood and element, but it is shaped by emotion. All the books you've read on us, all that learning, and not one has taught you restraint."

Cassius breathed out slowly and kept his hands to himself, turning to Dorian instead of rising to take the bait, ignoring Creed completely. "When do you leave?"

Dorian shrugged; their bottle still capped on the table before them. "Once we're done here."

"Where will you go?" Ever pressed softly, aware that Dorian had been tight-lipped about their plans, especially as the wake of the Blooded remained imminent and their saviour remained stubbornly asleep.

Dorian ran a hand through their shorn hair, now back to its natural blazing auburn, and said in weary tones, "Feng, first. Then Aura." They shrugged again, every rise bringing a familiar ache to their chest. "Anywhere after that, if you can be trusted to keep it together here and some great war doesn't break out."

Near the fire, Cassius let out an apprehensive laugh and stood. He gestured to Leon, who stood as well, and slid his embellished long coat over his shoulders; his dark hair was held back by jewelled clips instead of the wood and steel of the cursed crown.

"Yes, if true peace is to happen then we have a lot of work to do." He dibbed an affectionate kiss on Dorian's temple, and said, "Your Stormborn left us quite a mess."

Dorian twitched a smile, tinged with bitterness. "Ah, but you're alive."

The prince nodded and said solemnly, brushing a familial peck to Dorian's head in farewell, "Thank him for me if . . . when you can."

Cassius invited Ever and Creed to join him and they accepted, though whether they were going to do any work or just give Dorian some time, Dorian didn't know and didn't care. They only felt relieved that Jin slipped out behind them, leaving Dorian alone. They didn't want anyone to see this.

Uncorking the bottle, Dorian got up and crouched before the fire.

The rites of sorrow and honour belonged to those who were left behind, and while the rites for Lord James had been lacklustre at best, they were still more than Dorian thought he deserved. In their mind, they swore that he could be grateful that they had given him the opportunity to be toasted at all. So, he could forgive them for this.

Taking a swig of the cheap wine, Dorian wiped their mouth on the back of their flesh hand and considered the bottle clutched there.

"This is it, Father," they said bitterly to the flames. "Guess it sucks to be a traitor."

And they dumped the rest of the cheap wine on the floor, leaving the empty bottle on the table and dousing the fire without completing the rite. They left the teahouses, pulling their hat down low and their coat tightly around them, the rain splashing puddles on the streets, which would be frosted over by next rise.

They boarded the *Oathbreaker*, hidden in the estuary near the Starless Caverns beneath Kernon's Seat, and the call to the crew went up from Alice to make the ship ready, as by evenspan they had "best be underway". By nightrun, Dorian was sailing on open waters, leaving the capital, Cassius and the original captain of the *Oathbreaker* far behind.

Shye was dreaming of the *Oathbreaker*. The roll of the ship beneath his old bunk, the rock of the waves and water outside and the breath of a wind giving way to frost, instead of the sun-balmed breeze that he remembered best.

Pain was not unusual in Shye's dreams, and the twinges that took his breath away as he sat up couldn't dislodge the hazy liquidity of his body, but the bandages that wrapped his chest and shoulder were new and oddly coarse against his dream-skin. His bare feet hit the floor, legs shaking as he levered himself upright using the front of a chair facing the bed as leverage.

Muse seemed to be playing a violin somewhere beyond the door, and the quartermaster's cabin around him was unusually clean, with all his trinkets tidied and put away. His chest seized in a brief flash of panic when he realised his green cloak was nowhere to be seen, but it quickly faded as a hint of memory pushed at the back of his skull, but he couldn't reach it. In a dream, it wouldn't matter if he went up on deck without it.

Shye heaved himself towards the door and through the soupy mist that seemed to drag him back to the bed.

"This is a Strange dream," he muttered to himself, fighting to open the door, almost falling through it and ending up bracing himself on the wall beyond to stay vertical.

He moved drunkenly through the bowels of the ship. The wood warmed beneath his fingertips as he traced them on the walls for balance, following the call of Muse's sweet song up to the main deck. The smell of strong winds and brine grew clearer. Rising above him on the deck, Muse spilled music into the nightrun, his hair tinkling with the sound of bells.

The waves over the side were black, like the deepness, and shimmering with slits of moonlight. He fought the urge to slip into it and feel the swell and surge around him, although an idle unstuck thought said that it would likely be very cold down there.

A slide of blooming white and red caught in his periphery as he contemplated the waters, and Dorian swung onto the deck from the ratlines, grinning at Muse, washed in the pale silver of moonlight and the flickering yellow of the lanterns along the deck. Their shorn hair had lost Lord James's swished gentlemen's style, and it writhed in the wind; the ends tucked behind their ears. They shone in the violet night, with their loose white shirt brighter than the moon's run across the skies.

They joined Muse near the railing, and the sound of strings and bells rose on the winds. Shye took an aching step towards them.

Muse's song tapered into stillness.

"That was beautiful," Dorian said, an easy smile tucked into their charming mouth.

"You're beautiful," Shye heard himself say, somewhere far away.

He expected the Dorian of his dreaming to turn to him with that easy grin and say something teasing, but instead they whipped to him with shock written plainly on their face, which quickly gave way to pale worry.

Muse turned too, and seeing him, fumbled with his instrument.

It crashed to the deck and Shye stumbled forward – the image of Muse on the ground, his battered violin falling next to him, the shrill sound of a warning note in Shye's ears before blistering pain shattered – but had to stop and grasp at the railing as a hot, deep ache ripped through his back.

The cool steel band of a ring pinched on his fourth finger, and, blinking through his swimming vision, it glittered there, undeniably real on his hand. A white opal and labradorite seal with a light-trailed star at its centre. He held it up in front of his face to watch the moonlight catch on the newly forged surface.

Someone pinched his arm and he hissed, focusing beyond the ring to see Dorian's face looming in front of him, with Muse tucked anxiously behind their shoulder.

Shye pressed his ringed hand to their chest, startled to find it warm and solid beneath it, and confessed to them, "I think I'm dreaming that we eloped."

Dorian's concerned eyes crinkled a little in the corners.

"You're not dreaming, though you should definitely be in bed."

Shye wasn't sure that was true, especially as the cloying haze covering the night in a liquid film had yet to lift from him. But he wasn't quite sure how to explain the liquid state of nightrun to Dorian . . .

"Ah," he said instead. "But we are eloping—"

"No," Muse interjected quickly, "but you did destroy the Horned Crown."

Shye nodded. The memory was absent though the shadow of it remained; a hole of raw, pointed space in his mind and the echo of corrosive heat and burning light.

"And save the Empire, its prince and the Blooded," Muse continued with pride, as Dorian eased themselves beside him and pulled his weight half onto theirs.

He leaned gratefully into them. They pulled the hand that was clawing weakly into their shirt and twined their fingers together, propping them both up on the railing.

"Yer also a Dusk Lord," came a raspy call from the helm.

Shye gave a little backwards wave to the voice, who had to be Edge, and flopped his hand back down. He was starting to think this wasn't a dream after all.

Dorian skidded a finger over the cool seal of Shye's ring.

"Cassius made it for you before we left, with the help of Jin's father."

He nodded once, feigning realisation and said teasingly, "Oh, *so Cassius and I are . . .*"

Dorian huffed and shook their head in mock threat, and he felt a furtive smile crack across his lips, while Muse looked on like he wanted to cuff him across the head for playing dumb but wasn't sure he was allowed.

"There have always been four Dusk Lords and if one is lost, and one clearly is, then another must be appointed. I think it's why Creed didn't acknowledge you after Tanith abandoned you and he found you, aside from the Creed name not having a lot to offer you at the time. This way, you wouldn't be bound to his position and could come into your own. Surely no one deserves the title more than you."

Dorian raised the ring to their mouth and kissed it, bowing their head to show the respect words could not express for Shye and everything he'd done. Something in their eyes sparked with a heated longing for him and wicked unravellings started to shine in their eyes, spilling a burst of warmth into Shye's gut as they raked him up and down with it. But then they caught on his bandages and the wicked glint gave way to a rare softness.

Dorian reached out and pushed Shye's wild, unbound hair behind his ear. "I'm glad you woke up."

Shye tried to hide the flush that bloomed in him, and he returned with a truthful if teasing, "You're better than any dream I could have."

Muse gagged from where he had wandered on the other side of the deck.

Looking out across the dark waves, Shye caught Edge at the helm and the teasing wink he sent them. Beneath the shift of waves, he could hear snoring coming from below and the hum of Mercy in the galley.

The wind gave a slow caress to his skin and he shivered.

Dorian's hand that was not caught up in his, glimmered and flared, a mess of veined black opal and sunstone twining across their palm and down their fingers, up to the inner crook of their elbow. The whole thing was a tapestry of stained glass and melded flesh.

Shye reached for it and they flinched back, before letting him trace the lines and whorls of colour, touching the pads of their fingers to his and then to his lips to feel the Strange combination of cold glass and warm skin.

"So where are we going?" he asked, letting the fluid feel of world sink beneath his consciousness.

Dorian didn't answer for a moment, their head bumping to rest on his for a second before they reluctantly untangled from his grip and fished an imperial assignment from the sling sewn inside their shirt. They handed it to him, still sealed shut by Cassius's stamp.

"He made you an emissary to the Blooded, though I imagine the last, and now first, of the Dusk Lords will be much more, given time."

They reached up to trace his cheek with their gem-studded fingers. "First, we go to Feng."

"Right."

His cheeks pinked a little as Dorian's fingertips slipped from his cheek to his jaw.

"And then to Aura." Their fingers dipped to his collar, and the heat in Shye's gut shuddered at the smooth skim across his skin.

"Of course."

Dorian smirked, looking pleased with his reaction, and took their fingers away. They pulled off the railing to stand in front of him, bracketing his body with their arms, heat shielding him from the bellows of the wind.

"After that, wherever."

Shye hummed and leant forward to rest his head on Dorian's shoulder, his back starting to stiffen. Dorian hauled him up and held him close, the ship swaying under them, and the lantern lights flickering at the edges of their vision.

Muse and Edge shared a disgusted glance at the pair of them, and the violinist struck up once again, sending his music over the waves and into the dark nightrun cloaking the ship.

"Wherever?" he asked excitedly.

He smiled and pulled out of Dorian's hold, towing them up towards the helm where Edge was holding court with the *Oathbreaker*'s wheel.

Dorian followed clumsily, laughing as the wind whipped past them, and they nodded, slinging their arm around his waist as they watched the sea barrel by; an ocean of dark and endless deep, split with light.

They hummed into his mouth as they leaned in to kiss him.

"Here and there, all across the sea and land, the Blooded will be waking. They will need you and they will need Cassius. Wherever your wind calls you, that's where we must go."

The musicians in the ballroom several levels below were striving hard at their work, so much so that Cassius could still faintly hear them as he snuck away from the party he was meant to be hosting and into his office in the imperial wing of the palace.

He regretted telling Shye that peacetimes left a prince ample time for reading. Now that the falls had stopped for a time, the party season had officially begun, and it wasn't as if his people had forgotten what their prince looked like simply because he no longer wore a crown. It had been a difficult endeavour to get away and he was sure it wouldn't be long before Ever Locke, his Huntsman and newly appointed adviser, sent the newly restored Ezra Creed to drag him back to the ballroom for appearance's sake.

Shrugging out of his costume coat, he slung it over the back of the chair and took a seat before a desk scattered with papers, held down in piles by the books they related to, which were left open to various important pages. His royal seal was sitting where he left it, on its side next to a half-used wax stick. Idly, he righted it.

Sighing, he pulled a sheaf of papers from the pile and hefted one of the tomes closer, holding his breath against the puff of dust that wafted from the crinkled, yellow pages.

In his mind, he hoped for Dorian's sake that Shye's stubborn sleep had ended and that they had reached Feng together. Either way, he trusted them to deliver the sealed letters he had assigned them with. And if Ezra was mourning his position as captain of the *Oathbreaker*, the restoration of his lands and the restructuring of the capital had kept him busy enough that Cassius had yet to see any evidence of it.

Inking his pen, he read quickly over the notes Ever and Leon, though mostly Leon, had left for him during the day. It was easy to find records of the first king's laws, patchy though they were in places, but the ancient laws from an Old World were proving much more difficult to trace. Without them, Cassius wasn't sure he could move forward with the subtlety they needed to make this work. To code the presence of the Blooded into law. To create a new capital and court out of the old, one where Dusk Lords and human princes ruled in alliance, so that Shye and Dorian could feel free to return and Cassius could sleep at night without the shadow of his father's suppression in the back of his mind. Without the memory of Tanith's attempt at a second one and his own failure to do anything about it sticking to every thought and action.

Rewriting ancient laws was one thing, but rewriting the turn of the world was another, and to do it would take a thorough understanding of how they had failed it in the past.

Cassius's pen scratched furiously as he picked up the translation Leon had left for him, pieced together from copies of ancient Feng laws and histories passed along by Creed's Feng contacts.

Both the humans' place among the old empire and the Dusk Lords' place among Camillus's court had been cursory honours; a farce on each part to maintain control of land and state. Ceding that control in order to make those honours real might end up taking more time than Cassius would be given.

He could not, in good faith, be the imperial king everyone expected, but Mistral wouldn't wait forever, and neither would the Blooded. And Cassius was embarrassed to find he'd spent a lot of time reading the wrong damn things.

A gruff cough interrupted his train of thought and his pen skittered off the page, splashing ink onto his fingers. He looked up into two pairs of eyes watching him, one of laughing green and the other of yellow-specked hazel.

He'd gotten more time than he'd expected but he grouched anyway, "Patience, Creed. I'm trying to make you a prince among men. Leon, good to see you, please come in."

Creed smirked and crossed his arms over his chest. The gesture creased the crisp black coat he wore; the cuffs and hem embellished in silver with little ostentation. It was the same design as the one he'd worn the run when he'd tried to steal the crown at the end of a gun, if now much sleeker and cleaner. Though the dress code was distinctly costume, Cassius doubted any of his guests minded Creed's distinguished sartorial roguery.

Cassius had asked his tailor to dress him for the season. The coat they had returned with glimmered with frosted gems and mist stone; the first natural samples seen since Mistral's mines in the Wild Mountains had dried up in the reign of one of Cassius's ancestors.

The tailor didn't need to know Cassius had made them himself, rather than stumbling upon a lucky find in the Brightspir's treasuries.

They had made him an outfit that embodied both rain and darkness and although it hadn't been exactly what he'd meant, he was rather pleased with the work. At the same time, it was understated enough that no one had noticed when he'd tried to leave the ballroom.

Well . . .

He shot a warning look to Creed when it appeared he was about to speak.

Almost no one.

Creed sniped back at him, coming over to the desk, ignoring the look. "And I was looking for one, but, to my surprise, he was gone."

Cassius huffed but reluctantly put aside his pen and scrubbed the ink stains off his fingers. "I have work."

Ezra was no more impressed with that excuse now than he had been for the last span. "This rise you gave Feng and Aura their independence; next you will give us ours."

Cassius looked beseechingly at Leon, who remained lingering in the doorway and answered him with a raised brow. Pointedly, he didn't help Ezra shuffle him back to the ballroom. Instead, he shrugged at Ezra and helped himself to a chair, seemingly content to cast aside his role as backup almost immediately. Cassius passed him his cup of wine in thanks.

He watched carefully as Ezra sauntered over and removed Cassius's jacket from the back of his chair, dropping it into his lap. "Right now . . ." he continued provokingly.

"Yes?" Cassius asked wearily, shrugging on his coat and wondering how soon he'd have to begrudgingly let Ezra frog march him to the door. A fizzle of suspicion was growing in Cassius as the exchange went on. Leon looked very comfortable in his seat. Creed had not stopped smirking and his movements were profoundly unhurried.

Ezra paused, frowning with consideration, and then shrugged as well, doing nothing to force Cassius back towards the faraway strains of music and laughter.

"Well, I'm not sure, but I heard something about fireworks."

His green eyes flashed eagerly but he did nothing more to make Cassius leave except fetch him a glass of wine since he'd given his original to Leon and open the draperies to the balcony, letting a swirl of moonlight in. Grabbing his own glass, he turned a chair towards the expanse of the nightrun sky and sat down next to Leon, propping his feet up on the desk.

"It'd be a shame if we missed them."

Cassius was grateful to his tailor when the first cool sweep of frost shuddered jarringly through a room that had no fire or brazier to warm it, and as long as Creed wasn't making him leave, Leon certainly seemed to have no intention to . . . he looked at his pen and picked up his wine instead.

He inclined the glass in their direction. "I suppose it would . . . To ending the world as we know it."

Leon clinked his into Cassius's with a grin. Outside, the pop and fizzle of fireworks spiked across the sky, spidering colour over the horizon.

Ezra laughed and saluted Cassius back, "To saving it."

SNEAK PEEK AT DUSK LORDS
BOOK TWO
CHAPTER ONE

CASSIUS WAS ON HIS WAY TO WAR, A WAR HE WAS FIGHTING WITH WORDS and deeds, deception and persuasion. It was less bloody than one fought with weapons but no less dangerous for a prince who ruled a kingdom that both was and wasn't his. If he were to slip, if he gave too much away, showed too much or too little favour and revealed himself to be anything more than the prince of his father's empire, then his hold on Mistral would vanish and its resources with it. This was a war he had accepted and prepared for.

But the world was not satisfied. For all his work, it had sent him another test. One no one had predicted.

"Your Highness, the council is waiting."

The scrivener who called him stood sheepishly in the doorway to Cassius's office and had been there for some time, waiting for leave to speak until they could wait no longer.

Cassius looked up from the reports piled on his desk, medicas's reports, medical texts, inventories of local surgeries and lists of consulting practitioners taking over the usual papers of business and governance.

"I am waiting too," Cassius replied, standing and indicating for the scrivener to leave with confident authority. "Tell them I will be along shortly, plead for patience if you must. At this time, they must understand, I am very busy prince."

He sent the scrivener scurrying away, just as Jin came pelting down the halls towards his office. He came skidding to a stop, a recent growth spurt turning his limbs awkward and graceless, and Cassius's mood darkened when he saw that Jin had brought no letter with him.

"Nothing," he snapped.

Jin huffed and shook his head, ignoring Cassius's tone and the ire that was not meant for him.

"It's been two seasons without word." Cassius allowed himself to fume for a moment, before recollecting himself. His sighed after a moment, furious features softening a little, and nodded at Jin, the fire dying.

"Thank you for checking, Jin."

He touched the back of two fingers to Jin's forehead and scolded, "But if you have no news for me, why did you run? I can't tell if you're heated from that or from . . ." Cassius paused and took his hand back, continuing with concern, "or because you've caught it."

Jin shook his head vigorously, still catching his breath. "Not sick, feel fine, no symptoms. Just, I knew the council was sitting and I didn't—" Jin finally caught his breath in time to finish. "I didn't want to make you late and for them to blame you. After last time, when they joked that the sickness was the former king's revenge for restoring and protecting unworthy families, I thought someone might be getting suspicious, rather than just taking a shot at Creed."

"Creed has made himself an easy target for my purposes and he is a diversion that seems to be working on the council's minds. I doubt we are revealed just yet," Cassius imparted thoughtfully, though he felt a smile threaten at Jin's dedication and followed with a stern, "Don't waste your energy and provoke my concern so lightly next time."

He gestured for the boy to follow him as he left the office. As Cassius's assistant and primary scrivener, Jin was required to accompany him to the meeting, but Cassius needed to know first if there had been any word from Shye and Dorian. There had not.

Cassius's fingers slipped into his pocket to pull out the letter he had composed while waiting for Jin to return.

"You will not be required in this meeting. Remember, before you think about protesting, that I am your prince and theirs and, as long as they believe I'm human, I am above reproach. I need you to take this to Lord Payne, it needs to be sent on the swiftest tide to Feng and then to Aura with those we trust. If he hears nothing by end of season, he is to follow. We don't know where Shye and Dorian are, but we have to hope they made it as far as Aura but no further."

He held out the letter for Jin to take.

"They may not know it yet, but Shye and Dorian have a new mission."

Jin took the letter and, with a quick bow, pelted off again. Heaving a tired sigh and rubbing his cheeks to bring some colour into them, so the council would not know of his sleepless nights, Cassius carried on towards the council chambers.

"They have their unenviable mission," he muttered darkly to himself as he approached the doors behind which his latest battle lay, "And I have mine."

Dear Cousin,

We have arrived in Aura. We meet the city captain soon to present her the formal declaration of independence from the lands of Emin Rif and its (former) crown. I write former because according to the representative of the quarter in which we've docked – known as the Keel – the quarters voted under the watch of the third city captain to disregard most imperial rule. Apparently, each quarter – Keel, Rudder, Shrouds and Nest – have a vote on important matters within the city and each quarter appoints a representative for the people, while the city captain acts as overseer. I suppose it makes sense to treat the city the same as a ship, most of it is made of the same material and while half of its supports are sunk into a sandbar and the shallows of the Nest, the rest just disappear into the sea. It's certainly a sight worth seeing, it really does seem to be a floating city. You won't be surprised to learn that most of the population is Blooded here or that with such an indifferent attitude towards the rule of the previous empire that we heard nothing of my own tempest until he blew our way. Write to you with more soon. And in your next letter, more news and less complaining about Creed's teasing. Alice has taken to her new role with enthusiasm, so you have to keep him.

Dorian

Dorian crumpled the letter in their hand and then smoothed it out again, a number of crinkles old and new scarring across the words. With grim optimism, Dorian refolded the unsent letter and lit a taper, melting half a wax stick on the seal of the folder paper and stamping Shye's ring into the cooling patch of royal blue. They dropped the letter into the pocket of their coat, as if they had a real intention of actually sending it this time, instead of shoving it back into the draw they left it in, under the writing implements they brought out every time they tried to do this.

Dorian had gotten used to the rocking of the *Oathbreaker* in dock, but all previous attempts to write had ended up in the fire all the same. Enough for Dorian to stop pretending the motion of the ship still had anything to do with it.

Still, Dorian tried.

"Dear Cousin," Dorian began before sighing and slumping back in their chair as they struggled to find the words to explain how deeply their situation had changed since they had left Feng. Finally, they simply ripped off the top of the paper and tried again.

"Dear Cassius . . ."

They were no more able to continue this letter than they had been able to post the first, which had been written spans ago. But Dorian had promised themselves to make the attempt at least once a day until they could or until the wind returned to whisper their next destination. Shye's wind.

The *Oathbreaker* gave a sudden, great roll, splashing ink from the bottle all over the paper, eating Dorian's pathetic attempt with easy disdain.

Dorian watched the ink creep before scoffing, "Saves me the trouble, I guess," and tossed the ruined paper into a waste bin stacked full of similar sad pages. Standing, they began the familiar tramp from the Captain's cabin – graciously loaned to them – up towards the deck. Sunlight spilled down from above as they rose into the lightrise and fresh air finally greeted them. Ahead of them at the bow, a figure stood, swaying to and fro with the movement of the ship, his hair glinting white and near luminescent under the strong sunning.

Dorian began to make their way towards Shye as though drawn inevitably by invisible string, stopping only briefly to as they passed Muse on railing, the man's golden eyes focused on the water at the edge of the horizon.

"We going anywhere?"

Their eyes flicked to Shye, watching him suddenly clamber onto the railing, holding a rope line for balance, eyes roaming, face tight with concentration. Muse moved to watch him too.

Shye's eyes slowly closed but he did not lose his look of concentration as his body strained outwards, leaning over the water.

Muse shook his head, "No word yet."

Dorian sighed and continued over to Shye. They waited below the railing as Shye leant out, searching, until something in Shye's face gave way, his breath seeming to stutter before his body began to dip dangerously over the side and Dorian jumped forward and towed him by the waist back onto the deck.

"Careful," Dorian admonished, stumbling back with Shye in their arms.

Shye's eyes were dazed, but hope bloomed in Dorian's chest as he looked around and said, "I thought I heard . . ."

A breeze rose around them, tangling up Shye's hair, and his expression crashed into disappointment and shame with such speed it stung Dorian to see it, before crushing their budding hope under its heavy weight.

Shye rubbed his eyes and continued, "It was nothing. I didn't hear anything. I'm sorry."

Dorian's heart ached for him and their hands at Shye's waist squeezed a little in comfort.

"I know you've been sleeping badly, evidently worse than I thought if you're close to falling overboard, but you do not need to apologise to me. Your wind will return, perhaps, it just needs a rest, as you do."

Shye shook his head, eyes turning to the sea and the breeze that rattled through the furled sails, "No, it's still here, I can still feel it. It just has nothing to say. And without it, I have no idea where we're supposed to go."

Shye nodded once to himself and said, "We should head back to Mistral," accepting the circumstances with a wretched serenity that inspired both envy and aggravation in Dorian because they could never face their truths so easily and worse, it reminded them of the ease of his surrender to them. For Shye that surrender had been necessary and strategic, but under this sun it tasted too much of defeat.

Which was why they said, "No. We'll give it a little longer."

"What?" Shye questioned, with the flash of a bright smile appearing from the cloudiness of his expression. "Until Cassius sends the Huntsman after us to fetch us back?"

Dorian could see thoughts turning over in his head, the guilt of their circumstance briefly abating.

"Precisely."

Basking in the warmth of that brief smile, Dorian squished themselves closer to Shye, arms banding around his waist until the two were properly pressed together.

"Besides, perhaps this silence simply means that we are where we are meant to be. In this city you once called home under this lovely sunning, where we can swim the sea and relax for a bit before worrying about what's coming next after destroying my cousin's crown and overpowering various murderous family members . . ."

Dorian held Shye's gaze, watched his pupils dilate as they brought their face closer with every word until they finally kissed him. His lips moved softly against theirs, Shye's hands finding their way beneath Dorian's coat, and Dorian was just about to suggest they retire to their cabin for a spell when a rough voice coughed loudly beside them.

Shye pulled away hastily, a little red-faced and self-conscious, and Dorian turned to face Edge, a satisfied grin curling at the edge of their mouth.

Edge stared back, dead eyed, unusual pale purple bags sagging under his lifeless glare, turning his handsome face haggard.

"Get off my ship if yer doing that rubbish."

"It's not your ship," Dorian quipped back quickly, hoping to engage Edge in another battle of retorts and insults, with the expectation of actually wining a round at some point against the man.

Unusually, Edge didn't take the bait and simply said, "Ain't yours either," his eyes dodged past Dorian to Shye, and he continued brusquely, "Move. Some of us ain't waiting on the wind to give us work to do."

Some of the clouds returned to Shye's expression but he hopped out the way without complaint, pulling Dorian towards the gangway by the arm, muttering, "Sorry, we'll go," at Edge as they passed.

"Ignore Edge," Muse called as Shye continued to tow Dorian off the ship. "He's just grumpy. Woke up on the wrong side of the hammock."

Muse paused and then muttered a final, "Just like everyone else," and yawned.

Dorian turned to Shye, "Am I the only one getting a good rest come nightrun on this whole boat?"

Shye didn't answer them, instead saying with a tired smile, "It's a ship, not a boat," and, lacing his fingers through theirs, he began to pull them off towards the Shrouds Quarter.

"I hope you're taking me to somewhere where we can rent a room?"

Dorian looked sideways at Shye and winked, squeezing his fingers. Accepting Dorian's public attention was something Shye was still getting used to, as Dorian was still getting used to having a hand that was cool as the glass that held it together and lent them more stares than they usually sought, especially when it was wrapped up in the grasp of a Stormborn.

Dorian sensed that Shye was reaching his limit for the rise. After all, that kiss on the ship would never have happened in full of the crew if Shye hadn't been comfortable with it, comfortable with Dorian and the thing between them. A season ago in Feng, he'd still been cautious and the sentiment between them had been new in full expression. So, though Dorian teased, they didn't stop him or act offended when he blushed and pulled his hand free, arms crossing across his chest. But Dorian's own hand did seize for a moment, stuck because they hadn't started to let go with enough time to make a smooth transition, before it relaxed.

Though, Dorian didn't really mind the odd sensations of glass meeting skin or the staring – having courted enough of the last before they fused glass into their skin to preserve the functionality of their hand – but they weren't sure they'd ever adjust to having one hand that didn't work as deftly as the other.

"I was actually going to take you diving for offerings."

Dorian's previous thoughts stalled as excitement zipped through them and they hastily shelved those thoughts of alone time with Shye to be retrieved later.

"For the Nain?" Dorian clarified quickly.

Shye nodded, his eyes brightening at Dorian's sudden peak in energy, his arms coming down by his sides. Dorian carefully snatched his hand back, with enough stillness to allow him to pull back if he wanted, and pretended to be considering the offer, as if they'd ever say no.

"Will it involve taking your clothes off?" They asked at last, with a terrorising grin.

"Maybe," Shye answered with a bold lie to their face, a smaller, happier smile digging its way into the corner of his mouth and staying there. His eyes didn't flinch from theirs and Dorian had to admire it, from someone whose disposition was a truthful one.

Delight and anticipation bubbled up within them, warming their whole body, and they couldn't help but laugh a little and gesture forward with their linked hands, black opal and sunstone flashing with the motion.

"Then lead the way."

BEFORE YOU GO
WANT BONUS SCENES?

Sign up for my **newsletter** to receive updates, anecdotes, announcements for new books, **and to download** *Five Lords Bonus Bits*!

Also, if you liked this novel, please consider leaving a review. Reviews help the author and new and future readers. So if you enjoyed it, let us know!

SNEAK PEEK AT FIVE LORDS BONUS BITS

Captain Ezra Creed: A Moment in the Past

EZRA CREED WAS DRUNK. HAD BEEN FOR NEAR SEVERAL SPANS NOW AND he had no intention to be any improved several spans hence. His coat was still singed and stank like smoke, and he was expecting a hunter to walk through the door any moment. He was ready to welcome them in.

There was surely no other way he'd be getting off this stool.

Courting a Stormborn: An Interlude in Feng

Dorian's heart fluttered in a way that would be embarrassing if anyone else knew about it. It fluttered despite the nearly endless expanse of stone steps that stretched before them, but it didn't care as long as Shye continued to pull them up by a hand gripped tight onto theirs.

The Society for Aromatic Sereni-tea: An Incident in Mistral

It was a truly miserable frostfall in the capital. Edge sniffed for the thousandth time as the wind rocketed through the city streets, the sound lost under the sheets of chilling rain hitting the glass parasol that Butler was holding over their heads.

"Tell me again why we're waiting out here like this? For once, I think I'd be more comfortable on the ship," Butler rumbled. "And you've already got a cold."

ACKNOWLEDGMENTS

While I may be self-publishing this book, it has received some mighty and enthusiastic help along the way. Thank you to Frank & Co Readers for doing my first beta read and manuscript assessment. Thank you to the Expert Editor for my second manuscript assessment and first copy edit.

When it came to getting a final line edit and proofread, I could not be more thankful to have encountered Element Editing Service, through a Google search no less, and Kat Betts, who did incredible work.

Kat, the comments you left peppered throughout my manuscript to let me know you were enjoying it were amazing and so appreciated! I'm so excited to work with you again on the next book!

To my friends who are so supportive and enthusiastic, you have all the gratitude in the world and all my love. I'm so lucky to know you all. A special thanks to those of you who looked at this manuscript in the early days; I hope you can appreciate how far it's come with your help and that of these wonderful people above.

Lastly, thank you to all the readers who made it this far and to all who will in the future. I hope you've loved the adventure as I much as I have.

ABOUT THE AUTHOR

F. Malbeck is an Australian indie author and proud queer person of Aboriginal descent. Hailing originally from rural New South Wales and Wiradjuri Country, F. Malbeck moved to Melbourne, Victoria, with its treacherous weather, at a young age and has since given into the dark side that is Melbourne's seductive gridded CBD layout and multiple theatres full of musicals, unlikely to ever willingly give them up.

Between working on their PhD, working at their day job, and writing mostly on the weekend, F. Malbeck likes to believe they are as organised and efficient with their time as any a true god of productivity, but in reality they're usually found ruining their spine, hunched over their laptop like any other goblin with an internet connection, with the posture and sitting position of L from Death Note. Throughout it all, there is always a cup of tea within reach.

www.ingramcontent.com/pod-product-compliance
Lightning Source LLC
Chambersburg PA
CBHW031435240626
47154CB00001B/277